RANDOM HOUSE

LARGE PRINT

FAULT LINE

FAULT

FAULT LINE

A NOVEL

BARRY EISLER

R A N D O M   H O U S E
L A R G E   P R I N T

Copyright © 2009 by Barry Eisler

Published in the United States of America by Random House Large Print in association with Ballantine Books, New York.
Distributed by Random House, Inc., New York.

The Library of Congress has established a Cataloging-in-Publication record for this title.

Cover Design: Marc Cohen
Cover photograph (San Francisco Bay) © Justin Lightley/Getty Images

ISBN: 978-0-7393-2833-0

www.randomhouse.com/largeprint

FIRST LARGE PRINT EDITION

10 9 8 7 6 5 4 3 2 1

This Large Print edition published in accord with the standards of the N.A.V.H.

For Naomi, Dan, and Maya, with love

FAULT LINE

1 LOOKING UP

The last thing Richard Hilzoy thought before the bullet entered his brain was, **Things are really looking up.**

He was on his way to the Silicon Valley offices of his lawyer, Alex Treven, who had arranged a meeting with Kleiner Perkins, the Midases of venture capital who could increase a company's value a hundredfold just by offering to invest. And now Kleiner was considering writing a check to **him,** Richard Hilzoy, genius, inventor of Obsidian, the world's most advanced encryption algorithm, destined to render all other network security software obsolete. Alex had already applied for the patent, and if things worked out with the VCs, Hilzoy would be able to rent office space, buy equipment, hire staff—everything he needed to finish commercializing the product and bring it online. In a few years he would take the company public, and his shares would be worth a fortune. Or he'd stay private, and become to security software what Dolby was to sound, raking in billions in licensing revenues. Or Google would buy him—they were into everything these days. The main thing was, he was going to be rich.

And he deserved it. Working for chump change in an Oracle research laboratory, drinking Red Bull after Red Bull late at night and shivering in the deserted company parking lot for tobacco breaks, enduring the taunts and laughter he knew went on behind his back. Last year his wife had divorced him, and boy was the bitch ever going to be sorry now. If she'd had any brains she'd have waited until he was rolling in money and then tried to shake him down. But she'd never believed in him, and neither had anyone else. Except Alex.

He walked down the cracked exterior steps of his San Jose apartment building, squinting against the brilliant morning sun. He could hear the roar of rush hour traffic on Interstate 280 half a block away—the **whoosh, whoosh** of individual cars, trucks grinding gears as they pulled on from the entrance ramp at South Tenth Street, the occasional angry honk—and for once, having to live like this, right on top of the freeway, didn't bother him. Even the cheap bicycles and rusting barbecues and stained plastic garbage containers crammed together against the side of the adjacent building didn't bother him, nor did the reek the autumn breeze carried from the overflowing parking lot Dumpster.

Because Alex was going to get him out of this sewer hole. Oracle was a client of Alex's firm, and Hilzoy was Alex's contact on patents there. Hilzoy hadn't been overly impressed initially. He'd taken one look at Alex's blond hair and green eyes and figured him for just another pretty boy—rich parents, the right schools, the usual. But he'd recognized soon enough that Alex knew his shit. Turned out he wasn't just a lawyer, but had degrees from Stanford, too— undergraduate in electrical engineering, same as Hilzoy, and a Ph.D. in computer science. He knew at least as much programming as Hilzoy, maybe more. So when Hilzoy had finally worked up the nerve to pull him aside and ask about patenting Obsidian, Alex had gotten it right away. Not only had he deferred his fees, he'd introduced Hilzoy to a group of angel investors who had put in enough money for Hilzoy to quit his day job and buy the equipment he needed. And now he was poised to take money from the biggest swinging dicks of all. All in the space of a single year. Unbelievable.

Of course, there were aspects of Obsidian that the VCs might not like if they knew about them. They might even have found them scary. But they wouldn't know, because there was no reason to tell them. Obsidian could protect networks, and there wasn't a Fortune 500 company out there that wouldn't pay out the wazoo for that. That's what VCs understood. The rest . . . well, that would all just be his little secret, a kind of insurance policy to fall back on if Obsidian's intended uses weren't enough to command the proper sums.

He looked at his watch. He was nervous about the meeting. But there was time enough for a cigarette; that would calm him down. He stopped at the bottom of the stairs and fired one up. He took a deep drag, then put the pack and the lighter back in his pocket. There was a white van parked next to his car, an '88 Buick Regency he'd bought after selling his Audi during the divorce. HUMANE PEST CONTROL, the van said. He'd noticed it here, what, three times in the last week? Four? He'd seen a rat once, under the Dumpster. And there were roaches. Somebody must have made a stink with building management, and now the idiots were trying to show they were doing something about it. Whatever. Pretty soon that would all be someone else's problem.

There were some scares along the way, existing inventions Alex was concerned might prevent them from getting a patent. And something about a possible secrecy order from the government, which could slow things down. But so far Alex had always found a way around the problems. The patent hadn't been issued yet, but the application itself was bankable.

Hilzoy had been worried at first about describing the source code in the patent application because anyone who got hold of it would know the recipe for Obsidian, but Alex had assured him the Patent and Trademark Office maintained all applications in strict confidence for eighteen months, at which point they'd have a good idea about whether a patent would be forthcoming. And once the patent was issued, it wouldn't matter whether people knew the recipe or not—they couldn't use it without paying him the big bucks. And if they tried to, Alex would sue them into the ground. That's right, people, you want to play, you got to pay.

He paused in front of the Buick and got out his keys. What a piece of crap. It had over a hundred thousand miles on it and every one of them showed. It was the kind of car you could piss all over and no one would even notice. A Mercedes, he thought, not for the first time. Or maybe a BMW. Black, a convertible. He'd have it detailed four times a year so it would always look new.

The pest control guy got out of the van. He was wearing a baseball cap, coveralls, and gloves. He nodded to Hilzoy through a pair of shades and moved past him. Hilzoy nodded back, glad he didn't have to kill rats for a living.

He took a drag on the cigarette, then tossed it away, enjoying the feeling of wasting it. He blew the smoke up at the sky and unlocked the car door. Yeah, baby, he thought. Oh yeah. Things are really looking up.

2 ONE SHOT

Alex Treven was pacing in his office at the law firm of Sullivan, Greenwald, Priest & Savage. Outside the window was an expanse of hard blue sky and the gentle curves of the Palo Alto hills below it, but Alex was oblivious to the view. It took him five steps to reach one sun-dappled wall, where he would stop, pivot, and repeat the process in the other direction. He counted steps, imagining he was wearing down a path in the green carpet, trying to distract himself with trivia.

Alex was pissed. Hilzoy, who ordinarily was even more punctual than Alex, had picked today of all days to be late. They were going to see Tim Nicholson—Tim frigging Nicholson!—and the Kleiner partner wasn't going to be impressed if Hilzoy couldn't make a first meeting on time. And it wasn't going to make Alex look good, either.

He checked his watch. Well, they still had thirty minutes. Hilzoy was supposed to get here an hour early for a last rehearsal of the pitch and some role-playing, but they could dispense with all that if they had to. Still, where the hell was he?

His secretary, Alisa, opened the door. Alex stopped and fixed his eyes on her, and she flinched. "I've called him at least twenty times," she said. "All I get is his voice mail."

Alex resisted the urge to shout. This wasn't her fault.

"Go to his apartment," he said. "See if you can find him there. South Tenth Street in San Jose. I forget the exact address, but it's in his file. Keep trying him on the way and call me when you arrive. We've still got a little time before I have to cancel the meeting and we look like idiots."

"What do you—"

"I don't know. Just call me as soon as you get there. Go."

Alisa nodded and closed the door. Alex returned to his pacing.

God, don't let him screw this up, he thought. **I've got so much riding on it.**

Alex was a sixth-year associate at Sullivan, Greenwald, getting close to that delicate "up or out" stage of his career. It wasn't as though anyone was going to let him go; his blend of science and patent law expertise was too unusual, and too valuable to the firm, for him to ever have to worry about unemployment. No, the problem was much more insidious: the firm's partnership liked him exactly where he was, and wanted to keep him there. So in another year, two at the most, they'd start talking to him about the benefits of an "of counsel" position, the money, the seniority, the flexible hours and job security.

It was all bullshit to him. He didn't want security; he wanted power. And power at Sullivan, Greenwald, he knew, came only with your own client base, your own book of business. If you couldn't eat what you killed, you'd always be dependent on the scraps from someone else's table. That might have been fine for other associates. But it would never be enough for him.

Which was why Hilzoy was so damned valuable. Alex had grasped the potential of Obsidian in a way he knew few other people could—not from Hilzoy's pitch, but by actually getting under the hood and examining the fundamental design. It had taken maneuvering, and a level of political skills he didn't even know he had, to convince the partners both to defer the firm's fees and to list Alex as the originating attorney. Behind their Bay Area casual attire and the first-name basis with the secretaries and paralegals, these guys were all sharks. When they smelled blood in the water, they wanted the kill for themselves.

Alex's mentor was a partner named David Osborne, a shrewd lawyer but with no formal tech background of his own. Over the years, the strategic patent-counseling side of his practice had grown increasingly dependent on Alex's technical acumen. He made sure Alex's twice-yearly bonuses were the highest the firm could give, but in front of the clients he always managed to take credit for Alex's own insights. He put on a confident show in his trademark cowboy boots and fuchsia T-shirts, but inside, Alex knew, Osborne felt threatened by people he suspected had more potential than he. So despite the periodic noises he made about backing Alex for partner "when the time was right," Alex had come to believe that time would never come. Partnership wasn't something they gave you, Alex had decided. It was something you had to take.

So after several secret meetings with Hilzoy to ensure that he really did own the Obsidian technology, or at least that no one could prove otherwise, Alex had taken a deep breath and walked down the short stretch of expensively carpeted corridor that separated his medium-sized senior associate's office from Osborne's gigantic partner's version. Both offices were in the main building, the massive round structure the partners liked to refer to as the Rotunda but that was better known among the associates as the Death Star. An office in the Death Star rather than in one of the two satellite buildings conferred a certain degree of status—the kind of thing that mattered a great deal to Osborne and, Alex had to admit, to himself, too—as well as putting its occupant at the geographical center of the firm's action.

Outside Osborne's door, he had paused to collect

himself in front of the massive wall display of Lucite tombstones commemorating work done for Cisco, eBay, Google, and a hundred others. There were framed photos of Osborne with various Valley luminaries, with the celebrity CEO of a major telecom Osborne had recently landed as a client in a major coup, and even one with the prime minister of Thailand, where Osborne traveled three or four times a year to work the project-finance practice he had developed there. Alex tried not to think of the kind of power and influence a person would accrue in doing all those deals and knowing all those players. The trick was to convince yourself of the opposite—that the person you were about to face in negotiations was beneath you, needed you far more than you needed him—and Alex knew the tombstones and photographs were as much about causing people to flinch and abandon negotiating positions as they were about bragging rights.

He had psyched himself up, gone in, and made the pitch. The balance was delicate—it had to sound interesting enough to make Osborne want to say yes, but not so interesting that he'd be tempted to try to claim the origination for himself. After all, if this went well, the patent would be just the beginning. It would also involve a ton of corporate work, and that was Osborne's specialty more than it was Alex's.

When Alex was done, Osborne leaned back in his chair and put his cowboy boots up on the desk. He scratched his crotch absently. The relaxed manner made Alex nervous. It felt like a feint. He knew that behind it, Osborne was already calculating.

"What's my client going to say about this?" Osborne asked after a moment, in his nasal voice.

Alex shrugged. "What can they say? The invention doesn't have anything to do with Oracle's core business or with Hilzoy's day-to-day responsibilities there. I've already checked the employment contract. Oracle doesn't have any claims."

"What about—"

"He invented it at home, on his own time, using his own equipment. We're okay optically, too."

Osborne smiled slightly. "You did your homework."

"I learned from the best," Alex said, and then immediately wished he hadn't. Osborne would probably twist the comment in his mind until it became **You've taught me so much, David. I owe you everything.**

"Tell me how you met this guy," Osborne said after a moment.

"He called and asked if I could advise him about something he was working on at home," Alex said. He'd rehearsed the lie so many times that he remembered it as though it had really happened this way. "I met him at a Starbucks and he showed me what he'd been doing. I thought it looked promising so I took it from there."

It wasn't the answer Osborne had been hoping for, of course. If Alex had told him the truth—that he and Hilzoy had first discussed Obsidian while Alex was at Oracle on firm business—it would have presented an opportunity for Osborne to make a stronger **But for me, this wouldn't even have come to you** argument. Alex expected Osborne would probably check with Hilzoy, discreetly, if he ever got a chance. But Alex had prepared Hilzoy for this possibility. For both their sakes, the more this thing seemed to have happened outside of Oracle and Sullivan, Greenwald, the better.

"I don't like it," Osborne said. "The client will say you met this guy through them. Even if they don't have a legal case, I'm not going to risk pissing off a client like Oracle for something that's pretty small-time by comparison."

"Come on, David, you know every company ever born in the Valley at some point had a connection to a big established corporation that was somebody's client. It's just the way it works. And Oracle knows it, too."

Osborne looked at him as though considering. Probably enjoying the ability to take his time and make Alex squirm on the carpet before him.

"Let me have this one, David," Alex said, a little surprised by the firmness of his tone.

Osborne spread his arms, palms up, as though this went without question, as though he hadn't spent every minute since this conversation began looking for a way to freeze Alex out. "Hey," he said. "Who's your daddy?"

It wasn't an answer, or at least not a definite one. "Hilzoy is mine?" Alex said. "I'm the originating attorney?"

"It seems fair."

"Is that a yes?"

Osborne sighed. He swung his boots off the desk and leaned forward as though he was ready to get back to whatever Alex had interrupted. "Yes, it's a yes."

Alex permitted himself a small smile. The hard part was over. Now for the really hard part.

"There's just one thing," Alex said.

Osborne raised his eyebrows, his expression doubtful.

"Hilzoy . . . went through a nasty divorce last year. He doesn't have any money."

"Oh, for Christ's sake, Alex."

"No, listen. He can't afford our fees. But if we incorporate him, take a piece of the company—"

"Do you know how hard it is to get the partnership committee to go for that kind of speculative crap?"

"Sure, but they take your recommendations, don't they?"

This was a gambit Alex had learned in years of negotiating for clients. When the other side pleaded that it wasn't their decision, that they had to check with the board or the management committee or Aunt Bertha or whoever, you engaged their ego, and then their desire to be consistent.

Osborne was too experienced to fall for it. "Not always, no."

"Well, this time they should. This technology has promise. I've examined it personally, and you know I know better than most. I'll do all the work myself. Not instead of everything I'm already doing. In addition to it."

"Come on, Alex, you're already on track to bill over three thousand hours this year. You can't—"

"Yes I can. You know I can. So what we're talking about is a percentage of something for the firm—something that could be big—in exchange for effectively no investment. The partnership committee won't listen to you when you propose that?"

Not if, when. Osborne didn't respond, and Alex hoped he hadn't pushed it too hard. Osborne was probably wondering, **Why is he willing to sacrifice so much for something so speculative? Is this thing going to be bigger than he's letting on?**

Alex tried again. "The committee listens to you, right?"

Osborne smiled a little, maybe in grudging admiration of how well Alex had played his hand. "Sometimes," he said.

"Then you'll recommend it?"

Osborne rubbed his chin and looked at Alex as though he was concerned for nothing but Alex's welfare. "If you really want me to. But you know, Alex, this is the first matter you've ever originated"—**First one you've ever let me originate, you mean**—"and if it doesn't pan out, you're not going to look good. It'll show bad judgment."

Bad judgment. At Sullivan, Greenwald it was the ultimate, all-purpose opprobrium. Anything that went wrong, even if it wasn't the attorney's fault, could be attributed to bad judgment. Because if the attorney had good judgment, he would have seen it coming no matter what. The bad thing wouldn't have happened on his watch.

Alex didn't respond, and Osborne went on. "All I'm saying is, for a risk like this, you want a margin for error, a cushion to fall back on."

Alex was disgusted with the way Osborne presented all this as though he were Alex's best friend. He knew he was supposed to say, **You're right, David. You take the origination. Thanks for protecting me, man. You're the best.**

Instead he said, "I thought you were my cushion."

Osborne blinked. "Well, I am."

Alex shrugged as though that decided it. "I couldn't ask for better protection than that."

Osborne made a sound, half laugh, half grunt.

Alex took a step toward the door. "I'll fill out the new client form and a new matter form, run a conflicts check."

This was it. If Osborne was going to try to overrule him, he'd have to say so now. If he didn't, every day that passed would create new facts on the ground that would be harder and harder for Osborne to get around.

"If we're not taking any fees," Osborne said, "I still have to take this to the committee."

"I know. But I feel confident they'll listen to you." Alex looked at Osborne squarely. "This is important to me, David."

Unspoken, but clearly understood, was, **So important that if you screw me, I'll be working at Weil, Gotshal next week, and you can find someone else to make you sound as smart with your clients as I do.**

A beat went by. Osborne said, "I don't want you working on this by yourself."

Alex hadn't been expecting that and didn't know what it meant. Had he just won? Had Osborne caved? "What do you mean?" he asked.

Osborne snorted. "Come on, hotshot. How are you going to ride this to where you want it to take you if you don't have any associates working under you?"

Alex hadn't thought about that. Mostly he worked alone. He liked it that way.

"Look, it's a little early—"

"Also," Osborne said, "how are we going to justify a big piece of this guy's company if we've only got one lawyer on it? We want him to know he's being treated right."

Alex didn't know whether to laugh or what. Osborne was practically telling him to pad his time. But if this was what it took for Osborne to feel he'd won a little victory in the midst of the way Alex had played him, fine.

"I see what you mean," Alex said.

"Use the Arab girl, the good-looking one. What's her name?"

Alex felt a little color creep into his cheeks and hoped Osborne didn't notice. "Sarah. Sarah Hosseini. She's not Arab. She's Iranian. Persian."

"Whatever."

"Why her?"

"You've worked with her before, right?"

"Once or twice."

Osborne looked at him. "Three times, actually."

Christ, Osborne was no tech whiz, but when it came to who was billing for what, he was all over it.

Alex scratched his cheek, hoping the gesture seemed nonchalant. "Yeah, I guess so."

"You said in your review she's 'unusually confident and capable for a first-year.'"

The truth was, the description was an understatement. "That sounds right."

"She's smart?"

Alex shrugged. "She has a degree in information security and forensics from Caltech." He knew Osborne might sense a mild put-down in this, but was annoyed enough not to care.

"Well, she's not busy enough. Use her. Build a team. Do you have a problem with that?"

Why was he pushing it this way? Would the extra lawyer give Osborne a greater claim, maybe to supervise the work, start taking it over, something like that?

Or was he just having fun, teasing Alex, forcing him to work with Sarah because he knew—

"No," Alex said, cutting off the thought. "There's no problem."

Osborne had pitched the partnership committee as promised about taking on Hilzoy, and the committee had okayed the arrangement. Osborne told him there had been opposition, but Alex suspected that was bullshit. For all he knew, Osborne might not have needed to pitch it at all. Maybe the committee loved this kind of shit—sure, get the associate to bill even more hours, while we keep the profits if his work turns into anything. Maybe Osborne had just positioned it as some Herculean task so Alex would feel in his debt afterward.

It didn't matter. Alex didn't owe anybody. He'd gotten this far by himself. His parents were gone, his sister was gone, his sole remaining family was his prick of an older brother, Ben, who had caused everything and then run away to the army after their father had . . . after he had died. Alex hadn't talked to Ben since their mother's funeral, eight years earlier. Even then, with nothing left but the two of them, Ben wouldn't say where he was or what he was doing. He just showed up for the ceremony and left, leaving all the details to Alex, just as he'd left Alex alone to care for their mother during the last year and a half of her life. After he'd finished the probate—again, all by himself—Alex had sent Ben an e-mail explaining his share of the estate, which was pretty big, as their fa-

ther had done well and there were only the two beneficiaries. Ben hadn't even thanked him, just told him
to send the paperwork to an address at Fort Bragg,
North Carolina, saying he'd sign it when he could.
For all Alex knew, right now Ben was in Iraq or
Afghanistan. Sometimes Alex wondered whether he
was even still alive. He didn't care. Either way he was
never going to talk to him again.

Goddamn Hilzoy. Alex hated that he needed him,
but he did. Because if Obsidian was even half as suc-
cessful as Alex expected it to be, the seed money was
going to be followed by a second, third, maybe a
fourth round of financing. After the acquisition or the
IPO, the firm's share would be worth a fortune. And
Hilzoy would never forget who got him there. All the
legal work afterward, and all the billing for it, would
be Alex's and his alone. His name would be indelibly
linked with Obsidian, he would be the lawyer who
represented the hottest company of the year, maybe
the decade, and then the David Osbornes of the world
would be begging for the crumbs from **his** table.

Assuming Hilzoy hadn't already blown it for them.
Did he understand just how busy these VCs were,
how many proposals were pitched at them every single day, how few they actually followed up on? You
get one shot for these people's attention, Alex had
told him, just one shot.

If Hilzoy screwed this up, Alex was going to kill him.

3 A SIMPLE UNDERSTANDING

Ben Treven sat motionless at the edge of a wooden chair at the Hotel Park Istanbul, watching the rainy afternoon street two stories below through tattered gauze curtains. The room was small and spartan, but its size and furnishings couldn't have mattered less to him. The window was open a few inches, and from time to time the interior quiet was broken by the sounds of the city without: car tires thumping over the antique cobblestone streets and splashing through potholes; the practiced touts of rug merchants calling out to passing tourists from in front of their small shops; the haunting notes of the muezzin, entreating the faithful to prayer five times daily between dawn and dusk.

In addition to letting in the sounds of the street, the open window kept the room cold. When the moment arrived, he would need to move quickly, and he was already wearing deerskin gloves, a wool cap, and a fleece-lined, waterproof jacket. His hair was naturally blond, but the false beard he wore was black. With the hat on, no one would notice the discrepancy.

The warm clothing would be useful in the rain and against the December chill, of course, but that was only part of it. The gloves prevented prints. The hat obscured his features. The jacket concealed a suppressed Glock 17 in a cross-draw holster on his left side.

On the coffee table next to him was a backpack containing clothes, two sandwiches, a bottle of water, a first-aid kit, ammunition, false travel papers, and a few other essentials. Other than the backpack, there was no trace of the room's occupant, nor would there be when he was gone.

He was there to kill two Iranian nuclear scientists, Omid Jafari and Ali Kazemi. Ben knew a lot about the men: their real names, the names they were traveling under, the details of their itineraries. He knew they were in Istanbul for a meeting with a Russian counterpart. He knew they were staying at the Sultanahmet Four Seasons, which is why he had taken this room at the Park, directly across the street. He had copies of their passport photos and had recognized them immediately when they arrived from the airport in one of the hotel's BMW limousines three days earlier. He knew the two men who accompanied them at all times were with VAVAK, Iran's feared secret service, and that the VAVAK people, in addition to being well trained, would be motivated. If one of the scientists were kidnapped or assassinated, or if one of them defected, as Ali Reza Asgari, the Iranian general and former deputy defense minister, had done not so long before, the man who let it happen could expect to be executed.

He knew considerably less about the Russian: not much more than a real name, Rolan Vasilyev—which he probably wasn't traveling under anyway—and that he was coming to Istanbul to meet the Iranians. Washington had been pressuring Moscow about Russian nuclear assistance to Tehran, and presumably the Kremlin had decided it was too risky to bring the Iranians to Russia, even under false names. Istanbul was a good neutral corner: about midway geographically, with good air links, and security services focused more on ethnic Kurds than on Russians or Iranians.

Each morning since they had arrived, the Iranians and their VAVAK minders had gotten into one of the hotel limousines and returned after dark. Ben figured these trips were for meetings with Vasilyev and would have liked to follow them to learn more, but the likely costs outweighed the benefits. Alone in a car or on a motor scooter, he would be relatively easy to spot. Even if he weren't spotted, catching them in a venue that enabled him to do the job and depart without trouble would require an unrealistic amount of luck. He might have tried taking them as they arrived at or departed from the hotel, but the front and interior of the Four Seasons were quietly replete with cameras, doormen, and security personnel. It just wasn't a good place for a hit, which was part of the reason they had chosen it in the first place.

It didn't matter, though. His gut told him something would open up. After all, the Iranians were in town for seven days, and what did that mean? Probably that they expected to be done with their work in four, or maybe five. Country and culture were irrelevant: when the government or the corporation or anyone else was footing the bill, bureaucrats and other worker bees could always be expected to overestimate the time they would need for meetings. Especially when the meetings required their presence in a city as enticing as Istanbul, and at a hotel as fine as the Four Seasons.

In fact, the choice of hotel increased Ben's confidence about what was coming next. Because if the Iranians could persuade the bean counters to spring for the Four Seasons, cost was obviously not a consideration. If cost wasn't a consideration, they could have stayed at any hotel in the city—the Pera Palas, the Ritz-Carlton, even the second Four Seasons, recently opened on the Bosporus. Ben had checked with all of them, and they all had rooms available. They all offered more or less the same level of luxury and security. The question, then, was, why this hotel?

The answer, Ben thought, was location. All the other luxury properties were in Beyoglu, the newer part of the city, north of the Golden Horn. Only the

Sultanahmet Four Seasons was a five-minute walk from the city's most storied attractions: the Blue Mosque, Hagia Sophia, Topkapi Palace, the Grand Bazaar. And if Ben was right about location being the deciding factor, he was confident the Iranians would take at least a day, and probably more, to see those walking-distance sights. When they set out from the hotel on foot, Ben could get behind them. From there, an opportunity would present itself. All he had to do was wait.

Which was fine. Waiting didn't bother him. He liked to wait, in fact, liked the simplicity of it. Waiting was the least complicated part of an uncomplicated job.

Periodically, he received orders. The orders were always short and direct, and he had extremely wide latitude in determining how to carry them out. He could ask for whatever equipment he needed, and the equipment would promptly turn up in a dead drop as though by magic. There was no questioning, no red tape, no oversight.

The only real constraint this time was that Vasilyev was off-limits. During the early years of the Cold War, trying to remove the other side's pieces from the board was considered just another part of the game. Eventually, like rival mafia families, everyone had figured out the bloodshed was more expensive than it was worth, and a kind of shadowy détente had settled in. Now, no one wanted to be responsible for breaking the truce, for a return to those bad old bloody days.

He tried not to be irritated by the restrictions. After all, it wasn't like the Russians were matching Uncle Sam's restraint. They had killed that guy Victor Litvinenko in London with polonium. And there were all those dead journalists, too—Anna Politkovskaya, Paul Klebnikov, too many to keep up with. Ben thought he could make a pretty good argument that Ivan was getting more aggressive precisely because of Uncle Sam's overzealous devotion to the rules, but that kind of shit was above his pay grade and it wasn't as though anyone would listen to him anyway. But if he could, he would have asked someone what had happened to "You're either with us or you're with the terrorists." He supposed it had been just another empty slogan from another lying politician.

They were all liars, actually. The left was naïve, thinking you could follow the niceties and still fight effectively against the kind of fanatics America was up against. And the right was hypocritical, thinking you could take off the gloves and still occupy the moral high ground.

Yeah, the left couldn't understand the nature of the fight; the right couldn't accept its true consequences. But Ben didn't care about the niceties, he didn't care about the moral high ground, he cared about **winning.** And the way you won was by being the hardest, dirtiest, deadliest motherfucker the enemy could ever have imagined in his worst nightmare. Christ, what good were rules if they made you lose the fight? What all the armchair analysts couldn't get their minds around was that when your tribe is attacked, you do what you have to do to win. You win by any means necessary. Later there could be a victor's justice, fine, but first there had to be a victory.

The thing was, most Americans wanted nothing more than to be safe. Maybe it hadn't always been that way, in fact he suspected things had once been different, but these days America had become a nation of sheep. Which to him was a pretty sorry way to live, a way that represented everything he'd joined the army to get away from; but that was American culture these days, and someone had to keep the sheep safe from the wolves. He understood at some level that the bullshit restrictions and the second-guessing just came with the territory. Still, it was galling to be put in a position where he was more afraid of CNN than he was of al Qaeda.

A BMW 750L pulled up in front of the Four Seasons and a doorman with an umbrella moved forward to open the door. Ben tensed, but no, it was an Asian couple, not the Iranians. He settled back onto the chair and resumed his waiting.

No one had told him where the intel behind this op had come from, of course. But from the quality of the information on the Iranians, and its paucity regarding the Russian, Ben suspected an Iranian mole—possibly in the country's nuclear program, more probably in the security services. An asset in the nuclear program would have known the scientists' names and itineraries. He might even have known about the VAVAK minders. But only someone in charge of security would also have access to the false names and papers under which the men would be traveling, and to their passport photos. Also, understanding the likely fate to which he was condemning them, someone in the nuclear program would have found it harder to give up the scientists. After all, they would have been colleagues, men another scientist would know personally. Betraying your country is easier to rationalize than betraying a friend.

It was interesting. At one point, Uncle Sam had been more inclined to render the Jafaris and Kazemis of the world to friendly governments like Egypt and Saudi Arabia, where they could be interrogated with proper rigor. But then the CIA had screwed up the rendition of Abu Omar from Milan, leaving a paper trail so egregious an Italian magistrate had issued arrest warrants for the thirteen CIA operatives behind it, and then "plane spotters" had started to unravel the whole secret rendition network. The Pentagon had decided it was better to act more discreetly, and more directly. No one took the CIA seriously anymore anyway, not since the DCI had been made subordinate to the new director of national intelligence and the agency had been saddled with the problem of those nonexistent Iraqi WMDs. If you wanted actionable intelligence now, and if you wanted the intelligence acted upon, the Pentagon was the only real player in town.

Ben knew all this, but he didn't really care. He wanted nothing to do with politics, national or organizational. Hell, the politicians didn't even know men like him existed, and if they suspected, they knew better than to inquire. The military didn't invent "Don't ask, don't tell." It learned it from Congress.

So basically, things were copacetic. There was a lot of work, and he was good at it. It all involved a simple understanding. If he fucked up, he would be denied, disowned, and hung out to dry. If he continued to achieve results, he would be left alone. It was the kind of deal he could live with. One where you knew the rules, and the consequences, up front. Not like what his family had pulled on him after Katie. Not that any of that mattered at this point anyway. They were all gone now, except for Alex, who might as well be gone, and good riddance, too.

Another BMW pulled up. Ben leaned forward so he could see more clearly through the curtains, and bingo, it was the Iranians, their first time back to the hotel before dark. This was it, he was sure of it, the chance he'd been waiting for. He felt a hot flush of adrenaline—a familiar, pleasant sensation in his neck and gut—and his heart began to thud a little harder.

The Iranians headed into the hotel, one VAVAK guy forward, the other aft. Ten to one they'd be on their way out within an hour, two at the most.

He stood and cracked his neck, then started doing some stretches and light calisthenics. He'd been sitting a long time with nothing but quick bathroom breaks. That was fine while he was waiting. But the time for waiting was done.

4 WAITING ROOM DOORS

Alex's mobile phone buzzed. He checked the display—Alisa—and opened it.

"You find him?" he asked.

"No. I'm in front of his apartment, though, and there are police cars everywhere. There are a lot of people standing around. They're saying someone was murdered."

Alex felt an odd numbness take hold behind his ears. He could hear a faint buzzing, like the sound of a fluorescent light. "Oh, shit. Is it—"

"I don't know. I tried talking to one of the officers, but he'd only say it's a crime scene, which anyway I can tell because there's orange tape all around the building. But they're not letting anyone inside and I can't see anything from where I'm standing."

"Who's saying someone was murdered?"

"Some of the people standing around watching.

Maybe they're wrong, though. Maybe it's just a rumor."

The numbness was spreading now. His breathing seemed very loud.

He wanted to drive down there himself, but knew that was irrational. It wasn't likely he could see or learn anything Alisa couldn't. And what if this whole thing were a gigantic coincidence? What if Hilzoy called or showed up right now—**Sorry, caught a flat, and can you believe it, right in a dead zone where I had no cell reception! Of all the crappy luck**—and Alex wasn't here? He would have turned a potential no-harm, no-foul situation into a catastrophe, all through his own bad judgment.

No, he couldn't let that happen.

He took a deep breath and slowly forced it out. Concentrating on his breathing settled him, a little.

"Stay there," he said. "See if you can learn anything else, and call me right away if you do."

He clicked off and checked his watch. Twenty minutes. In his M3, with the right luck on traffic lights and traffic cops, Alex could get to Kleiner's offices at the top of Sand Hill Road in six minutes. So fourteen minutes before he had to pull the plug. He'd still look stupid, canceling at the last minute, but better than not showing up at all. Would he ever be able to get another meeting with these guys after screwing up the first? Probably not, at least not without using Osborne's or some other partner's connections. And Osborne would know what had happened, would know how much Alex needed him. He would charge for the favor accordingly.

Damn. Damn. Damn.

His office felt suddenly confining. He needed to move, to think. He walked out into the corridor, where he could increase the ambit of his pacing. He turned the corner, and—

There was Sarah, heading in his direction. **Shit.**

He didn't want to talk to her right then, didn't want to have to explain. He hadn't invited her to the meeting. She was too outspoken at times, and while he respected her gumption in private, he didn't trust her to know her place in front of a roomful of VCs. Hilzoy was his show, and he didn't want anyone else in the limelight.

Anyway, even if Sarah were as prim and proper as a first-year should be, she was still bound to be a distraction. Everyone would get one look at her lustrous black hair, caramel skin, and ripe lips and wonder why Alex had brought her to the meeting. Were they involved? Was he hoping for something?

Well, yeah, of course he was hoping for something. And it wasn't just that she was gorgeous. Part of what made him crazy was that she did nothing to flaunt it. She used hardly any makeup, kept her hair tied back, and favored skirts hemmed below the knee. But Alex saw her several evenings a week in the firm's gym, where she typically wore some kind of yoga outfit, and her body was so lusciously long and curvy that Alex had to look away for fear his own body would betray his thoughts. Sometimes, late at night, in the bedroom of the house he had inherited from his parents and lived in still, he would close his eyes and take himself in hand and imagine himself with her, imagine what he wanted her to do, how she would do it, and even more than her beauty it was the existence of those fantasies, and the way their presence in his mind would linger into the next day, that made him awkward with her, made him err in the direction of feigned disinterest and even disdain lest she suspect his secret.

But she didn't seem the least bit interested. And even if she were, what would people say if a senior associate, someone who God willing would be up for partner soon, were dating a first-year ten years his junior? And what would happen if he made partner? What would he do then? A partner couldn't be involved with an associate, at least not publicly. There were trysts at Sullivan, Greenwald, of course, enough to keep the rumor mill spinning full-time, but those people were already partners, they could afford to be known as pigs. Maybe when Alex had made it to the top of the heap he'd hit on hot associates, too, maybe even summer associates, for Christ's sake, but not now. He didn't need complications like that. He had to stay focused.

"Alex," she said, a little surprise in her voice. "Where's Hilzoy? I thought you would have—"

"He's not here. I . . . I don't think he's coming."

"What about the meeting?"

She seemed genuinely concerned, not at all resentful that he'd excluded her. He felt a pang of gratitude, and of guilt. He wanted to say something, something real, but . . .

"Alex?" she said.

He looked at her and wondered whether he'd been blushing. He was about to excuse himself, but realized that would seem weird. Maybe he should just bring her up to speed on Hilzoy.

"Can you help me kill twelve minutes?" he said.

They went back to his office and closed the door. He told her what had happened, how Alisa was at Hilzoy's apartment now.

"Oh my God," she said. "You think he's, you think—"

"I don't know what to think. But I have a bad feeling."

His words surprised him. He never talked about his feelings—or anything else the least bit private—with anyone in the office, and especially not with Sarah. Well, he was under stress right now. This thing with Hilzoy—**Oh no. Oh please God no**—it was just bringing up some bad memories, that was all.

They talked more. Something about Sarah, some wellspring of empathy in her brown eyes, made him feel better. There was something so . . . comforting, when someone could look at you like that, when someone made you feel she understood you completely and was completely on your side. He sensed she would know what it was like to stare for hours at the swinging waiting room doors, desperate for news and at the same time terrified of what the news might be.

He cleared his throat and glanced at his watch. The meeting started in five minutes. Hilzoy could show right now and it would still be too late.

But Hilzoy wasn't going to show. Not today, not ever. Alex could feel it, a sad, sickening weight in the pit of his stomach. He knew the feeling. He remembered it.

"I better call the VCs," he said.

5 OOPS

Ben sheltered from the rain under one of the elegant porticos of the Blue Mosque, surrounded by scores of chattering tourists and keeping an oblique eye on the mosque's exit, fifty feet away. The Iranians had gone in ten minutes earlier, having walked from the hotel exactly as Ben had hoped. He knew from his earlier reconnaissance of the area that there was only one exit, so he hadn't followed them in.

The people around him conferred over their guidebooks in a dozen languages and snapped non-stop photos of the soaring minarets and massive semidomes and rows of ablution spigots. Ben kept his hat pulled low and the jacket zippered over his chin, his breath fogging before him. This wasn't an ideal place to do the job—it was too open, there were too many potential witnesses, it was too close to where he had been staying—but if an opportunity presented itself, he would take it, and he didn't want to be recognizable afterward in some idiot tourist's photos.

During their stroll from the hotel to the mosque, the scientists had showed no sign of security awareness. The VAVAK guys, though, were reasonably sharp. They had stayed one ahead and one behind the scientists, never letting the gap between their positions close to below twenty-five feet. Dropping one at point-blank range would mean having to engage the other from a distance, and possibly allowing the scientists to escape in the meantime. Going after the scientists first would mean giving the VAVAK guys an extra second to get their shit together and then an opportunity to engage from two different directions. The ideal was to drop all four almost instantly and walk away clean, and the VAVAK guys were naturally trying to make something like that as difficult as possible.

In addition to their tactical positioning, the VAVAK guys were also obviously surveillance conscious, but here they were operating at a disadvantage. Ben was pretty sure he knew their likely destinations—the major attractions of Sultanahmet and Seraglio Point—and their likely routes, so he could afford to lose visual contact from time to time. Also, the area was crowded with tourists, many of whom would be walking from one spot to the next in the same sequence the Iranians were following. Under the circumstances, multiple sightings of the same person wouldn't mean much. Toughest of all, about half the hundreds of people in the area were hunkering under black umbrellas and keeping their heads down against the chill and the rain, as Ben was, which made it hell to pick out individuals.

But Ben was operating under one significant disadvantage: he was alone, while the people he was using for concealment were mostly in pairs and groups. So from time to time he made sure to consult his own guidebook with studied fascination, to jot down some notes about the mosque's six minarets and turreted corner domes and special entrance for the sultan, to shoot a few photos, and to otherwise blend as much as he could with the tourists around him.

When the Iranians emerged, one of the scientists and one of the VAVAK guys headed down the steps and turned left while the other two remained under the portico. Ben instantly understood why they were splitting up: the scientist had to hit the head. He knew the restroom they were going to use, too, and it would have been ideal: small, secluded, at the bottom of a flight of stairs at the corner of the mosque grounds. But if something went wrong, he might come out of this with only half the job done, maybe less. No, better to wait for the right moment when he could catch them all closer together.

The scientist and the VAVAK guy returned after a few minutes, and Ben followed them to Hagia Sophia, waiting near the exit again while they were inside. Their next stop was Topkapi Palace, and this time one of the VAVAK guys waited outside. This confirmed for Ben what he already strongly suspected: the VAVAK guys were armed. Topkapi was home to a priceless collection of jewel-encrusted Ottoman swords and crowns and thrones, and there was a metal detector at the entrance to prevent anyone from bringing in hardware for a robbery. Ben figured the guy who was waiting was holding both their guns while the other accompanied the scientists inside. He was half tempted to hide the Glock somewhere and follow them in, but dropping all three barehanded would have presented something of a challenge. Not to mention all the cameras, the single point of egress, and the guards with submachine guns. No, there would be a better opportunity. He waited outside the massive palace gates, haggling with merchants, shooting a few photos, occasionally sneaking a peek through the entrance to make sure the VAVAK guy was still there. He watched the people coming and going carefully in case there was a countersurveillance unit involved. The intel hadn't mentioned it, but intel was never perfect and you had to be careful. He didn't see anything that rubbed him the wrong way.

After Topkapi, the Iranians headed west through the gathering dusk. Ben thought he knew where they were going: either the Grand Bazaar or the Spice Bazaar. If he was right, his opportunity was coming.

They wandered down narrow cobblestone streets

through alternating pools of darkness and light, the sound of their footsteps echoing on the stone walls to either side and mingling with the conversation and laughter of shoppers and passersby. What sky was visible was a dull, dying gray. The rain had stopped, but it was still humid and cold, and a sheen of perspiration gleamed on the peeling façades of souvenir shops and carpet stores and food stalls, all crammed side by side under sagging awnings and rusted escarpments. Ben kept well back, pausing when the Iranians paused, moving when they moved, staying cool, staying patient, knowing something would open up.

The sounds around them were suddenly drowned out by the evening muezzin chanting out the **adhan,** the call to prayer. Ben's Arabic wasn't as strong as his Farsi, but he understood the words:

God is greatest.
I bear witness that there is no lord except God.
I bear witness that Mohammed is the
messenger of God.
Make haste toward prayer.
Make haste toward welfare.
God is greatest.
There is no lord except God.

The Iranians stopped at a small, undistinguished corner building recognizable as a mosque only from the minaret near its entrance. The scientists took off their shoes and went inside, accompanied by one of the VAVAK guys. The other waited outside. Ben smiled. Maybe they were willing to put their faith in God, but not their security. He hung back and waited.

Fifteen minutes later, they emerged and continued northwest. **Come on,** Ben thought. **The Spice Bazaar. You know you want to.**

They moved along Marpuccular Cad, the road that provided the southwest boundary of the bazaar, then onto Tahtakale Cad, still moving northwest. They paused from time to time to examine the wares of the various shops, but didn't go inside. The VAVAK guys maintained their tactical positions. **Come on,** Ben thought. **Come on.** Despite the cold he could feel himself perspiring.

He followed them right onto Uzunçarşi Cad, his breath starting to quicken slightly. It was full dark now. He'd been afraid they were going directly to the Galata Bridge, but now it looked good, it looked like it was the Spice Bazaar after all. He tightened the cords on the backpack and squeezed his left arm against the satisfying bulk of the holstered Glock.

He stayed with them until they turned right onto Hasircilar Cad, the main street of the Spice Bazaar. All right. This was what he'd been waiting for.

He turned and dashed down the middle of Tahtakale Cad, paralleling the route the Iranians were now on, dodging cars and trucks, staying off the sidewalks to avoid the thick clots of pedestrians. The backpack was secure. The weight of the Glock felt right.

He cut left on Yeni Cami Cad, then left again on Çiçek Pazari Sok, now on a collision course with the Iranians. The jostling crowds were thick and he had to slow. He passed stalls filled with enormous mounds of spices, their yellows and oranges and reds and greens impossibly bright under the incandescent bulbs strung up above them. Tables were piled high with candies and honey-soaked pastries and fruit. The air was thick with the mingled aromas of spices and coffee and tobacco smoke. Peddlers cried out warnings above the din as they maneuvered pushcarts around clusters of shifting shoppers.

At the corner of Tahmis Cad and Hasircilar Cad he could see them coming toward him, about forty feet away. His heart was beating hard now. He checked his perimeter and sensed nothing amiss.

He moved left, pausing in front of one of the corner windows of Kurukahveci Mehmet Efendi, one of the city's oldest coffee shops. Ben had been here a half dozen times during reconnaissance, and there were always at least ten people lined up at its two corner windows waiting to buy quantities of the house-roasted beans. It was a logical stop for the Iranians. Even if they didn't stop here, though, they were going to pass right by. He would be able to see them through the store's windows.

He moved back, pretending to examine the colorful cookware in the stall adjacent to the coffee shop.

He pulled the hat down low and unzipped his jacket. His heart was hammering.

A minute later, the first VAVAK guy appeared through the adjoining corner window. He made a right and stopped not ten feet from where Ben stood. The scientists were in front of the adjoining window now, lined up with a dozen other people to purchase some of Kurukahveci's famed beans. He couldn't see the second VAVAK guy, but it was a safe bet he was somewhere a short distance behind them.

Ben closed his eyes for a moment and took a deep breath, then let it out. Another. And again.

He pulled a guidebook from one of his pockets and slowly walked past the VAVAK guy while examining it. He didn't consider what he was about to do. He focused on the book.

At the corner in front of the coffee shop, he looked left. There was the second VAVAK guy, as he had expected, behind the scientists, twenty feet away.

He looked straight, then right, just another addled tourist trying to orient himself. He detected no problems.

He dropped the guidebook back in his pocket and headed back to the first VAVAK guy. He walked past his position without looking directly at him. He saw in his peripheral vision that the VAVAK guy was watching him now. It didn't matter. It was too late.

He passed by the VAVAK guy's left side. As he did, he let his right hand drift inside his open jacket. By the time he was three steps past the VAVAK guy, the

Glock was out. He pivoted counterclockwise, stepping through with his right foot, and brought up the Glock from five feet away.

The VAVAK guy had just enough time to widen his eyes. Ben pressed the trigger. There was a quiet **pffft** and a neat black hole appeared in the VAVAK guy's forehead. His head jerked and a spasm passed through his body. Then his knees buckled and he slid to the ground. Ben was already moving past him. He rounded the corner.

The scientists were at the window now. The second VAVAK guy saw Ben moving past them, the Glock at his side, approaching with unmistakable intent. Someone from around the corner screamed.

The second guy reacted instantly, reaching inside his jacket, but an instant was all he had and it wasn't enough. Ben was too far away to be sure of another head shot. He brought the Glock up in a two-handed grip, put the front sight on the VAVAK guy's chest, and pressed the trigger. **Pffft.** The VAVAK guy jerked back. Ben kept walking straight at him. He fired again, center mass, and the VAVAK guy staggered. Ben adjusted his aim and the third shot blew out the man's left eye.

There were new screams. People started to scatter. The scientists turned from in front of the coffee shop window, their expressions confused, not understanding what was happening, looking for the source of the trouble. The first one didn't even see Ben walking at him from ten feet away. Ben shot him in the head.

The second one had just enough time to raise his hands, either in self-defense or in supplication. Ben put a single round directly between his eyes and was moving past him before his body had even hit the ground.

He glanced left and right as he moved. People were screaming and fleeing. He didn't see any heroes. No one was even looking at him. They were all just trying to get the hell out of there as fast as they could. He kept his chin down and his eyes forward, the Glock close at his side.

Suddenly he sensed something out of place, someone who didn't fit in with the crowd's panicky rhythms. He glanced ahead and saw a stocky Slavic-looking guy standing motionless and watching him intently. Ben pulled up short. They locked eyes. No question the Slav was a professional. It was in his face, his posture, his balanced demeanor.

They stood like that for one frozen second, each trying to determine the other's intent. Then the Slav's nerve broke. He cut left, reaching into his jacket as he moved. Without thinking, Ben brought up the Glock in a two-handed grip. He fired three times, moving closer with each **pffft,** walking the shots in. The Slav crumbled to the ground. He managed to get his gun out, too late. Ben drilled him in the head from less than five feet away.

He moved off and cut down an alley, his head swiveling, searching for problems at his flanks, badly rattled. Jesus Christ, he hadn't seen that guy at all.

Fucker had been standing right there like a ghost when the whole thing went down. If the crowds hadn't left him stranded like driftwood at ebb tide, Ben never would have noticed him. And goddamn it, if the guy had shown the presence of mind to get his weapon out a second earlier . . .

He swapped a fresh magazine into the Glock and kept moving. He knew these streets from reconnaissance and made sure to keep to dark ones until he was well away from the Spice Bazaar. Along the way he stripped off the fake beard and discarded it in a Dumpster overflowing with waste. He lost the black hat and replaced it with a red one. The jacket was reversible. He shrugged it off, turned the inside out, and was suddenly wearing yellow instead of blue. He would get rid of the gun later, when he was sure he was safe.

He began to circle toward the Galata Bridge, back among blissfully ignorant crowds again. He would walk across, catch a cab to Haydarpaşa Station, then a train to Ankara, his original arrival point, which would make for a safer departure, as well.

He heard sirens in the distance. They were heading away from him. He let out a long breath. He was okay. No one was following him and no one could connect him with what had just happened. Istanbul was a city of over ten million people. He was a needle in a haystack, a drop in the ocean. He kept moving, just another tourist again.

Damn, though, who was that guy? Bastard had almost gotten the drop on him, no question.

Well, he hadn't. Some days you eat the bear, and some days the bear eats you.

The bear.

He stopped. Holy shit, was that guy Russian?

He sure looked Russian. Well, it wasn't Vasilyev, he was certain of that. The guy had been a pro, no question, not a scientist or other civilian. Maybe someone connected with Vasilyev, though. Yeah, who else would have been ghosting along behind the Iranians? And why else would the guy have delayed so long before going for his weapon? Because he was thinking he wasn't the target, maybe. But maybe because he was thinking he was immune, at least until he'd seen Ben's eyes. After all, no one was going to drop a Russian agent. You'd have to be crazy.

Son of a bitch. Maybe he hadn't killed **the** Russian, but he had a feeling he'd just killed **a** Russian.

He thought, **Oops,** and in the giddy, adrenaline-charged aftermath, the thought was hilarious. He pushed the back of his hand over his mouth and shook with silent laughter.

He hoped the brass wasn't going to be too pissed.

6 IMPLACABLE

Once he'd canceled the meeting, Alex felt a little calmer. It was like running late to catch a plane—the stressful part was racing around, hoping you might still make it. Once you knew the plane was gone, you could relax, accept it, come up with an alternative.

Except there was no alternative to Hilzoy. Hilzoy was a once-in-a-lifetime ticket.

He worked on a few other matters, but he couldn't get Hilzoy out of his head. He wanted to find out what would happen to the patent application if Hilzoy were . . . gone. Presumably it would be treated as part of Hilzoy's estate, and pass to his descendents or beneficiaries. But who would those people be? Alex didn't know the first thing about Hilzoy's family, other than that he was divorced and had no kids. Was there any way to salvage this thing without Hilzoy, with just the patent?

His mobile rang. He checked the readout. It was a blocked number, but he was so hungry for news he answered anyway.

"Alex Treven."

"Mr. Treven, this is Detective Gamez of the San Jose Police Department. Am I reaching you at a convenient time?"

Alex's heart started kicking. "Uh, yeah, it's a fine time. Is this about . . . is it about Richard Hilzoy?"

There was a pause on the other end, and Alex wondered whether maybe he shouldn't have said that.

"There's been a crime," Gamez said, "and we'd appreciate it if you could come down to the station to answer a few questions."

"Sure," Alex said. "When?"

"Right now would be best."

"Sure," Alex said again. "Just tell me where you are."

"Two-oh-one West Mission Street. Use the front entrance and ask for Detective Gamez."

"I should be there in about a half hour. Can I just ask you—"

"Let's talk when you get here," Gamez said. "A half hour, right?"

"Right," Alex said, and the line went dead.

He started tidying up a few things on his desk, then realized he was being ridiculous. He was afraid of what he might learn, that was it, and was looking for a reason to delay. Or maybe he was seeking to impose some order on the universe by straightening up his desk. **Please.**

He headed out. "I just got a call from the police," he told Alisa as he walked past. "I need to go down to the station."

"Is it Hilzoy?" she called after him.

"We'll find out."

He plugged the address into the M3's nav system, then followed it onto Page Mill Road toward 280. As he crossed Foothill Expressway, he remembered reading about some bicyclist who had died nearby about a year earlier. A freak accident, a broken neck. The memory increased his certainty that something really had happened to Hilzoy. He knew life was like that, knew it firsthand. Just when everything was fine, when it couldn't be better, fate liked to reach out and remind you of exactly how tenuous it all really was.

He wondered why Gamez would be calling him. It had to be Hilzoy. But how had the police known to call him? And how had they gotten his mobile number?

Then he realized. Hilzoy's mobile. The appointment with Alex and the VCs would have been in the electronic calendar. And Alex had called him, what, twenty times that morning? All those calls, and Alex's number, would have been in the log.

He tried to imagine what the appointment and all those logged calls would look like to the police. He wondered if he could be a suspect. Jesus.

San Jose Police headquarters was a fortress, all concrete blocks and ninety-degree angles and dark reflective windows. The two benches in front were bolted to

the cement beneath and did nothing to leaven the for-
midable atmosphere of the place. Even the trees and
plantings felt more like camouflage than decoration.

Alex took a deep breath, walked up the cement
stairs, and entered a lobby. It was more of the same:
bulletproof glass, surveillance cameras, heavy high-
tech-looking metal doors. A half dozen people were
plopped down along two rows of metal chairs, all of
them wearing the kinds of expressions you might expect on someone about to be called in for a nice long
root canal.

Waiting rooms. He hated them.

A woman who looked like she might be there to
answer questions was standing behind the reinforced
glass. Alex walked over and said into the intercom,
"Hi, my name is Alex Treven, I'm supposed to ask for
Detective Gamez. I think he's expecting me."

"Treven?" she asked, and when Alex nodded in
confirmation, she said, "I'll call him and let him
know you're here."

Twenty uncomfortable minutes later, a guy came
through the interior door and looked around the
room. He was about six feet and muscular under his
gray suit jacket and dark tie. He had close-cropped
black hair, and with the coloring and the name, Alex
figured he was Latino.

Alex stood up and looked at him. The guy said,
"Alex Treven?"

Alex nodded and walked over. "Hi, you're . . . Detective Gamez?"

"That's me." The man didn't offer to shake Alex's hand. "Sorry I kept you waiting—we've had a lot of information coming in on this case and it's keeping us jumping. Let's go inside where we can talk."

Alex followed him in. He wanted to ask about the case but decided it was better to say less. Besides, he figured he'd know more soon enough, one way or the other.

They took an elevator to the second floor, then walked down a short corridor. The place felt governmental to Alex, though he couldn't articulate exactly why. Maybe it was the functionality of the decor. Fluorescent lights overhead, drop ceilings, plain tile floors in the hall. They passed a few open doors, and the sounds of conversation from within were muted, serious, as though the people inside were hard at work. Alex was struck by the size of the facility, by the amount of manpower and other resources the government obviously could bring to bear on a problem if it wanted to. There was something . . . implacable about the place, and Alex found it intimidating.

They turned right through an open door. There was a sign overhead—something like CRIME INVESTIGATION UNIT. Alex didn't quite catch it before they had gone through. Inside was a large carpeted area with about a dozen cubicles. Alex could see people working at a few, but no one looked up.

Gamez led him into a small room to their right, maybe eight feet by six. The ceiling was low. A table, three chairs, and no shadows under the harsh fluorescent lights. All the noise without seemed to die in the room, and Alex wondered if it was soundproofed.

Gamez closed the door and they sat facing each other. He pulled a notepad out of his pocket and fixed his eyes on Alex. "When we spoke on the phone, you asked whether this was about Richard Hilzoy. Why did you ask that?"

Alex was mildly taken aback by the guy's abruptness. "We had an important meeting this morning and he didn't show up. I called him a bunch of times, then sent my secretary down to his apartment to see if she could find him. She said it was surrounded by police, and someone said someone had been killed. I was worried it was Richard. Is there a reason you won't just tell me? I'm his lawyer, I'm concerned."

Gamez was looking at him closely. After a moment, he said, "Richard Hilzoy was murdered this morning in the parking lot of his building."

Murdered. Even though Alex had suspected the worst, and thought he'd been prepared for it, the news shook him.

"Damn," he said. "How . . . what happened?"

"I have a few more questions I'd like to ask you," Gamez said. "Your meeting this morning. Who was it with? What was it about?"

Alex answered Gamez's questions. Gamez wrote things down in a small notebook. Occasionally he asked Alex for clarification. Sometimes he circled back to something Alex had said earlier. He confirmed that it was the appointment in Hilzoy's calendar, and the multiple calls in the phone log, that led the police to Alex. Alex realized Gamez wasn't just looking for general information, but that he himself actually was a suspect, and even though he knew he had nothing to worry about, it was unnerving to sit in front of this cop who was thinking that maybe just a few hours earlier Alex had killed someone.

At one point, Gamez asked Alex if he knew whether Hilzoy was using or dealing drugs.

"No," Alex said. "I mean, I didn't know him that well, but I never saw him . . . saw any sign that he was using drugs. And he didn't seem like the kind of guy who would be dealing them. Can I ask why you're asking?"

Gamez pursed his lips. His cheeks expanded, then he blew out a long, slow breath.

"We found a substantial amount of heroin hidden in Hilzoy's car."

"Heroin? Are you serious?"

Gamez looked at him. The look said, **Do I not look serious?**

Alex was trying to process it all. "You think . . . he was killed because he was dealing drugs?"

"It's possible."

"Yeah, but . . . I mean, why wouldn't whoever killed him take the drugs?"

The moment he said it, Alex felt foolish. He was no cop, and he didn't want Gamez to think he was second-guessing him.

But Gamez only shrugged. "Someone searched his apartment. Most likely looking for the dope. The way it was hidden in the vehicle it could have been over-looked. What about enemies? Did Hilzoy have any?"

"I don't think so. Well, he was divorced last year and it sounds like it was a little messy, but I don't know any more than that."

After another hour of Q&A, Gamez closed his notebook. "I appreciate your cooperation," he said. "Just one last question, and it's really a favor because it helps us rule things out and saves us time. Would you mind giving us a DNA sample before you go?"

Alex's eyes widened. At some point, Gamez had asked him if he'd ever been in Hilzoy's car or apart-ment. The answer was no, thank God, and now Alex understood why he'd been asking.

Gamez was looking at him closely again. Alex was suddenly aware that this guy interviewed people, maybe dozens of them, every single day. He had probably been lied to more that morning, and by ex-perts, too, than Alex had been lied to in his life.

Alex shrugged. "No, I don't mind, if it helps. What do you need me to do?"

There was really nothing to it. A consent form, a cotton swab rubbed against the inside of his cheek, and that was that. Gamez walked him back down to the lobby. He handed Alex a card.

"If you think of anything else, please give me a call," Gamez said. He held out his hand. "And I'm sorry about your client."

Alex sensed from the gesture and the words that Gamez had pretty much ruled him out. He shook Gamez's hand. "I hope you catch who did it."

"We'll get him," Gamez said, and left.

Hilzoy was dealing drugs? At a level where people were murdered over it? Alex couldn't believe it.

Well, Hilzoy was tight for money after the divorce. Maybe it had made him desperate. But how could he be so stupid?

Or maybe he had lost his nerve. Maybe that happened to some people when they got so close to the thing that could make their dreams come true.

Getting into his car, he looked back at the station. With the mirrored windows, it looked as impregnable to understanding as it did to attack.

He thought of the cool way Gamez had said, **We'll get him.** He should have been comforted by the man's confidence. Instead, there was something chilling about it.

7 SO LONG AS THEY FEAR US

Ben spent three days in Ankara. He wasn't in a hurry, and didn't want to cross a national border until some of the potential heat from Istanbul had evaporated. The hit was all over the television news and in the English-language dailies. The Iranians had been identified as such, but there were no reports of their affiliations beyond nationality. The fifth guy was a total unknown. Ben assumed he'd been operating sterile, carrying no passport or other identifying documents, and if no one claimed him, he would remain, at least to the public, the Turkish equivalent of a John Doe.

He'd checked in immediately with his commander at JSOC, the military's Joint Special Operations Command, an African-American named Scott "Hort" Horton. Horton was a legend in the black ops community, a veteran of countless campaigns both public and secret, a swashbuckler who had ridden on horseback with the mujahideen in Afghanistan, fought with the Contras in Nicaragua, and personally led clandestine small-unit hunts for bin Laden in Pakistan's northwest tribal regions, a man of impeccable patriotic credentials who could trace his military ancestry all the way back to the Fourth United States Colored Infantry, which fought with Major General Edward Ord's Union Army of the James at the decisive Battle of Appomattox Court House. Horton was a colonel and Ben only an E-8 master sergeant, but despite the difference in their age, rank, and service, and despite the near reverence Ben felt for the man, Ben addressed him as Hort. Members of the unit called one another by their first names or call signs regardless of rank. There was no saluting, either, or much other regular military behavior. They didn't need it. They were too small, too irregular, and too specialized for the spit-and-polish discipline and hooah spirit that kept the regular army cohesive. And although they wouldn't have said it in so many words, they were also too elite.

Every one of the unit's members had been through the same brutal feeder system: Airborne, Ranger, Special Forces, and Delta, or the marine or navy equivalent. A candidate needed a personal recommendation from someone already in the unit before being invited to try out, and at least three confirmed combat kills. Most, like Ben, who had been blooded in Mogadishu, had many more than that. Once selected, candidates were put through MOTC—the CIA's Military Operations Training Course—then subjected to a variety of grueling physical and psychological tests, culminating in something known as "the Final," which Hort was reputed to have designed himself, in which the candidate was drugged, hooded, flown to a third-world country he had never visited and whose language he didn't speak, and left with no money, passport, or anything else but the clothes on his back. His objective was to carry out a designated clandestine act that would involve a prison term if it were discovered, then return to the United States undetected. Only men who had passed every test, including the Final, were accepted into the unit. There were three areas of specialization: signals intelligence, human intelligence, and the shooters. Everyone had crossover skills, of course, but Ben was primarily a shooter.

Over the years the unit had been known by a variety of names: Foreign Operating Group, Intelligence Support Activity, Centra Spike, Gray Fox, and quite a few others. The frequent name changes were part of JSOC's ongoing efforts to persuade government bean counters that the elite unit was being reformed following inquiries into the latest assassination or other covert op du jour. An ambassador would protest that he hadn't been briefed, someone from the Senate Select Committee on Intelligence or the Armed Services Committee would ask what the hell was going on, the Pentagon would tell JSOC it had better behave, JSOC would say sorry and give the unit a new name. Egos would be massaged, faces saved, consciences salved. But the program itself never really changed. Because the truth was, the more restrictions Congress and the brass laid down on "white" special ops units like the Green Berets, the greater the need for "black" units like Ben's. It was a demand-side problem, and thank God there were men who would always find a way to create a supply.

Ben briefed Hort about the way it went down in Istanbul, using a pay phone and a portable scrambler that fit over the mouthpiece of the receiver. He told him about the Russian.

"You sure he was Russian?" Hort asked in his gravelly baritone and cultured coastal drawl.

"Pretty sure," Ben said. "He had the Slavic cheekbones and pale skin, and that flat expression, if you know what I mean. Plus he was standing there like he was untouchable."

"Right up until you touched him."

"He was going for a weapon."

"Don't worry, son, I believe you. No chance he was Israeli? They would have loved to take a crack at the two you sent to Valhalla."

Ben thought about that. He'd even wondered at one point whether someone had considered handing this op off to the Mossad. Probably someone had, but with their better intel inside Iran, the Israelis might have figured out who the mole was, and no one would have been willing to take that chance, even with one of America's closest allies in the dreaded global war on terror. Plus there was always someone at JSOC lobbying for use of U.S. resources. They'd invested an enormous amount training—in fact, creating—Ben and a few others like him, and what was the point of having an attack dog if you didn't sometimes let him off the leash?

"I'm thinking he was FSB," Ben said. The FSB was the Federal'naya Sluzhba Bezopasnosti, the Russian successor to the Soviet KGB.

"I hope not," Hort said. "Those guys are like the mafia. Hell, with all those former KGB **siloviki** in office, they **are** the mafia."

"What do you want to do?"

"I'll see what I can find out. But don't worry, even if he was FSB, it's not going to be obvious who did it. The other two had a lot of enemies."

The Iranian enemies Hort was referring to were the Israelis. In fact, while he was in Istanbul, Ben had been eating food brought directly from Israel. If the op went sideways and he was killed, or if he was captured and used the cyanide pill he was carrying, there would be an autopsy, his stomach contents analyzed. Best for things to point in the direction of Israel. JSOC had laid down a few other false clues, as well, nothing too heavy-handed. Not a very nice trick to play on a friend, but the Israelis were realists and would understand. Anyway, what could Russia really do to Israel that it wasn't doing already? Sell arms to Damascus? Deliver nuclear fuel to Tehran? And what could Iran do? Back Hezbollah? Blow up another Argentine synagogue? Yeah, one thing the Israelis had going for them was clarity. Their enemies couldn't hate them more than they already did. Ben wished the U.S. could be equally clear-eyed. What did Caligula say? **Oderint dum metuant.** Let them hate us, so long as they fear us.

He went back to waiting in his room. He didn't go out much. There were periods in his life where he would go days without even speaking, where his whole world would shrink to no more than the dimensions of the walls around him. Sometimes he withdrew so thoroughly, the only thing that would bring him out of it was the buzz of his pager.

He thought about hate. America was hated overseas, true, but was pretty well understood, too. In fact, he thought foreigners understood Americans better than Americans understood themselves. Americans thought of themselves as a benevolent, peace-loving people. But benevolent, peace-loving peoples don't cross oceans to new continents, exterminate the natives, expel the other foreign powers, conquer sovereign territory, win world wars, and less than two centuries from their birth stand astride the planet. The benevolent peace lovers were the ones all that shit happened to.

It was the combination of the gentle self-image and the brutal truth that made Americans so dangerous. Because if you aggressed against such a people, who could see themselves only as innocent, the embodiment of all that was good in the world, they would react not just with anger but with Old Testament–style moral wrath. Anyone depraved enough to attack such angels forfeited claims to adjudication, proportionality, even elemental mercy itself.

Yeah, foreigners hated that American hypocrisy. That was okay, as long as they also feared it. **Oderint dum metuant.**

True, there were downsides to the fear. After the U.S. took out Saddam Hussein, every bush-league enemy of America out there realized he needed an insurance policy. Because if Saddam had had a few nukes and had demonstrated the insanity or even just the minimal resolve to use them if attacked—and who would bet against a guy who had gassed his own people?—the U.S. would have stood down for sure. The Iranians understood this. It was part of why they were trying so hard for a nuke of their own.

He smiled. Well, they'd suffered a bit of a setback recently, hadn't they?

But killing the scientists was mostly just buying time. America was the world's richest, most networked, most technologically advanced nation, with unparalleled military superiority. Nukes might be enough to check a power like that, but that didn't mean America's enemies weren't also looking for a checkmate. The Chinese were experimenting with antisatellite technology, looking for a way to put out America's eyes in space. For the Russians, it was all about cyberwarfare, with their massive denial-of-service attack on Estonia a trial run. The Iranians and other third-tier powers . . . who knew? In a thousand garages and bunkers and secret laboratories all around the world, motivated men probed for weakness. When they found it, they would exploit it.

Luckily, there were hundreds of guys in the bowels of the Pentagon whose job was to ruminate over all the possibilities, imagine, predict, monitor, counter. Of course, there had been people assigned to figure out how to protect America from asymmetrical threats pre-9/11, too. But there were more of them now, and they were better motivated. The Defense Department had even formalized some of it, turning the Eighth Air Force into something called a Cyber Command, tasked with training and equipping forces to conduct network defense, attack, and exploitation. Ben hoped they were doing their job.

Well, he was doing his. He was proud of that. If his folks were alive, maybe they would have been proud, too.

Maybe not, though. He'd always been the black sheep. There was a reserve about him, a stillness at his core his parents found vaguely discomfiting and other kids mistook as a kind of cool. The stillness had made him popular, and that unsought, effortless popularity, along with the friends and dates and parties that came with it, had acted to balance the stillness and to some extent conceal it.

His father had been an engineer with IBM, and the family had moved three times when Ben was a kid—first, Yorktown Heights in New York; then Austin, Texas; and then Portola Valley, in California's Silicon Valley, a stone's throw from the San Andreas Fault. Ben had a knack for football and wrestling, and sports were always a good way to quickly get accepted in a new school. His younger sister, Katie, never had a problem, either. She was a beautiful girl with a radiant smile and nothing but goodwill in her heart, who had it in her just to naturally like everyone, and naturally enough, everyone seemed to like her in return.

Alex, the youngest of the three, was the problem. He was shy and awkward everywhere but in the classroom, where the little teacher's pet would have an answer to every question and never made a mistake. Alex's constant need to show everyone how smart he was would invariably attract the attention of a bully, and then it would fall to Ben to straighten the bully out. The bully would typically have an older brother, and the brother would always have friends. Usually it took three or four fistfights before Ben established that even if his younger brother was a dipshit, that didn't mean people could pick on him. During these periods, when Ben had to make things clear to people, he often found himself suspended from school. His parents were appalled. They demanded explanations, but what could Ben really tell them? Alex, with his instant aptitude for science and school, was his father's favorite, and the old man wouldn't have understood that it was precisely Alex's showing off all the time in class that was causing the problems. A few times, after Ben had violently interceded on his behalf, Alex thanked him, but Ben didn't want his thanks, he just wanted him to stop provoking people by acting like he was smarter than everyone else. Ben would tell him that, but Alex never listened. And so it went on, Ben angry at Alex, the parents angry at Ben, Ben even more angry at Alex as a result, and Alex, awed by his big brother, confused and resentful at his aloofness and ire. The only emollient was Katie. She would soothe Ben and comfort Alex and try to explain to their parents, and although Martin and Judith Treven could never accept Ben's ready embrace of violence as a solution, no one could stay angry long when Katie was advocating for peace.

He hadn't known it at the time, but family was a fragile thing. Like a house of cards. Some cards, no doubt, could be pulled out without much affecting the overall structure. Others, when they were removed, caused a shudder, and then another card popped out, then two more—and then the whole thing collapsed, just like that. All from a single mistake, from one little lost card.

But none of that mattered anymore. What happened had happened, and now, looking back, it all seemed unavoidable, not a collection of random events at all but rather the insidious and inevitable workings of destiny itself. He wondered sometimes whether that feeling of destiny was a trick, a narcotic the mind offered up to anesthetize remorse and re-

gret. After all, if it didn't just happen, but had to happen, it couldn't have been your fault. Destiny was like
a freight train, and who the hell could stop that?
Trains just went wherever the tracks led them. So at
the time it had looked like a car, sure. But it wasn't.
Really, it was a train.

8 THE FLAVOR OF THE FOOD

Sarah had gone back to her office so Alex could call the VCs and cancel the meeting. The poor guy looked crushed. Well, who wouldn't? He never said anything about it, but she knew if the Obsidian technology turned out to be as good as it looked, Hilzoy would become a very important client of the firm. For a sixth-year like Alex, coming up for partnership, originating a client like that had to be a big deal.

She spent two hours analyzing some prior art for one of the senior litigation associates. There were no interruptions, and she was glad of it—she still wasn't used to managing her time in six-minute increments, and long periods devoted exclusively to a single matter made it easier to keep track. She made a note of the time and thought about getting some lunch.

She got up and adjusted the blinds. At midday the sun moved into position and made the office too warm. Not that an overabundance of sunlight was anything to complain about.

Outside her window, a soccer game was in progress on a field that had lain barren until recently, when some sort of Superfund cleanup had converted it to its current use. She pulled the blinds open a bit and watched for a moment. Her window was impressively soundproofed and she couldn't hear the game, but she imagined the players were laughing.

No, she really had nothing to complain about. An office with a view in a great location, nice furnishings, a secretary. The work was reasonably interesting and she was good at it. The position conferred a certain degree of status, too, although she wouldn't have wanted to put it that way out loud. And of course she was making an obscene amount of money for a twenty-six-year-old. Still, at times the feeling that somehow she had just stumbled into it all troubled her. Just because you were good at something, and it paid well, was that sufficient reason to do it?

Her parents would have laughed at the question, and indeed they had before she'd learned to keep her doubts to herself. But of course, they were from a different generation. They had met as college students in America, where they had come to study and to perfect their English as was the custom among the sons and daughters of well-off Iranians of the day. Her father, Emaan, was pre-med and planned to become an ophthalmologist. Her mother, Ashraf, was studying nineteenth-century English literature and wanted one day to become a professor herself. They married while still in school. Their parents were pleased with the match, and their future looked bright.

Then came the revolution, and the seizure of the U.S. embassy. Amid talk of war, President Carter froze Iranian assets. Their families lost everything. Forget about tuition—it was all they could do to find a way to eat and pay the rent. Ashraf took a job as a waitress. Emaan sold eyeglasses at an optician's shop. They worked their butts off and saved money by sharing a two-bedroom apartment with another Iranian couple who had been similarly afflicted. Eventually, they had enough put away to buy out the optician. Now they owned five eyeglass stores in the Bay Area and some real estate, too, and were damn proud of it. Once, when Sarah had told her father she wanted a job that paid psychic income, he had laughed and said, "Silly child, don't you know that financial income **is** psychic income?"

She understood his point. But she had more opportunities than her parents did, opportunities they had given her. Wouldn't it be wrong not to take advantage? Shouldn't she build on the foundation they had provided?

And besides, she thought she had seen sadness behind her father's laugh.

She tried to ignore it, but she couldn't shake the feeling that there was something more for her, if only she could figure out what.

And that was her problem: all her dreams were inchoate. She didn't know what she wanted. There was a longing inside her, but she couldn't name it. It could be quietly corrosive, feeling so strongly something was there yet unable to express or even identify it. She wondered which was worse: betraying a dream or being too shallow even to have one?

And then she would tell herself she was being silly. She was hoping for too much, that was the problem. She should just be satisfied with all the good things she had.

Sometimes she wished she had a sibling she could confide in. But times had been hard when she was born. Her parents didn't think they could afford another child, and by the time they could, Sarah was already ten. They didn't want to start all over again.

The one thing that really interested her was politics. She read everything, across the political spectrum—newspapers, magazines, books. Blogs especially. There were some great ones out there, and with their diversity and spontaneity she trusted them much more than she did the mainstream media, which was controlled by corporations or driven only by a hunger for access to whoever was in power, or both. The voracious reading was a kind of hobby that had started in high school and intensified as she got older. But what was she supposed to do with it? Look at how Obama's opponents had tried to smear him by falsely suggesting he was Muslim. Or the way they'd destroyed that Iranian-American businessman,

Alex Latifi, with textbook malicious prosecution in Alabama. What would people make of an Iranian-American woman who really was Muslim, who in fact found passages of the Koran breathtakingly beautiful? Her given name was Shaghayegh, for God's sake, after the Persian flower—Sarah was just a nickname. Shaghayegh Hosseini, vote for me . . . Really, she had a better chance of being sent to Guantánamo than of being elected to office.

She had been a freshman at Caltech when the planes struck the Pentagon and Twin Towers. After, she had been approached by recruiters from all over the federal government: FBI, NSA, CIA, the newly formed Department of Homeland Security. They were all desperate for people who could speak the languages of the Muslim world, and Sarah, whose Farsi was fluent, seemed to be popping up on all their computer lists. She was intrigued by the notion of a top-secret security clearance, by the chance to fight the fanaticism that was poisoning the culture she came from. But her parents had been against it. Having endured the revolution and everything that came after, they had been badly afraid of another backlash. The Hosseinis were American now, and didn't want to do anything to draw attention to their origins. Education was the key to success in America, her parents assured her. They had long since accepted that she had no interest in becoming a doctor, but she had a strong aptitude for science—advanced placement courses in high school, early acceptance to the information security program at Caltech. Why not go on to a law degree? With a combination like that, she could do anything. And so a kind of compromise had been born.

She loved her parents and wanted to make them happy, but there was a part of her too that resented their obsession with education and status, with the way they used her as a vehicle to pursue their own truncated dreams. That kernel of resentment led to her first real act of rebellion—an American-as-apple-pie boyfriend named Josh Marshall, whom she started dating as a sophomore when he was a junior, and to whom she lost her virginity that same year. Josh was a nice guy, from a nice family, and with good prospects, but he wasn't Iranian, and although there wasn't much her parents could do to stop her, she knew they were quietly appalled. And that was good. She was finally going after something **she** wanted.

The romance lasted until Josh graduated, when he left for Tucson and a job designing missile systems with Raytheon. They saw each other a few times that summer, but when the senior-year fall semester began, Sarah told him she was just too busy to keep it up. She pretended to be full of regret, but the truth was, she'd gotten bored. Although he was generally a confident guy, Josh had always been intimidated by her, and uncertain of himself as a result. It was as though he didn't quite believe he deserved her, that she was doing him some kind of favor by seeing him.

She'd always felt the relationship was on her terms, that she was the one ultimately in control, and in the end she'd been proven right.

The pattern had continued at Berkeley's Boalt Hall. She'd been at the law school less than a month when she got involved with a second-year, another Anglo-American, this one named John Cole. And later, when John graduated and left for a job with the Justice Department in D.C., Sarah, who had grown bored with her new relationship in much the same way she had grown bored with the previous, again used the occasion as an excuse to end it. After, she wondered about her motivations. Both had been good boyfriends, at least in an all-appropriate-boxes-checked kind of way. But both had been guaranteed to be unacceptable to her parents, and both had come with a kind of built-in expiration date. Was she stacking the odds against herself? And why would she do that?

Had she loved them? She told them she did, after they breathlessly declared the same to her. But although she felt a deep affection, especially for Josh, who after all had been her first, she didn't know if she could really call it love. She wondered if it was not only the expiration date that drew her, but also a certain blandness to the flavor of the food. Maybe she was afraid to taste something that might ignite some latent appetite, an appetite she sensed inside herself but for some reason sought to deny.

The sex had been good, though. Or good enough,

anyway. True, she couldn't seem to come with either of them, but it didn't really matter. Just the contact was nice, and she liked having someone to sleep with. And when she needed to really get off, she could always lock the bathroom door, take a hot bath, close her eyes, and touch herself the way she needed to. In her fantasies, she would be at the back of a lecture hall, or surrounded by a crowd at a bar or a party, or in the library stacks late at night. There was always a man whose face was indistinct, but who she knew was watching her, and there was something simultaneously appreciative and arrogant in his gaze. She would challenge him, demand to know who he was, what he thought he was looking at. He would smile and say, **I know what you want.** She would laugh at his presumptuousness and say something like, **Oh, really?** The laugh was supposed to make him wilt, but it didn't, and his smile would grow broader, and she would feel he was silently mocking her. **You don't know the first thing about me,** she would say. He would come closer then, and in a low voice say that of course he knew things about her, and he could prove it if he wanted to. His insolence would enrage her, and she would demand, **Prove it how?** He would come very close then, and she would try to move back, but there was always something blocking her, and then his body would be against hers and his mouth would be at her ear and he would whisper, **I know how you like to be touched . . . like this, and like this, and like this . . .**

She shook her head and let the blinds fall shut. She needed lunch. Maybe she'd ask Alex. She was curious if he'd heard anything else about Hilzoy. And he looked like he could use a little company.

He was an attractive guy, and she wondered about him sometimes. But he'd probably make partner soon, and if she were involved with him at that point they'd have to break it off. She chuckled. Yeah, he was right up her alley. Another good-looking, all-American guy with the right kind of résumé and an automatic expiration date. Perfect.

Anyway, he didn't seem interested, although she had to admit that was part of the attraction. She was used to men wanting her. They weren't very good at concealing it, and most didn't even try. It was funny, too, because she'd been a strange-looking kid, with widely set eyes and lips way too full for her face, and her features hadn't come together until late in high school. She was grateful for that. If she'd been born beautiful, it would be like being born rich. Everything would have been too easy. As it was, her looks always felt like an improbable, unexpected gift, something she'd happened across by accident, not something she'd been granted by right.

It was ridiculous, really, that she would be interested in the one guy in the firm who seemed not to be interested in her. But he had qualities she liked. He was good to work with, for one. He always explained things clearly, and he wasn't intimidated by her technical knowledge, unlike various other associates she'd worked with. And he was certainly serious. Even too serious—she saw him in his office whenever she came in early or left late, and he didn't seem to have much of a life outside the firm. She thought she detected an odd sort of . . . sadness behind the seriousness, and it intrigued her. She imagined how she might respond if he made a move, then laughed at the thought. He wasn't interested, and that was probably for the best.

But no harm in just asking him about lunch. She was going out anyway, she would just check in about Hilzoy and then mention that she was going to grab a bite, maybe at Straits Café, the Singaporean place, and if he was hungry . . .

She walked down the corridor to his office and poked her head in, but he wasn't there. His secretary, Alisa, saw her and said, "He had to go to the police station."

Sarah raised her eyebrows. "The police station? Is it about Hilzoy?"

Alisa shook her head. "He didn't say."

Sarah nodded and said, "He never does, does he?"

She walked off, thinking maybe she would just grab something from the firm cafeteria. Yeah, that was probably for the best.

9 SADLY ETERNAL

Alex got to the office at six o'clock the next morning. He hadn't slept well, but at least he'd come up with a course of action. The first step was to check in with the Patent and Trademark Office. The group director of Technology Center 2130—the PTO examination group responsible for computer cryptography and security—was a Stanford grad named Hank Shiffman, whom Alex had been friendly with when they were students. Having a friend like Hank inside was huge—he was smart enough to really get what Obsidian was about, and he knew all the bizarre inner workings of the patent office, too. Hank and 2130 hadn't officially received the application yet, but Hank had been keeping Alex unofficially apprised of its progress since it had first arrived at the Office of Initial Patent Examination. The last Alex had heard, the application had been forwarded to the Depart-

ment of Defense for national security review. A security review was routine for an invention dealing with
cryptography, and unless the DoD decided to issue a
secrecy order—a huge pain in the neck but, thank
God, highly unlikely—the application would soon
pass muster and be assigned to a formal examiner in
Hank's group.

It was nine o'clock in Virginia, where the PTO was
located. Alex called Hank and got his voice mail.

Damn. Hank was always at his desk early. Well,
maybe he was in the bathroom or something.

The message said to press zero to speak to an operator. Alex did. A moment later, a woman asked,
"How may I direct your call?"

"I'm trying to reach Hank Shiffman."

There was a pause. The woman said, "Ah, could
you hold on for just a moment?"

Alex waited, wondering why the woman had
sounded so uncertain about something so mundane.

A moment later, another woman's voice came on,
throatier than the first, the tone more businesslike.
"Hello, this is Director Jane Hamsher, Computer Ar-
chitecture, Software, and Information Security. May
I ask to whom I'm speaking?"

Alex thought for a moment. The information
Hank had been feeding him was back-channel. He
didn't want to create a problem for his friend.

"This is Alex Treven," he said. "I'm a friend of
Hank's from Stanford."

There was a pause, then the woman said, "I see.

Then I'm sorry to be the one to tell you that Hank passed away yesterday."

Alex had one long moment during which he was certain he had heard wrong. He replayed the woman's words in his head, trying to arrive at a construction that made sense. Nothing did.

Finally he managed to blurt out, "What . . . what happened? How?"

"Apparently, it was a heart attack."

Alex thought of Hank, a vegetarian and a demon on the squash court. "But . . . Hank was totally healthy. I mean, I don't think I've ever known anyone that healthy."

"I know, it's been quite a shock to all of us. It seems it was something congenital, but they're still trying to work it out. We're all going to miss Hank. He was a good man and very capable."

She was easing away. Alex thought, **Well, nothing to protect him from if he's dead,** and said, "The thing is, Hank was . . . advising me on a cryptography application on behalf of a client. I wonder if there's someone else there who could give me an update?"

There was a pause. "Hank was the examiner?" the woman asked, her tone doubtful.

"No, it hadn't been assigned to a group yet. As far as I know, it's still at OIPE, and subject to Defense Department review—"

"Well, as soon as it's cleared the review, OIPE will assign it to a technology group, probably 2130 from your description. We'll be in touch at that point."

Damn, not quite the sympathetic reaction he'd been hoping a bereaved friend would rate. "Right," Alex said. "Thank you."

"Not at all. And again, my condolences."

He hung up. Time for a Plan B. Trouble was, with Hilzoy dead, he was already at Plan B. And it didn't seem to be going well.

First Hilzoy, then Hank. Unbelievable. It was like Obsidian was cursed.

He thought about what to do next. He still needed to find out who stood to inherit the rights to the patent if—when—it was issued. Also to roll up his sleeves and thoroughly assess the technology—the benefits, the limitations, all possible applications in various potential markets. Up until now, Hilzoy had been the best pitchman for Obsidian as something you could build a company around. With Hilzoy gone, Alex would need to be able to talk that talk.

He went through Hilzoy's file and was unsurprised to find no information on family. All right, he'd put Alisa on this. Contact the ex-wife and figure out who were the closest relatives—the likely beneficiaries under a will, or the most likely to inherit if Hilzoy died intestate.

Finally, the technology itself. Hilzoy always left a backup DVD of the latest version with Alisa when he visited the office. Alex went out and retrieved it, then popped it into the bay of his laptop. When the program booted, Alex was surprised to hear music coming from the laptop's tiny speakers. He didn't recognize the tune—something instrumental. He listened for a minute, then found a command to turn it off. It was creepy, imagining Hilzoy listening to it while he worked on Obsidian. Maybe it was one of his favorites.

He started performing the various applications, describing them as he worked, pretending he was talking to a VC. "Did you see how fast Obsidian encrypted a five-gigabyte video file? Well, it scales, too. We've tested it up to five terabytes, and we think it can go further. And not just video, of course not. Any data. Any platform. And the decrypt process is just as quick. Watch this . . ."

He kept at it for an hour, immersed, lost to the outside world. He had to be able to do this. He had to.

There was a knock on his door. He called out, "Yeah."

The door opened and Sarah walked in. "Hey," she said, her tone and accompanying expression suggesting she was not entirely pleased.

"What is it?" Alex asked, startled to see her, his mind still more than half occupied by Obsidian.

She sat down and looked at him. "Has it not occurred to you that other people might be concerned about what happened to Hilzoy?"

Alex frowned. Why couldn't she just act like a first-year associate was supposed to? She couldn't just barge in here, plop down in a seat like his office was her second home, and start interrogating him.

"Look—" he started to say.

She leaned forward, her elbows on his desk. "You blew out of here and went to the police station yesterday. What was that all about?"

Alex forced himself not to glance down at the alluring bit of décolletage he sensed in his peripheral vision. All right, maybe she had a point. "He was murdered," he said.

Suddenly her expression was soft again. "Oh my God, I can't believe it."

He thought he should just tell her he was busy. Convey his displeasure with her failure to show him the appropriate deference. He'd always been deferential when he was a first-year. What was wrong with her?

Instead, he said, "There was a bunch of heroin in the trunk of his car. Some kind of drug deal, they think."

"Heroin? Hilzoy? Come on, he was a geek. That doesn't make sense."

"I guess you can never tell."

She leaned back as though she intended to stay awhile. "The police called you because . . . they thought you might know something?"

For a moment Alex hesitated, and then he surrendered. Hilzoy, then Hank . . . it was so weird, he just needed to talk to someone. He told her about the cell phone connection that led the police to him, about the Q&A at headquarters, even about the DNA test. He hadn't been planning to say so much; in fact, he hadn't planned on saying anything. He sensed that in doing so now he was taking a chance, the risks of which he didn't fully understand and certainly couldn't control. The feeling made him feel slightly dizzy, almost nauseated.

"Have you told Osborne?" she asked, when he was done.

"No. He's in Bangkok until tomorrow. I'll tell him then."

"Won't he want to know right away? You could send him an e-mail."

Alex laughed. "If it's not his client, Osborne could give a shit, believe me."

The moment the words were out, he wished he hadn't said it. He always knew to be tight-lipped about that kind of thing—you never knew how something innocuous could get distorted and amplified in the retelling. He hated that she could have this effect on him.

But Sarah only smiled sympathetically. "So, what's going to happen to the patent?"

Alex ran his fingers through his hair and sighed. "I'm trying to find out."

She glanced at his laptop. "Is that what you're doing there?"

"A little, yeah. Taking Obsidian for a test drive. Trying to see how it does without Hilzoy behind the wheel."

She nodded. "Well, if you want a copilot, just ask me."

He looked at her, trying to read her expression.

What did the offer mean, exactly? Was it just about work, or . . .

He felt himself blushing. Goddamn it.

"Thanks," he said. "I'll let you know."

She smiled and stood. "Sorry I barged in on you. I was just really curious, you know?"

Alex nodded and forced himself to stay in his seat. He wasn't going to see her off as though she were a damned partner.

She flashed him that beautiful smile again and left, closing the door behind her. Alex expelled a long breath. After a minute, he opened the laptop and returned to experimenting with Obsidian. But he couldn't get his focus back. This whole situation . . . it was just stirring up memories.

Alex had been a freshman at Menlo Atherton High School the night Katie died. He was sleeping, and was stirred to partial wakefulness by the sound of the phone ringing. He wondered vaguely why someone would be calling so late, then started to drift off again, knowing that whatever it was, his parents would take care of it. And then, a moment later, he was shocked to full consciousness by the most terrible sound he'd ever heard. It wasn't a loud sound, but it made him sit bolt upright anyway, his hands shaking, all the warmth suddenly gone from his body.

The sound was his mother. Six syllables, all in a quavering, unnaturally high voice, the words themselves eclipsed and irrelevant beside the naked terror in her tone.

"Oh no. Oh please God no."

Alex sat frozen in his bed, holding the covers close, more frightened than he'd ever been in his life. What could make his mother sound that way? Who was on the phone?

A moment later, his father appeared at his door. He flicked on the light and in a quiet, commanding voice Alex had never heard before said, "Alex, get dressed. We have to go to the hospital."

Alex shook his head, not understanding. The hospital? Who was sick?

"Dad—"

"Now!" his father said.

They piled into his dad's car, his mother in the passenger seat, Alex confused and afraid in back, and screeched backward out of the driveway. The moment they hit the street his dad spun the wheel and locked up the brakes and Alex was thrown forward. He didn't even have his seat belt on yet. Then his dad floored it and he was thrown back again. He got his seat belt on with shaking hands just as his dad fishtailed right at the end of the street, nearly slamming Alex up against the door.

His dad kept driving like a madman, and his mother, who was never shy about opining on his dad's driving, especially when she deemed it unsafe, didn't say a word. Alex was suddenly aware he needed to take a leak. He'd been so frightened, and they'd left in such a hurry, he hadn't even realized.

"It's Katie," his father said as though remembering

for the first time that Alex didn't even know what the hell was going on. He slowed at a red light and swiveled his head to check for traffic, then rocketed through. "She was in an accident."

Alex felt tears well up and forced them back. He heard an echo of his mother's voice in his mind and knew all at once the sound would reverberate inside him forever.

Oh no. Oh please God no.

"I don't understand," his mother said, and Alex could hear she was crying. "Where's Ben? I thought you were going to tell him—"

"I did tell him," Alex's father said. "He was supposed to drive Katie home. I told him specifically."

Alex tried to understand what this was about. Earlier that day the whole family had returned from two days at the California State Wrestling Championships in Bakersfield, where Ben had won the 171-pound weight class. Ben had been ecstatic, so happy he had even surprised Alex by hugging him in front of everyone in the stands. Some kids were throwing Ben a party that night. It was for seniors and juniors, so Ben and Katie were going. No one had told Alex more than that. They never did.

"Maybe Wally drove her," Alex said in a small voice, trying to be helpful. Wally Farquhar was Katie's boyfriend. He was a senior and had a fancy black Mustang. He never gave any sign of even knowing Alex existed, and Alex didn't like him much. He had the sense his parents weren't so crazy about Wally either.

There was a long silence, and Alex wondered if he had said something wrong. After a moment, his father spoke, his voice unrecognizably grim. "Wally was driving."

No one said anything the rest of the way. It was as though the fact Wally had been driving had decided something, something both awful and permanent.

Alex wanted to know more, but he was afraid to ask. Katie was in a car accident . . . but she would be okay, wouldn't she? And why wasn't Ben driving her? His parents said he was supposed to. He wasn't able to articulate the feeling, but he sensed strongly that Ben had done something wrong, and that whatever it was, if Ben hadn't done it, none of this would be happening.

But maybe it wasn't happening. Maybe he was still asleep at home. Maybe the ache in his bladder, his dad's crazy driving, the sound his mother had made, this whole sickening lurch in their lives, maybe it was all just a terrible dream.

His father screeched to a stop in front of the Stanford Medical Center emergency room entrance and cut the engine. His parents jumped out, slamming the doors behind them, and Alex realized they weren't going to a parking lot, they were leaving the car right here. How was he supposed to know that? No one had even said anything to him, and it felt like they were just leaving him.

He got out. The night was cold and quiet and he could see his breath fogging, could see swirling cones of vapor under the sodium lights in front of the building. The façade of the hospital seemed to glow in the darkness around it, the building's edges indistinct. His sense that this could be a dream deepened.

He ran inside and pulled up next to his parents. His father was talking to a black woman in a window, a nurse or a receptionist. Katie Treven, he was saying. We're her parents. Where is she?

The woman looked at some paperwork in front of her, then at Alex's father. "She's in surgery, sir."

Surgery. Alex's mind was flooded with visions of masked doctors in bloody gowns, white-hot operating room lights, trays of gleaming metal instruments, and the thought of Katie at the center of it all, right here, right now . . .

"We need to see her," Alex's mom said, her voice equally frightened and firm. "Where is she?"

The woman looked at Alex's mother, and though her expression wasn't without compassion, Alex recognized something unmovable in it. He could sense how many times the woman had danced these steps, how accustomed she was to dealing with this situation.

"Ma'am," she said, "I understand how upset you are. But you're not permitted into surgery. It's a sterile environment, and if you went in it could only hurt your daughter, not help her. Please, just have a seat in the waiting room. The doctor will be out shortly."

Alex watched his parents' shoulders slump, and they all shuffled off, meek and scared and dejected. He wondered for a moment how he could have known about the nurse. The nature of the insight felt new to him, and not entirely welcome.

There was something sadly eternal about the small rectangular waiting room, with its smell of antiseptic and rows of upholstered chairs and television flickering in the corner. The television was playing too quietly to be heard and Alex wondered what was the point, and then he realized: it was to remind people that this room wasn't the whole world, that whatever horror had summoned them here, there was still life outside. He was struck by the thought, by the newfound **adultness** of it, as he had been by his insight into the nurse, and for some reason the fact that he could suddenly understand such a thing frightened him.

They found three adjacent chairs and sat. Alex looked around. A dozen or so people were in there already. None paid Alex and his family the slightest attention. A Latina cradled a little girl's head in her lap, cooing softly. A little boy Alex supposed was the woman's son slumped against her shoulder, asleep. An old man in a flannel shirt moaned to himself, clutching a bloody rag against his arm. They all looked like they'd been there forever, and Alex wondered briefly if his family now looked the same.

He wanted to take his mother's hand but saw that she and his father weren't touching, so maybe that meant he wasn't supposed to. "I have to . . . I need to go to the bathroom," Alex said. His mother offered only a tiny nod in response, and Alex felt guilty that he had to do something for his own comfort.

When he returned, his father had gotten up and was pacing. His mother sat so still she might have been carved from marble. Certainly her face was white enough.

Alex sat and stared at the swinging doors he assumed led deeper into the hospital. He tried not to think about Katie, about how they were operating on her. They must have given her anesthesia, right? At least she wasn't in pain.

Every twenty minutes or so his father would go to a pay phone in the corridor and call home. After the fourth such foray, he came back and said, "I got Ben. He's on the way."

His mother looked up. "Where was he?"

His father shook his head. "I don't know. I didn't want to get into a discussion. I just wanted to get him over here."

Less than ten minutes later, Ben burst into the waiting room, and Alex felt a wave of reassurance at the sight of his tough, broad-shouldered big brother. At least they were all together now. It could be hard to talk to Ben, and Alex knew Ben didn't exactly like him, but his brother had always protected him. Alex felt he would protect him now, too, protect all of them.

"What happened?" Ben said. "How's Katie?"

"Where were you?" his mom said, coming to her feet and closing on him. "You were supposed to drive her!"

"What?" Ben said.

His father stepped in and grabbed Ben by the arm.

"I told you, you were supposed to drive her home from the party."

"You did not," Ben said, shaking his head. "You said I should have Katie home by midnight."

"What did you think I meant?" his father said, his voice rising. "You were supposed to drive her!"

Alex looked around from his seat. The previously stupefied denizens of the waiting room had stirred to partial awareness and were watching this drama unfold.

"I thought . . . you know, she was supposed to be home at a certain time," Ben said. "She's younger. Wally said he would drive her, so I thought—"

The room was silent.

Ben asked, "Where's Wally?"

His father said, "Wally was driving. He's dead."

Alex felt a rush of fear at those two last words, at their stark finality. He understood that whoever had called must have told his parents. But . . . how could Wally be dead? Alex had just seen him, what, three days ago?

Ben looked like he'd been hit in the stomach. "Katie . . . Katie said it was okay."

His father's voice got louder. "I think I made it perfectly clear that you were supposed to drive your sister home, Ben! You!"

Ben shook his arm loose and stepped back. He looked at his father, then his mother. "What are you, blaming me for this? This is my fault?"

"She wasn't supposed to be in Wally's car!" his mom said, and burst into tears.

They all stood that way for a long, frozen moment. Ben turned and walked out.

"Ben!" his father called, but Ben didn't even glance back. "Ben!"

His father started to go after him. Alex heard the swinging doors open and looked up to see a guy in green surgical scrubs coming through. The guy said, "Katie Treven's family?"

Alex's parents rushed over to him. Ben turned and came back in the room. Alex, terrified, forced himself to stand.

"We're Katie's parents," Alex's father said, his voice low, his jaw hardly moving. "How is she?"

"She's in post-op," the guy in scrubs said, and Alex's mom's hands flew to her mouth, stifling a sob. She sagged against his dad. His dad was breathing in and out like a locomotive. Tears were suddenly running down his face.

"I'm Dr. Rosen," the guy in scrubs said. "Let's go somewhere we can talk."

Dr. Rosen led them to a small room off the waiting room. There were chairs, but no one sat.

"Your daughter sustained severe trauma to the head," Dr. Rosen said. "There was bleeding, and we had to operate to relieve the pressure."

Alex's mom had a fist pressed so tightly to her mouth her arm was shaking.

"Is she . . ." Alex's dad asked, but he couldn't finish.

"We've done everything we could," Dr. Rosen said. "But I have to caution you, at this point I'm not optimistic about Katie's chances. You have to prepare yourself for the worst."

A sound escaped from Alex's mom's throat, high-pitched, something like a hiccup. She twisted her fist savagely against her lips.

Alex felt the tears well up again and this time he couldn't stop them. He glanced at Ben. His brother's mouth was a thin pale line. Of the four of them, he was the only one not crying.

"Can we see her?" his dad whispered.

Dr. Rosen nodded. "Of course. She isn't conscious, though. She's bandaged and there's a lot of bruising. She's also intubated—a tube in her mouth."

Alex understood that Dr. Rosen was telling them all this to prepare them. He was glad for the warning. He wanted to be strong. Maybe he couldn't be as strong as Ben, but he wanted to try and he knew he needed every advantage.

Dr. Rosen led them down a corridor and into a private room. Ben was behind their parents. Alex, frightened and unsure of himself, brought up the rear.

For a second, Alex thought there had been a mistake, Dr. Rosen had taken them to the wrong room. The person in the hospital bed was unrecognizable—the head wrapped with bandages, the mouth agape around tape and a plastic tube, the eyelids shot purple and swollen shut.

And then, through the bandages and bruises and battered flesh, he recognized Katie. **Katie.** The tears didn't just well this time, they spilled from his eyes in a hot rush.

His mother dropped to her knees next to the bed and took Katie's hand. "Oh baby," she whispered. "My sweet baby. My baby."

His father moved around to the far side of the bed and took Katie's other hand. He didn't speak. Katie didn't stir.

Alex felt himself sweating. Why did they keep the room so hot? And his breath was coming very fast. He couldn't seem to slow it down.

Ben turned and looked at him. He put an arm around Alex's shoulders and gently led him out of the room.

They stood in the hallway, not speaking. Alex realized he was hyperventilating and he couldn't stop crying.

Ben eyes were still dry. He tousled Alex's hair. "You going to be okay?"

Alex nodded, but the compassion in his brother's gesture and voice made him cry harder. After a couple of minutes he had it mostly under control. The trick was to not think of how Katie had looked in that bed. How diminished and hurt and vulnerable. How . . . vacant.

Alex wiped his face against his sleeve. "Why didn't you drive her?" he asked. It was all he could think to say.

And suddenly Ben was right up in his face.

"I . . . didn't . . . do . . . anything . . . wrong!" he said, his voice rising to a shout.

Alex started crying again. Ben stalked off.

A little while later an alarm sounded from Katie's room. A whole team of doctors and nurses converged, and Alex's parents had to go out. Alex was too scared to ask what was happening. He thought he knew anyway and didn't want anyone to tell him he was right.

Ben came back. They all paced wordlessly.

Alex wanted someone to touch him the way Ben had when he led him from the room, but it seemed like everyone was keeping away from everyone else. His father kept trailing his fingers back and forth along the wall, as though trying to anchor himself to something. His mother had her knuckles knotted into her hair and looked like she was about to pull out fistfuls. Sometimes a shoe would squeak on the linoleum floor, but other than that the corridor was horribly silent.

Alex lost track of time. After a while, Dr. Rosen came out. Alex saw his face and instantly knew—another newfound, unpleasant adult realization.

"I'm very sorry," Dr. Rosen said. "We did everything we could. I'm sorry."

Alex saw the tension just go out of his mother's legs, and Ben leaped forward to support her. His dad was saying, Oh God, no. Oh my Christ, no. Dr. Rosen was telling them something about donating organs, and he was so sorry to press but Katie could give the gift of life to others, and they had to decide quickly. Alex tried not to think about what it meant that they might take Katie's organs, but he couldn't help imagining.

His parents went back into the room to say good-bye. Ben lingered for a moment, and Alex thought maybe he didn't want to leave Alex behind. But then he turned his back on Alex and followed his parents in. Alex wondered whether it was because he was mad at what Alex had said. But why **hadn't** he driven Katie? He was supposed to, his dad had said so. Why?

Alex stayed outside. He couldn't go in there again. He just couldn't. He didn't want to see his sister dead. He wished he hadn't gone in before. He couldn't get the image out of his mind.

Alex's recollections of the rest of the night were mercifully unclear. He remembered his parents fighting about Katie's organs. His father saying it's what Katie would have wanted, and how would they feel if it were Katie who needed the transplant? His mother shouting that they weren't going to cut up her little girl. In the end, they didn't sign the forms. Alex was secretly relieved.

There were more fights in the days after, and although they mostly happened from behind his parents' closed bedroom door, Alex could hear plenty. Funeral arrangements. Where Katie should be buried. More about the organs, even though it must have been too late for that. Most of all, it was about Ben not driving her and whether Alex's dad had told him to.

Alex had never heard his parents fight this way, and it scared him. He wondered if it was possible they could even get divorced. He had friends whose parents were divorced, but he'd never thought it could happen to him. His parents had always seemed to love each other.

There was a funeral at Ladera Community Church, a burial at Alta Mesa Memorial Park in Palo Alto. Over five hundred people came to the funeral—teachers, neighbors, Ben's friends, Alex's friends, the entire junior class. Everyone loved Katie.

Come on, he thought. **Drop it. Focus.**

But it was hard to focus. The truth was, bad memories never died. No, at best they were quiescent, just waiting for the right circumstances to pop up like an evil jack-in-the-box and say, **Miss me? Don't worry, I'm still here! And I'm not going anywhere, either. Never, ever.**

He wondered whether it was like this for other people. Did everyone grapple with shit like this when they were stressed?

He wondered for a moment about Ben, about whether he was ever bothered by any of it. Yeah, right. The irony was stunning—the guy who caused all of it, including what happened afterward, probably slept like a baby at night.

10 KING OF THE WORLD

Ben was getting bored in Ankara. Waiting for a target was one thing; he had a sniper's patience for that. But waiting for information was different. Hort still hadn't been able to find out anything about the Russian, if in fact the guy was Russian, and had told him to stay put until they'd cleared it up. So he read and worked out twice a day and visited a few famous archaeological sites.

The Ankara Citadel was impressive, he had to admit. He went early one morning on a whim. It was set on a hill a kilometer high, and the city below was invisible, covered in mist. He thought of the people who had built it, gone now, but having managed to cleave a monument to a mountain in however much time they had.

He thought of his parents. **See, guys? I'm getting some culture. I told you I would.**

He smiled. Their ideas of culture had always been different from his. They'd been dead set against the army from the time he'd first started talking about it in high school. His father wanted Ben, who showed none of Alex's aptitude for science, to be a lawyer. Ben found the proposition about as attractive as an offer of a lobotomy and a lounge chair.

His father had pressured him to apply to college. "Why not keep your options open?" the old man had argued. "Give yourself a choice. If you get into a good school, you can take advantage. And you can always join the army afterward, as an officer. Then you'd have all the advantages and opportunities of a college degree plus the military."

Ben knew what the old man was really thinking: **By the time you've graduated from college, you'll have outgrown all this silliness.** He was just trying to keep Ben on the "right" track long enough for Ben to get stuck in the grooves.

There had been recruiters at Ben's football games and wrestling matches, and he knew there was interest at Stanford, Berkeley, Michigan, Penn, a few other places. But his grades weren't so hot. He figured he could apply to some schools to placate his dad but that in the end nothing would come of it. Then he could say, Hey, I gave it a shot, but it didn't work out. Hello, army.

It almost worked. But the old man was on the Board of Trustees at Stanford, which also happened to be the school most interested in Ben's football prowess, and he pulled some strings. Ben was accepted. Then the old man started in with a new pitch: Stanford will be great. You'll actually be able to play there, whereas at one of the higher-ranked schools you would have been red-shirted your first year anyway. Plus it's the best education, it'll serve you well as an army officer.

Ben knew the old man had a point, but he just didn't want to go to school so close to home. In fact, he wanted to be far from home, overseas far. He couldn't exactly explain why. It wasn't that he didn't love his family, and the Bay Area was a good place to live, and Stanford was a good school, and yeah, he could play football there and wrestle, too, but . . . he just wanted more for himself, something fresh, something he felt he was cut out for in a way his dad and certainly Alex never would be. There was something special inside him, he could feel it, and going to college three miles from the house he grew up in . . . it was wrong. It would have been like betraying himself, in a way he couldn't quite understand, let alone articulate to his dad.

He had decided, fuck it, he wasn't going to Stanford or anywhere else; it was his life and he was joining the army. He had talked to a recruiter and found out he could be guaranteed a slot in Airborne, which was the feeder to Ranger Battalion, which could lead to Special Forces—everything he'd always wanted, everything he knew he could be the best at. He would learn languages, train indigenous forces, have adventures ordinary people could barely imagine. He decided he would break the news to his parents right after the States. He'd be facing the best wrestlers in California there, and he couldn't afford any distractions.

He'd been seeded eighth, which meant in the first round he would face the top seed, an undefeated guy named Musamano who was built like a bull, and no one had figured Ben to survive even into the semifinals. But Ben had thought hard about what his opponents knew about him, what they would be expecting. He was known as a single wrist and half nelson guy, effective, but meat and potatoes. Standard. A little predictable. He started wondering what would happen if he threw Musamano a few curves.

He thought about what he would do to stymie someone who wrestled the way he did. Keep the arms rigid, he thought. Palms on the mat, head up. That denies the opportunity both for the single wrist and for the nelson.

But defending with that posture must create new vulnerabilities, right? The more he thought about it, the more he thought he could surprise people by attacking with a cradle, either near side or far, it wouldn't matter. With their hands planted and heads up, overcompensating against the expected nelson and wrist attack, they'd be vulnerable.

He didn't want anyone to know what he was doing, so he practiced his new moves only at home, on his father and on Alex. His father didn't have much patience for it but tried to be a good sport. Alex was too small and had no experience, but Ben could use him as a training dummy. He'd tell Alex what to do and how to move, to try to escape and resist this way and that way. Alex complained about the rug burns, but to his credit, he never refused. And by the first day of the tournament, Ben felt ready.

Musamano took him down immediately in the first round and rode him for the rest of the period. But Ben was on top at the beginning of the second, and Musamano braced for Ben's attack exactly as Ben had hoped. Ben slammed in a crossface with his left hand and dropped his right deeply into Musamano's right inner thigh, spiraling out clockwise way past Musamano's head, surprising him, twisting him up. Musamano's right arm crumbled and one quarter of his stability was gone. Ben heard a roar from the crowd and felt something surge inside him: it was working! But he pushed the excitement away. He wasn't there yet.

He spiraled out even more aggressively and sliced the crossface in harder, digging in so savagely he could feel Musamano's teeth on his forearm right through the guy's cheek. Musamano grunted and straightened his right leg to brace, and there it was, it was now or never. Ben dropped his right hand in behind Musamano's right knee and changed directions, springing over Musamano's back and landing right next to him on his right. He shot his right hand in deeper and took hold of his left wrist, tunneled his head into Musamano's right temple, and tried to roll right. He could feel Musamano brace hard in the other direction and for one second Ben thought he didn't have the leverage, he was going to lose the grip. But then Musamano was moving, arcing over Ben and onto the mat, his shoulders down, the cradle in place. Ben heard another roar from the crowd, louder this time, and Musamano bucked and arched but Ben sank the cradle deeper, angling Musamano's shoulders onto the mat, squeezing with everything he had.

He wedged a knee under Musamano's lower back and gritted his teeth, squeezing, squeezing. The sound from the crowd was outsized now, not just cheers but the din of a thousand stomping feet reverberating through the floor and walls, but he was only dimly aware of it. He might have heard a whistle blow but it didn't mean anything to him, he just kept working Musamano's shoulders to the mat, choking him, trying to pin him or kill him, he didn't care which. Then he felt strong hands tugging at him, prying him away, and it was only then he realized he'd done it, he'd pinned Musamano. It was over, he'd won.

He released the grip and rolled to his feet. His arms were shaking. The auditorium was pandemonium now. He looked over and even his ordinarily restrained parents were on their feet, shaking their clenched fists over their heads, whooping at the top of their lungs. Alex and Katie were jumping up and down and shouting. He grinned and looked at Musamano. The wrestler was getting slowly to his feet. He looked stunned. He looked beaten.

The referee took each of their wrists, walked them

to the center of the mat, and raised Ben's arm. The crowd went crazy again. Ben couldn't stop grinning. He'd done it. He'd beaten Musamano. He felt like king of the world.

After that first-round upset, his other opponents were psyched out. He could see it in their eyes and their postures the moment they stepped on the mat. He was the guy who had pinned Musamano, for Christ's sake, and although he'd learned in one of his classes that **If A can beat B and B can beat C, A can beat C** is a logical fallacy, he knew people still felt it in their guts. He pinned his way through the rest of the tournament. No one could stop him.

It had been the best two days of his life.

And then. And then. And then.

He shook the thought away. At least his parents had meant well. Fucking Alex, though, Alex never said, "It's okay, Ben," or, "It wasn't your fault, Ben," or, "I know how much pain you're in over this, too, brother."

Well, the hell with him. The last time Ben had heard from Alex, he was in law school. Before that, it was some computer Ph.D. program. All those degrees, and what did he ever accomplish? He'd never gone anywhere, never even really left home. By now he'd be a rich lawyer, the kind of ignorant, ungrateful yuppie who never got his hands dirty and looked down his nose at soldiers. That was the only good thing about their parents, about Katie, being gone. He didn't have to deal with Alex anymore. And he never would again.

11 HAUNTED HOUSE

Alex spent so much time on Obsidian in the afternoon that he had to stay at the office until almost midnight to catch up on other work. He went straight to bed when he got home, but he couldn't sleep. He tossed and turned for an hour and wasn't even beginning to feel drowsy. Finally he decided the hell with it, he'd take a hot bath. Sometimes that helped.

There was a little moonlight coming in the windows, so he kept the lights off. He turned on the faucet, then eased himself in and sat, gritting his teeth, wincing as the hot water crept over his legs and up to his stomach.

He turned off the tap and the room went suddenly quiet, the only sound a few last drops falling from the faucet to the water below, breaking the silence like a dying metronome.

He splashed a little hot water onto the porcelain

behind him to warm it up, then eased back. He slid
down until his chin was just touching the water and
closed his eyes, thinking this was good, this was what
he needed. After a few moments, the dripping
stopped and everything was utterly noiseless.

It was funny to think this was the same tub where
his mom used to wash them as kids. Some people
would say it was weird that he still lived in the house
where he grew up, and he supposed they had a point.
He'd never even left town for any of his degrees, and
the only different addresses he'd had since he was a
teenager were a collection of dorm rooms, which in
retrospect felt like just a break, a vacation from this,
his only real home. Sometimes he thought he should
have taken more chances, explored a few more possibilities. But after the thing with his dad, and then his
mother got sick, what kinds of chances was he supposed to take? And as for living in this house, well,
yeah, you could say it was the safe alternative. But on
the other hand, after everything that had happened
here, it had taken a lot of courage.

After Katie's funeral, he and Ben had gone back to
school. Alex focused on his studies, Ben stayed after
every day for track and field. Katie's absence was
huge—an oppressive, constant, almost physical
force, a void touching everything in their lives.
Katie's jacket on a hook in the foyer, slowly collecting
dust. Katie's shampoo in the shower, the amount of
amber liquid in the bottle unchanging. Katie's empty
chair, staring at them at the dinner table. Alex

thought this was where the idea of ghosts came from, this was what it meant to live in a house that was haunted.

Some of the fights Alex overheard were about what to do with Katie's things. One day he came home and her room was empty—a desk, a chair, a stripped mattress and bed. Alex closed the door behind himself and checked her closet, her drawers. Everything was gone. It was like Katie had just . . . vanished.

He looked around the empty room, dumbfounded. He remembered how once, when he was a little kid, he'd broken the arm off one of Ben's G.I. Joes, which Ben had specifically forbade him to touch. Petrified, he'd gone to Katie. He remembered the way she had smiled and shushed away his tears and helped him glue it back. And no, of course she wouldn't tell, not even Mom and Dad, pinkie promise. And when Ben had noticed anyway and confronted Alex, Katie said it was her fault, she had done it. And Ben had just let it go. Alex wondered if Ben knew—after all, what was Katie doing with a G.I. Joe?—and thought maybe Ben just couldn't stay mad once Katie stepped in. She was like a force field against anger and hate and accusations.

He dropped to his knees beside the bed, buried his face in the denuded mattress, and sobbed her name over and over. Where was she? How could she be gone, without even any evidence that she'd been there? It was impossible. He couldn't get his mind around it.

He cried until his throat was raw and his back throbbed, until he was so exhausted and drained he couldn't feel anything anymore. Then he stood and took one more slow look around the room.

Katie was gone. And if something like this could happen to Katie, who was as joyous and good and alive a person as Alex had ever known, who liked everyone and laughed at everything and had not a single enemy, then the best thing you could say about the universe was, it was random.

But randomness was merely a logical possibility. What Alex felt in the deepest places within himself was different. In his gut and his bones, he knew the universe wasn't random, or indifferent, or in any way benign.

The universe was hostile. You couldn't count on anyone against that. And Alex wouldn't forget it.

He lay in the tub for twenty minutes and was just thinking it was enough, he could sleep now, when he heard something downstairs. It sounded like the mail slot in the front door. These days he was never home when the mail came, but he knew the sound well enough from when he was a kid. This time it was softer than he remembered—**stealthier?**—but he recognized it just the same.

He sat up, water running down his back. Oh, come on. No one was looking through the mail slot at two in the morning. He was just keyed up, that was all, which was why he was in the bath in the first place.

Right. He was being silly. Even so, he sat very still for a moment, breathing silently through his mouth, his head cocked, concentrating on listening.

There was nothing. He was definitely being silly.

He closed his eyes and settled back. Maybe he'd soak for a few more minutes.

He heard a quiet click from downstairs.

His breath caught. He sat up and listened.

A few seconds went by. There was nothing.

It's an old house. The floor settles, joints groan. How often are you awake at two in the morning to hear anything? This is just what the house sounds like this late.

He let out a long breath. Christ, he really was jumpy. At this rate, he was going to have to stay in the bath all night.

He heard another sound. A quiet scraping, the movement of a rubber weather strip over a metal threshold. **The front door.**

Suddenly his heart was hammering so hard he could hear it echoing in his ears. He almost called out, **Who's there?** but managed to stop himself. **Who do you think is there?** he thought, fighting panic.

A burglar. There was no other explanation. If he called out, it might scare him away. But if it didn't . . .

Without thinking, he placed a shaking hand on the edge of the tub and eased himself soundlessly out. Water ran down his body onto the floor and he was suddenly freezing. He thought frantically of what he might use as a weapon. Knives in the kitchen. Golf clubs in the garage.

Here, goddamn it. Something here.

His heart was thudding like a war drum. He fought to control his breathing.

There were some cleaning products in the cabinet under the sink. He didn't know what exactly; whatever the maid used. But there might be something. If he could just stay quiet, quiet . . .

He heard the sound of rubber over metal again. The front door, this time being closed.

He eased the bathroom door shut and quietly locked it. Even as he did so, he knew it was pointless. It was nothing but a little privacy button, you could pick it with anything. But he didn't care. He just wanted a barrier, any kind of barrier. He didn't dare turn on the light—it could be seen from under the door and probably through the edges, too.

He dropped down to his knees in front of the cabinet and opened it. It was dark inside. He felt around, his hands shaking. Toilet paper. A bar of soap. A plastic bottle.

He pulled the bottle out and rotated it until he could see the label. Toilet bowl cleaner.

He set it aside, thinking, **Come on, come on . . .**

Another bottle. Some kind of scouring powder.

He reached in again, his hands shaking so violently he was terrified he would knock something over and give away his position.

Mildew remover. That meant bleach, right? He

tried to read the label but couldn't make out the small print in the dark. He unscrewed the spray cap and sniffed. Immediately he jerked his head away and had to fight back a coughing fit. It smelled like pure bleach.

He stood and looked around the counter for something to put it in. Nothing. Not even a cup. The only thing he ever used this bathroom for was the bath.

A light flashed across the bottom of the door. A flashlight beam, cutting through the dark. He realized closing the door had been stupid. It had exposed where he was.

He felt paralyzed. He couldn't think.

Please, he thought. **Please, come on . . .**

He dropped down again and felt inside the cabinet. A scrub brush. More toilet paper . . .

His fingers touched something cold and hard. He pulled it out. A mug, a big ceramic coffee mug. The maid must have put it there, part of her cleaning supplies, or to rinse the tub or something.

The doorknob rattled.

God, oh God . . .

He backed away, shivering violently, and somehow managed to get most of the mildew cleaner into the mug. He set down the empty container as quietly as he could and took hold of the wall that divided the bath from the toilet, steadying himself. He held the mug in his right hand at waist level and ground his teeth together to keep them from chattering.

A second went by. Ten. Ten more.

Maybe he's gone. Maybe when he figured out someone was home—

The lock popped. The door crashed open and slammed into the wall. A dark figure stepped through. Alex saw a flashlight and maybe a gun, and then the light was in his eyes, blinding him. With a wild yell he flung the contents of the mug forward toward the figure's head. A long blob of liquid cut through the beam of the flashlight. The man cried out and stumbled back. Alex shot forward and slammed his shoulder into the man, knocking him on his back. He leaped straight over him and onto the stairs, taking the six steps in another leap. He grabbed his keys from the table in the foyer, yanked open the front door, and went tearing down the flagstone walkway to the driveway, where his car was parked, barefoot, naked, and still dripping from the bath. Somehow he had the presence of mind to hit the unlock button on the fob on the way. He practically dove into the car, slamming the door behind him and locking it. He was shaking so badly he had to use both hands to get the key in the ignition. He pushed the clutch in and turned the key. The engine growled to life. He popped the gearshift into reverse and used every ounce of rational thought he still had to force himself to let the clutch out slowly. He made it out of the driveway, shifted into first, and didn't think to shift again until he was doing forty at the end of the street and the engine was screaming so loudly it sounded like it might tear right through the hood of the car.

He got on 280 and at 120 miles an hour made it to San Jose Police headquarters in under fifteen minutes. By the time he arrived he had calmed down a little and was starting to think. Weirdly, the thing he was most grateful for was that he had a set of workout clothes in the trunk. Otherwise, what the hell would he do, barge into the police station stark naked in the middle of the night?

The parking lot that had been nearly full a day earlier was empty now, and he was able to scurry around to the trunk of the car and dress without anyone seeing him. It couldn't have been more than forty degrees out and he could see his breath fogging. By the time he walked through the lobby doors his teeth were chattering and he was completely broken out in gooseflesh.

He walked up to the information window, rubbing his palms furiously against his arms and shoulders to generate a little friction heat. "I want to report a burglary," he said. "Someone just broke into my house."

The woman behind the glass asked, "What is your address, sir?"

Alex gave her his Ladera address. The woman said, "Sir, that's San Mateo. You need the San Mateo County Sheriff's Office."

Jesus, what had he been thinking? San Jose had just been on his mind because he'd been here recently; he hadn't even thought about the jurisdiction.

"Right," he said. "Look, I surprised this person in my house. He had a gun and I just ran out. I got confused. Can you . . . I don't know what to do. Can you call the San Mateo police for me?"

The woman nodded and picked up a phone. She gave Alex's information to someone and hung up.

"Sir, the Sheriff's Office is sending a patrol car to your address right now. They're going to wait for you outside the premises and escort you in when you arrive. They'll ensure the premises are secure, take your statement, and collect any evidence."

Alex thanked her and went back to his car. When he got home, there was a police car waiting in front. He parked in the driveway and walked over. Two uniformed cops got out, one a tall skinny guy, the other with shoulders as wide as a refrigerator.

"Alex Treven?" the skinny one said.

"Yes, I'm Alex. Thanks for coming."

"No problem. I'm Officer Randol, and this is Officer Tibaldi. We understand you had an intruder in the house this morning?"

This morning . . . right, it was morning, technically. "Yes, that's right. I think he had a gun, but I didn't see that well."

"Okay. We'd like you to wait here while we go in and ensure the house is secure. Once we've done that, we can take your statement inside."

"Uh, yeah, sure, of course."

Alex waited while Randol and Tibaldi walked up the path to the front door, which Alex noticed for the first time was closed. He was surprised to see them draw their guns, then realized, of course, they had to

assume someone was still in there, no matter how unlikely.

Tibaldi tried the door, then called to Alex, "You're
going to have to unlock it."

Alex walked up and unlocked the door. Tibaldi
opened it, waited a moment, then went in, followed
by Randol.

The house wasn't huge, and in five minutes they
had turned on every light, opened every closet, and
looked under every bed. It was empty.

Alex told them exactly what had happened. He
showed them the bathroom. The tub was still full of
water. They examined the door and the lock, but
there was no evidence that it had been picked. The
room stank of bleach and the cleaner had gotten all
over the walls and floor.

"We're going to check the front door and have a
look around," Randol said. "Why don't you inven-
tory the house and see if anything is missing?"

Alex did. Nothing was gone or even out of place.
Even his wallet and cell phone were where he always
left them when he was home, on the table in the
foyer. He'd been so batshit scared when he ran out
that he'd grabbed only his keys and nothing else.

"The front door is intact," Randol told him. "No
sign of forced entry."

"Well, someone got in here," Alex said, feeling
foolish.

"I can see that. Is anything missing?"

Alex shook his head.

"Do you have any enemies, sir?"

"Enemies?"

"You know, were you doing something that made a husband jealous, or maybe you took something you weren't supposed to from someone you shouldn't have taken it from."

"No, nothing like that. Nothing. Are you saying this guy was looking for me personally?"

Randol shrugged. "Most burglars are pretty inept. The ones adept enough to break in quietly and without damaging anything are too smart to carry a gun. It ups the penalties if they're caught."

"Well, I'm not sure he had a gun. I told you, I didn't see that well. It was dark, there was a flashlight in my face, and I was pretty damn scared."

"All right. No gun, my guess is, someone broke in here hoping to burglarize the place, and when you surprised him, he got the hell out."

"And closed the door as he left?" Alex asked.

"Sure," Tibaldi said. "You'd be amazed at the weird things perps do. He probably thought if he closed the door, no one would notice he'd been inside."

Alex wasn't persuaded. If the guy had bolted out in such a hurry that he'd missed the wallet he'd gone right past on his exit, what had possessed him to take the time to close the door?

"Why would he break in if he knew someone was home?" Alex asked.

"How would he have known you were home?" Tibaldi asked.

"My car was right in my driveway."

Tibaldi nodded. "I noticed you've got several newspapers at the end of the walkway. Burglar thinks, 'This guy's not home—he caught a taxi to the airport.' Or whatever. Point is, he thinks the newspapers trump the car. You have to put yourself in the perp's shoes. They look for things like that. Newspapers in the driveway, mail in the mailbox, packages in front of the door."

"Why pick the bathroom lock, then? By then he knew someone was home."

Tibaldi shrugged. "At that point, he's committed. He's already made his decision, already committed a crime. Some mentalities, they'd rather double down than back off. Look, you have to accept that in all crimes, there's a certain random element. It's why conspiracy theorists love JFK's assassination and nine-eleven so much. You can't ever get all the threads to tie up neatly. There's always something that doesn't make sense."

Randol asked, "Did you get a good look at him? Could you describe him, pick him out of a lineup?"

Alex tried to picture what he'd seen. "It was dark. I . . ." What had he seen? Suddenly, he wasn't sure about any of it. He felt drained and useless.

"Black? White?"

Alex shook his head. "I don't know."

"Well, at least you scared him off," Tibaldi said. "Nice move, with the bleach. And you didn't lose anything."

Alex looked at them. "So you think this was just a random break-in?"

Randol didn't answer, and Alex realized he was assessing his own confidence in Alex's responses. After a long moment he nodded and said, "If he didn't have a gun, and you don't have enemies, that's what it looks like. I think you had a bad guy casing the neighborhood, he saw those newspapers, he took a closer look, he saw the door has only one lock, not even a deadbolt, which looks to be what, forty years old, I'm guessing?"

"Yeah," Alex said. "Probably that old."

"Watch this," Randol said. He stepped out and closed the door behind him. From the other side, Alex heard a rasping sound, then a click, and then the door opened.

"Damn," Alex said. "How did you do that?"

Randol handed Alex a thin piece of plastic, hard but flexible, about four inches by four. "Slide it between the door and the jamb, push back the mechanism, you're inside in less time than it takes to use a key. Get deadbolt locks. Have the jambs and frames reinforced. Make it harder for the criminal."

Alex didn't like the rebuke behind the words, but the man had a point.

Alex scrubbed a hand across his face. He was a weird combination of keyed up and exhausted. "Well, thank you very much for coming out in the middle of the night, or, whatever, I guess it's the morning," he said.

"Not a problem, sir," Randol said. "We're glad you're okay."

Alex left every light on after they left. He knew it was ridiculous, but he couldn't help thinking: **What if he comes back?**

But come on. A burglar coming back to the same house he got surprised at and ran out of earlier the same night? The police might be there, who knows what.

Ridiculous.

The way Randol had opened the front door, though . . . that was unbelievable. The miracle wasn't that Alex had gotten away tonight; it was that no one had tried to rob him until now.

Not that the guy would come back. But if he did, it wasn't like Alex could stop him. There was effectively no lock on the door, he didn't own a gun.

He remembered the sound the door had made as it slid stealthily open. How terrified and vulnerable he had felt in the bath.

The hell with it. He'd just stay at the Four Seasons in Palo Alto. He did enough business meals in their Quattro restaurant. Might as well sleep there tonight. If he stayed here, he would lie awake the rest of the night, imagining every joint that settled was a footstep, every whoosh of the gas heater the sound of the front door again.

He grabbed a change of clothes and looked through the front window long and hard before venturing out.

12 EMERGENCY

Alex slept fitfully for a few hours at the hotel. When he woke up, the brilliant Bay Area sun was shining through the windows onto the white bed linens. He scrubbed his face and thought about the night before. At the time, he'd been panicked and confused. He had thought it was just a burglar. But now, he realized he'd been missing something obvious.

The inventor killed, Alex's contact at the patent office dead, and someone breaking into his house, all in the space of what, thirty-six hours? You didn't have to be a conspiracy theorist to believe coincidences didn't happen like that.

What were those games he had liked to play in **Highlights** magazine when he was a kid? **What do these things have in common?**—that was one of them. There would be a bunch of seemingly disparate pictures, but if you looked closely, if you thought about it, you'd realize they all had right angles, or all began with the letter **A,** or whatever.

What Alex, Hilzoy, and Hank all had in common was Obsidian. Even if it was a coincidence, the overlap was obvious. The question was, why? What was it about Obsidian that led to someone wanting to kill for it?

No, it didn't make sense. Companies that wanted to acquire a promising technology or neutralize a threatening one did it with cash. It was easy, and it was legal. Hell, Hilzoy could have been had for under seven figures. That wasn't even a rounding error for players in the computer security field.

But whoever was behind all this, how did they even know about the technology? The patent application was secret.

Well, something could have leaked. Who knows who Hilzoy might have told? Who knows who saw what in the patent office? And it wasn't as if Obsidian was for Alex's eyes only at Sullivan, Greenwald. There was Osborne, for one, and of course Sarah.

He told himself he was probably being ridiculous, but better safe than sorry. He called Detective Gamez on the mobile number on the man's card. He told him about the break-in. He told him he knew it sounded crazy, but . . . What if Hank's death hadn't been a heart attack? How sure were they? Because the inventor and the examiner—it just seemed like quite a coincidence, no? To his surprise, Gamez didn't treat him like he was a nut job. He told him he would look into it and call Alex back.

Alex drove to the office. The first thing he did there was call a locksmith. It was going to be hard enough to sleep in the house after what had happened. Turning the place into a fortress would make it a little easier. Then he called a gun shop. Apparently, he could buy a gun but would have to wait ten days to pass a background check before picking it up. Shit, he'd always thought background checks were a good idea. But he needed something right now.

Gamez called him back. He said, "All right, I talked to the Arlington cops. They already autopsied Shiffman. The family wanted it—Shiffman was young and healthy, and the family was concerned there might be some genetic predisposition that could affect other members of the family."

"Well, what did the autopsy show?"

"Inconclusive. They think it might be something called Brugada syndrome."

"What's that?"

"Apparently it's a genetic condition that accounts for sudden death in otherwise healthy males, most of them in their thirties, often while they're sleeping. It's not that well understood."

Alex thought it sounded like something someone made up so doctors wouldn't have to tell the bereaved, **Sorry, we don't have a clue.**

"Do you know . . . is it likely they'll have any kind of definitive explanation?"

"They're doing genetic testing and a family history. But you want my opinion? No one's ever really going to know. Sometimes people just keel over and there's no explanation. It happens."

"So you think this was just . . . a heart attack?"

"I talked to the homicide lieutenant in Arlington. They examined Shiffman's apartment, routine for a death like this. No sign of forced entry. No evidence of a struggle. And there were no marks of any kind on the body. If that's a murder, I'd like to know how it was done."

"So you think I'm being paranoid."

"No, I don't think that. It's a hell of a coincidence, no doubt about it."

"I don't know what to do."

"Apart from the break-in, have you noticed anything unusual? Anyone loitering near your car in the office parking lot, anyone following you while you're driving, anyone outside your house when you leave for work?"

"No. Nothing."

"Well, you've got my number. Be alert, and if anything rubs you the wrong way, call me."

"Thanks."

"Not a problem."

Alex hung up and looked at the phone for a moment. Somehow the fact that Gamez was so sure

Hank had just died of a heart attack made him edgy again. Because the truth was, they didn't really know.

What if none of this was a coincidence? If someone was after him, they knew where he lived. They'd known where Hilzoy lived. They'd gotten to Hank. They would know where Alex worked. They'd know what he looked like—hell, his photo and professional bio were right there on Sullivan, Greenwald's Web site, available to anyone anywhere. So what was he supposed to do? Stop living in his house? Stop going to work? He thought he'd felt naked in the bathroom that night, but he felt more exposed now.

A thought was trying to bubble up from somewhere deep inside him. It felt more like an instinct, a reflex, than a thought. A single word, a syllable, and it was—

Ben.

No. Katie, then their father . . . and he'd visited home, what, twice while their mother was wasting away with cancer? She'd been in a coma for three days at the end, and Ben hadn't managed to get back to be with her even then. Too busy playing army to be with his own mother when she died. Didn't they have compassionate leave in the military? Jesus, it was a miracle the bastard had even bothered to show up for the funeral.

He blew out a long breath. His useless brother. Football hero. Wrestling star. G.I. Joe. But when the going really got tough, he was the invisible man. And now Alex was supposed to go crawling to him, begging him for his help?

Anyway, help how? What could Ben do?

He had a lot of training, Alex knew that. He'd been a Ranger in the battle of Mogadishu and had won a bunch of medals. Alex had seen the movie **Black Hawk Down** and couldn't imagine Ben, tough as he was, doing all that, but apparently Ben had. And after that he'd been a Green Beret or something. So for Christ's sake, if anyone could help . . .

The thing was, he didn't know how to contact Ben. There had been a mailing address at Fort Bragg, but four or five years earlier, the estate stuff he'd been sending to the address had started coming back to him unopened. Apparently, Ben had been posted somewhere new and hadn't bothered to mention it to Alex. And Alex was damned if he was going to ask.

Jesus, was Ben even still in the army? He seemed to love it; it was hard to imagine him leaving. But . . .

He went to the army's Web site and followed the links to something called militarylocator.com, which apparently enabled you to find anyone in any branch of the service. You had to register to use it. Alex started to type in his name and e-mail address, then hesitated. Probably he was being paranoid, but it couldn't hurt to be careful. He typed in **John Smith,** with a made-up e-mail address. A search box popped up: first name, last name, branch of service. He entered **Ben Treven, Army** and hit the return key. A new screen came up: **Ben Treven. Army, active duty. E-8. Bio, not available. Conflicts and operations,**

not available. Interests, not available. Unit affilia-tions, not available.

Well, two things seemed clear. First, Ben was still with the army. Second, whatever he was doing, the army wasn't inclined to say.

There was an 800 number for something called Military OneSource. He punched it in and waited. After a single ring, a woman answered.

"Cherine Nelson, how may I help you?"

"Hi, my name is Alex Treven," he said, feeling un-certain. "I'm trying to contact my brother, Ben. He's in the army, but I don't know how to get in touch. It's kind of an emergency."

Cherine gave him the 800 number for the army personnel center. Alex called the number. A man there told him he didn't have precise information about Ben's whereabouts, but could see that he re-ceived a message.

"If you don't know where he is, how are you going to get him a message?" Alex asked.

"Would you like to leave a message, sir?" the man responded, as malleable as a brick wall.

Alex hung up. He'd call back later if he had to.

There was one more possibility. Ben had an e-mail address their mom had used to stay in touch with him. Alex had used it, too, to keep him apprised of their mom's worsening condition, and of estate mat-ters after she died. It had been over six years, and even if it was still an active account, he didn't know whether Ben still checked it, and if he did, how often. But it was worth a try.

He opened a new message and typed Ben's Yahoo address in the To box. He thought for a moment, then typed "Emergency" in the subject line. He tabbed down and wrote:

Ben, last night someone broke into our house and tried to kill me. Two people I'm connected with have also been killed. I'm not paranoid and I'm not making this up. I need your help. Please call me as soon as you can. Alex.

He included his mobile phone number, then hit the send button. He waited a moment, then checked for new mail. No bounceback. Okay, the account was still active. But would Ben check it? And would he call even if he did?

13 DÉJÀ FUCKING VU

Ben was watching CNN in his Ankara hotel room when his mobile phone buzzed. He checked the readout, expecting a message from Hort. Instead, it was an e-mail. From . . . Alex?

He frowned, wondering what it could be about. He couldn't even remember the last time he'd heard from his brother. The estate stuff was long since done. He couldn't think of a reason they needed to be in touch. There were some cousins, an aunt . . . maybe someone had died?

He opened the e-mail and read the message, then read it again. He closed the phone and shook his head.

It was exactly like the shit in high school, the same old shit. Alex had done something he should have known better than to do, and now he needed his big brother to bail him out. Amazing. Déjà fucking vu.

Or more likely, it was nothing at all. To Ben,

Alex's claim not to be paranoid was evidence of the opposite.

So fuck him. If Alex really wanted his help, he should have sent a different message. It would have read, "Hey, Ben, sorry I've been such a self-righteous asshole all my life. I had no right to blame you for everything that happened to our family. Oh yeah, I'm an ingrate, too."

He stood up and looked at the phone. "You hear that?" he said aloud. "Here's a life lesson for you, little brother. Don't bite the hand and then ask it to feed you."

He started pacing. Who did the little hotshot think he was, anyway? Not a word for six years, and then he e-mails to ask a favor? Not even a **Hey, how you doing, Ben,** just a straight-up **I need your help, so call me.** What was Ben, a servant? Some kind of housekeeper, kept on call to clean up after the messes his prick brother made?

"Tell you what," he said. "I'll help you. You just pay me for it. Yeah, pay me. Servants get paid, don't they? Or do you think I'm your slave, is that it? You think I'm your slave now?"

He kept pacing. "Oh, and **our** house?" he said, wheeling and staring at the phone. "So it's still **our** house? Yeah, when you want to suck me into something, it is. You think I'm stupid, Alex? Is that what you think?"

He was breathing hard and he felt that crazy, joyous urge to fuck someone up, an urge that had gotten

him penalized so many times for unnecessary rough-
ness during his one season at Stanford that only his
father's connections with the Board of Trustees had
kept him on the team.

He couldn't remember the last time he'd been in a
fight, and he supposed that was good. Fighting was
the antithesis of anonymity, especially with a camera
and even video on every cell phone. But more than
that, he didn't really trust himself to fight anymore.
He wasn't sure he'd remember how. Fighting was essentially consensual. There were implicit rules, unspoken limits. But at this point, Ben was so
conditioned to lethality he was afraid that in the face
of even amateur violence he'd do what these days he
did, without pausing to think about it until after.

It wasn't a happy realization. Fighting had been a
good outlet for him, and he'd enjoyed it in a sick way.
Not being able to anymore—it felt like he'd lost a
part of himself, a part that, in retrospect, seemed
oddly innocent. Maybe because most of his fights
had been in high school. Maybe because high school
was mostly before Katie died.

He'd been at a party that night, thrown by two
popular girls from his class, Roberta and Molly Jones.
The Joneses lived in an Atherton house with a huge
backyard, and had parents tolerant enough to in-
dulge their daughters' periodic desire to throw a big
high school bash. No one had planned it, but after
the tournament, this one had turned into a kind of
unofficial victory party for Ben.

Of course, alcohol was forbidden. And of course, the kids always found a way to drink anyway.

Ben had a couple of beers, but he was taking it easy. He hadn't had a drink since wrestling season had begun four months earlier; he'd needed to drop ten pounds to compete at 171; and as giddy as he was, he was also beat from the tournament. With a combination like that, a couple of nursed beers was about all he felt he could handle. Besides, a lot of girls were giving him the look. He was more interested in hooking up than he was in drinking down.

At some point a major hottie named Larissa Lee told Ben she'd just broken up with Dave Bean, the guy she'd been going out with for as long as anyone could remember. It was past time, she said. She was glad. She wanted a change. The only problem was, she didn't have a ride home, but maybe . . .

"Uh, yeah," Ben told her. "Just tell me when you want to leave."

"How about right now?" she said, looking into his eyes.

Right.

They were halfway to his car when he remembered: his dad had told him he was supposed to get Katie home by midnight.

But that didn't mean actually take her home, right? He was older, he could stay out later. And this was his big night, and getting bigger by the minute. He just had to make sure Katie got home on time, that was it.

He told Larissa he'd be right back and hustled into

the party to find Katie. There she was, sitting with some of her girlfriends, laughing at something. Ben walked over, asked if he could talk to her for a sec. She got up and followed him a few paces away.

"Where's Wally?" he asked, looking around.

She smiled, maybe a little knowingly. "I don't know. Around somewhere. What's up?"

"Dad wanted me to get you home by midnight, but I was thinking—"

She laughed. "You were thinking you'd take Larissa home instead."

Ben was careful to keep his face neutral. "What do you mean?"

"Everyone knows she just broke up with Bean. And that she's got the hots for you."

There was a pause. The truth was, Ben had been with a lot of girls from his class, and some from Katie's, too. Some of them had boyfriends, but no one ever found out because Ben never said a word to anyone. He didn't want to hurt anyone's reputation. He didn't want to hurt his chances of being able to go on doing it, either.

He shrugged. "Hey, I think she just needs a ride, that's all."

Katie laughed again. "Yeah, sure."

Ben looked around, then back at Katie.

"Don't tell anyone, okay?"

She smiled. "Have I ever?"

Ben couldn't help smiling back. Katie was smart, maybe as smart as Alex. The thing was, somehow she never hurt anyone with it, never made anyone feel inferior or condescended to or anything. Whatever Katie had, you always felt she would use it to help you, that she was always on your side.

"So, uh, you think you can get a lift with Wally?"

"Sure."

"Cool."

He turned to go, then looked back.

"Hey, he hasn't been drinking, right?"

"No, he's cool."

For one second, Ben thought maybe he should just close the loop, check with Wally directly. Wally wasn't a bad guy, but he liked to party hard.

Then he thought of Larissa. Well, Katie said Wally was cool. She would know.

"Okay, then. Later."

He headed back to Larissa, Katie still smiling at him knowingly, indulgently, with all the warmth and goodwill that had always seemed to define her.

Okay, then. Later.

The strange thing was, if the accident hadn't happened, he probably wouldn't even remember that hurried conversation, or the way Katie's smile had lingered in his mind as he left. It wouldn't have meant anything. No one would have questioned his decision to let Wally drive Katie home. Why would they? He wouldn't have done anything wrong. Or even if he had, it would have been a misdemeanor at most. A tiny oversight. An obvious case of no harm, no foul.

But it **had** happened. The conversation turned out to be their last. And lasts, he had learned, were in retrospect always imbued with a significance they had utterly lacked at the time. Probably, he had come to think, everything was like that. Everything was significant, just camouflaged with banality until some terrible thing stripped the banality away, like skin torn off to expose raw, screaming nerve endings you hadn't even known were there.

He'd driven Larissa home. They had talked on the way but he couldn't remember about what. What he remembered was how smooth her skin was, the maddening shape of her breasts beneath her light sweater, the slight smell of her perfume in the car's interior. Most of all, he remembered the way she had been looking at him whenever he glanced over, a look that told him he could have whatever he wanted and she wanted it just as much.

"My parents should be asleep," she said. "But if you're really quiet, you could come in. They'll hear the door and think it's just me. They won't get up."

"I can be quiet," Ben said.

And he had been, much quieter than Larissa, in fact, whose mouth he'd had to cover not once, but twice while he whispered **shhhh, shhhh** as they were doing it right on her bedroom floor. It was a turn-on, exciting her so much she could forget herself that way, so much she would cry out not twenty feet from where her parents were sleeping, oblivious to it all.

Afterward, driving home, he couldn't stop smiling. She'd been good, she'd been so into it. It was like Bean hadn't been satisfying her or something. He half wondered whether she had cried out because she wanted him to cover her mouth, because she liked it, and even though he'd already come twice the thought gave him a hard-on. Man, there couldn't have been a more perfect end to a more perfect day.

When he pulled into the driveway, the first thing he noticed was that a lot of lights were on in the house. He glanced at the car's digital clock. It was nearly two in the morning. It didn't make sense.

Then he noticed his dad's car was gone. Uh-oh. Had Katie not made it home okay? Did his dad have to go get her? If so, Ben was probably going to be in deep shit.

He went inside and walked quietly up the stairs. The bedroom doors were all open. The lights were on in Alex's and his parents' bedrooms.

"Hey, what's everyone doing up?" he called out.

There was no answer. He poked his head in Alex's room. No one was there. The bedcovers were kicked off, though. Alex was always anal about making his bed just right, so he must have been sleeping in it tonight until . . .

"Is anyone here?" Ben called out again, now walking over to his parents' bedroom. It was in the same condition as Alex's, the lights on, the covers off.

"What the hell?" he said aloud, nervous now and telling himself there was no reason to be.

He walked down the hall to Katie's bedroom and flipped on the light. The bed was made.

Shit, Katie had never made it home.

No, he didn't know that, not for sure. All he knew for sure was that she hadn't gotten in her bed before . . .

Before what? Before they all piled into his dad's car and hauled ass out of there in the middle of the night?

But if Katie had called for a lift, why would they all have gone?

Suddenly he felt sure something was seriously wrong.

He walked down to the kitchen. No note, no nothing. Everything neat, the dishes all put away. Somehow the neatness, the order, was unnerving. It sharpened the incongruity of everyone's absence.

"Fuck," he said aloud. He had no idea what to do.

The phone rang. He spun and stared at it for a moment. He realized he was afraid to answer.

It rang again.

He hesitated, sensing he was trapped in some precarious in-between place, his life and its safe assumptions on one side, the end of it all on the other. On the other side of that phone.

It rang a third time.

Come on, just pick up the goddamned phone.
But he didn't.

It rang again.

He thought, **What if they hang up?**

His paralysis broke. He strode over and snatched up the receiver. "Hello," he said, his mouth dry.

"Ben." It was his dad. "Thank God. You need to come to Stanford hospital emergency room right away. Katie was in an accident."

A chill rushed through him. He tried to swallow but couldn't. "What? What happened?"

"Just come right away. Understand?"

"Okay. I'll leave right now."

"Drive carefully," his father said, and somehow, behind the two simple words, Ben sensed a bitter rebuke.

The rest of the night was a blur; the days after, a nightmare. His parents outright blamed him. Alex's silent, accusatory stare was worse.

Worst of all was the morning of the funeral. He was already crushed with grief and guilt and remorse. He was sitting at the desk in his room, staring at the wall, replaying the evening over and over again, imagining the thousand different things that could have happened, the thousand different things he could have, should have done.

There was a knock on his door. "Yeah," he called out listlessly.

It was his parents. It had been, what, forty-eight hours since Katie had died? They looked like they hadn't slept a minute since. Like something inside them had . . . broken.

They sat on the edge of the bed across from him. "Ben," his dad said. "What we said the other night . . . it wasn't right. It wasn't . . . correct."

Ben shook his head, afraid to speak.

"We're . . . devastated, honey, you know that," his mom said. She started to cry but managed to keep going. "When something like this happens, people sometimes blame others, even the people closest to them. Because if you blame someone, it's easier to believe someone had some control over what happened, that it could have been prevented." A quaver had entered her voice and she stopped, took a deep breath.

"But that's not right," she went on, her voice getting higher now. "Not everything can be controlled. Accidents . . . sometimes they just happen, baby, and it's not your fault."

She was crying harder now, her eyes pleading with him through her tears.

"If it was anyone's fault, it was mine," his dad said. "I wasn't clear when I told you about coming home. You didn't do anything wrong, Ben, and we were wrong to suggest that you did."

Ben looked at them. He understood what they were doing. He could even imagine the conversation that had led to it: **We have to protect him from the guilt. We can't saddle him with this, no matter how true it is. He's too young.**

The problem was, the way they were now trying to protect him made the guilt a hundred times worse. Their previous recriminations had made him angry, and the anger was at least partly protective. Now, with the recriminations lifted, his anger dissipating, the truth shone through with a new and awful clarity.

Because deep down, he'd known what his father really wanted. The old man didn't trust Wally and wanted to be sure that Ben—Ben personally—would get Katie home safely. Maybe he didn't spell it out to the last detail because he didn't want to seem overbearing, overprotective, but that's where he was coming from. Ben had just been looking for a loophole, that's all, because it was his night and he was the conquering hero and Larissa Lee wanted to fuck him. He'd known, but pretended not to.

Ben wanted to tell them no, it wasn't their fault, his dad had been clear, Ben had understood fine but hadn't wanted to listen. Admitting it, owning up to it, it was the right thing to do, no matter how hard it was.

He tried to say something, but . . . he didn't. Maybe he was afraid to speak, afraid that if he did, he would lose control. Or that he'd say something wrong and make it worse. So he said nothing instead. His parents kept crying. Eventually his mom got up and left, and his dad followed her.

Part of him understood they needed to have the rest of the conversation now, that otherwise it wouldn't happen ever. But another part of him whispered that his parents were already bearing as much as they could; he needed to leave them alone for a while. There would be other opportunities for him to admit his guilt, sometime in the future when it could be discussed to the tune of a little less confusion and agony.

And he'd listened to that second voice. Just as he'd listened when Katie had told him, **No, he's cool.** He'd listened to what he'd wanted to hear.

Jesus, two turning points in as many days. And he'd gone the wrong way at both.

Why weren't those turning points marked? LETHAL CURVE AHEAD. CAUTION. Something like that. Something that might warn you: Hey, the seemingly humdrum decision you're about to face? It's actually your whole fucking life.

Ben sighed and shook his head. Then he went out to find an Internet café and a public phone.

14 NO NONSENSE

There was a knock on Alex's door. Wanda, the receptionist, poked her head in.

"Alex, I have a call from someone asking for you who won't identify himself and insists that I should come get you personally and bring you up front to take the call there. What do you want me to do?"

Alex thought, **What the hell?** And then, **Ben.**

But why was he calling on the office line? How did he even know the number?

"Sure, I'll come take it," he said, as though it was the most natural thing in the world.

He walked down to Wanda's station. Wanda pressed a button and handed him the receiver.

"This is Alex," he said.

"I got your message." Ben's voice.

There was a pause. Alex said, "How did—"

"Give me a number to call you back on, something

not connected to you. The woman who answered the phone—is she carrying a cell phone? Ask her to borrow it."

Alex asked Wanda if he could borrow her phone for a moment. She gave him the number and he passed it along to Ben.

"I'll call you back," Ben said, and the line went dead.

Alex smiled at Wanda as he took her phone. "Paranoid client. New technology. Does something like this every time he wants to talk to me. I'll just be in the conference room for a few minutes. I'll be right back."

Wanda gave him a slow **ooo-kay** nod. Her phone was already buzzing as Alex stepped into the conference room and closed the door behind him. He opened the phone and said, "How did you know to call me here?"

"You're not in your office, are you?"

"No, I'm standing in an empty conference room. How did you know to call here?"

"It's the middle of the morning out there. Where else would you be?"

"I mean, how did you know where I work?"

"Your e-mail address has the domain name sullivangreenwald. I Googled the names."

Oh. He should have realized that. "Well, why bother? I left you my cell phone number. What's all this about?"

"I don't know what kind of trouble you've gotten yourself into, or with who. E-mail is insecure. Cell phone signals can be intercepted. Your office could be bugged, your line might be tapped. It's less likely someone would tap the general line into your office because that's not the line you would be expected to talk on. It wasn't perfect, but I didn't have a better way to respond to your e-mail. Okay?"

Alex was simultaneously rattled and reassured. Rattled at how easily someone could pinpoint his whereabouts. Reassured because obviously Ben knew all about this stuff. On top of both, he resented the lecture. He suppressed the feeling and explained what had happened.

When he was done, Ben said, "So you're saying the inventor was killed, the patent examiner was killed, and you were about to be killed, because of this new technology."

"You think that's crazy?"

"Depends."

"On?"

"On a lot of things. But three incidents in thirty-six hours . . . that's a lot of coincidence to swallow."

"I thought so, too."

"You talk to the police?"

"Yeah. They seem to think it's a collection of random events. It doesn't look like there's much they can do."

"So? What are you going to do?"

Why the hell do you think I'm calling you? he wanted to shout. **I don't** know **what to do.**

He fumed for another moment, then said, "I don't know."

There was a long silence. Ben said, "You have something to write on?"

Alex pulled over a notepad on the conference room table and picked up a pen. "Yeah."

"Turn off your cell phone and leave it off. You can check your voice mail from random pay phones. Stay away from home for a few days. Go to the bank—not your usual branch—and take out a lot of cash. Don't go to the places you usually go and don't use your usual routes. Check into a hotel. Pay cash for everything, don't use your credit cards, don't use your name. Don't allow yourself to wind up anywhere where there are no other people around. Stop being polite and start being suspicious."

Alex wrote fast. "I need to come to work—"

"What if you had the flu? What would you do then?"

"I'd still come in."

"I'll bet you would, too. Ever miss a day because you were sick?"

"No."

"Good. Then the boss won't give you a hard time. Be deathly ill with the flu for a few days. Tell them you're working at home. They'll expect you to be sleeping a lot, that's why you won't be answering your cell phone if someone calls."

"What good is this going to do? I'll just have to—"

"I don't know what you're up against here," Ben said, "assuming you're up against anything. But the smart thing is to act as if."

"Act as if what?"

"You still writing?"

God, he hated the way Ben cut him off. Like the

two extra seconds it would take to listen would be too much of a waste of his valuable time.

"Yeah, I'm still writing."

"First chance you get, go to a Web site. Nononsenseselfdefense.com. One word. Bring a cup of coffee, you'll be there a while. You need to get smart about paying attention to your environment and thinking like the opposition. That Web site is a good place to start learning how not to be a soft target."

"Fine, I'll go to the Web site. And I'll have the flu for a few days. Then what?"

"I'll be out there before then."

Alex was surprised. "You're coming?"

"I just said I was, didn't I?"

"But my cell phone will be off, how will I—"

"I'll find you."

The line went dead.

Alex looked at the phone for a moment, suddenly gripped by rage. He realized he was hoping to have it both ways—get Ben to come out here, but not have to actually ask him. And he'd managed it, too—except the way Ben had said it, it was as though he knew exactly what Alex was up to but had decided to humor him anyway.

And the way he'd hung up on him, too. Like the whole thing was such a pain in the ass for him he couldn't be bothered to even say good-bye.

That, or he just wanted to get off before Alex had a chance to say thank you.

Well, the hell with that. Alex wasn't going to say it.

15 FOR THE SAKE OF ARGUMENT

It all felt like paranoia, but in the end, Alex decided he'd better listen to Ben. He went home to meet the locksmith and get the front door taken care of, but after that he checked back into the Four Seasons. He called Alisa and told her he had the flu and would be working at home, probably for a couple of days. And he e-mailed Osborne, giving him the bare bones about Hilzoy and telling him he'd fill him in on the rest when he was back in the office.

Staying at the hotel wasn't bad. It was luxurious, the food was good, and he liked the fitness center. And what the hell, it wasn't as though he ever took a real vacation. This was as close as he was likely to get. He checked out nononsenseselfdefense.com, and Ben had been right. There was a lot of information, and even though the subject was pretty alien to him, it seemed to make good sense.

The problem was, everything that had happened in the last few days was beginning to feel . . . weird, improbable, like an odd smell he could dispel if he could just get back to his normal life. He was surprised at how strong the urge was to go into the office, see the usual people, take the usual calls, go home at the end of the day. It was as though he'd been told not to scratch at a scab, and the itch was now driving him crazy.

He started to wonder if he'd blown the whole thing out of proportion. Was it so hard to believe Hilzoy had been dealing drugs? And Hank—sad as it was, young people did have heart attacks from time to time. And the police certainly seemed to think the break-in at his house was a random thing. Maybe it all had been just a giant coincidence. Add a big case of the nervousness it all induced, and it was no wonder everything had started to smell like a conspiracy.

On his second evening there, he was having a solitary dinner in the hotel's restaurant when he looked up to see Ben walking toward him. He knew it was Ben from the walk even before he saw the face. It was a wrestler's walk, slightly bowlegged, but more than anything else it was confident, relaxed, the kind of walk you see on someone who not only thinks he owns the place but is probably right about it. Alex had always been jealous of that walk. When they were kids, he'd secretly tried to imitate it.

He stood and tried to think of something to say, but all that came out was, "Ben."

Ben was wearing jeans, boots, a dark shirt, a wool

jacket. A leather bag was slung over a shoulder. His brother didn't look much older. He still had the line-backer's physique, that air of readiness and **Don't mess with me.** His hair was longer and he had a stubble of beard; that was new. He was looking around the restaurant as though assessing it, and Alex realized from what he'd read on the nononsenseselfdefense Web site that Ben was evaluating the environment tactically. So people really did this stuff. Up until that moment, Alex had half believed it was all a game.

Ben turned his eyes on Alex and looked him up and down. "How you doing, Alex?"

Alex wanted to hold out his hand but didn't. "All right. You?"

Ben nodded. "You were sitting with your back to the wall. You went to the Web site?"

"How did you know how to find me here?"

"I told you I'd find you."

"How?"

Ben glanced around again. "There are, what, three good hotels in Palo Alto and Menlo Park? And this is the newest and the best. It was the first one I called. You're checked in under your own name. I told you not to do that."

"I'd already checked in—"

"And your car's parked in the general parking lot."

"So?"

"You should use the valet. Waiting for you in a car parked near yours would be the best way to get to you here."

"How did you even know which car is mine?"

"All it takes is access to the DMV. Whoever you're having a problem with wouldn't even need that, they might have just watched you getting in and out of it elsewhere. Circle the parking lot checking plates . . . **bam.** Nice little M3, by the way."

The way Ben said it, it all sounded obvious. But how was he supposed to know? He wished he could catch Ben trying to figure out what prior art to use in a patent application, or how to code in C++, or a dozen other things. He could make him feel stupid, too.

"Another thing," Ben said. "You're parked way down at that slope, at the exterior of the parking garage. It's deserted down there. How easy are you trying to make things for the bad guys? You could have at least parked at the top, near the office complex, where people are coming and going."

"The parking lot was full when I got here," Alex said, seriously beginning to resent the lectures. "Top to bottom. It was business hours. It must empty out at night."

He thought, **Now he's going to tell me I should have thought of that.** Instead, Ben said, "I could use something to eat. Mind if we switch seats?"

Alex got up and Ben took his seat. Ben picked up Alex's plate of half-eaten food and moved it across the table. Alex said, "You want to get a menu?"

"Nah, I'll just have what you're having."

A waiter came over. Alex said, "Another wild

mushroom ravioli with Taleggio. And another glass of the Sophie's Rows."

"No, no wine," Ben said.

"Very good," the waiter said, and moved off.

"You don't like wine?" Alex said, knowing it was stupid but feeling it was a personal rebuff all the same.

"Not really, no. Especially not after a long trip."

"Where are you coming in from?"

"Europe."

"Did you not know Europe is a continent?" Alex asked, letting the full sarcastic **Hello?** into his tone.

Ben looked at him and didn't say anything, and Alex felt a wave of satisfaction.

"I mean, you might as well say, 'I came from somewhere on earth.'"

Ben was still looking at him. "If I want you to know more," he said, "I'll tell you."

"Yeah, I won't hold my breath."

"That's the smartest thing you've said tonight."

Alex turned away, pissed. At Ben, for being such an asshole. And even more so at himself, for having called him in the first place. God, was he really that desperate?

Unfortunately, he really was.

After they ate, they went up to Alex's room. Alex noted that Ben had a certain way of walking. He moved slowly, as though he was just taking his time, and his head seemed always to be sweeping back and forth. And he left a large margin when he went around corners, as though to give himself more time and space to see what was on the other side of them. There was nothing ostentatious in any of this; in fact, it was subtle, and Alex realized he wouldn't have noticed at all if Ben hadn't told him to read about it.

Alex unlocked the door and went in first. Ben hung back, and for a moment, Alex was a little thrown by his deference in waiting. But then he came in and checked out the room—closet, bathroom, under the bed—and Alex realized the wait had only been tactical, a way to let Alex run into trouble first, if there was any. And before Alex had a chance to digest what all that might mean, Ben was back to his usual ways. He plopped into the sleek upholstered chair overlooking Highway 101 as if Alex were visiting him, and said, "All right. Any additional incidents?"

Alex swallowed his confusion and irritation and pulled over the desk chair so they were facing each other. "No."

"How are you feeling?"

"How do you mean?"

Ben shrugged. "An intruder in the house in the middle of the night . . . even if it was random, that's unsettling."

"Well, I feel unsettled."

There was a moment of quiet. Ben said, "That was pretty good presence of mind you showed there, improvising a weapon."

Alex nodded, looking at him.

"Tomorrow, I'll want to see the house and your office. For now—"

"I thought you said I had to stay away from the usual places?"

"You do. I'll be with you tomorrow, that's different. For now, I want you to tell me more about the technology. Obsidian, it's called?"

Alex told him. When he was done, Ben said, "So, why would someone not just buy this thing? Why would someone kill the inventor, the patent examiner, and the lawyer who applied for the patent?"

"Because . . . they don't want anyone to even know about Obsidian?"

Ben yawned. "Sounds like it, from what you've told me."

"It still doesn't make sense. This isn't the kind of stuff that's dual use, nuclear capable, whatever. It's a security algorithm. It's just a better way of protecting networks. It's like someone trying to kill a guy for inventing, I don't know, a better door lock."

"Well, who's against better door locks?"

Alex thought for a moment, then said, "Burglars."

"There you go. Maybe you're dealing with someone who's able to break into houses just fine the way it is. He doesn't want better locks. Or he wants to be the only home owner with a lock as good as this one, so burglars will be someone else's problem. Or maybe there's a use you don't know about, something someone else spotted."

"So you think there could be something to this?"

Ben rotated his head, cracking the neck joints. "Maybe, maybe not. The inventor seemed to be dealing heroin. That's a high-risk profession. The patent examiner had a heart condition—"

"Yeah, but couldn't something like that be faked? I mean, like someone killed him, but made it look like a heart attack?"

"That kind of thing is easier to do in the movies than it is in the real world. Supposedly there was a guy once, Japanese or half or something like that, who could reliably bring it off, but I think he's a myth. Anyway, people say he's retired."

"What if he's not? Just for the sake of argument, say the patent examiner was killed. Say whoever broke into the house was trying to kill me."

"Okay, for the sake of argument. The patent guy was killed. But the guy who broke into the house wasn't trying to kill you."

"What do you mean? Why would—"

"I can think of several reasons, but killing you, at least right then, wasn't one of them."

"You're not making sense."

"Alex, he knows where you live. If he knows where you live, he knows where you work. You get to work early, right?"

"Why do you think that?"

"I wouldn't have to be your brother to know you're the kind of person who gets to work early. Parking lot pretty empty when you arrive?"

"Usually, yeah, I guess."

"Well, there it is. Wait for you in the deserted office parking lot, one shot to the head, drive away."

"Jesus."

"A soft target like you . . . if whoever it was wanted you dead, you'd be dead now a dozen different ways. Breaking into your house would be unnecessarily risky and complicated."

"Then why?"

Ben shrugged. "Privacy. To interrogate you."

"Torture me, you mean?"

"Call it whatever you want. You said your car was in the driveway, so he knew you were home. He wanted you in a controlled, private environment where he could take his time. When he was done, he probably would have killed you."

"Just like that?"

Alex meant the question to be sarcastic, a nonchalant response to hide his discomfort. But Ben's eyes drifted up and to the left, as though he was seriously considering. "Not just like that. He probably would have made you drive someplace where he could do it and get rid of the body."

"What? Why?"

"No body would tie together all the story elements. Afterward, I'd drive the car to a bus or train station. Maybe plant some signs of heroin. Plant a few more clues. The story then becomes, 'Lawyer mixed up in drugs gets spooked when police question him about the drug-related death of his client-slash-drug-dealing partner. He disappears himself because he feared exposure, or that he was the next target, or whatever.' Yeah, it would all make sense. Police are busy, no one's going to dig deeper than that, not without a body."

"How would you get rid of the body?"

"You don't want to know."

Alex imagined himself dead, with some faceless guy leaning over him holding a saw; or wrapped in a plastic bag and thrown down a well; or weighted with chains and plummeting down through cold, murky water, the pressure incredible, the light of the world racing away above him . . .

"How do you know these things?" he said. "I mean, you really know, don't you?"

Ben got up and walked over to the window. He stood there, looking down at the silent traffic. After a moment, he said, "Let's start with who knew about the invention. Was it public knowledge?"

Alex felt a chill run down his back. "No," he said, after a moment. "The patent application stays secret for eighteen months, and then, absent an exception, it's published."

"And you were still inside eighteen months, so the application was secret."

"Right. We filed a year ago."

"But some people knew about it. Who?"

"A lot of people. The PTO, for starters."

"Who?"

"Patent and Trademark Office. Also a bunch of people at the firm. And the angel investors and venture capitalists I contacted for funding. Plus . . . anyone Hilzoy might have told, I guess."

Ben walked over to the other side of the window. "Three targets: you, the inventor, the examiner. Lots of people could have known about any one of you and your connection to the technology. But someone knew about all three. There's a choke point in there. Who would know about the patent guy?"

"No one, really. His group wasn't even officially assigned to the patent yet, I just knew him from school. He was helping me unofficially, just status reports, that kind of thing."

"So his name isn't on any paperwork?"

"No, nothing like that. Just some off-the-record phone calls and e-mails."

"Well, somebody knew he was involved."

"How?"

"Don't know. Could be something as simple as a tap on your phone or a bug in your office. Or in his."

They were quiet for a moment. Ben yawned and said, "I need some sleep. We'll figure out more in the morning."

Alex felt awkward. He didn't want Ben to have to pay for a room. He'd already paid for a plane ticket. "Did you take a room here? Or—"

"I'll just crash on the couch, okay?"

One of Ben's little games. Acting like he was putting himself out, careful not to accept anything that could get in the way of the routine.

"Suit yourself," Alex said. "You flew a long way, right? All the way from wherever."

16 KARMIC KILTER

Alex woke up the next morning and noticed the sound of the shower running. He sat up and glanced at the bedside clock. Six-thirty. Looked like they were going to get an early start. He was surprised he hadn't heard Ben get up. Ordinarily, Alex was a light sleeper.

He walked over to the bathroom in his underwear and tried the door. It was locked. Damn, he had to take a leak. He knocked and said, "Ben, hurry up," and was immediately struck by how strange it was. They'd always shared, and often fought over, a bathroom when they were kids, and here they were doing it again.

He opened the blinds and looked out. The sun was just coming up and the sky was scudded with long pink clouds. He stood and watched for a moment, rubbing his bare shoulders. He felt disoriented. He should be in his house, getting ready to go to work.

The need to get to the office, to be back in his life, was strong.

The shower stopped. Alex turned and walked past the couch. Ben's bag was open on it. Alex saw clothes, a paperback book . . .

Was that a gun?

He looked closer. It was a gun, small and black. Jesus Christ, Ben had a gun? With him?

The bathroom door opened and Ben walked out, a towel around his waist, a bundle of clothes in his arm. "All yours," he said.

"You have a gun?"

Ben walked right past, barely looking at him. "Of course."

"With you?"

"Where else would I want it?"

Jesus, it was like the guy who answered **Why do you rob banks?** by saying, **That's where the money is.**

"What I mean," Alex began, then thought better of it. But wait. "If you're supposed to have it with you, why didn't you take it into the bathroom?"

Ben dropped the clothes he had in his arm onto the couch and like a magic trick was left holding another gun, larger than the one Alex had seen a moment earlier. "The other is backup," he said. "I wear it on the small of my back. I don't usually bring two into the bathroom."

"You can travel with them? On airplanes?"

"Sometimes. When I can't, I can have them waiting for me."

Alex wanted to ask more—**Waiting for you how? By whom?**—but decided not to. He couldn't get over the idea of his brother carrying a gun. Make that two guns. Of course, intellectually it made sense. Ben was some kind of undercover soldier. But still.

He used the toilet, brushed his teeth, showered, and dressed. Ben paused just before opening the door and said, "Here's what I want to do first. Give the valet this ticket and have him bring around my rental car. I'm going to stroll by your car and have a look around the places I would wait if I were hoping to ambush you. If someone's waiting and he or they don't look right, maybe I persuade one of them to take a ride with us."

"Persuade them?"

"Do I need to paint you a picture, Alex? Just drive the rental around. If I'm alone, pick me up. If I'm not, pop the trunk. Ask the right person the right questions in the right way and we can find out where your problems are coming from, and why. Isn't that what you want?"

"Yeah, but—"

"But what?"

"Look, I don't want to get mixed up in—"

"You're already mixed up in it. What you want to do is get out."

"What are you saying? You want me to help you . . . kidnap someone? In the parking lot of the Four Seasons Hotel in Palo Alto?"

"No, what are **you** saying? You expect me to do the dirty work for you? Is that it?"

"I don't . . ." He stopped, unsure what to say next. This was happening too fast. Ben wasn't really proposing to kidnap someone, was he?

Ben laughed. "You're just like the politicians, Alex. You want something done but you won't let people do it right. You think you can pick up a turd from the clean end? It doesn't work that way."

"That's not what I'm—"

"Yes, it is. I'm sick of liberals who've never even seen a gun, let alone handled one under adrenal stress, trying to crucify cops for not shooting the knife out of the bad guy's hand. Trying to prosecute soldiers who put an extra bullet into Achmed after he goes down, never even thinking to ask whether it was that extra bullet that stopped the fucker from detonating an explosive vest. You can live in that fantasy world if you want, but how about just a little bit of gratitude for the people who make it possible for you? Who do all that dirty work so you can go on pretending you're clean?"

"What do you want, a shiny gold star?" Alex said, louder than he'd been intending. "You volunteered for what you do, right? You get a salary, don't you? Sure, I'm glad people join the army so I don't have to, but I could say the same for people who mine coal. Why do you deserve special dispensation?"

Ben shook his head. "But you don't tell miners how to mine, do you? You don't tell them to try doing it without getting coal dust under their nails. So where do you get your amazing expertise about my business? I have to put up with that shit on CNN all the time and I'm not going to put up with it from you."

They stood looking at each other for a moment. Alex thought of a few rejoinders. But they all felt childish, and what was the point, anyway?

Ben glanced at his watch as though longing for some other place to be. "I'm going to walk past your car now," he said, "just to see if anyone is waiting there to kill you. I'll check the lobby, too. Give me a one-minute head start so we don't get seen together." He handed the valet ticket to Alex, checked through the peephole, and left.

Alex waited a moment, fighting the urge to pick something up and throw it, then went out. He took the elevator down to the lobby, looking around cautiously as he emerged. It was empty. Christ, was this what it was going to be like from now on? Constantly wondering whether some guy reading a newspaper in a lobby was there to kill him? He didn't think he could live that way.

He gave the valet the ticket. The guy left and was back in two minutes with a gray Taurus. **Anonymous looking,** Alex thought. **This is how Ben lives.**

He got in and drove around the corner. Ben was standing near the M3, alone. Alex pulled over and Ben got in. He said, "Drive me to your office. Go south on Page Mill, not the direction you would take from the house."

Alex almost asked how Ben knew where the office

was, but then remembered: he'd checked the Web site. And of course he knew the terrain. He'd grown up here, too.

They drove in silence. When they got to the Sullivan, Greenwald parking lot, Ben said, "Drive past wherever you usually park but don't stop. Let's see what we see."

Alex did as he asked. It was just after seven, and there weren't many cars in the lot.

"See that one there?" Ben asked. "The Jaguar. See how the hood and the windows are covered with dew? That's been there all night. No one could see out of it. For us that means it's safe."

"That makes sense."

"What we're looking for is a car that was driven this morning. Most obviously, one that has the engine running to keep the occupant warm and the windows from fogging up. But I don't see anything that applies."

"But most of these cars don't have dew on them."

"Right. They were driven to work this morning, by early risers like you. The point is, they're empty. So far, so good. Now drive around the block a few more times so I can see the perimeter, then park somewhere you don't usually park and use an entrance you don't usually use."

They parked and went inside. Ben moved cautiously, the way he had in the hotel. He kept pausing and looking around as though gauging something.

"Key card access," he said, and Alex wasn't sure if

he was talking to Alex or himself. "That's an obstacle. Plus, if you don't belong here, where do you set up inside? People coming and going, risk of discovery even early and late, so you can't control the environment. So the parking lot is your best staging area. Multiple entries and exits. But likely the target solves that problem by always using the same one. Yeah, no doubt, I'd go with the parking lot."

They walked up a set of stairs in the Death Star. Ben said, "Don't say anything inside your office until I tell you it's safe."

"Safe to—"

"Just don't say anything."

They walked down the long, green-carpeted corridor. The light was on inside Osborne's office, and as they passed, Alex glanced inside. Damn, Osborne was in there. He looked up at the sound of footsteps.

"Alex!" Osborne called out. "I didn't expect to see you. How are you feeling?"

"Uh, better," Alex said. "What are you doing here so early? You're back from Thailand?"

"I'm always here early," Osborne said. He gestured toward Ben. "And this is . . ."

"My brother, Ben."

Osborne stood up and strolled over, cowboy-boot slow. "I didn't know Alex had a brother." He held out his hand. Ben waited a long second, then shook it.

"I don't get out to California much these days," Ben said.

"No? Where do you live?"

"I do volunteer work with the Missionaries of Africa."

Osborne looked taken aback. Alex thought, **What the hell?**

"Africa," Osborne said. "Hmm."

"Yes, we provide food, clothing, shelter, new sources of clean water, medicine, pastoral care, education . . ."

Osborne looked more nonplussed than Alex had ever seen him. "Really," he said.

Ben smiled. " 'Suffer the little children . . . for such is the Kingdom of Heaven.' Matthew 19:14. Don't you agree?"

"Nothing more important than children," Osborne said. "Well, don't let me keep you." He offered a sickly smile and went back to his desk.

Alex and Ben went down the hallway. Alex was steaming. What the hell was that about? Osborne was going to think he had some kind of religious zealot for a brother. He wanted to say something, but they were almost at his office and Ben had told him not to.

They went in. Ben held a finger to his lips, then pointed at the door and rotated his hand as though turning a key. Right. Alex closed the door and locked it. Ben set his bag down on Alex's desk and took out something that looked like a radio. He attached a corded wand to it and started walking around the office, pointing the wand here and there. Alex realized: **Damn, he's checking for bugs.**

After a few minutes, Ben turned his attention to Alex's phone. He checked the receiver, the line, and the unit itself.

Ben set the detector down on Alex's desk. He looked out the window for a moment, then closed the blinds. "Your office is clean," he said.

Alex noticed the unit's red indicator light was still on. "You're leaving it on?" Alex asked.

"In case there's a bug that was turned off while I was looking for it, and that gets turned on later."

"You really think someone could have bugged my office?"

Ben shrugged. "We're doing things for the sake of argument, remember?"

"You carry that equipment with you all the time?"

"What are you getting at?"

Alex shook his head. "I don't . . . I don't know how you can live like this."

"I'd be dead if I didn't."

"I mean, it must be exhausting."

"It just seems that way to you because you don't know what to look for. You don't have any filters."

"What were you looking for out the window?"

"A place someone could set up a laser to read conversations off the window glass."

"You can't be serious. You can really do that?"

"It's not easy, but it can be done. No sense taking chances."

Alex sat down in his chair, glad Ben hadn't taken it already. If he hadn't been playing with his equipment, he probably would have. "Why did you say all that stuff to Osborne about being a missionary?"

Ben laughed without mirth and took one of the chairs on the other side of the desk. "I didn't like the smell of that guy. I didn't want to talk to him. He's your boss, right?"

"How could you tell?"

"I just could."

"Yeah, well, all the more reason not to make him think my brother's a fanatic."

"It was the right thing to tell him to cut short the conversation. Fat cats who spend their days collecting five hundred dollars an hour to move paper around don't like to engage people who do charity work. It makes them feel their lives are shallow."

"You think my life is shallow?"

Ben looked around the office. "You've been gone a couple of days, right? Anything seem out of place here to you?"

Alex wasn't going to let him just pretend he didn't hear. "I said, you think my life is shallow?"

There was a pause. Ben said, "It doesn't matter what I think."

"No, I want to know."

"I don't know, Alex. You live in the same house, you work in an office five miles away from it, you went to college and graduate school and law school all at the same place, all right here . . . I mean, have you ever done anything different? Ever taken a risk?"

Alex could feel his ears burning. "So what? Stanford was the best school. And you know what kind of tax hit you take in California when you sell a house?"

Even as he said it, it sounded lame. But fuck Ben, not everything was about taking risks.

"You think you're a big risk taker," he said. "But you want to know what I think?"

Ben glanced away as though bored. "Not really."

"You sucked in school, you quit college, and you couldn't have cut it in the Valley. You stumbled into the only thing you seem to be any good at, and ever since, you've been making a virtue of necessity. You don't do what you do because it's worthy and important. You do it because you don't know how to do anything else."

Ben unwrapped a piece of chewing gum and put it in his mouth. He extended the pack to Alex. Alex wanted to slap it out of his hand.

"Anything seem out of place here to you?"

Alex stared at him for a moment, then decided to drop it. "Let me see," he said.

As soon as he started looking, he noticed it. There had been eight stacks of paper on his worktable. One of them was missing now. The one on Hilzoy.

"What the hell?" he said. He started poking through the piles, confirming what he already knew. It was as though the Hilzoy paperwork had just been . . . deleted.

"What is it?" Ben asked.

"My file on Hilzoy. Obsidian. It's gone."

"You sure?"

"It was right here on this table. This is where I keep active matters."

He looked through his filing cabinet. "Yeah, it's gone."

He sat down and called Osborne. "David, you didn't borrow any files from my office, did you?"

"Why, is something missing?"

"David, is there a reason you can't just give a straightforward answer to a question?"

The second it came out, he couldn't believe he said it. Even Ben was looking at him with surprise.

There was a pause. Osborne said, "No, I didn't borrow your files." And hung up.

Ben said, "I wouldn't worry about him thinking I'm a zealot. You can probably piss him off all by yourself."

Alex didn't answer. It had felt good to snap at Osborne. He'd half expected Ben to be impressed by it, too . . . except now Ben was criticizing him, or mocking him.

Well, whatever. He had a right to be cranky. And he was getting tired of taking shit.

"Could anyone else have borrowed that file?" Ben said.

"Well, there's Alisa, my secretary, but she never takes anything without putting it back before she goes home."

"Why don't you take a look around her station to make sure?"

Alex got up and checked. No documents. He came back and sat down, shaking his head.

"Anyone else?" Ben said.

Alex thought for a moment. "Sarah, I guess, the associate who was helping me on it. But she wouldn't take something from my office. Or if she did, she would have left a note or a message, or something."

"Check with her anyway."

Alex called Sarah on her mobile. "Hey," he said. "Sorry to bother you so early."

"No problem. I'm just pulling into the parking lot. What's up?"

There weren't many people who got to the office earlier than Sarah. Alex was one of them.

"I can't seem to find some of my files on Hilzoy. You didn't borrow anything, did you?"

"Of course not. I would have told you if I had."

"Yeah, I figured. Just wanted to be sure. Thanks."

He clicked off and shook his head at Ben. Ben said, "We still doing things for the sake of argument?"

Alex swallowed. First his house, then his office . . . what the hell was this?

"No," he said. "Something is going on here."

"What would they get by taking your paperwork?"

Alex thought for a moment. "Nothing. We still have chron files, there's tape backup . . . and I could probably duplicate a lot of what's missing from e-mail correspondence, if it came to that."

"Have you checked your e-mail?"

Alex fired up his terminal and went through the correspondence. "Jesus Christ," he said. "It's all missing. All my files of the Obsidian source code."

He went out and checked the chron file. He couldn't find it. He double-checked, cross-referenced. Nothing. Obsidian was gone.

He came back to his office. "Someone took it all," he said. "Everything. It's all missing."

"What about the tape backup?"

"I don't know how to check that. I'll have to talk to someone in IT, when they get in."

"Trust me, the tape backup is gone, too," Ben said.

"How do you know?"

"Someone came in here in the last couple of nights and ran a professional black bag op. They'd done their homework. They knew to scrub your working files, your chron files, and the relevant e-mail correspondence. You think they overlooked something as obvious as tape backup?"

Alex sat silently, dumbfounded. He had no idea what to do.

"Here's the question, then," Ben said, looking at him. "Why are you getting a pass?"

"What do you mean?"

"They killed two people on two sides of the country. One of them, apparently, in a very sophisticated way, so that it looked like a heart attack. They could have killed you anytime. Why haven't they?"

"Well, I'd sure like to know."

Ben drummed his fingers along his thigh. "I think they made a mistake."

"What do you mean?"

"The perfect is the enemy of the good. And they were trying to be perfect."

"Hey, Ben? I don't know what you're talking about."

"Somebody wants this invention. No, that's the wrong way to put it. They don't want anyone else to have it, meaning they don't want anyone else to know about it. Now put yourself in their shoes. Disappearing the invention is your goal. What do you do?"

"Well, you can't, it's too—"

"If you had to. What do you do first?"

Alex thought. "The inventor," he said after a moment.

"Okay. In the current sequence of events, who died first?"

"The inventor."

"What next?"

"I'd say it's a toss-up between the patent office and the lawyer prosecuting the patent."

"They did the patent guy before you. Maybe they got to talk to him before he died. They wanted to talk to you, too."

"What the hell is this about?" Alex said.

Ben ignored him. "But you got away. They were watching you, and suddenly you're not at work and you're not at home. What do they conclude from that? That you're lying low. And when they realized that, they shifted priorities. What would you have done in their shoes?"

"I don't know . . . paperwork, I guess. Documentation."

"There you have it."

"But what would that get them? Patent applications are electronic now, the entire recipe is in PAIR, the Patent Application Information Retrieval system. To access it, you need a digital certificate and password. I mean, it's—"

"Check it."

Alex brought up the PAIR Web site, logged in, and entered the patent application number. There was nothing for that number.

"What the hell?" he said.

"Gone?"

Alex tried again, this time by docket number, and then by customer number. Nothing. He looked at Ben and shook his head wordlessly.

"See?" Ben said. "They were going after the people before they went after the documents. You interrupted the sequence of their op, so they shifted priorities. And the fact that they were able to instantly vacuum up the paperwork means they were ready to do it—they just preferred to delete you first if possible. You get it? It's like trying to clean up a mess. If you can't reach one spill, you take care of something else and come back to the part you couldn't reach later."

He paused, then said, "That girl, Sarah. You said she was helping you with this?"

"Shit, yes. You don't think—"

"Is she mentioned anywhere in the patent application? Are there other ways people could know she was involved?"

"Yes to both."

"Is there an attorney of record or something like that listed in a patent application?"

"Yeah, that would be me."

"Well, if they know she's junior, it means for targeting she's tertiary."

"You mean—"

"Every element of an operation carries potential repercussions, things that could go wrong and abort the op. So you want to start with the most critical targets. Like you said, that means first the inventor, next the examiner, next you. It's only after you've taken out the primaries that you'll risk complications by going after the junior associate who helped apply for the patent. Understand?"

"Yeah. You think she's in danger now."

"She would be if I were running this thing."

"Well, we have to warn her."

"Who 'we,' white man?"

"I don't know this stuff. I'll sound like I'm out of my mind. She won't listen to me. She's . . . stubborn."

"That's her choice."

"Damn it, at least help me talk to her. How are you going to feel if something happens to her?"

"I'm not going to feel anything one way or the other. It's not my problem."

Alex couldn't believe what he was hearing. "Wow, how did you get so cold?"

"You give any money to charity lately, chief?"

"What does that have to do—"

"You know, the Smile Train, for kids with harelips? Malaria No More? Care.org for childhood malnutrition? How about SaveDarfur.org? Just a few dollars a day, Alex, no more than the price of your daily latte habit, and you could be saving hundreds of lives."

"It's not the same."

"You're right about that. Because what you're asking me to do involves possible danger to myself. What you refuse to do on your own wouldn't even inconvenience you."

"How do you know so much about those charities?"

"I study up on them so I can point out hypocrisy when I meet people like you."

Alex sensed he was onto something and wasn't going to let it go. "You donate to them, don't you?"

"What if I did?"

"Why? To atone for other things you do? Trying to rejigger the cosmic ledger?"

Ben laughed. "You're like a little kid trying to understand adult experience. Just go back to the pencil pushing and leave the burden of the real world to grown-ups."

"Yeah, I'd really like to do that, Ben, except one of the grown-ups seems to have taken it into his mind to kill me. But right, that's not your problem. Sorry to bother you."

"That's right, it's not my problem. You're just another of my charities."

Alex stared at him, amazed. The really amazing thing, though, was that after all this time, his callousness could still be shocking. But why would it be? When had Ben given a shit about anyone but himself?

"So let me make sure I understand. You give money to charity organizations for the benefit of remote people you'll never have to know or touch. But when someone right in front of you needs your help, you can't be bothered. Is that the way it works?"

They stared at each other for a long moment. **The hell with it,** Alex thought. He picked up the phone and dialed Sarah's extension.

"Sarah? Can you come down to my office right away?"

"This is bizarre. I can't find—"

"Just come now. We'll talk about it here." He hung up and looked at Ben. "She's on her way. If you can't be bothered to even talk to her, you better leave now—unless you want to use my computer first, to donate money to one of those organizations you like. You know, so you won't be out of karmic kilter."

Ben said nothing. He watched Alex and chewed his gum, his cheek muscles jumping.

17 EXACTLY WHAT I TELL YOU

It was the weirdest thing. After Alex had asked about his Hilzoy file, Sarah thought to check hers, too. And it was gone. She was just going to call him when he beat her to it.

She grabbed her coffee and walked down to his office. She knocked, then went to let herself in. The door was locked. That was odd, especially because Alex had just called her to tell her to come.

"It's locked," she called out.

"Sorry," Alex called from within. A second later, he opened the door. Sarah walked in, and as Alex closed the door behind her, she noticed a man standing against the wall. "Oh," she said, with a start.

The man looked like a bigger, tougher version of Alex. The same blond hair, the same attractive green eyes. He was chewing gum and watching her, and there was something edgy about him, something that made her uncomfortable.

"Sarah," Alex said, "this is my brother, Ben. Ben, this is Sarah Hosseini."

His brother. Of course—she should have realized immediately from the resemblance. But why was he looking at her that way? As though he was . . . assessing her. Not sexually, either, she didn't think. His gaze was too dispassionate for that. Too tightly controlled.

"Hosseini?" Ben said, raising his eyebrows.

"Yes," Sarah said, looking at him directly, not liking his tone. There was something knowing in it . . . even accusatory.

"Famileh shoma az shomaleh iran hastand? Man ye zamani yek khanevadeh hosseini mi shenakhtam ke az mashhad bodand."

She was totally taken aback. He had just asked her in perfect Farsi whether her family was from Masshad, a city in the north. He said he had once known a Hosseini from Masshad.

"Na famileh man tehrani hastand. Hamantor ke khodet midoni hosseini esmeh rayeji ast," Sarah replied. No, my family is from Tehran. Hosseini is a common name. As I think you must know.

Alex said, "Are you—is that Farsi?"

"Yes," Sarah said, not taking her eyes off Ben.

"When did you learn Farsi?" Alex asked, looking at Ben.

"Correspondence course," Ben said, still looking at Sarah.

"Your brother speaks like a native," Sarah said. "I don't think he learned through a correspondence course. He's trying to be cute, although I don't know why. It's actually kind of rude on such short acquaintance."

Goddamn him, the way he was looking at her. She was not going to blink.

"Yeah, he does that sometimes," Alex said. "I wouldn't have subjected you to it if it weren't really important."

Ben smiled at that and walked past her to one of the chairs. The smile said, **Sure, you can win our little staring contest. Congratulations.** It was infuriating.

Okay, she told herself. **Drop it.** She sat down next to Ben.

"On the phone," Alex said, "did you start to say something was missing?"

"Yes, my file on Hilzoy. It was weird because you had just told me you couldn't find yours. What's going on?"

Alex looked at Ben and said, "Oh, man."

"Do I need to be worried about something?" she said.

She felt Ben looking at her. "Depends on how smart you are," he said.

She looked at him. "Assume I'm smarter than you."

He shrugged. "Then you should be very worried."

"Sarah," Alex said, "I think you and I might both be in danger."

Alex talked and Sarah listened, resisting the urge to interrupt him with questions. It was hard to know what to think. She didn't doubt the things he claimed had happened were true. She knew about Hilzoy, of course, and she could easily confirm the rest. Nor did she doubt Alex really believed there was some kind of conspiracy at work. But there had to be a rational explanation, right? People didn't kill over inventions in sunny, civilized Silicon Valley. They bought and sold, sometimes they sued, but killing?

When Alex was done, Sarah looked at Ben. "What do you have to do with all this?"

Ben shook his head. "Nothing, really."

"Ben's in the army," Alex said. "He knows this kind of stuff."

"The army?" Sarah asked, still looking at Ben. "You must know a lot."

The corner's of Ben's mouth moved just slightly, as though he found her terribly amusing and wasn't quite able to conceal it. "I know a few things," he said.

"Oh, I'm fascinated. Tell me."

This time, he cocked his head and smiled. She had never seen a more patronizing look.

"Oh, come on," she said. "Won't you at least try to bring me up to speed on how driving a tank, or shooting a rifle, or requisitioning supplies, or whatever it is you do, qualifies you to 'know this kind of stuff'?"

Ben's eyes narrowed slightly. He watched her, his gaze as forceful as it was quiet, and Sarah had the sense of tremendous pressure and tremendous control in uneasy equipoise. There was something dangerous about this man and she realized she was foolish to push him. But at the same time, that façade of tight control, and the condescension that so far was all he had permitted her to see . . . she couldn't just let it go.

"I don't drive tanks," he said, after a moment. "It's been a while since I shouldered a rifle. And I don't requisition many supplies."

"You must be very special, then." God, what was she doing? Why did she want so badly to . . . what? Provoke him? Rattle him? Trip him up somehow? Force a crack in that carefully constructed façade of condescension?

"Oh, I'm really nothing special. Not compared to, say, a lawyer. I mean, you guys, you're the special ones. Top of the food chain. People like me, we're just humble servants."

"Guys," Alex started to say, but Sarah cut him off.

"Tell me then," she said. "What kind of service do you perform?"

"I just keep people like you safe, that's all. It's nothing important, really."

She caught that. Keeping her safe wasn't important. "How, then? All you've told me is what you don't do."

He paused as though considering. "I neutralize threats so lawyers can go on earning big bucks and swilling overpriced lattes. It's a dirty job, but some-one's gotta do it."

He wasn't just showing her condescension, she realized. Condescension was what was he was **intentionally** showing her. Beneath that, implicit, was an entire worldview in which people like Ben were martyrs and people like Sarah were yuppie sheep, in-grates, whatever. **Play to that,** she thought, knowing she was being immature and possibly even danger-ously foolish, but too fascinated to see what would happen to stop herself.

"How noble of you. What sorts of threats, though? And how do you neutralize them? It all must be very dangerous." She didn't hold back on a single iota of the contempt she felt.

"Various," Ben said. His expression was still neu-tral, even bored, but there was something in his eyes—engagement? resentment? anger?—that made her feel she was getting to him. "Mostly Axis of Evil types. Iraqis, once upon a time. North Koreans." There was a pause, then, "Iranians."

"Iranians," she said, feeling her face go hot. "They must be the most evil of all."

"Hard to trust," he said, chewing his gum. "You never know what they're up to."

"Well, I'm glad you two are getting along so well," Alex said. "That ought to make our job of staying alive for another day much easier."

Damn it, he was right. She was playing an idiot's game, and what did that make her?

"Wait a minute," she said. "Do we have any remaining records of the Obsidian source code?"

Alex shook his head. "I don't think so. They got everything, even the application in PAIR."

"Shit," she said.

Ben looked at her. "What?"

"If we had the source code," she said, "we could have published it."

"Of course," Alex said. "SourceForge, or Slashdot—"

"Not just the tech sites," Sarah said. "We could have written to every political blog out there—Talking Points Memo, Unclaimed Territory, No Comment, Balloon Juice, Hullabaloo, the Daily Dish, Firedoglake. We could have documented the people who were killed, the break-in at your house—"

"That's why they moved so fast after they blew their shot at Alex," Ben said. "They had to eliminate any chance you might have gone public. This whole thing is about keeping the invention secret."

"That's what the government does," Sarah said. "Bottle things up. Information wants to be free. The government wants to control it."

Alex sighed. "Yeah, well, without the source code, we can't free anything. We'd sound like a couple of crackpots peddling a conspiracy theory."

"Sure," Ben said. "And then eventually, when you turned up dead anyway, assuming anyone even noticed when it happened, there would be no proof. No proof, no story. The main thing is, the invention would still be secret."

They were quiet for a moment. Ben looked at Alex. "You must know something," he said. "Otherwise they would have just killed you and vacuumed up the documents right after. But they didn't. They wanted information from you first. What was it?"

"How should I know?"

"What do you know? What could they have suspected you know?"

"I don't know."

"Think. They knew all about your firm's filing system, electronic and hard copy. They knew which lawyers were working on the case. They knew about PAIR, and how to access it. These are all quantifiable, procedural things. Formal things. Systems. What would have unnerved them is the possibility of something idiosyncratic, something outside the system, something hard to predict. What would that be? What would they be afraid they were missing? A personal laptop? An unofficial backup file? Do you have anything like that?"

"Yes!" Alex said. "Hilzoy used to leave a backup of the latest version with my secretary whenever he visited the office. Catastrophe insurance, keeping a copy in a remote location. It's on my laptop now. I've been playing around with it."

"That's exactly the kind of thing they were afraid they might miss," Ben said. "Exactly what they were planning to grill you for. Does it have the source code on it?"

"No, it's just executable," Alex said. "It's like a software program you would buy in a store. And Hilzoy's notes."

"Well, can you reverse-engineer it?" Ben asked.

"No," Sarah said. "I mean, maybe theoretically you could, but practically speaking, no."

"No backups of the source code?" Ben asked.

Alex shook his head. "They got all of them."

"Well, what would happen if you posted the executable version?"

Alex shrugged. "I don't think it would give us a lot of credibility. On the surface, it's just a slick way of encrypting data. Since Hilzoy died, I've been experimenting with it and I can't find anything about it that would be worth killing for. So posting it as proof of some kind of conspiracy would just get us a big yawn."

They were quiet for a moment. "Well," Sarah said, "what are we supposed to do now?"

"I see three possibilities," Ben said.

Alex and Sarah looked at him.

"First," Ben said, "you could do nothing. It's possible whoever is behind all this feels the risk/reward ratio has changed. They've vacuumed up the source code. They've deleted the invention from PAIR. They've eliminated the inventor and the patent guy. And they don't know about the backup disc, although it was the kind of possibility they were trying to foreclose. They might feel comfortable enough at this point to stand down."

"How likely is that?" Alex asked.

"I wouldn't say very," Ben said. "They started this op going after people. Doing so involved a lot of logistics and a lot of risk. That suggests the people aspect of their op is important to them. What you did at your house forced them to change the sequence of the op, but it doesn't change the value of the targets."

"And now I've had time to discover the missing paperwork," Alex said, "and the other missing items. To put together pieces. Meaning if there was some kind of backup they missed . . ."

Ben nodded, then inclined his head toward Sarah. "Exactly. Also, they might have let her live because she wasn't important enough to kill. But now they have to figure that you could have warned her about what's going on. You know more now than you did before. They might reassess her threat level as a result."

Sarah tried to control her irritation at the way he was discussing a threat to her life as though she wasn't even in the room. "Well, possibility one doesn't sound very promising," she said. "What's the second possibility?"

"The second possibility is that you come up with a meaningful explanation of what makes Obsidian worth killing for. You'll be a step closer then to knowing who's doing the killing."

"I've tried," Alex said. "I couldn't find anything."

"Who's threatened by it?" Ben said. "Or who stands to gain? Existing security software companies?"

Sarah chuckled. "You mean software companies are killing people? Please."

Ben looked at her. "Please what? Please don't tell you anything that might save your life at the cost of puncturing your little bubble of naïveté?"

"Come on, Ben," Alex said. "Companies don't kill people."

"And you're basing that conclusion on what evidence?"

"What about the government?" Sarah said. "Maybe the NSA doesn't want networks to be more secure than they already are."

Ben chuckled. "I really don't think the NSA—"

"What, you don't think the NSA would kill people? And **I'm** the one living in a bubble? I bet you don't think the president would arrest an American citizen on American soil and hold him without granting him access to an attorney or charging him with a crime or otherwise adhering to constitutional requirements. I bet you don't think the government would wiretap Americans without a warrant, either. I bet you don't think—"

"You don't know the first fucking thing about what I think."

"—that the government would cook up intelligence to start a war. I bet you don't think the government is run by people who've gotten as far as they have in politics by learning to rationalize all kinds of corruption, in the name of the greater good. Are you telling me these things don't go on, every single day?"

She stopped, breathing a little hard. She hadn't meant to make a speech. But she'd gotten through to him. That little f-bomb wasn't part of the control curriculum, was it?

"You know what?" he said. "If a few laws need to get bent to save lives, they get bent. That's just the way it is."

"Yeah? Who determines which laws get bent? And how much? If you can break some laws, why not others? Where does it stop? What does the law even mean?"

"Here's an idea for you," he said, chewing his gum lazily. "Instead of blaming America first for everything that bugs you, why don't you consider some other possibilities? If it's not too much of a strain."

"Like who?"

"How about the mullahs in Tehran, for a start? You wouldn't believe the shit they're up to."

Sarah knew he was baiting her again and tried to stay cool. She wanted to say, **I'm American, you fucking racist, and I hate the mullahs,** but knew that's what he wanted, he wanted to make her angry. After that, he would tell her she was just being emotional, adding sexism to the list of qualities she already loathed him for.

"Absolutely," she said, channeling her anger into sarcasm. "Let's make sure Iran is on the list. After all, every country with a GDP the size of Finland's is a grave threat to our national security. I mean, did you see it on the news? Two Iranian nuclear scientists were assassinated last week in Istanbul."

"Really?" Ben said. "I must have missed it."

"Yes, and their bodyguards, too. Even though we have a law—Executive Order 12333—that prohibits assassination."

Ben shrugged. "What can you do? Iran has a lot of enemies."

"Sure, and maybe we subcontracted the job to one of them, just like we used to subcontract torture to get around our laws against that. Until we started doing it ourselves. You see what happens when it's okay to break the law a little? It starts getting broken a lot."

"I admire your idealism," Ben said, with a paternalistic smile that made her want to punch him.

Alex said, "You mentioned a third possibility. What is it?"

A moment went by while Ben examined a cuticle. Then he said, "You don't want to know about that one. It's the one that doesn't have a happy ending. And right now, it's looking the most likely. I get the feeling you two are going to keep your heads in the sand until someone shoots your asses off."

How could he talk that way about his own brother? How could he care so little? Was it an act? After all, he was here, that must mean something.

"What about the police?" she said.

Ben looked at her. "What about them?"

"We could tell them about the missing files."

"Sure you could. What do you expect they would do at that point?"

"I don't know. Recognize something really is going

on here, just like we have. Devote additional re-sources. Protect us, maybe."

Ben shrugged. "Well sure, then do it."

She glared at him. She wanted to slap that insou-ciance right off his face.

"Okay," she said after seething for a moment, "tell me what I'm missing."

Ben sighed. "You're not looking at things from the other side's perspective. Here, the other side is the police. Alex already ran his conspiracy theory past them, isn't that right, Alex?"

"Well, I wouldn't call it that," Alex said. "And any-way, that was before—"

"Before what? Before you claimed some files went missing? They'll think it's a stunt. They'll think you're trying to find a way to be taken seriously. They'll start to take a very close look at you in a way you do not want to be looked at."

"But my files are missing, too," Sarah said.

"Right. They'll think Alex took them so you would corroborate his claim."

"They wouldn't think that," she said, realizing she sounded petulant. She just didn't want him to be right.

"How many police do you know?" Ben asked. "Do you know how they spend their time, how they look at the world? Let me tell you what a San Jose homi-cide detective is focused on. Gangs. Teenagers dead of gunshot wounds. Witnesses afraid to cooperate. Trying to keep a lid on all that. That's his world. The shit you've gotten mixed up in? That's what he goes to the movies to see. That's as real as he thinks this kind of thing is. And even if he did believe you, what then? What do you think—you're going to get a protective detail from the San Jose police?"

Damn it, he was right. But . . .

"Someone took those files from our offices," Sarah said. "How did they get in?"

"I can think of several ways," Ben said. "Why?"

Alex sat forward in his chair. "Right—the key cards. They're all individually encoded. So if you wanted to, you can tell who's been coming and going, and when."

Ben shook his head. "Even if they had help on the inside, you're not going to find out who with a key card."

"Why not?" Sarah said.

"Everything else they've done has been too thorough. They're not going to make a mistake that obvious."

"How else could you get in and out at night?" Sarah asked.

"Look, you wouldn't have to be Houdini to slip past the receptionist during business hours and hide in a bathroom or wherever until the place had emptied out. There wouldn't be any electronic evidence of that."

"But they knew exactly which offices to go to," Sarah said.

"Your names are on the wall outside them. Not that

anyone would need even that. This wasn't planned overnight. They've been studying your firm's filing system, they've been watching you, for months."

"Even so," Alex said, "I think we should contact security."

"No," Ben said.

"Why not?"

"First, like I said, it's a waste of time. Second, you've introduced me to enough people in your firm as it is. I don't want the attention."

Sarah, pissed, started to say, **Sorry to put you out,** but managed not to.

"You trust your boss?" Ben said. "The cowboy?"

Alex wanted to say, **I don't trust anyone.** Instead, he said, "Why? You think he's involved?"

Ben shrugged. "He was here early this morning."

"He keeps odd hours. Anyway, why would he do it?"

"How should I know? He's your boss."

"He's making seven figures a year. I don't think his motives would be financial."

Ben laughed. "Is it ever enough?"

The room was quiet for a moment. "All right," Sarah said, "option two. What are we talking about exactly?"

Ben looked at Alex. "Can you work with that backup file?"

"Of course," Alex said.

"Then do it. Grab a few days' worth of gear, find a secure place to hole up, forget about everything else, and figure out what's so special about this technology."

"It doesn't sound like much," Sarah said.

"It's not. But it beats Alex waiting around for someone to put a bullet in the back of his head."

She realized he was only talking about Alex holing up. What was she supposed to do? Two people were dead. Someone had stolen something from her office. They'd hacked the PAIR system, they'd broken into Alex's house. The thought of the only two people in the world who understood what was happening just leaving her was frightening.

"Yeah?" Alex said. "What's Sarah supposed to do?"

Sarah was so grateful she had to force herself not to smile at him.

"The same thing you're doing," Ben said. "Lay low. Wait for you to figure out what the technology really does."

"I can figure that out faster with Sarah than I can alone."

Sarah blinked. Did that just come from Alex Treven?

Ben shook his head. "I think it would be more secure if—"

"If what?" Alex said. "If we separate? I don't see how. And you said it yourself: the thing that's ultimately going to make us secure is knowing why someone wants this technology badly enough to kill for it."

Ben scratched his cheek. "All right. Suit yourself."

Alex looked at Sarah. "Can you disappear for a few days?"

She let out a long breath. "Maybe if I were sick . . . you've been sick, right? The flu?"

"Until this morning, anyway," Alex said. "Osborne saw me on my way in."

Sarah tried to smile. "I guess I could catch what you had. And you could have a relapse."

Alex looked at Ben. "What about you?"

"What about me?"

Alex sighed. "Can you spend a little more time on this? A little more time with Sarah and me?"

"I don't think you really need me."

Alex put his palms on his desk as though seeking support, or trying to steady himself. "Yes, Ben, we do. We're just a couple of lawyers, as you noticed. Look how fast you found me the last time I tried to 'hole up' on my own. Someone else could do the same. We need to stick together."

Ben looked out the window. He clenched a fist. The knuckles popped.

"Stick together," he said.

Alex looked at him. "That's right."

Ben nodded. "All right. But you two have your jobs, and I have mine. Your job is to figure out the technology. My job is everything else. I'm in charge. You don't question me. You don't lecture me. You do as I say. This is my world you're in now, not yours. Understood?"

Alex said, "Fine."

Ben looked at Sarah. Sarah returned his stare—**fucking control freak**—but said nothing.

"Understood?" he said again.

"I understand you," she said.

"Yeah," he said. "I understand you, too. Let me see your cell phones."

Sarah thought, **Now what?** But she said nothing. She handed Ben her phone. Alex did the same.

Ben turned each unit off and dropped them into a leather bag on the desk. Sarah said, "What are you doing?"

"You don't question me," Ben said.

"I do if you just take my phone. And just because I'm not supposed to question you doesn't mean you have to get off by never offering an explanation, either."

Ben chuckled. She wanted to slap him.

"I know it's hard for you to accept this," he said, "but someone has gotten seriously into your lives. Your homes and workplaces. The cars you drive. The places you go. The things you do. Are you getting it now? I can guarantee you that if I were the one hunting you, I'd be glued to your cell phone signals unless you were giving me something even easier to follow. Do either of you have any kind of emergency roadside assistance or concierge service subscription along with a car GPS?"

Sarah nodded and saw Alex do the same. That word he'd used so casually—"hunting"—had chilled her.

"Well, congratulations. I'd be all over that, too. You say you're ready to disappear for a while, but you don't know how to do it. It's not supposed to be easy. You're going to have to give up a few conveniences. Okay? Do you need any more explanation than that, or do you get it now?"

They were all quiet for a moment. Sarah realized what he was saying made sense, but still resented the way he said it.

"What do we do?" Alex asked.

Ben looked at Sarah. "Exactly what I tell you," he said.

18 BETTER LUCK NEXT TIME

They went to the Four Seasons in Ben's rented car, Alex driving, Sarah shotgun, Ben in back. Ben was pissed. He'd been back for, what, twelve hours? And he'd already lost control of the situation.

He didn't trust the girl. She was obviously political, and it wasn't inconceivable she had an uncle or a cousin in one of the security services. It would have been easy enough for her to make a call—hey, Uncle Ahmad, you should take a look at this technology I'm trying to patent. It's the kind of thing you told me to keep an eye out for. Yeah, maybe it was unlikely, but he knew Iran's cyberwarfare efforts were real.

And someone had taken those documents from Alex's office. Someone who knew where to go, or who had been given some very precise information. There had to be someone on the inside. Who else had the connection? And who else would have the motivation? The fact that she claimed to be missing documents, too, only made him suspect her more.

It was a huge risk to bring her along now, but he didn't really have a choice. He'd seen the way Alex was looking at her, and he could tell the idiot was half in love. Well, he couldn't exactly blame him. He had to admit she was attractive. But Christ, she was a handful. He shouldn't have said anything about Iran; it could only serve to tip her off. But sanctimonious and naïve was a combination guaranteed to piss him off.

And he didn't like that comment about the Istanbul hit at all. Yeah, it had been all over the news. She was Iranian, she was political, she would have seen it. But still.

Anyway, he was going to get Alex out of his latest mess. Not that Alex deserved it, but Ben was going to do it anyway because that's the kind of guy he was, even if Alex couldn't recognize it. And now his little brother had made it clear that it was a package deal: he had to help the girl, too. Christ, he should have seen it coming. It was just like Alex: suck him in, get him committed, and then tell him, **Oh, just one other little thing . . .**

Overall, he gave the situation a suck factor of about 9.8, but there was a tiny silver lining. If the girl really was working for the other side, he could use her as a conduit for false information—essentially as an unwitting double agent. He'd have to take extreme care because she'd also have plenty of accurate information she could pass along—their current location, for example—but if he could control for that downside, he might be able to use her to draw her people into an ambush. He started thinking about how.

He had Alex take them to the Wal-Mart on Showers Drive in Mountain View. Ben picked out wool hats for them. Sarah wanted to know why.

"I want to make us a little harder to recognize, and a little harder to remember. Just in case. Is there a downside?"

"I'm just asking," she said, "or do I have to obey without question?"

Ben tossed her a hat. "You just have to obey."

He paid for the hats and a prepaid phone. On the way out, he entered the number in his speed dial. He handed the unit to Alex. "This is if you need to call me, and for me to call you. No other uses, no other calls. Understood?"

They understood.

As they pulled off 101 onto the University Avenue exit that would take them to the hotel, Ben said, "Don't pull into the hotel parking lot. Take the next right, Manhattan Avenue, and park it there."

"Why?" Alex asked.

"Your car and her car are compromised. I don't want—"

"My name is Sarah," Sarah said, turning to look at him. "Use it. Stop talking about me as though I'm not here. It's rude."

Christ. "Well, I wouldn't want to be rude."

"No, you obviously **do** want to be rude, otherwise you wouldn't be. Which is why I'm telling you to cut it out."

"Yes, ma'am."

She shook her head slightly as though in disgust, then turned away again. All right, maybe he'd been too hard on her. He wasn't even sure why, exactly. It wasn't going to help him use her to set up the opposition, assuming she really was playing for the other team. She just pushed his buttons. He was already carrying Alex, he didn't need to shoulder her weight on top of it.

"Your car and Sarah's car are compromised," Ben said. "I want to make sure this one stays clean."

Sarah looked back at him again. "You think someone's at the hotel?"

"I doubt it. But like Alex said, I found him here. Someone else could have done the same. If there's a problem, it'll likely be waiting at Alex's car. You can't just sit around a hotel lobby forever without attracting suspicion. So for now, we'll stay clear of Alex's car and go in carefully, just in case. Got it?"

She nodded and turned away. Alex said, "What do you mean, 'for now'?"

Ben opened the Wal-Mart bag. "One thing at a time. Put your hats on."

They all pulled on the hats. Ben also slipped on his gloves. Dressing for an op was always easier in the cold.

They got out and walked, squinting against shards of morning sun slicing through the spaces between the buildings they passed. Manhattan Avenue was inaptly named: in fact, it was a quiet tree-lined street fronted by a few small lower-rent apartment complexes and a coin-operated laundry—artifacts of what the neighborhood had been before the sparkling hotel and office complex had been erected next door. Ben led the way back to the main entrance and into the hotel, scanning as they moved. He detected no problems.

A silver-haired guy in a charcoal suit by reception waved to Alex. "Hey, Alex. Nice to see you here. Breakfast today?"

"Hey, Tracy, no, I'm staying with you this time. Some work being done on my house."

The guy smiled. "Nice to have you with us."

They kept moving.

Ben was incredulous. "Who the hell was that?" he said.

"Tracy Mercer. The manager."

"You know the manager?"

"I do a lot of business meals here."

Ben wondered how someone so smart could at the same time be so galactically stupid. "Didn't I tell you to stay someplace where no one would know you?"

"Well, yeah, but . . ."

Ben shook his head. "Forget it," he said. Was Alex a moron? Did he have a death wish?

They went to Alex's room, and while Alex collected his gear, Ben looked out the window at the highway below and the massive sprawl of an Ikea shopping complex on the other side of it. None of this had been here when Ben was a kid. East Palo Alto had been a no-go zone then, unless you wanted to buy pot, and even then you wouldn't go at night. Times had changed. He was amazed that Alex could casually take advantage of something like this. This hotel had to be at least four hundred dollars a night, and Alex was using it as a safe house without giving a second thought to the bill. It was almost funny, the different economic strata they found themselves in. Of course, Ben's half of their parents' estate wasn't insubstantial, but he never touched that money. In his mind, it didn't even exist except as a last-ditch insurance policy should the shit he dealt with every day ever manage to squarely connect with the fan.

They headed back down to the lobby. Sarah said, "I need to use the bathroom."

An alarm went off in Ben's head. "No."

She looked at him. "No?"

"Not now. We're not secure here. We need to keep moving. You'll have to hold it in."

She cocked her head and her eyes bored into him. "For how long?"

He wanted to say, **Until I fucking tell you you can let it out.** Instead, he said, "Ten minutes. Can you manage that?"

She didn't answer, and he took that for a yes. Christ, he could almost see smoke coming out of her ears.

Well, tough shit. He was about to do another pass near Alex's car, and the last thing he needed was for her to duck into the restroom, borrow a cell phone, and warn someone what was up.

Alex checked out—no sign of the manager this time—and they went back to Ben's car, Ben scanning for danger along the way. "Drive again," Ben told Alex. "There's a Starbucks just on the other side of 101. Sarah can use the bathroom there. Then come back and swing around the hotel parking lot past your car. I want to have one more look at it." By the time they got to the Starbucks, if the girl made a phone call it wouldn't make a difference.

"You sure that's a good idea?" Alex asked.

"I doubt anyone's there," Ben said. But sooner or later, he knew, someone would be. Either at Alex's car, or at the office, or back at his house. Or at the girl's car. Or at her house. And every one of these ambush points was therefore also a place for a counterambush.

Alex and Sarah drove off. Ben pulled the hat low and walked back into the hotel parking lot. He walked past the hotel entrance, his head swiveling, checking all the places he would have used himself.

He cut through the parking garage so he could come out closer to Alex's car. If anyone was there, the shortcut would give them less time to react. He turned the corner and bingo, there was a burly white guy with a shaved head leaning against the parking garage just ten feet past Alex's car. The guy was wearing shades and smoking a cigarette, and wore a black, waist-length leather jacket.

Although his mind grasped it all in a kind of instant shorthand rather than in conscious thoughts, Ben understood all the things that were wrong with this picture. This was the western side of the garage, and this early in the morning it was all in shadow, so no need for the shades. It was too early for an office worker to be taking a nicotine break, too, and anyway why would the guy walk all the way down here for a smoke? And the waist-length jacket would be perfect to conceal a shoulder, waist, or hip carry.

Ben walked casually toward him, his heart rate beginning to accelerate. He glanced around and didn't notice anyone else, but there were some cars parked in a row and he couldn't see into all of them. He couldn't be sure the guy was alone. He didn't think about what he was about to do. He'd learned at the Farm that you can't just play a role; you have to live it, you have to **believe** your cover. So in his mind, he was just another business traveler, heading out early to his car. Deep down, walled off in such a way that it wouldn't surface and show itself in his expression or behavior, he was aware of the bald guy's hands, and would have his own weapon out, the usual Glock 17 in a waistband holster, if the hands went anywhere Ben couldn't see them.

"Excuse me," Ben said as he approached. He pinched his thumb and forefinger together and cupped his hand as though he were holding a cigarette behind it. "Do you have a light?"

The bald guy looked at him but didn't respond. Ben was glad he'd gone through the garage and come in from below where Alex had parked. The fact that the guy was still leaning against the wall indicated he'd been surprised. An operator would never keep a posture like that in the face of a possible threat. Now, if the guy tried to attack, he'd first have to kick off from the wall. It would take him a long time. The rest of his life, in fact.

"Haven't seen you here before," Ben said, stopping a couple of yards short of him. "And I know most of the smokers in the complex because in the People's Republic of Palo Alto you can't even smoke near a building entrance. Can you beat that?"

Still no answer. Maybe the guy didn't speak English. Maybe he did, and didn't want anyone to hear or remember an accent.

For a lot of reasons, noise and potential witnesses not the least of them, Ben didn't want gunplay. But just a little closer and he could drop the guy quietly with his hands.

"Is there a problem?" Ben said. "Do you not speak English?"

There was a pause, and then the guy said in a deep, gravelly voice, "I speak English."

The accent was heavy. The accent was Russian.

The submerged part of Ben's mind that was in tactical mode served up a loud helping of **Oh shit, not again.**

They looked at each other for a long, suspended

second. The world was suddenly silent, everything slipping away but the tension between them. Ben could feel himself decloaking, emerging from under the gauzy, innocent façade he had hidden inside to get this close. He knew the bald guy was seeing it happen. The guy remained perfectly still, but Ben recognized something coiling in his body now, a readiness to move, a hyperalertness that hadn't been there a moment earlier.

Ben braced to rush in and at the same instant the guy kicked off from the wall, his right arm blurring toward the left side of his jacket. Ben leaped forward, simultaneously body-slamming the guy and jamming up his right arm. He groped for the guy's wrist and whipped his left elbow around into the guy's right temple. The shot connected with a satisfying **thwack** and the cigarette went tumbling through the air. Ben found the wrist and shot in another hard elbow and the guy staggered. The guy was trying to get his wrist free now, either because he'd accessed a weapon or just to protect his exposed right side, Ben didn't know which and he wasn't going to let go to find out. They twisted around and the guy was now between Ben and the wall. Ben took a half step back and head-butted the guy in the face, then braced and slammed his left shoulder into the guy's sternum, getting his entire hundred and ninety behind it, hitting him the way he'd once hit blocking dummies and backpedaling quarterbacks, nailing him into the wall, driving the breath out of him. He hit him with another elbow, then another. Suddenly the guy was heavy, and Ben realized there was nothing holding him up but Ben and the wall behind. Blood was gushing out of the guy's nose and his eyes were rolled up in his head.

Ben yanked the guy's right arm away from his body just in case and took a cautious step back. The guy went straight down like one of those imploding Las Vegas hotels. Everything was still utterly quiet—an effect, Ben knew, called auditory exclusion, caused by adrenaline. Adrenaline caused another kind of exclusion, too, this one visual, brought on in part by a hyperfocus on the threat at hand. The trained reflex was to scan, and Ben did so now. Which is when he saw another guy in a dark jacket getting out of a brown sedan two up from Alex's car. This guy was in sunglasses, too, and at least as big as the first. The guy's arm was already inside his jacket, already coming out, and Ben thought, **Shit, shit, shit . . .**

The second guy's gun came out. Ben lunged left and dropped to a crouch, accessing the Glock as he went down. The guy's shot went high. Ben put three rounds into his chest before the guy could get off another shot. The guy went down. Ben detected movement to his right—the first guy. He spun and put two rounds into the guy's head. He snapped left again and saw the second guy on his back, still moving, the gun on the ground inches from his hand. Ben put the Glock's sights on him and walked over. So much for not making noise. He figured he had a half minute before he had to beat feet.

"Kto vy?" he asked, in Russian. Who are you?

The guy didn't answer. His sunglasses had gotten knocked off and he was watching Ben with an expression of pained surprise, as though he couldn't quite figure out how all this had happened.

Ben kicked the gun away. **"Kto vy?"** he said again.

Still no answer. Blood was spreading on the concrete sidewalk underneath the guy's torso. Ben heard an odd slurping sound and realized the guy had a sucking chest wound.

"Tell me who you are and I'll call you an ambulance," Ben said.

The guy gave a weak chuckle that dissolved into a gurgling cough.

Yeah, well. He had never been a good liar in these situations. He glanced around. No one was coming.

"Do svidaniya," Ben whispered, and put a last round into the guy's forehead. The guy's body shuddered once as though he'd been shocked, and then the rigidity, the human cohesion and coherence, was just gone, leaving an inert mound where a moment ago had been a man.

Ben squatted and checked the guy's pockets. Son of a bitch, a wallet. He grabbed it, thinking, **Hallelujah.** He checked the other guy and he had one, too. **Come on, man, gotta boogie . . .**

He stuck his head inside their car. No key in the ignition, and he saw why: the ignition lock was broken off. They'd stolen the car and hot-wired it. Smart. A description of the car or a license plate would be useless.

Nothing else. No syringes, no restraints, nothing. They hadn't been here to grab Alex, then. They were going to drill him and go. Anyone who saw it would have described two guys in shades, if that, and an irrelevant car. An unsolved murder, which police would probably figure had to do with drugs because look what had happened to the guy's client just a couple of days earlier. Ben looked at the two corpses and thought, **Better luck next time, assholes.**

He holstered the Glock and walked toward the gated service entrance that accessed Manhattan Avenue. He climbed over the gate and pulled out his cell phone while he walked. Alex picked up immediately.

"It's me. Don't go back to the hotel. I'm walking north right now on West Bayshore, parallel to the freeway. You know where it is?"

"Of course."

"Good. Take Woodland back to Euclid, Euclid to West Bayshore. Drive normally."

"Why wouldn't I drive normally? What's going on?"

"Everything's fine, just do what I told you."

He clicked off. Two minutes later, he heard a car approaching from behind. He glanced back, ready to go for the Glock, but it was Alex. Alex pulled up alongside him and Ben got in, saying "Go" before he even had the door closed behind him.

"What happened?" Alex asked.

"Just drive. Nice and slowly. Through Menlo, then over to 280. I'll tell you more as we go."

Sarah turned and looked at him. "There's blood on your face," she said.

Shit, must have been from when he head-butted Ivan. Ben looked in the rearview and used some spit to wipe it away.

"Not your blood," Sarah said.

Ben smiled, feeling giddiness starting to kick in, knowing he had about ten seconds before he got the shakes.

"That's the best kind," he said.

"What the hell happened?" Alex asked again.

They were coming up on a do-it-yourself car wash on Oak Grove. "Pull into the car wash," Ben said, "and pop the trunk. I need to get out for a minute."

Alex pulled into one of the bays. Ben jumped out and took the car's real plates out of the trunk. He used them to replace the set he had stolen and put on the car before first going to see Alex at the Four Seasons. He put the stolen set in his bag and took out an unused gun, another Glock 17. He would ditch the tainted gun and the plates later, when the girl wasn't around to know where.

He got back in and Alex drove off. "You changed the license plates?" Sarah asked.

"Had to. People in that neighborhood would have heard gunshots. I'm sure plenty of them were looking out their windows. A few of them might have noticed you picking me up, even though that was a few blocks from where the shots were fired. A very few might even have written down some of the license plate number. No reason for us to take a chance like that."

"Shots fired?" Alex said. "Jesus, Ben!"

Sarah said, "Where did you get the plates?"

"I borrowed them."

Alex turned to look at him. His eyes were wide. "Did you . . . I mean, you shot someone?"

"Eyes on the road, Alex. Do your job. Let me do mine."

Alex faced front and said, "I don't believe this. I don't believe this is happening."

"There were two of them, amigo," Ben said. "Waiting in a stolen car parked right next to yours. You think they were there to wish you Happy Birthday?"

"But you just saw them, how could you possibly know—"

"Alex. Stop talking and drive the fucking car."

That shut him up. The prick. Not even an inkling that maybe he could say something like, **Wow, Ben, thank you for taking care of the two guys who if you hadn't been here would already have killed me. I appreciate it.**

"Where are we going?" Sarah asked.

"The city," Ben said. "We're going to stay at a hotel for a little while. You two are going to do your thing with the technology. And I'm going to follow up on what I just learned."

"What did you just learn?" Sarah asked.

Ben hesitated. He still didn't trust her. The Russian guys didn't feel like government to him. Government guys wouldn't have had wallets on them, they would have been operating sterile. And they would have been sharper about their positioning near Alex's car. They wouldn't have let Ben get as close as he had.

His guess was they were Russian mafia. Which meant either that the Russian mob was after Alex's technology or, more likely, that the mob was being used by someone else as a cutout. It wouldn't be the first time. Look at the way the CIA had used the mob to go after Castro in the sixties. It certainly wasn't unthinkable that the Iranian government would contract out a job to Russian gangsters. The two countries did enough sub-rosa work together. He'd just seen it firsthand in Istanbul.

And he had another problem now, too, which he should have considered more carefully earlier. The girl, whom he didn't even know, whom Alex had forced him to bring along, was now a material witness to a double homicide. True, she didn't actually see him pull the trigger, and he'd been careful not to confirm any of Alex's hysterical allegations, but the information she did have could be plenty damaging.

But he had to tell them something. Otherwise, they'd be groping in the dark when they tried to get inside the technology. And he wanted the girl to understand that the threat she faced wasn't something the police could protect her from. He had to discourage her from the temptation, which he knew would arise repeatedly, to default to good, civilian behavior, implicating him in the process.

"I heard them talking," Ben said. "They were Russian. Can you think of any reason the Russians would want Obsidian?"

Sarah said, "Russians? Russians are mixed up in this?"

Ben nodded. "Sounds like the two of you treed a bad one."

Alex said, "What do you mean?"

"I see two possibilities. One, they were FSB. That's the new KGB. Which would mean the people who want you dead are the Russian government."

Sarah glanced back at him. "What's the other possibility?"

"They were Russian mafia."

"Great," Alex said, shaking his head but at least keeping his eyes on the road. "The people who want us dead are either the KGB or the Russian mob."

"I doubt your problem would be with the Russian mob directly," Ben said. "My guess is, someone gave them a contract. Could be the FSB. Could be someone else. So again, can you think of any reason the Russian government would want Obsidian?"

They were all quiet for a moment. Alex said, "None particular to Russia."

"Well, keep the connection in mind as a new data point. I'm going to check with my people and see if I can't learn more about who they were working with. Or working for."

19 RITUAL

They drove in silence through Menlo Park, onto Sand Hill Road, and then onto 280. Ben watched the rolling green hills pass, the sky above hard blue and studded with bright white clouds. It was surreal.

He rarely had to deal with the aftermath of a job. Ordinarily he just walked away, instantly severing the connection with what was left behind. But now he had . . . all of this. The crazy thing was, a part of him was enjoying it. Maybe it was the giddy aftereffects of what had just happened, but the whole situation was a hell of a challenge, and he'd managed it pretty well so far.

They passed Crystal Springs Reservoir, a stretch of sparkling blue. Ben had chosen 280 over 101 because its slightly more meandering route would give him more time to think on the way to the city. But he was glad now for the views, as well. He'd forgotten how beautiful a highway this was. Even when he had been a kid here, 101 had been an eyesore—an unending stretch of billboards and sound walls and industrial buildings backed up ass-forward to the very edge of the highway.

"Why the city?" Sarah asked. "Why not an airport hotel? That would be anonymous, right? And there are dozens up and down 101."

"You just said why," Ben told her.

"Because it's the first thing I thought of?"

"That's right. It's the first thing someone will key on if they start widening their search."

There was a second, more important reason, but Ben didn't mention it. San Francisco would give him better opportunities to test the girl and surprise anyone who acted on the information he was going to feed her.

"I don't know about anyone else," Alex said, "but I haven't had breakfast. Can we stop somewhere for a cup of coffee, maybe a muffin?"

"Whatever you want," Ben said.

"I know a place," Sarah said. "Ritual Coffee Roasters, on Valencia, in the Mission. Take the San Jose Avenue exit, then bear left on—"

"I know how to get to the Mission," Alex said. "Just tell me the cross street."

"Between Twenty-first and Twenty-second."

Ben didn't like that Sarah had just selected the place they were going, but he couldn't find a tactical reason to object. She didn't have a cell phone. She couldn't warn anyone of anything. So unless Ritual Coffee Roasters was in fact a front for some diabolical organization of which Sarah was a secret member, they would probably be okay there.

Briefly.

Ben noticed the place first from the crowd in front of it—a line stretching twenty feet out of the store, mostly twentysomething hipsters with facial hair or piercings or both. Overhead was a red sign punctuated by the white outline of a coffee cup with a star above it that reminded Ben vaguely of the flag of communist China. It took them ten minutes to find a place to park because the street was jam-packed and Ben refused to let Alex park the car illegally, even if they were just running inside. He would rather eat a bullet than have the time and place of his vehicle logged by a bored city cop issuing a parking ticket.

Ben looked around while they stood in line. The neighborhood was funky: two- and three-story buildings in green and yellow and pink façades; stores with names like Lost Weekend Video and Aquarius Records and Beadissimo; ethnic restaurants and bodegas cheek by jowl with a foreign-car repair shop, a coin-operated laundry, an "environmentally friendly" dry cleaner, whatever that meant.

"They better serve some damn good coffee," Ben said.

"It's worth it," Sarah said. "You'll see."

The line moved faster than he had expected. It was loud inside—music with a heavy beat throbbing through ceiling speakers; the hum of fifty conversations from scattered tables and couches and stools along the bar; the thump and steam of espresso being pulled by hand. Every third person was using a laptop, all of them Macs, and there were a lot of different hair colors, including fuchsia and magenta. Overall the place was a little hip for Ben's tastes, but he had to admit there was nothing self-conscious about it all and the smell of roasting coffee made up for any shortcomings he found in the ambience.

One of the baristas, a twentysomething white guy with a full beard and a Panama hat, smiled in their direction. "Hey, Sarah," he said, and Ben thought, **Goddamn it, she's known here?**

"Hey, Gabe," Sarah said. "The usual."

"Two of these in one day? Someone's gonna have to talk you down." Gabe glanced at Ben and Alex. "Your friends . . . ?"

Alex ordered a latte and a muffin; Ben, suppressing his anger, got something called the Guatemalan Cup of Excellence. Alex pulled out his wallet and Ben made sure he paid cash.

They waited at the end of the bar. "What did I just tell you about going to places where you're known?" Ben said. "The manager of the Four Seasons, now this . . . you guys are unbelievable."

Sarah raised a hand to her ear and then pointed to the ceiling, indicating the music. "Sorry?"

He put his mouth close to her ear and repeated himself.

"Oh, shit," she said. "Sorry, you're right."

Christ, he thought. How could people be so stupid?

They waited. The barista put the coffees on the counter. Ben went to reach past Sarah for his and she flinched. And then he realized.

She was afraid of him. She could pin him to what police would prosecute as a double homicide, and she was afraid of what he might do now. She took them here so she would have witnesses.

He was simultaneously impressed by her thinking and appalled at what lay behind it. When had he reached the point where a girl, someone who in all likelihood had done nothing wrong, looked at him and feared for her life?

A Delta guy he had known in Mogadishu once told him that you can tell the kind of warrior you are by the way the people you're sworn to protect react to you. Are they reassured by your presence, or are they afraid?

Jesus.

He took a sip of coffee and nodded appreciatively. "It's good."

"Yeah."

He waved a hand in no particular direction. "You, uh, you live around here?"

"This is my neighborhood place," she said, stirring sugar into her coffee.

Right, got that the first time.

"You don't mind the commute?"

She looked at him, and he could feel her trying to

make up her mind. "It's not so bad," she said, after a moment. "A straight shot down 280. It's worth it, to live in San Francisco. Didn't you grow up here?"

"Not in the city," he said, looking around. Very unlikely anyone would know about, or key on, the place she bought her coffee. But he wasn't going to rule it out, either. "The Peninsula. Portola Valley."

"Yeah, but this is still your city, right?"

"I haven't been here in a long time," he said, and looked away. The truth was, being in the city was making him uncomfortable, though he couldn't articulate exactly why. Not an operational thing . . . something else. He pushed the feeling away, thinking he would examine it later.

They sat in back, where the music was quieter, on a couple of black leather sofas next to a mound of 150-pound burlap coffee bags and a giant roasting machine. There was a back door, open, and Ben looked through it before sitting. It led to a courtyard filled with bicycles, presumably the employees', some potted plants, and assorted bric-a-brac, all surrounded by a fence. You could get over the fence fast enough, coming in or getting out. He would keep an eye on it.

"Where are we going to stay?" Alex asked.

Ben had been trying to work that out. He wanted something big enough to be anonymous, but not so big that it would have a lobby bustling with conventioneers, where someone could easily set up for an ambush. Not that it would come to that, most likely, but he'd learned the easy way in training and the hard way in combat that a good defense is always layered.

The other requirement was, he wanted to be in a part of the city he knew. Which narrowed things down more or less to North Beach, a neighborhood of mostly low buildings painted in light colors that dated back to 1906, when much of the city had been rebuilt after the devastating earthquake and ensuing fire of that year. The area had once actually been a beach, but landfill had long since extended the city northeast into the bay and now only the name served as a reminder of the area's past. It was where he and his friends had gone on weekends when they were in high school, sneaking into Little Italy bars that were lax about checking ID, chowing down on late-night dim sum in adjacent Chinatown, reveling in the neon tackiness of the girlie bars and adult bookshops. The neighborhood had probably changed a lot since then, but at least he would know its broad contours. That would give him an advantage.

"What about that place in North Beach?" he said. "Corner of Broadway and Columbus. Something Motor Inn, if it's still there. Blue building, lot of glass?"

"You're not serious," Sarah said.

"What's wrong with it?"

"It's a total pit, that's what's wrong with it. You'd have to be desperate."

"Have you not gotten the memo? You are desperate."

"I'm not that desperate."

Alex said, "What about the Four Seasons?"

Ben didn't even know there was a Four Seasons in the city. It must be new. "Where is it?" he asked.

"South of Market," Sarah said.

Ben shook his head. It was too far for his purposes. "No good. Alex just stayed at a Four Seasons. I don't want any patterns."

"All right," Alex said. "The Ritz-Carlton."

"Jesus, the two of you have expensive tastes. You ought to write a book. Five-star-hotel safe houses. You don't know the manager there, do you?"

"No, I've never stayed there."

Actually, the Ritz-Carlton would work. It was on the edge of Chinatown, a half mile from the heart of North Beach.

They drove over. While Alex and Sarah waited in the marble-floored, Oriental-carpeted lobby, Ben used a credit card registered to one of the legends he traveled under to reserve two connected rooms on the fourth floor. He asked for two key cards to each room, and gave Sarah only one.

"I'll pay you back," Alex told him.

"Yes, you will," Ben said.

The rooms were deluxe—high ceilings, luxurious drapes, patterned carpets, elegant furniture. Nice views of Coit Tower and the bay, too.

"Here's the deal," Ben told them. "Alex and I will stay in this room. Sarah, you have the room next door. I'm going out for a few supplies and to run down the names of the Russians. You two get moving on Obsidian."

Sarah said, "I'm going to have to get some clothes at some point."

"We'll take care of that later," Ben said. "Let's see what kind of progress we make today."

"Give me ten minutes," Sarah said to Alex, and went through the connecting door to her room.

As soon as the door was closed, Ben said, "I don't trust her."

"What?"

"Somebody knew where those missing files were kept."

"Yeah, but you said yourself—"

"It's a question of probabilities. We need to be very careful with her."

"Ben, you sound . . . paranoid."

"Thanks for the compliment. Listen. I'm going to have a look around the area. While I'm out, keep the door locked and the privacy sign on. If someone knocks, do not answer."

"What if they don't go away?"

Ben reached around and freed his backup from its holster. He stood up and showed Alex the gun. "Have you ever used one of these?"

Alex's eyes went wide. "No."

"It's very simple. This is a Glock 26. Nine-millimeter, which is a relatively small round but also relatively quiet. Although to you, it would sound like a cannon. There's no safety you need to worry about.

There's already a round in the chamber. Point it at the target and squeeze the trigger. Keep it in your pocket and don't play with it. That's it."

Alex nodded, looking uncomfortable. The sad truth was, by the time Alex got his balls sufficiently in an uproar to use the gun, it would probably be too late. Training was at least as much about mental and emotional readiness as it was about physical skill. But what else could he do? He couldn't leave Alex naked.

"Keep your finger off the trigger and out of the trigger guard until you're ready to shoot," Ben said. "Don't ever point the gun at something unless you're ready to shoot it. You'll be fine."

"I don't feel fine," Alex said.

"Trust me, you'll feel better when you have something to shoot back with."

He closed the curtains, then walked over to the desk and ripped a sheet of paper off the notepad by the phone. He folded it in quarters, then used a strip of duct tape from inside his wallet to tape it over the peephole on the door so that it functioned as a flap. "Now if you need to look through the peephole," he told Alex, "the person on the other side won't know you're there. With the curtains closed, you won't cast a shadow under the door. Just get up close before you move the paper out of the way."

"You really live this way. I can't believe it."

"I'll be back in about an hour. Call me on my cell phone if anything comes up." He wrote down the number and left.

20 IN ANOTHER THOUSAND YEARS

Ben stopped at the front desk and asked if there had been any calls from the room Sarah was in. He was ready with a story in case the receptionist asked, something about his spendthrift cousin Sarah who had a habit of running up phone and room service charges and pissing off their grandfather, who was footing the bill, but the receptionist just told him no, there hadn't been.

Good. She hadn't tried to call anyone. At least not yet.

"As it turns out," he said, "we're going to need one more room. Hopefully on the same floor?"

"Certainly, sir. Let me see what we have available."

They were in luck—there was a third room, right across from the ones they were in. He took two key cards for the extra room, keeping them in separate pockets clockwise alphabetically. Alex front left; Ben front right; Sarah back. A little thing, like folding the edge back on a roll of duct tape, but it would save time when it counted.

On the way out, he scoped the lobby. Small, only a couple of sitting areas, all in view of the concierge and the front desk. Not an easy place to set up and wait. There was an adjacent tearoom, up a few marble stairs and visible from where he stood. A woman was playing a harp in the corner and the gentle sound of it couldn't have been more incongruous.

He walked outside and looked around. There were a few cars parked in front of the hotel, all of them empty, and it looked like getting a spot in the street might take a sniper's patience. Not a place you could plan to wait in a vehicle. And the surrounding buildings were all residences. Again, not usable for a seat-of-the-pants ambush. Between the lobby and the street, Alex had picked a reasonably hard-target hotel. Albeit for all the wrong reasons.

He circled the block and then headed north, getting his bearings. The white double spires of Saints Peter and Paul Church were aglow in the midday sun, the blue of the bay behind them, Angel Island and the green hills of Tiburon beyond. He went down the dank stairs of the Stockton Street Tunnel. The concrete walls were covered with graffiti and piss stains. A sign warned of video surveillance. **Yeah, thanks for the heads-up.**

He crossed California, and the vibrating sound of the cables sliding along in their metal tracks made him remember an early trip to the city, with his parents and Alex and Katie. His dad explained to everyone that the reason they were called cable cars was that they were actually pulled along by metal cables. Ben and Katie played dumb and kept asking, **What? Why are they called cable cars?** Alex was too young to be wise to the joke, and their father, ever the engineer, too earnest. Alex and their dad kept trying different variations of the obvious—**They're called cable cars because they're cars and they're pulled by cables**—their accompanying gesticulations growing increasingly emphatic, until finally the others dissolved in laughter, crying out, **Oh,** that's **why they're called cable cars!** Their dad chuckled with them then, realizing they'd been putting him on. Only Alex refused to share in the amusement, probably because in his insecurity he suspected he was the source of it.

He continued up Stockton into Chinatown, joining a thick, slow-moving mass of pedestrians squeezed between produce stands and souvenir shops on one side of the sidewalk, and newspaper vending machines, street signs, and parking meters on the other. A low-level cacophony surrounded him: storekeepers hawking their wares in Chinese, honking horns, traditional stringed music blaring soullessly from speakers strung from the underside of awnings. The air was laced with the smells of herbal elixirs and diesel belching from buses. A cold wind sliced up and down the east-west streets, and the laundry hanging from shadowed tenement windows twisted back and forth in it like tethered ghosts struggling to break free.

He cut right on Clay, then ducked left into a nameless alley strewn with garbage containers and rotting wood pallets, its walls scarred with dark splotches of paint covering the graffiti underneath. A few pigeons marched spastically away from him, searching for scraps. The air was moist and fetid. He leaned against the wall and waited three minutes. The faces that passed the alley were all Asian. No one followed him in, and no one paid him any attention. He moved on.

When he felt he'd gotten comfortable with the layout of the area, he went back to the hotel, watching his back, checking the likely ambush points as he moved. He checked in at the front desk again. No calls made from either room. Okay.

He tried his key card at Alex's room and it didn't work. Good—Alex had engaged the secondary lock. "Alex," Ben said. "It's me. Open up."

Alex opened the door and Ben went in. Sarah was standing in front of the television. "You're on channel four," Alex said. "KRON, the Bay Area news station."

Ben watched. A double homicide outside the Palo Alto Four Seasons. Unidentified victims. Police following leads.

"I don't know why you think that has anything to do with me," Ben said. Sarah looked at him but said nothing.

Ben picked up the remote and turned off the television. "The two of you are here to do a job," he said, not bothering to prevent the irritation from creeping into his tone. "Watching the news doesn't improve your situation. Figuring out Obsidian does."

Sarah looked at him and he thought she was going to say something smart. But she didn't. She just walked over to the desk and sat down in front of one of two open laptops. Shit, he'd been so focused on the possibility of Sarah making a phone call, he hadn't even thought to check her bag for a laptop. He'd locked the front door and left the windows wide open.

"This is your setup?" Ben asked, walking over and looking at her screen. No e-mail or chat application open, but that meant nothing. It would have taken her all of thirty seconds to send a message, and he had no way of knowing.

"We're just getting started," Sarah said. "We linked the two laptops together as a local area network. We'll use the LAN to encrypt files with Obsidian and send them back and forth."

"What's the music?" Ben asked. Something was coming from one of the laptops. He hadn't been aware of it while the television was on.

"'Dirge,' by a band called Death in Vegas," Sarah said. "Hilzoy built an MP3 file into Obsidian and a command to play it when the program opens. We were listening to see if there was more to it than just a song Hilzoy liked."

"Is there?"

"Doesn't seem like it."

"Well, he picked an appropriate title. Let's get back to work, okay?"

"Okay," Sarah said, without any of the feistiness he had learned to expect from her. Her flat tone gave him another unpleasant emotional wince, like the one he'd felt at the coffee place. But you know what? It might not be the worst thing she was a little afraid of him, afraid of what might happen if she did something stupid like try to contact the police with information about what had happened outside the Four Seasons that morning.

"I need to go out again," Ben said. "Not sure for how long. Call if there's a problem."

He headed north from the hotel, then had a cab take him to Baker Beach, the northern extremity of the city, where the Pacific Ocean ended and the San Francisco Bay began. He took off his shoes and walked across the soft sand, which was pleasantly warm from the sun. A cold sea breeze whistled through the air, and from somewhere on the bay a ship's horn sounded, long and plaintive. A jogger with a golden retriever pounded along at the tide's edge, but other than that the beach was empty of all but driftwood.

He walked down to the water, the Golden Gate Bridge looming a quarter mile off to his right, steep sea cliffs topped with houses sporting multimillion-dollar views on his left. For a moment, he looked out over the Pacific and gave himself over to the timeless rhythm of waves crashing against rocks and packed wet sand, the roar of impact, the hush as the water receded and gathered, the roar again. He wondered what it must have been like here, this very spot, a thousand years earlier. Take away the houses and the bridge and it was all probably the same as it was now. The sky and the water; the sound of the wind and the waves; an ocean with another name, long since forgotten. He smiled, thinking that in another thousand years it would be like that again.

He'd come here a fair amount in high school. It was a good place to smoke a joint, and a better one for sex. At the foot of the sea cliffs there was a rock formation you could climb. At low tide you could drop down into its center and do whatever you wanted, hidden from the world. Ben climbed the formation now, surprised at the immediate familiarity of the hand- and footholds, and more so by the heavy sadness their presence stirred in his memory. The tide was too far in and he couldn't climb down to the formation's center, but that wasn't his purpose. He stood at the top, reached into his bag, and took out the Glock he'd used at the Four Seasons that morning. He looked at the gun for a moment, then disassembled it and pitched the components far out into the water. A moment later he slung the license plates in, too. Doubtful any of it would ever be found. Even if it was, the gun was untraceable, and the salt water would long since have scoured away any DNA evidence.

He headed out to the road and caught a cab back

to North Beach. The broad outlines of the neighborhood were the same, but he'd known the area before
only by night and there was something off about it in
daylight. It was like seeing the working girl who'd
gotten you so hot the night before without her
makeup the next morning. Clubs with names like
Roaring Twenties and the Garden of Eden and the
Condor Topless Bar and the Hungry I clustered together like drunks sleeping off a collective hangover,
their neon signs inert, bleached in the sunlight, the
innumerable gray wads of gum ground into the sidewalks before them the only evidence of the restless
crowds they attracted at night. A homeless man in a
raincoat the color of lichens stopped in front of a trash
can and began picking through it, oblivious to Ben's
presence. Ben peeled a twenty out of his wallet and,
when the man looked up, handed it to him. The man
looked at it, then smiled at Ben, revealing dark and
ulcerating gums. Ben watched him shuffle off and
thought, **What difference does it make, anyway?**

He found an Internet café and pulled out the dead
Russians' wallets. The driver's licenses identified
them as Grigory Solovyov and Yegor Gorsky. He got
no hits. Well, maybe one of the alphabet soup agen-
cies had something on them.

He had a thought—a way of testing the girl. What
was the name of that club across from Vesuvio . . .
Pearl's, something like that? He searched for Pearl's
San Francisco and got it on the first try: Jazz at
Pearl's. Someone named Kim Nalley would be

singing songs of love there at eight o'clock that night. **Okay, Kim,** he thought. **Sing one for me.**

He went out to a pay phone and called Hort, using the scrambler as always. "Anything turn up about that Russian in Istanbul?" he asked.

"Nothing. Nobody's claimed him. I would have let you know otherwise."

"Yeah, I know. The main reason I'm calling is, I just saw something on the news and thought, what the hell, maybe it's connected."

"What is it?"

"Two Russians got shot to death this morning in Palo Alto. Well, the part about their being Russian isn't on the news. I found out about that another way."

There was a pause. Hort said, "I can't help noticing you're calling from San Francisco."

"Just passing through. Couple of personal things to take care of."

"I'm not going to ask you if you had anything to do with these two dead Russians."

"Good, then I won't have to tell you."

"They came after you?"

"No. Not me."

"Then why do you think it was connected?"

"I don't. It's . . . just a lot of Russians lately. You want their names? I'm hoping you can tell me a little more about who they are. I think they were Russian mafia, but there's nothing publicly available and it's probably going to be a while before the police can identify them."

"Go ahead."

Ben gave him the names. Hort said, "All right, as soon as I learn something, I'll call you. It might take a while. It's still hell getting the FBI and CIA to share information."

"Yeah, I know."

"Nice job in Istanbul, by the way. Intercepts indicate the Iranians are apoplectic. They think it was the Israelis."

"Well, that's good."

"Yeah. I'll let you know what turns up on the Russians."

Ben hung up and walked away. For a moment he felt purposeless, and found himself heading up Kearny, one of the city's famously steep streets. Something still felt off to him, but he couldn't quite place it. He paused at Filbert, just below Coit Tower, and looked out at the city to the west. This was another spot they'd liked as kids. Unlike Columbus and Broadway, the heart of North Beach, with its restaurants and clubs and traffic and neon, the neighborhoods above were quiet and almost entirely residential. He remembered standing here at night, the Transamerica Pyramid behind him and Coit Tower just above, listening to the sounds of distant traffic and watching the river of headlights flow across the Golden Gate Bridge, and he would feel like he could have all this, not just this city but a hundred others like it that for now he could barely imagine, cities and places that were only hinted at and yet

also somehow promised by the twinkling neighborhoods below him and the endless dark of the Pacific
beyond.

And then he realized what was bugging him about
being in San Francisco. When he used to come here
as a kid, the visits were always fun and exciting, full
of enthusiasm and innocence and stupid optimism.
He had grown up down the Peninsula, where Alex
still lived, and being back there hadn't strummed any
contrasting emotional chords, maybe because he was
somehow hardened to it. San Francisco, it seemed,
was different. He knew he'd changed since he'd left
the Bay Area; that had been almost twenty years earlier, and who doesn't change in twenty years? And
with the shit he'd seen and done, he knew he'd
changed more than most. But being back here made
him realize the person he used to be hadn't just
changed, he was actually gone, and this was the first
time he had paused to consider whether that long-
ago person's disappearance might be grounds for sadness, maybe even for grief.

He cleared his throat and spat. It was stupid to
come back here. Well, Alex hadn't left him much
choice, had he?

He headed back down Kearny and then over to
Molinari's, an Italian deli he used to like at the corner
of Columbus and Vallejo. He bought sandwiches and
headed back to the hotel, checking in at the front
desk on the way. Still no calls. But that didn't prove
anything. The girl was smart, he could see that, and

she might even have figured he would check at the desk to see if she'd used the room phone. If she wanted to contact someone, she'd use the computer.

Alex let him in. He saw the bag and said, "That smells great. We were just talking about lunch—can't believe it's already almost three."

Ben handed out the sandwiches. Sarah asked, "Molinari's?" When Ben nodded, she said, "Good place."

He didn't like that she knew the city. It gave her an advantage. "Any progress?" he asked.

"Not yet," Alex said.

They ate sitting on the floor. When they were done, Ben said, "Sarah, do you mind if I lie down in your room? I need to shut my eyes for a while, and the two of you will be talking in here."

"It's fine," she told him.

He grabbed his bag and walked through the common doorway, closing and locking the door behind him. He'd almost been hoping she would protest, or say she had to go in there first, or do some other thing that would bolster his suspicions. But nothing. Still, he took the opportunity to quickly and quietly search the room. Again, nothing.

He thought he would nap for maybe twenty minutes, but when he woke he realized from the weak light coming through the window that he'd slept much longer than that. He checked his watch. Damn, it was almost six o'clock. He'd slept nearly three hours. Still on Istanbul time, he supposed. But he was glad he'd been out so long. He'd obviously needed it.

He opened the common door and looked in. Alex and Sarah were still in front of their computers. He walked in rubbing his face. "Anything?"

Alex shook his head. "No. Nothing yet."

Ben nodded and walked into the bathroom. He showered and changed into an oxford-cloth shirt. Before leaving the bathroom, he hid a key card for the extra room under a drawer. He would call Alex and tell him about it later, when the girl couldn't overhear.

He walked back out into the room. They were still working the computers. Good.

"There's an eight o'clock show at Jazz at Pearl's on Columbus," he told them. "I'm going to catch it and I'll be back after."

"Since when do you listen to jazz?" Alex said.

Ben looked at him. "Since when was the last time we talked about music?"

He covered the half mile to the corner of Columbus and Broadway on foot in fifteen minutes. He could have made it in five, but he made a few aggressive moves on the way to ensure he was alone. He didn't go into the club. The truth was, he didn't know the first thing about jazz, Kim Nalley, or anything else, and if Sarah, who increasingly struck him as an astute observer, had probed even a little, she might have found some suspicious lack of depth in his musical knowledge. But she didn't. He was good to go.

He crossed the street, his back to the club, and went into Vesuvio, the venerable Beat generation bar next door to an equally famous Beat landmark, City Lights Bookstore. Vesuvio was one of the bars Ben and his friends had occasionally managed to sneak into back in high school. He looked around and had the weird sense he had gone backward in time. The place hadn't changed at all—the long wooden bar and pleasantly cramped tables; subdued chandelier and sconce lighting that made you feel you were entering a secret cave; Beat memorabilia plastered on walls the color of tobacco smoke. The air smelled faintly of beer and coffee. It felt like twenty years ago, and for a moment the contrast with the present was almost paralyzing.

A grizzled old man in a gray tweed coat sat at one of the booths, nursing a beer and reading a newspaper and looking as permanent a fixture as the tiled floor and the accumulated bottles behind the bar. A jazz number was playing in the background, piano and sax mixing with the disparate chords of conversation from the people sitting at the bar and surrounding tables. Ben walked past them, then took the narrow staircase in back to the dimly lit second floor.

He was in luck. One of the window seats looking out over Kerouac Alley and Columbus was open. He sat down and had a perfect view of the double doors and red awning that marked the entrance to Pearl's. He checked his watch. Seven o'clock. If something were going to happen, it would happen in the next hour, two at the most. A waitress came by and he ordered a coffee.

If the girl were tied into this, she would let someone know where Ben could be found. Unless Ben had killed all of them, which he doubted, he expected they still had local resources. If he was right, one or maybe two men were going to show up at Pearl's. If it were two, one would wait outside to ensure the target could at best spot only one of them. If it were one, he would of course go in alone, and then emerge after confirming Ben wasn't inside. If they showed, Ben would move out and follow them, and improvise from there.

What he was looking for was something that would be hard to articulate, but—what was it that Supreme Court Justice had said about obscenity?—he would know it when he saw it. The men would be alert and aware of their environment. Their expressions would be deliberately casual, but their postures would be possessed of purpose. Their clothes would be dark, bland, and without any identifying logos. There would be a look in their eyes he would recognize even from across the street. It was the same look in his.

He sipped his coffee, watching car traffic flowing up and down Columbus, noting pedestrians. The sky went from indigo to black; the street, from daylight to neon. Around seven-thirty, Pearl's started filling up, mostly with casually but well dressed couples who were of no interest to him. Eight o'clock came and went, but he didn't see what he was looking for. Well, he'd wait until the end of the show. If nothing happened, it wouldn't prove anything. The girl might still be involved; maybe her people just couldn't mobilize fast enough. After all, they'd lost two players that morning. It was possible they were having trouble putting together a full team now.

At a little before eight-thirty, he saw an attractive, dark-haired woman in a waist-length black leather jacket coming up Columbus. He looked closer. Son of a bitch, it was Sarah.

He watched her go into Pearl's, not knowing what to make of it. It didn't make sense. He could imagine her being an insider on whatever kind of operation Alex had gotten himself into trouble with, but not being an active part of it. He looked up and down the street, but saw nothing out of place.

There wasn't much time to think. He would just have to make it up as he went along.

He took out his cell phone and called Alex. "Just checking in," he said. "Everything okay?"

"Yeah," Alex said. "Nothing new. No breakthroughs. We just called it a night. Sarah went out to buy a change of clothes."

She hadn't told Alex she was going to Pearl's. He wasn't sure what that meant.

"I want you to do something," Ben said, watching the double doors through the glass. "There's a room key under the bottom drawer in the bathroom. It's

for an extra room I took—758, right across the hall.
Use it. Don't stay where you are."

"Why? Is something wrong?"

"No, everything's copacetic. I'm just being sensible, or you can call it paranoid if you want. I just
don't want you to be where she knows you'll be until
I'm back."

"Ben, I work with her. I know her. She's not mixed
up in this."

"Yeah, everyone thinks they know everyone. But
you know what, I flew halfway around the world to
help you. Why don't you help me make it not a
wasted trip, okay?"

There was a pause, and Ben could imagine Alex
fuming. Yeah, well, tough shit if he didn't like hearing the truth.

"Yeah, okay," Alex said.

"One more thing. Lock the connecting door and
leave all the lights on. And leave the closet and bathroom doors open."

"Anything else?" Alex said. Ben heard the sarcasm
and tried not to let it irritate him. Was it really so
hard to understand that Ben didn't want to come
back to a room he couldn't easily clear?

"Why don't you just acknowledge that you'll do
it," he said.

"Yeah, I'll do it."

"Good. I'll call when I'm back." He clicked off and
pocketed the phone.

A minute later, Sarah walked out of Pearl's and

starting heading southeast on Columbus, back the way she had come.

Ben opened one of the casement windows. "Sarah," he called.

She stopped and looked around. A bus went by and for a moment she was gone in a roar of diesel.

"Sarah," he called again. "Across the street. In the window."

She looked up and saw him. She gave a small wave of acknowledgment.

He looked around again and detected no problems. What she was up to? Keep him at Pearl's while someone else visited Alex? Could be that. Well, Alex was safe for the time being.

She couldn't be here to do him herself. No, it didn't figure. He could imagine her being an access agent, something like that, but not a trigger puller. He didn't read her that way.

Still, if he was wrong, the penalty for missing would be high.

"Come on over," he said.

21 INSUBSTANTIAL

Alex had yawned three times in an hour, and the last two had been infectious. Sarah looked at him and said, "We're going in circles. I say we call it a night."

Alex fixed her with that unreadable gaze of his, then something in his face seemed to soften. "You're right," he said. "We need to come at it from a different direction to see what we're missing, and that's not going to happen without a break. Are you hungry?"

She had thought he might ask, and was ready for the question. "No, I'm okay. I'm just going to go out and buy a change of clothes. I guess I'll see you in the morning?"

He nodded. "Seven o'clock too early?"

"No, it's good. I doubt I'm going to sleep well anyway. This is all too crazy."

She went to her room through the common doorway, stripped off her clothes, and got in the shower.

Something had been building up in her all day, and if she didn't deal with it, she thought she might explode.

The day had started out weird and then had become downright frightening. Her files missing. The strange call from Alex. Then this guy in his office who she could tell was dangerous in some way, who turned out to be Alex's brother. When they'd told her what had been happening, she was concerned, but not really frightened. Looking back, she realized her relative sangfroid was the result of a lack of understanding. She didn't really believe she was in danger. Yes, she understood the police probably couldn't help, but she had agreed to go with Alex and Ben and try to figure out what was so valuable or dangerous about Obsidian almost as a lark, a kind of adventure, a break in the routine. And then Ben had come back to the car outside the Four Seasons with blood on his face, and she'd seen the report on the news, and she realized that Alex's brother was someone who could kill two men—gangsters, it seemed—with about the same level of difficulty most people faced when pouring a cup of coffee. Could kill? He **had** killed them. There was no other explanation.

And what was she doing now? Had he made her, or had she made herself, in any way an accessory? She'd taken criminal law her second year of law school and had purged her mind of all of it about five minutes after graduating and taking the bar exam. She didn't know how bad this might be for her legally. And legally might be the least of it.

She knew he didn't trust her. And the way he looked at her, the way he'd casually walked over to see what was on her laptop screen . . . was he afraid she would freak out, go to the police? And what would he do if she did?

There were two ways she could deal with it. She could keep her mouth shut and hope it would somehow be all right. Or she could confront the problem directly.

She left the hotel and headed north on Stockton. The night was cold and clear and a crescent moon hung low in the sky. Chinatown was quiet, most of the stores closed now, hidden behind corrugated metal gates. Some of the gates had doorways, a few of which were open, and through them she caught glimpses of families eating dinner and friends playing cards, caught the smells of cooking rice and sweet pastries and the sound of laughter and conversations in a musical language she wished she could understand. Some of the doorways revealed steep, narrow staircases that ascended beyond the angle of her vision, and she wondered what rooms they led to, who traversed them every morning and night, what lives were lived in the secret spaces at their top.

She passed a street mural celebrating the Chinese railroad workers. Paper lanterns set at its base flickered, shivering in the breeze. She turned right on Pacific, looking up at the old wooden buildings, their balconies painted green and red, the eaves turned up in the Asian fashion. An old man was closing up his store at the front of one of them, an herb shop whose windows displayed glass jars filled with ghastly specimens that might have come from the earth or the sea or somewhere else entirely. He waved and smiled toothlessly at her as she passed, and she nodded and smiled in return.

She emerged onto Columbus, and the quiet of the somnolent Chinatown evening ended abruptly with the traffic and neon of North Beach. There it was, Jazz at Pearl's, a first-floor club with windows on the street and a doorway under a red awning. She crossed the street and went inside, explaining to the doorman that she had no reservation but she was supposed to meet a friend here . . . could she just take a quick look around?

It was a small place, maybe thirty people, soft carpet and red-hued lighting and small round tables covered in white linen. A voluptuous black woman was singing "Need My Sugar" with piano and bass accompaniment, and the audience was toe-tapping heartily along with it. Ben wasn't there. Maybe he was in the bathroom? She waited five minutes and then gave up, surprised at how disappointed she was. If she didn't confront him, if she didn't get past this, she didn't know how the hell she was going to sleep tonight.

She had just turned left onto Columbus, thinking maybe she'd grab a bite at Café Prague before finding a Walgreens or something else open at night where she could pick up a change of underwear and a few other items, when someone called her name. She looked around, seeing no one. A bus went by. Had she imagined it? And then she heard it again. She looked up and saw Ben, in the second-story window of Vesuvio. "Come on over," he called.

She felt an odd burst of pleasure that she couldn't quite place—excitement? relief?—and crossed the street.

She went inside and immediately liked it. She supposed it was weird that she lived in San Francisco and had never been inside Vesuvio, but she'd never been to Alcatraz, either. It was one of those places, well known to tourists, you figured would always be there and you'd get to it eventually. Not that she'd been in too much of a hurry. In her imagination, the place was more of a Beat museum than a real bar someone might want to go to for a drink, but the atmosphere struck her immediately as authentic and she was glad she'd been wrong.

She went up to the second floor and walked alongside the balcony overlooking the bar below. The ceiling was close overhead, maybe seven feet, and painted dark brown or black. There was some light from the street but other than that it was so dim she found herself squinting. A few indistinct groups were talking and laughing around tables in booths. She made out Ben's shape against a window, silhouetted by the neon sign of the Tosca Café across the street. He was sitting away from his table, his feet planted on the floor. There was something about him that always seemed . . . ready. For what, she wasn't sure.

"What are you doing here?" he asked as she approached.

She stopped in front of the table but didn't sit down. "I wanted to talk to you."

He nodded and looked out at the street, then back at her. "Do you have a problem with my putting my hands on you?" he asked quietly.

She shook her head, thinking she had misunderstood. "What?"

"I'm not going to be comfortable sitting here with you if I don't pat you down. I'm sorry, but that's the way it is."

She didn't know what to make of it. Was he serious?

As she stood there, trying to take it all in, he got up and stepped close to her. He leaned in close, and she realized this was for the benefit of anyone who might be watching, to obscure what he was really doing. She caught a whiff of the hotel's soap, and something else underneath it, something masculine she couldn't otherwise place. She felt his left hand move inside her coat and slide up her right side, the palm of his hand firm against her kidney, her ribs, the edge of her breast. Then his right hand was doing the same on the other side. He pulled her against him and ran his hands lightly across the small of her back and over her hips. She felt her heart beating fast and told herself it was because she was angry.

He took a step back and glanced around the bar, then knelt in front of her and quickly ran his hands up each of her legs, ankle to groin. She heard her breath moving forcefully in and out of her nose.

He stood and looked at her. She glared back. "Satisfied?" she asked.

He nodded and sat, with no indication she should do the same.

The insolence of it, and her failure to do anything effective in response other than a single lame word of sarcasm, made her so angry she imagined herself picking up a chair and swinging it at him like a baseball bat. "Stand up," she said.

"What?"

"Stand up," she said again.

He did.

She stepped in close and looked into his eyes. "We better both be careful, no?"

She slipped her hands inside his blazer and ran them slowly up his sides. She could feel the warmth of his skin through his shirt, the muscles underneath. She never took her eyes from him. He wanted to play it mocking and insolent? She could play it that way, too.

She knelt in front of him and touched him with the same clinical ease, the same sense of entitlement, that he had used on her. Then she stood and put a hand on his stomach. It was hard and flat and she could feel it expanding and contracting slightly with his breathing.

"I guess you're unarmed," she said, still looking into his eyes.

He put his hand over hers and started pushing it lower. She couldn't believe it . . . what was he doing, one-upping her? But she wasn't going to blink first.

Lower. Her heart was pounding but she wouldn't look away.

Her hand stopped at a hard protuberance just above his groin. She realized what it was—a gun, in some kind of special concealed holster.

"Maybe I can trust you after all," he said.

She glared at him. "Why?"

"Because nobody, with even the most rudimentary training, could have done such a lame pat-down. Maybe you are just a lawyer."

"And maybe you're just an asshole."

"Oh, I'm a lot more than that."

His hand was still covering hers. She pulled it away and sat down. After a moment he joined her.

"Well? What did you want to talk about?" he asked, his tone and expression casual enough to suggest that he didn't really care.

She looked at him for a long second, anger seething inside her. "Forget it," she said, and stood to go.

He was out of his seat with such liquid speed it amazed her. He caught her arm. "Why?" he said. "You mad because I patted you down? Because I didn't get turned on when you did the same to me?"

"Getting turned on is a human quality. I don't see it in you."

"Listen. I don't know you, so I don't trust you. It's not personal."

"The hell it's not. You trusted me fine right up until you heard my name. So don't tell me it's not personal."

"Why don't you sit down and I'll buy you a drink."

"I'll buy my own drink."

Ben glanced over her shoulder. "All right, buy one for me, too."

She looked, and saw the waitress standing behind her.

"Bombay Sapphire martini," Ben said. "No olive, no vermouth."

The hell with it. She nodded to the waitress. "Make it two."

They sat. Ben said, "You going to tell me why you're here?"

She felt her heart beating and it made her angry again. She hated that he could be so cool with her, and that at the same time he made her nervous. And she was scared about what she was going to say next.

She cleared her throat. "It's . . . about the Four Seasons. I'm thinking about what you're thinking, putting myself in the other person's shoes, the way you said to do. And if I were in your shoes, I'd be afraid that I might . . . go to the police or something. I'm afraid of what you might do to prevent that."

He looked at her for a long moment, and she thought she saw something play across his eyes in the diffused light from the street. Sympathy? Regret?

Then he glanced away. "When we're done with this, you'll look back and it'll seem like it never happened."

She didn't follow him. Was he telling her not to worry? He wouldn't . . . hurt her?

"How do you know that?" she said.

"I just know. This is all weird to you. Like something that's happening to someone else. When it's over and you're back to your life, it'll be like waking up from a dream."

She looked at him, trying to read his expression. "You're right," she said. "It does feel like that. But . . . how do you know?"

He shook his head and looked away, and she thought, **Because you never woke up.**

The waitress brought their drinks and Sarah paid for them. They sipped in silence for a few minutes.

"Why do you speak such good Farsi?" Sarah asked, switching languages.

"You already know why," Ben said, also in Farsi.

"I don't like what you do," Sarah said, switching back to English.

Ben laughed. "That's okay. I like it fine."

"You like violence?"

He shrugged. "It's a tool for a job."

"The craftsman doesn't enjoy his tools?"

"Why did you become a lawyer? Because you enjoy lawyering?"

She looked at him, surprised at the way the question went to the heart of her own doubts. "I don't really know why. Maybe just because I was good at it. Why did you get into your line of work?"

For a moment his expression was oddly blank, and then he looked away. "It's a long story."

They were quiet again. Sarah said, "Tell me something about yourself."

"Like what?"

Actually, she didn't know. The words had just come out. She hadn't planned them, and didn't know what she was asking exactly.

"I don't know. Just . . . something you can tell me. Not something about work. Something personal. So I'll feel like I at least know you a little."

He shrugged. "I like to pull the wings off flies. It's just a hobby, but I'm thinking about going pro."

She shook her head, realizing it was a waste of time, feeling foolish for even having tried. "Are you married?" she asked. "Do you have a family?"

There was a pause, and she thought he wouldn't answer. But then he said, "Not anymore."

"What happened?"

"Nothing happened. She was Filipina. I met her in Manila. When we got back to the States, I found out she wasn't who I thought she was."

"Maybe she found out the same thing about you."

"I'm sure she did."

"Kids?"

A long moment went by. He said, "A daughter. They live in Manila."

She couldn't help being intrigued at his obvious reluctance, and more by his ultimate willingness to answer. "You don't see them?"

He shrugged. "It's a long way away."

"But that's not why you don't see them."

He took a long swallow of gin. "What about you? Boyfriend?"

She shook her head. "There was someone in law school. But not now."

"Why not? They must go crazy for you at your law firm."

"Why do you say that?"

He looked at her. "Are you fishing for a compliment, or are you really that blind?"

She felt herself blushing, half in anger, half in embarrassment. "I just haven't met anyone."

"No, that's not it."

"What do you mean, that's not it? How would you know? You don't know anything about me."

"I know a lot about you. It's my job to know things about people."

"Yeah? What do you know?"

"I know that when a woman as beautiful as you is unattached, it's not because she hasn't met anyone. It's because she doesn't want to."

"And why wouldn't I want to?" she asked, resisting the urge to shift in her seat.

"A lot of reasons. You got to the office at, what, seven o'clock this morning? So you want to make a big splash as a lawyer. A boyfriend would be a distraction. And if people in the office knew you had a boyfriend, they wouldn't hope as hard. If they didn't hope as hard, you couldn't subtly manipulate them as much."

She couldn't believe what she was hearing. "You're pretty sure of yourself."

"You asked."

"What else?"

He took another swallow of gin. "You know any guy you get involved with is going to lose his perspective. You know because it's happened before. He'll probably want to get married right away to lock you in while he can. You can't abide that because you want to keep your options open. Not about men, about your life. You don't know what you really want to do. What you want to be when you grow up."

"Yeah?" she said, ignoring the provocation. "And what do I want to be?"

"I don't know. But it's not a lawyer."

"How do you know that?"

"Because if you wanted to be a lawyer, you wouldn't have responded so quickly."

She shook her head, saying nothing. His cockiness enraged her . . . but at the same time, she had to admit the things he was saying weren't so far off.

"You want to know why you don't see your family?" she asked.

"I'm sure you're going to tell me."

"It's because you can't stand an attachment. You can't bear to have someone depend on you. Why is that? Did you disappoint someone along the way, let someone down?"

"You don't know what you're talking about."

"Yes, I do. If I didn't, you wouldn't have been so

quick to argue. It was a departure from your usual style of smug silence."

He smiled. She couldn't tell if it was the usual condescension, or if he was saying, **Touché.**

"What is it? You think your daughter is better off with no father than with one who might be unreliable? What is it, a kind of inoculation? Preemptive disappointment?"

He took a sip from his glass. "Just drop it."

"Why? More fun to get in someone else's head than to have her get in yours?"

"You're not in my head."

"Tell yourself again. Maybe it'll help you believe it."

He looked at her, his expression baleful, and she thought again of tremendous pressure and tremendous control. What was it about him that made her want to know what was behind the control, that made her want to increase the pressure to the point where the control would crack? Why had she become so invested in stirring him up? Because he had belittled her? Made some arguably racist remarks? He was petty, and she was allowing him to make her petty, too.

She knew the words were right. Yet they were having no impact at all on her feelings.

Ben drained his glass. "Another?"

She polished hers off, too, fighting the urge to grimace. "Your turn to buy."

He ordered them two more. She wondered if it was a good idea. She was already buzzed from the first.

But there had been a challenge in his offer, and she wasn't going to back away from it.

You see how stupid you're being? she thought. But once again the words had no effect.

They sat in silence for a few minutes. The waitress brought their drinks and moved off. Sarah took a sip and glanced out the window, musing, enjoying her buzz. She liked the bar. She liked sitting in the gloom, watching the street outside as though from some kind of secret aerie. Pearl's was right across the street; she could see the entrance clearly.

And then it hit her. Damn him. Goddamn him.

"You never went to Pearl's," she said. "You announced you were going there because you thought I might follow you. You came here to watch and see if I did."

He shrugged. "Something like that."

"Something like that . . . I get it, it wasn't me you were expecting, it was what, the other bad people? The Iranian terrorists I work for?"

"I have a suspicious nature, remember?"

"You know what? You're full of shit. No one's suspicious of everyone, not even someone like you."

"You need to get out more often."

"I get out plenty. You spent time here when you were a kid, didn't you? It's why you wanted to stay in the city instead of at an airport hotel. And you wanted proximity to North Beach, too, right? Because you know the layout, you knew you could set something like this up. You expect me to believe this is just routine for you? You do it for everyone?"

"I do it when I need to."

"You'd be doing it if I weren't Iranian?"

"Like I said, I do it when I need to."

"Why don't you just admit it's because I'm Iranian, that you have a problem with that?"

"I don't have to admit anything to you."

"Of course you don't. You don't even have to admit it to yourself. Not if you don't have the balls."

He put his hands on the table and leaned forward. "Listen, honey. You don't live in the real world. You live in a fantasy. And if something intrudes on your little delusion—if you actually have to acknowledge one of the serving class that makes your lifestyle possible, if you get even a hint of a notion of what has to be done on your behalf so you can live the way you think you deserve to—you have a moral-outrage hissy fit. Forgive me if I find it hard to take you seriously."

He leaned back and finished his gin in one long swallow.

"You're right," she said. "What I really need to do is wander the earth unfettered and alone, killing people along the way who need killing, wallowing in the tragic nobility of my sacrifice. Oh, and I'll have to abandon my family, of course. That's obviously part of enlightenment."

She leaned back and emptied her glass as he had his. The gin scorched her throat and burned its way into her belly. She squeezed her eyes shut and shuddered with the effort not to cough.

When she opened her eyes, he was looking at her. He was extremely still and she had no idea what he was thinking. Had she hurt him? She'd been trying to and suddenly regretted it. What he'd said to her had been mean, no doubt, but she wondered if what she had just done in response hadn't been outright cruel. The one didn't justify the other. She wanted to apologize but sensed that doing so would make it worse. Acting as though she knew she had hurt him, and was now trying to make him feel better, would be twisting the knife.

"I think I've had too much to drink," she said, hoping he would read it as the oblique apology she intended.

"I'll walk you back to the hotel," he said. She'd been expecting an insult, something about her inability to hold her liquor, maybe, and the fact that he seemed to have lost any enthusiasm for that made her wonder again if she'd gone too far.

They headed down Columbus, then into Chinatown. The moon was higher now, the wind colder than it had been earlier. In the useless, yellowish glow of the streetlamps, objects seemed indistinct, insubstantial; cars and signs and storefronts melded together, tenebrous elements possessed by the dark.

She noticed his head moving as they walked, looking left and right, even checking behind them when they crossed a street or turned a corner. **You could**

never sneak up on him, she thought. **You'd have to hit him head-on.** The thought felt odd to her and she realized she was drunk.

The hotel was pleasantly warm, the glow of light from chandeliers and wall sconces fuzzy at its edges, the sound of their footfalls on the carpet like muffled heartbeats in the silence. In the elevator they said nothing, and she was very aware of his closeness. He walked her to her room and waited while she fished her key card from her jeans. She opened the door and turned to him. "I want to ask you something," she said.

"Yeah?"

"Does Alex even know?"

"Know what?"

"That he has a niece."

There was a pause. He said, "I don't know why he would."

"You never told him, then."

"We don't talk."

"Why not?"

"Do you have brothers or sisters?"

She shook her head. "No."

"Well, it would be hard to explain, then."

"Try."

"It's a long story."

"Do we not have time?"

"We don't. You need to get a good night's sleep so you can work on Obsidian tomorrow. And I have something to do tonight."

"What?"

"I'll tell you in the morning."

She wanted to say more. More than that, she wanted him to come in. Really wanted him to. But she was afraid to ask.

They stood there for a moment. He looked away and said, "You know Alex is in love with you."

Whatever she'd been expecting, it hadn't been that. "What? He is not."

"Yeah, he is."

"He told you that?"

"No. He would never tell me."

"Then how do you know?"

He sighed. "He's my brother."

Why was he telling her this? Was he saying . . . he wanted to come in but didn't want to hurt Alex? They were so out of touch Alex didn't even know about Ben's child. Why would he care? And anyway, Alex wasn't in love with her, that was ridiculous.

"I have no idea what to say to that," she said.

He smiled, but his eyes were sad. "Say good night."

She looked at him, waiting. Then she said, "Good night."

And then he was walking away. His arms moved, and suddenly he had a key card in one hand and a gun in the other. She thought, **What the hell?** He opened the door and in one fluid movement was gone, the clack of the lock closing behind him the only evidence that an instant before he'd been there.

She stood for a moment, feeling drunk and confused and oddly bereft. He needed his gun to go into his hotel room at night? He was crazy. He must be crazy.

She waited a moment, but he didn't come back out.

She went inside. Nothing had happened. She told herself that was a good thing.

22 INFINITE LOOP

Alex had left the room as Ben told him, and it took Ben only a minute to confirm that he was alone. Everyone had bedtime rituals. Some needed a bath; others, a cup of tea. Some liked to read in bed; others, to listen to music. Ben preferred a room sweep with a Glock in a two-handed, chest-level grip.

He sat at the edge of the bed and thought about what to do. Damn it, what had he been thinking? He'd almost . . . Christ, he didn't know what he'd almost done.

It's the pressure, man. The shit outside the Four Seasons this morning . . . It was just a delayed combat hard-on, that's all. And two straight-up all-gin martinis.

Yeah, maybe. But that didn't change the fact that he'd been a nanosecond from kissing her. Kissing her. Hell, if he hadn't managed to walk away there was a better-than-even chance he'd be in her room right now and kissing would be the least of it.

He glanced over at the common door. She was right there, on the other side, probably looking at the door herself. If he knocked, she would answer. The way she'd been looking at him . . .

He scrubbed a hand across his face. He was being criminally stupid. He'd heard of guys getting caught in honey traps. He'd always thought of them as fools, and now he was on the verge of being one.

She'd gotten to him. Somehow she had. The shit she'd said about his family . . . half of him wanted to fuck her, the other half to smack her. What did she know? He didn't see his daughter—**What are you, afraid to say her name? Ami. Your daughter's name is Ami**—he didn't see Ami because what kind of father could he have been to her? The things he did could be lived with only in silence and solitude. What was he supposed to do, just wash the blood off his hands and then come home to **Hi, honey, how was your day? Fine, sweetie, killed two terrorist moneymen in Algiers and got away clean. Lucky, too, because if I ever fuck up, the U.S. government will disavow all knowledge of my activities, and if I haven't managed to swallow a cyanide capsule, I'll certainly be imprisoned and tortured to death. What's for dinner?**

Please. It was best for them. He was no kind of husband, and he wasn't going to be any kind of father, either. He couldn't have people depending on him. He just needed to be alone.

So why did it bother him so much that Sarah was afraid of him? He should welcome her fear; it was his best chance of keeping her in line, of keeping her mouth shut about what had happened at the Four Seasons that morning. **Oderint dum metuant.** And why had he been so moved by the way she had admitted her fear to him? He should have done something to reinforce it, and instead had wound up stammering out some horseshit about how it would be like none of this had ever happened. Comforting her. For Christ's sake, he had . . . he'd actually tried to comfort her. He must be out of his mind.

The bottom line was that he didn't know the first thing about her. Not really. Treating her with anything other than skepticism and suspicion was his dick talking and nothing more. What he needed to do was jerk off and go to sleep and forget what had almost happened tonight.

Almost. That was the key word. Okay, he'd been tempted, who wouldn't be? She was beautiful, there was no sense denying it. And there was something about her that . . . affected him—that, one minute, made him want to protect her; and the next, made him want to shove her up against the wall and put his hands on her and shut her up by covering her mouth with his own.

Put his hands on her. He hadn't meant anything by it when he'd patted her down in the bar—he'd been too focused on the possibility she might have a weapon. But as soon as he was satisfied she wasn't carrying, he'd relaxed, and it was as though some other guard had dropped, too, because the way she'd looked into his eyes while running her hands up his sides and down his legs . . .

He blew out a long, hot breath. But he hadn't acted on it. No harm, no foul.

On top of it all, he felt guilty. But why? It wasn't as though there was anything between Alex and Sarah, and even if there was, he didn't owe his brother anything.

So why had he told her about Alex? Maybe he'd been trying to distract her. Maybe he'd been trying to explain why even though he wanted to, he couldn't.

The room phone rang. He picked up the receiver and said, "Yeah," thinking, **Sarah?**

"I was wondering if you were back yet." Alex.

"Yeah. Just got here."

"Did you see Sarah? She went out awhile ago."

He hesitated. "Yeah, I saw her. She's in her room. Listen, I need to go out again. I'll come over there and brief you."

He hung up, checked the corridor through the peephole, then walked across the hallway to the third room.

"How was Pearl's?" Alex asked him.

For a second, Ben forgot he was supposed to have been there. "It was fine," he said. "You get anything done?"

"Not really. We were experimenting with using Obsidian in different environments. No breakthroughs. And nothing in Hilzoy's notes to help us. At least not that we've been able to recognize and use. I'm going to play around a little more on my own."

"All right. I need to go out, do a few things."

Alex raised his eyebrows quizzically. "What?"

Ben shook his head. "Just this and that. Day job stuff." He didn't distrust Alex, but Alex didn't need to know, either, and operational security was operational security.

"Whatever," Alex said. "Anyway, there's something I was thinking about. When this is done, I was thinking maybe you and I . . . we could go to the cemetery."

Ben frowned. "Why?"

"Just to pay our respects. You haven't been around in a while. When was the last time you visited Mom and Dad's graves? Or Katie's?"

"I never visited them."

"That's kind of my point."

Here we go again, Ben thought. **Judging me. This time for not sharing his superstitions about genuflecting over a clod of dirt.**

"I don't do graves," Ben said, tamping down his temper. "But if you want to, that's fine. Knock yourself out."

"You know, I don't think I'm asking too much—"

"Yes, you are. You're asking too much. Like always."

"What's that supposed to mean?"

Ben felt his temper slipping away like a greasy cord. "It means I almost ate a bullet today that was intended for you, and I don't feel like a lecture now about how I'm a bad son and brother because I won't pop over to the place where my parents' and sister's bodies currently serve as worm food."

Alex's jaw tightened. "Don't talk like that."

"Like what? They're dead, Alex. They're gone. They don't exist."

"Yeah? What did you do when they did exist? You were too busy to be with Mom even when she was dying!"

Ben felt a sort of heavy, angry surprise, and shook his head as if to clear it. How could this be happening? All the years, all the distance, and here they were, trapped in some kind of infinite loop. "What did you say?"

Alex started to take a step backward, but then held his ground. "You heard me."

Ben paused, forcing the anger back. "I was there for her," he said after a moment. "And she knew it."

"She didn't know it. All she knew was that you were too busy running around playing G.I. Joe to even be with her when she was sick."

"I called her every goddamn day, Alex, and she understood why I couldn't come back. She told me not to come."

"You can't recognize a politeness bluff? What did you want her to do, beg you to come? Fucking beg you? And you wouldn't have, even if she did!"

"Oh, and you took care of her? I didn't see you taking any time off from law school."

"I didn't have to take time off! I was there almost every day!"

"Alex, you're so full of shit. You were there because you could be, because you could get all your studying done sitting with her in a hospital room. If you were with her it was only because it didn't interfere with your almighty fucking career plans. You didn't stay home to take care of her, you stayed home because you were afraid to do anything else."

Alex's voice drifted up a notch. "I was with her when she died. I was holding her hand, not sleeping like a baby in a different time zone."

"She was unconscious for a month before she died, and no one knew when she was going to go," Ben said, the anger building, trying to get around him. "She wouldn't have noticed whether I was there or not."

"She noticed," Alex whispered, nodding. "She could tell."

"She couldn't tell shit!" Ben shouted. "Her brain was shot full of tumors, she was doped to the eyeballs, the hospital could have burned down around her and she wouldn't have fucking known it! Why don't you just admit that you were there for yourself, not for her, and you wouldn't have been there at all if you ever had the balls to do anything else? Mom being sick was the best excuse anyone ever gave you to just stay at home and never go anywhere else!"

"Yes, I would have been with her! I was lucky I

didn't need to take time off from school, but I would have, and that's more than you can say."

"Tell yourself that. Whatever makes you feel better."

"Listen to the way you talk about her," Alex said. "You don't even miss her, you prick."

"I miss her," Ben said, automatically, but the truth was, he didn't. He never thought of her. Of any of them. What good would it do?

"Yeah? Do you miss Dad?"

"Don't go there, Alex. You're not going to like what happens if you do."

"You ever wonder why he did it?"

"I'm warning you, Alex." What the hell? He couldn't remember the last time he'd warned someone of anything. He hated warnings, real or bluff. When you're going to do it, you do it. You don't alert the other side so they can get ready. What was it about being with his brother that made him think and act like a teenager again?

"You want to know what I think?" Alex said.

"No. Not even a little. Just shut the fuck up now."

"I think when you gave up, he did, too."

Ben felt the blood drain from his face. He could see himself grabbing Alex's neck and smashing his face into the wall again and again. His muscles bunched with the urge—**Do it just do it beat the smugness out of the little shit teach him once and for all what happens when you fuck with the wrong people**—but something held him back. Barely.

He needed to get out. If he stayed, he was going to hurt Alex.

And that would be bad because . . . ?

He turned and walked out of the room. Alex might have called from behind him, he wasn't sure. The hallway was rimmed with red and he could hear a ringing in his ears.

He'd never wanted to kill someone as badly as he did right then. Well, the night was still young.

23 OUTTHOUGHT

Ben drove south on 280, the cruise control set for seventy because with the rage still coursing through him he couldn't trust himself not to speed. It was late and traffic was light. The hills glowed faintly under a high crescent moon.

He had already decided to do one more thing tonight, and he was going to do it. Most likely nothing would come of it anyway, but by God he was going to stick to the plan no matter how hard the little shit tried to get under his skin.

He forced all the bullshit out of his mind and concentrated on tactical considerations. He started to feel better. This is who he was. This is what he was good at.

They'd sent someone for Alex at the hotel. Meaning they knew he was moving around. Meaning they probably wouldn't bother making another run at his house. But there was a chance they might, depending on how healthy their numbers remained after they'd lost two at the Four Seasons. If they had no other leads, they might go with the only information they had: work address during the day; home address at night. He imagined himself in their shoes, whoever they were. He would know it was unlikely the target would reappear, but nor was it impossible. Alex was a civilian. It would be hard for him to break out of the patterns and habits of his daily life. He'd be in denial, too. Eventually the two could combine—an item left at home that he realized he needed, a moment of wishful thinking, and the target might reappear at a known nexus. Ben had seen it happen before, and had been there to take advantage of it.

He'd seen at the Four Seasons that the objective of their operation had changed. It was no longer about interrogating Alex first; now it was a straightforward elimination. Under the circumstances, the question then became: Knowing what you know about Alex, where would you lay an ambush at his house?

The answer was easy. The house and a detached garage formed an L at the end of the driveway, with a wooden gate separating them and leading to the backyard. Wait behind the gate. You'd have perfect concealment, and line of sight over the whole drive-way. When Alex gets home, it doesn't matter whether he parks in the driveway or the garage. All you need to do is step out from concealment, blow his brains out with a suppressed pistol, and walk to whatever quiet side street you'd used to park your vehicle. Thank you for playing; next contestant.

If someone were waiting there, his attention would be focused on the driveway and, to a lesser extent, the street beyond it. He wouldn't be thinking about the backyard. It wouldn't occur to him that someone might know this terrain, and use it. Someone who, say, used to cut through the backyard, and the neighbor's yard behind it, on his way to and from school every day.

He got off 280 at the Portola Valley–Alpine Road exit and headed south on Alpine past the low-slung wooden buildings of the Ladera shopping center, where his mom had bought groceries and his dad made sure the cars were gassed up and the tires full. His parents' house—Alex's house—was on a cul-de-sac called Corona Way, one of many such small streets in a neighborhood dotted with rambling houses and large, hilly lots. He made a right on La Mesa Drive, then a left on Erica Way, uneasy at how comfortable the turns were, how familiar the landscape.

There were some cars parked on the tree-lined streets, Lexuses and Mercedes and Volvos that looked like they belonged. He cruised by them slowly, checking the interiors. They were all empty, the windshields and hoods covered in evening dew.

He pulled over and killed the headlights, then opened up his bag and took out a pair of night-vision goggles. Night Optics USA D-321G-A, about six grand a pair if you could find them outside the military. And small and lightweight enough to make a perfect stocking stuffer. He adjusted the headgear and clicked on the unit, and suddenly the world was in sharp, green focus. Rock and roll.

He turned left on Escanyo Way, a cul-de-sac roughly paralleling Corona and separated from it by two winding rows of houses and yards and a thicket of trees. The street was empty of cars and there were no streetlights. He parked alongside a stand of redwood trees between two houses—the Levins' and the Andrewses', he remembered, if they even still lived here. Alex used to play hide-and-seek out here with their kids. He made sure the car's interior light was set to the off position and got out, easing the door closed behind him.

The air was cold and moist and smelled of conifers and peat moss. He closed his eyes and stood with his head cocked for a moment, listening. The wind rustled in the tops of the trees, carrying with it the faintest **whoosh, whoosh** of the thin traffic on 280. How many nights had he snuck out, or in, along this very route, nights that smelled and sounded exactly like this one? He remembered standing in this very spot, taking a drunken leak among the trees, hoping his parents were deeply asleep, coming up with stories in case they weren't. And then there was the time—

Enough. Focus.

Right. He eased the Glock out and headed up the

grass at the extreme edge of the Levins' front yard. He moved slowly, placing each foot carefully toe-heel against the damp grass, pausing after each step to look and listen.

It took him four minutes to cover the fifty feet to the wooden fence enclosing Alex's backyard. It wasn't a high fence, only six feet, built less for privacy than to contain the family dog, Arlo, a mildly neurotic poodle their mother had doted on but whom Ben had mostly just tolerated, and who in any event had long since shuffled off that mortal canine coil. He stood on his toes in the shadows of a clump of oak trees and looked over the fence. He could see the spot at the corner of the house and garage as clearly as though someone had thrown a spotlight on it. It was empty. He glanced around the yard. It was exactly as he remembered. The clubhouse their father had built them when they were kids. The hot tub no one ever used. It was like Alex was living in some kind of family museum. It was pathetic.

He scanned the yard and, seeing no one, put the Glock back into the holster and pulled himself carefully up onto the fence. He turned sideways, eased over his right leg, then his left, then slowly lowered himself to the ground. He brought out the Glock again and waited, looking and listening. Nothing.

Most of the yard was covered in wood chips or gravel. He avoided those areas, keeping to the grass, staying in the shadows. Step. Stop. Look and listen. Step. Stop. Look and listen.

The spot by the garage was so perfect an ambush point that once he had confirmed it was empty he doubted anyone was here. Probably they were short on manpower at this point. Or they figured Alex wasn't coming back tonight. Or both.

Still, best to be certain. The only other spot that would make any sense as an ambush point was the opposite corner of the house, which faced the street at the end of a narrow dog run framed by the house on one side and the fence on the other. You could stand at the front corner in the dark and still see the street, then head back toward the garage when you saw a car turn in.

He moved carefully toward the house, stopping at the raised wooden deck that led to a pair of sliding doors and the kitchen. Step. Stop. Look and listen. He hunkered low, taking advantage of the cover and concealment the deck offered, and began to move laterally.

He was almost at the left corner of the house, and getting ready to take a quick peek past the edge, when he heard a voice from behind him, quiet but cutting with deadly intent through the silent night air.

"Don't turn around. I'm wearing goggles, too. I'm behind cover, and there's a laser dot right on your spine."

Ben had a nanosecond to decide whether to instantly turn and engage or to comply. The calm confidence in the voice, and the facts it had just articulated, persuaded him the second choice was better. For now.

He remained motionless. Where was the guy? From where the voice had come from, he must be behind the hot tub.

"Drop the gun and lose the goggles," the voice said. "Move very, very slowly. The laser is attached to a Taurus Judge."

Ben knew the model—a revolver that could be chambered with .410 shotgun ammunition, rifled to disperse the shot and shred a fist-sized hole from twenty feet out.

In instant mental shorthand, his mind processed the available information. The accent was American, the diction idiomatic. He understood Ben knew firearms, otherwise he wouldn't have been able to count on the mention of the Taurus having the desired effect. He didn't want Ben dead—yet—otherwise he'd be dead already.

So they wanted something from him. He would find out what soon enough. In the meantime, he had a few advantages. Very small, under the circumstances, but better than nothing at all. He closed his eyes.

"Drop the gun and lose the goggles," the voice said again.

He waited, figuring he'd get one last warning, using the extra seconds to think, to give his eyes more time to adjust to the dark he would face without the goggles.

He understood the nature of his mistake. He'd assumed they would be laying an ambush for Alex, a civilian. Instead, they'd been ready for an operator, him, and adjusted their tactics and positioning accordingly. He was furious with himself for failing to have foreseen this. After they'd lost two at the Four Seasons that morning, they would have known there was serious opposition. They'd outthought him. And outplayed him.

Then he realized. The girl. Goddamn her. Goddamn himself, for letting his guard down. She was plenty smart, smarter than you'd have to be to figure out what he was planning on tonight. She'd made a call, after their little moment in the corridor. And that clueless pat-down in the bar . . . she played dumb like a pro.

"One more chance to lose the gun and the goggles, and then I put you down."

Without turning, Ben extended the Glock away from his body, moving very slowly as though trying to reassure the guy of his docility, but in fact giving his closed eyes precious seconds more to adjust. The Glock dropped to the wet grass with a quiet thump.

"Now the goggles. Slowly."

The empty holster felt like a hollow in his guts. The knowledge that Alex had his backup made him want to puke. Slowly, slowly, he loosened the headgear and eased off the goggles. He opened his eyes. He had a little night vision back. But not enough.

Not yet. He extended the goggles to his side and let them fall.

"Where's the one who lives here?" the voice asked.

Thank God he'd put Alex in the extra room. They must have checked the one where the girl thought he was sleeping. It was something, but it wouldn't last. In just a few hours, Alex would wake up and probably knock on Sarah's door. Without Ben to warn him, he'd be toast.

He didn't answer. The guy had given him three tries on the gun and goggles. Now that Ben was disarmed and running blind, the guy could be expected to be at least that patient again.

"Where is he?" the voice asked.

"I don't know," Ben said.

"We don't want to hurt him. He has something we need. If he hands it over, he walks away. Simple."

If he hadn't been a hair away from being eviscerated with buckshot, Ben might have laughed. He knew what the guy was doing: helping Ben rationalize giving Alex up. **Don't help us, and you die,** went the implicit calculus. **Do help us, and your brother will be fine.** Easy, right?

"I really don't know," Ben said. He shifted his eyes left, then right. Things were coming into focus now in the faint moonlight. And he knew the layout, knew it by heart.

"Let me tell you how it's going to be," the voice said. "You tell me where he is. I make a phone call. Some people go talk to him. You and I wait here, in his nice, warm house. When the people call me back to tell me they have what we need, we all go away, and everyone lives happily ever after. Sound good?"

This time, Ben did laugh. "Yeah. Like a fairy tale."

He was five feet from the corner of the house, a gap that in his present circumstances looked as wide as the Grand Canyon. There was something just on the other side he could use. Assuming it was still there, of course. If it wasn't, even if he made it around the corner, he was dead. But Alex hadn't changed anything else. And regardless, it was his only chance.

"Listen, buddy, you're in a bad spot, I know. But here's the way it is. Maybe I'm bullshitting you. Maybe I'm not. But trust me on this, okay? When I ask you again? This one more time I'm going to ask you? If you don't tell me something I can work with, the thing you'll see a second later, the last thing you'll see ever, will be the mist that used to be your insides."

Without letting any sign of it come to the surface, Ben tensed to move faster than he had ever moved in his life. Then he laughed, long and hard and with a confidence he absolutely didn't feel. The laughter was inappropriate and incongruous, and no matter how good the guy was, trying to process it was going to momentarily suck up a few precious neurons.

"Something funny?" the voice said.

"For me it is. He's in the tree right over you."

The instant the last word was out of his mouth, Ben dove for the corner like he'd been shot out of a cannon. And it worked: the laughter, the momentary shift in the guy's focus to what was going on above him instead of in front, and good old action beating reaction—it was just enough. He hit the deck on his stomach like he was sliding into third base and heard the boom of the Taurus behind him, felt lead flying through the air just above his head. He rolled in close to the house, got his feet under him, and dove forward again.

The woodpile. There was always a tarp-covered half cord or cord of firewood here, stacked parallel to the side of the house and two feet away from it because his dad didn't want termites to have an easy jump from the wood to the foundation. And it was still here, thank God, not as much as he remembered but chest high. He scrambled to his feet and turned, his back to the house. He flexed his knees and dropped his hips low, getting his head and body below the top of the pile. He brought his palms up against it, his elbows in, his forehead pressed against the protruding ends of the logs.

And then the guy made a mistake. In his fear that Ben might clear the fence and escape, and in his confidence that Ben was effectively blind now, he followed in too fast. Ben tensed, forcing himself to wait the extra second, to let the guy narrow the gap, and then blasted up and through the wood like an offensive lineman crashing into a blocking sled. Two-foot lengths of hard white oak—splits, rounds, and everything in between—exploded out. Ben charged out behind them. He heard a heavy thud, heard the guy cry out, and then he was on him, wrapping his left hand around the barrel of the gun and twisting hard to the left, driving the other hand into the guy's throat, shoving him backward, slamming him back into the fence. The gun went off again but the muzzle was pointed away from him and then he felt the guy's trigger finger break and the gun tore free. He reversed direction instantly, bringing the gun in muzzle-first in a hammer fist grip, driving it into the guy's temple like he was pounding in a nail. The guy spun away and doubled over, his hands suddenly invisible, clearly reaching for a backup weapon. Ben took the Taurus in his right hand, put the front sight on the guy's back, and rolled the trigger. There was a flash from the muzzle and the gun kicked in his hand. The guy's body jerked as though he was trying to shrug something off, then he dropped to his knees. Ben kept the gun on him and moved in, wanting to shoot him again but hating the thought of the noise of a fourth discharge.

There was no need. The .410 ammunition had shredded the guy, and in the pale light of the moon Ben could see blood flowing from all over his back. The guy groped a hand around to the gore, then held it before his face. "Fuck me," he whispered, his tone faintly wondrous, and pitched face-forward to the ground.

Ben moved in, keeping the gun on the guy. He turned him over with a foot and checked for a pulse in this neck. Nothing. He was done.

He retrieved the goggles he had dropped and got

them back on, then picked up the Glock. He went back to the guy and pulled the goggles from his slack-jawed face. Caucasian, close-cropped hair, about thirty, maybe younger. That didn't tell him anything. His tactics had been good, though, at least until he'd followed Ben around the corner of the house. But that could be excused—he wouldn't have had a way of knowing how well Ben knew the terrain. And his equipment was good, too. The Taurus, of course; and his goggles were Night Optics, like Ben's.

He crouched next to the body for a moment, sucking wind, trying to clear his head and figure out what to do. A series of snapshot images clicked open and closed in his mind: Tossing a baseball with his dad. Throwing a Frisbee to Arlo. Katie, laughing, throwing barbecue sauce at him after he'd squirted her with a water gun. He looked down at the body and for a moment was paralyzed by the colliding past and present.

Come on, he thought. **Focus.** Three shots fired. Pretty damn loud. The lots were big in Ladera, though, typically separated by fences and trees that would suppress some of the sound. Could be people slept through it all, or convinced themselves it was something other than gunshots, or thought it might be gunshots but figured someone else would do something about it. Could be someone picked up the phone and called the police. He couldn't afford to wait around to find out.

He went through the guy's pockets quickly, not expecting anything. This one was better than the Russians. He was a pro. It wasn't like he was going to be carrying a business card.

A bunch of spare Taurus rounds. Useless. A Sure-Fire E1E mini light. Same. And . . .

A car key. No rental agency fob or other identifying characteristics, but it belonged to a Volvo. He'd seen a few Volvos parked on the streets on his way in. A good bet one of them belonged to his new dead friend here. Or if not, then another one, somewhere within, say, a one-mile radius from the house. After all, the guy didn't parachute in here.

He dragged the body back behind the hot tub. He took the guy's goggles and the Taurus—the less physical evidence left at the scene, the better—and headed back over the fence and to his car. He drove away with the headlights off, switching them on again only when he was back on Erica. He parked far back in the Ladera Center parking lot. There were only two streets in and out of Ladera, and from here Ben could see both. If the police came, he would quietly drive away.

He waited, watching and thinking. Leave the guy, or move him? There were risks either way. If he left him, it wouldn't be long before someone saw the body. And a body in his brother's backyard was too close a connection to himself. Okay. This guy had to go for one last ride and be found somewhere else, if he was ever found at all.

After a half hour with no sign of police, he drove

back to Escanyo and parked as he had before. He crossed the yard, hopped the fence, and walked over to the woodpile. He grabbed the tarp that had been covering it, got the guy onto it, and dragged him back to the fence. The tarp was plastic and sledded easily across the wet grass. At the base of the fence he rolled the guy into the tarp, managed to scoop the package up onto his shoulder, and then, using both hands and his head, shoved it over the side. From there it was an easy drag to the car.

He passed two Volvos parked in the street on the way out. Both times he hit the remote unlock button on the key he had taken from the dead guy, hoping for a bit of luck. No good either time. Okay, take care of business and come back later. Too risky to drive around looking for the guy's car with his body cooling in the trunk.

Two minutes later he was back on 280, heading north. He made two stops: first, San Andreas Lake, where he punched the necessary holes in the body to prevent it from floating and then dumped it, along with the guy's pistol and goggles and the knife he used for the aeration; second, a Dumpster in the Mission, where he unloaded the bloody tarp. Then he drove back to the hotel, smiling grimly at the prospect of the girl. Wasn't she going to be surprised to see him now.

24 VIRUS

After Ben had left, Alex opened his laptop again and continued to work with Obsidian and Hilzoy's notes. But his focus was shot.

Maybe he shouldn't have said anything about the cemetery. But it wasn't his fault that Ben couldn't handle it. A simple suggestion, a request, that his brother pay his respects, and Mr. Tough Guy has a purple fit. What was Alex supposed to do, walk on eggshells out of fear that Ben might blow up at the slightest provocation? It was ridiculous.

He felt sick and exhilarated at the same time. Sick because he'd said some harsh things, things he hadn't thought of in a long time and had never dared articulate before. Exhilarated because it was high time Ben heard them. Most of all he was angry—furious, in fact—that Ben, who'd pulled the world's greatest disappearing act while their mother was sick and dying, would now accuse Alex of taking care of her only because it had been convenient for him, because it was some kind of excuse not to go anywhere or do anything else.

Convenient? I wish you could have been there to hold her head while she puked her guts from the chemotherapy. To watch her waste away until she looked like a prisoner of war. Trying every stratagem to get her to take just one more bite. Come on, Mom, it's good, just one more, can't you? No? You want something else? I'll make you something, it's not a problem. Or I could run down to the deli at the shopping center. Just tell me, Mom. Just eat something. Just a bite. Please. Please, Mom.

They'd hired a nurse, but she hadn't been there all the time, and Alex had cleaned up more than one mess when his mother had lost control of her bowels, and then had to try to comfort her afterward, had to try to find ways to ease her shame and shore up her collapsing dignity.

He remembered her feeble laughter at his feeble jokes. **Come on, Mom, what are you talking about? You used to do the same for me, remember?** Remembered his despair when he realized she was only pretending he had made her feel better to make **him** feel better, remembered this as one of the black instants when he understood, really understood, she was going to die.

Mostly she'd been tough, but still, sometimes the

façade would suddenly crack and out of nowhere she'd be crying. **I'm scared, honey. I'm scared. Look at me, big brave Mommy.**

He closed his eyes and rubbed his temples. It was amazing, the clarity of the moments, of the images, that lived in his mind. Months would go by, years, without anything from that horrible time surfacing, and then here it was, in total-recall high definition, all at the flick of a switch.

Yeah, you could have tried looking into her eyes when she cried, while you lied to her about how it was going to be all right. And you could have cried yourself to sleep afterward, because everyone you loved was dying and you couldn't handle this again. Except you had to. You had to. Because no one else was there. That was convenient, too, asshole.

His screen saver kicked in, an image of a galaxy or something, infinite black studded with distant stars and swirling violet nebulas.

The hell with it. He wasn't getting anything done on Obsidian. He got up and started pacing.

It wasn't just that Ben, underneath all his war medals, was a chickenshit that bothered Alex. It wasn't even his hypocrisy in suggesting that Alex had cared for their mother just because he could, while he himself had done nothing. It was his refusal to acknowledge, in his acts if not in one repentant word, that he was the cause of so much of what had happened. If Ben could just admit that, maybe Alex could let it go. But the way Ben acted as if he hadn't done anything wrong . . . that made it even more wrong.

Their parents had been wrecked by Katie's death. It was as though her presence, her life, had been keeping them both intact, while without her, fault lines in their personalities had started to widen, hair-line fractures, previously invisible and irrelevant, now developing into deepening cracks and fissures until the whole structure had become unsound.

Initially, the change had been more obvious in his mother. She had thrown herself into community work: school fund-raisers, get-out-the-vote projects, church activities even though until that point she'd barely attended a Sunday service. She'd started talking a lot, too, and always needed a television or radio playing on top of it. She seemed always to be in motion. It was as though she couldn't stand stillness anymore, couldn't stand what might well up without a cacophany of manufactured distractions to obscure it and beat it down.

His father had the opposite reaction: never a talkative man to begin with, he'd grown increasingly taciturn. Bags had grown under his eyes, and he seemed to be physically shrinking, too, his shoulders slumping, his posture sagging, his gait tired and shuffling where before it had always been confident and brisk. He spent a lot of time at the office, and when he was home he was always working on some solitary project: waxing the car; repairing something in the garage; a ham radio hobby, conducted from his office behind a closed door. He communicated mostly in yesses and noes, in "sure"s and "okay"s. Ben was home a lot those days, and the only thing that really animated their father was arguing with Ben about staying at Stanford, waiting to graduate before joining the army. Other than that, he was so listless, so out of balance—just one wrong push, and whatever dark place his mind half dwelled in, he could fall into it entirely. What scared Alex most was his sense that his father wouldn't even mind if it happened.

And then stupid, selfish Ben, not even a year after Katie had died, announced he was dropping out of Stanford and joining the army. A month later, his father had taken a bunch of pills at the office. Alex had never gotten all the details, but he gathered his father had planned the whole thing carefully so as to be found by a colleague and spare his family that trauma. As though a little trauma more would have made any difference.

He'd left a handwritten note. His mother had let Ben and Alex see it, and then she burned it. Alex thought that was strange at the time, but who could really say? What do you do with a suicide note?

He was so sorry, the note had said. So sorry, but he believed this was best for all of them. He couldn't bear the pain anymore. He couldn't bear thinking that maybe Katie needed him, and he wasn't there for her. The rest of them still had one another. He couldn't leave Katie alone.

Alex had only been a sophomore in high school, but living through losing Katie the year before had made him wiser than he would have liked about what people said and what they really meant. So he read between the lines of his father's little note. Why would his father think his dead daughter needed him more than his living wife and sons did? Could it have been that something had happened, someone had done something to make him feel useless? Maybe kicked out the one leg of support that was still keeping him standing—his desire to make sure his oldest son finished his college education before going off on his grand G.I. Joe adventure? That would have been too much to ask, wouldn't it? Just defer your big plans for a little while longer, Ben. Your father's fragile; your narcissistic, self-indulgent bullshit is about to shatter what's left of him.

Ben had stuck around for a few months afterward, but Alex knew it was for appearance's sake. One night, as the three of them shared a "family" dinner so funereal that even their mother's nonstop line of manic prattle couldn't dispel it, Ben broke the news that he couldn't defer his enlistment any longer. Something about training schedules, Airborne slots, whatever. Alex knew it was all bullshit.

After that, his only contact with Ben consisted of awkward moments on the phone when Alex made the mistake of picking up. Or his mother would pass on some bit of news with false good cheer after she had spoken with her eldest son, and Alex would pretend to be glad to hear. Ben had visited them, what, maybe a half dozen times after enlisting? Alex had dutifully shown up for those uncomfortable get-to-gethers because it would have killed their mother if he hadn't, his smiles so forced that sometimes the next day the muscles in his face would hurt. And then she had died anyway, and Ben had made the supreme sacrifice of actually showing up for the funeral, and then he was gone for good.

And now, after all the years of silence, after all the reasons Alex had to feel resentful, Alex gives the shitheel a chance to show just some remorse, some respect for the dead, and what does he do? Throws it back in Alex's face.

He stopped at the window and looked out at the lights of the city and the bay beyond, then went back to pacing. Well, what had he been expecting? His brother was a plague, a damn virus, and the illness he transmitted was other people's misery. Pretending he was some kind of missionary with Osborne, even though he knew Osborne was Alex's boss. Insulting Alex every chance he got. Insulting Sarah, too, sug-gesting she was part of whatever all this was about. All he ever did was cause other people pain.

He'd been glad when Ben went out to the jazz club that evening. It made him feel foolish to admit it, even to himself, but . . . he had been excited to spend some time alone with Sarah. Why, he couldn't say, ex-actly. It wasn't like anything was going to happen. Wasn't like anything could happen. Still . . .

She was smart, too. She'd come up with a lot of possible uses for Obsidian that day, and even though none of them had turned into the breakthrough they were looking for, each one showed a lot of creativity. She'd seen some possibilities in Hilzoy's notes, some notions for using Obsidian not just to encrypt a network but to encrypt messages sent between networks, and had figured out how to do it, too. But there were plenty of commercially available programs, like PGP, that already performed the same essential function just fine. They couldn't find an advantage Obsidian offered that was worth getting excited about, let alone killing over.

He wished, not for the first time that day, that he had access to the source code. It would have been hugely helpful. Of course, if they still had the source code, they could have just published it as Sarah had suggested and solved their problems right there.

He went back to his laptop. If some secret conspiracy had understood a valuable, or dangerous, hidden potential in Obsidian, how could Hilzoy, the guy who invented it, have missed it? There had to be something in his notes. There had to be.

25 A KIND OF MADNESS

Ben parked on California and walked back to the Ritz-Carlton. It was nearly three in the morning now, and the area was deserted. He wasn't expecting a problem outside the hotel. At this point, anyone waiting for him would likely be inside.

Russians that morning, an American that night. He wasn't sure what it meant. Different groups with an interest in Obsidian? Could be that. Could be whoever was behind this had run out of Russian contractors and had turned to someone else.

If anyone was waiting for him inside, he had a good chance of surprising them. The guy he'd killed at Alex's wasn't carrying a cell phone or a radio. That meant he wasn't expected to check in, at least not right away.

He'd been lulled after Vesuvio, thinking the girl was okay, being insufficiently tactical as a result. He'd been lucky. He wasn't going to rely on luck again.

The interior of the hotel was so still you could hear the silence. A lone woman greeted him at the reception counter, but other than that, the lobby, the bar . . . it was all deserted.

He took the elevator to the sixth floor, then the stairs down to four. He had his gun out the moment he was in the stairwell. Anyone he encountered on the stairs at this hour who wasn't dragging a mop and bucket wasn't likely to be friendly.

He hugged the wall on the approach to Sarah's room, then ducked low as he went past it on the remote chance someone was in there and looking out through the peephole. He pulled the goggles onto his head but not yet over his eyes. He had to account for every possibility now. Everything. Not just a human ambush, but something remote, too.

Getting his own door open was nerve-racking. Countering a threat from an emplaced IED required a totally different set of tactics than countering a threat from a human ambush, and pausing in front of his door to examine it for signs of the former left his ass badly exposed to the latter. Well, the doors were thick; unlikely someone would risk a shot through one of them. But still.

He found no wires or other signs of anything that would have closed a circuit when the door was open. The magnetic lock showed no signs of tampering. He slid his key card in with his left hand, the Glock held at chest level with his right. He eased the door open an inch and held it there, sighting down the Glock.

Nothing on the other side. No wires or anything else out of place around the doorjamb. He reached inside and flicked the master switch. The room went dark.

He let the door close and moved back down the hallway, away from the room. Could be someone was watching from outside. He'd circled the hotel on the way over, of course, but he could have missed someone. He didn't want that someone to see the lights go out at the edges of the curtains of room 767, wait one minute, and then remotely trigger an IED. Or at least he didn't want to be in the room when it happened.

He waited two minutes. Okay, if it was going to happen that way, it would have happened already. He went back to the door, pulled the goggles down, and went in, engaging the privacy lock behind him.

It took him three minutes to confirm that he was alone. Confirming no one had left him an IED love letter took another twenty.

He sat down on the floor, his back against the bed, and pulled the goggles off. He blew out a long breath. Christ, what a day. He ought to be exhausted, but he was still too wired to feel it.

Okay. One more thing, and then he could relax.

The girl.

There were three ways he could go in. First, through the common door, if she hadn't locked it from her side. Second, he could use his key card on the regular door, if she hadn't engaged the privacy lock. He wasn't optimistic that either of these would pan out. So the third option was the most promising: just kick open the common door. It was heavy wood, but it opened into her room, and the metal jamb around it would deform enough, and pull free of the surrounding frame enough, for his purposes.

He opened the door on his side, slowly, carefully, wanting to make sure there was nothing emplaced between the door on his side and the one on hers that could close a circuit. He was surprised to find that the door on her side wasn't just unlocked but was wide open. He was glad he'd left the room lights off and the goggles on. If he hadn't, he would have been instantly silhouetted.

He moved in carefully, not liking that the door was open, sensing a trap. In the green night-vision glow, he saw her on the bed. She was on her back, covered to the neck by the quilt, her long black hair spilling across the white linen pillows. Her right arm was back, resting just above her head. Her left was under the covers. He'd seen during the day she was right-handed, so having her strong hand in view, and seeing it was empty, was marginally comforting. She seemed to be sleeping, but she had played clueless in Vesuvio convincingly, too. He kept an eye on her while he silently cleared the room. It was empty.

He walked over to the bed and watched her for a moment. Her breathing was slow and even. She didn't stir.

He'd noted the privacy lock on her door was engaged. Which turned the open common door into a kind of funnel. He didn't like that at all. It didn't matter where he was going, he didn't like coming in the way he was supposed to.

Keeping the Glock on her, he eased aside the quilt and exposed her left hand. It was empty.

He pulled off the goggles, set them down, and flicked on the nightstand light. Her eyes popped open and she sat up violently in the bed, blinking and squinting and holding the quilt to her body. "What the hell?" she said. "What are you doing?"

"You sound unhappy to see me," he said, relishing the moment despite himself.

"You're fucking right I'm unhappy. You can't just come in here like this. What are you doing? What do you want?"

"Don't play dumb, sweetheart. I know you're good at it, but the act is getting old."

She looked at the Glock as though noticing it for the first time, as indeed probably she was. "Why the fuck are you pointing a gun at me? Are you crazy?"

He kept the pistol pointed at her. And because it was his own habit never to sleep farther than arm's reach from a weapon, he said, "Get out of bed."

"The hell with that. Get out of my room."

He took hold of the quilt and yanked it entirely off her. It flew to the opposite wall and slipped to the ground.

She leaped to the opposite side of the bed. "Get out of here!" she yelled.

She was wearing nothing but white panties and a

white camisole, and for a moment he doubted himself. But how many soldiers had made the same fatal
mistake about a sweet-seeming woman the instant
before she detonated a suicide bomb?

He circled the bed, keeping the gun on her. "Shut
up," he said. "And keep your hands where I can see
them if you don't want to get shot."

She stared at him, breathing hard. "You're crazy.
You're really crazy."

"You're right," he said, on her side of the bed now
and moving toward her. "I'm mad enough to do
something crazy, that's for sure. Three people trying
to kill me in one day? That'd make anyone crazy."

She didn't answer. No, of course she didn't. He
came closer. She backed into a corner, a wall to one
side, the nightstand to the left.

"You really had me fooled for a while," he said.
"I'll give you credit for that. But it's done now. The
guy waiting for me at Alex's house? He told me everything before he died. I had to work on him first, but
in the end, he talked."

"I don't want to know this," she said.

He stepped in closer. "Then you shouldn't have
gotten involved. But here's the good news for you. I
have one question. Answer it to my satisfaction and
you'll be okay."

"What question?"

"Who do you work for?"

"You're not making any sense!"

"See, that's not satisfying me."

And suddenly, she was advancing on him. "Will you stop looking at me as the enemy?" she yelled, jabbing him in the chest with a finger. "I'm Iranian, so that's all you can see! Everything that happens, you distort it in your mind to prove what you already want to believe! Why? Why do you need to believe I'm the enemy? What are you getting out of it?"

He was so surprised he almost took a step back, but then stopped. He was so sure of himself when he'd come in that he'd been expecting her to fold right away. Or to deny it unconvincingly, and then fold. What he hadn't anticipated was a counterattack. Especially one this loud, which could attract attention. He needed to regain control.

"Someone made a call tonight," he said. Keeping the gun on her suddenly felt silly. And at this range, and in her agitated state, there was even a risk of an accident. He slipped it back into the holster. "Someone who knew I was going to Alex's house. There was no one else but you."

"What are you talking about? I didn't know you were going to Alex's house. I didn't know where the hell you were going. All you said was you had something to do."

"You could have figured it out." As soon as he said it, it sounded weak. Christ, had that really been all he was going on? No, the guy asked where Alex was, too. But . . . could that have been because they didn't care about the girl? Alex was the primary, that was obvious. In fact, they might not even have known the girl

had gone into hiding. Whoever they were, their resources weren't unlimited. They might have been saving Sarah for later, if they gave a shit at all.

"So this person you say you tortured tonight," she
said. "What did he tell you? Nothing, that's what.
You're making this up. Making it up to scare me."

He hadn't said he'd tortured anyone, exactly, although he'd hoped the idea would frighten her. Regardless, something wasn't right here. Or rather,
something wasn't wrong. She was alone in the room,
unarmed, asleep or at a minimum doing a nice job of
pretending. It didn't make sense.

"Why did you leave the adjoining door open?" he
said.

"I felt like it."

Yeah, he knew she was up to something. "Why?"

"None of your fucking business!" she said. She
went to poke him in the chest again, and he snatched
her finger in his fist.

"I asked you a question," he said, squeezing hard
and backing her up against the wall.

"Go ahead," she said, grimacing. "Break it. Break
my fingers. Waterboard me. Isn't that what you do?
You torture people until they tell you whatever you
want to hear?"

Why had she left that door open? It had to be because she wanted to make it easy for him to come in
that way. But then why wasn't there anyone waiting
in ambush, why wasn't she armed? What was the
point? Why would she want him to be able to—

Oh, you idiot.

It all fit. It was all obvious. It was embarrassingly simple, and you'd have to be blind or, let's face it, fixated to have missed it.

He looked down, aware for the first time of how little she was wearing, how little was covering her. The shape of her breasts beneath the sheer material of the camisole, the smooth, caramel skin of her belly above her panties . . .

He let go of her finger and put his palm on the wall, next to her head. "Why did you leave the door open?" he said.

"I told you, none of your fucking business."

God, she was beautiful. He thought he'd noticed before, but he hadn't. Not like this.

"Why?" he said again, his voice lower.

"I'm not going to tell you," she said. She tried to go around him and he put his other hand against the wall next to her, boxing her in on both sides.

"I want you to tell me," he said.

"No."

Was she breathing harder now? He knew he was. He could see her nipples, hard through the fabric of the camisole.

He took a step closer and inclined his head so that his lips were only a few inches from her cheek.

"Maybe I already know," he said.

"You don't know anything about me."

"I know something," he said, moving closer.

She looked at him, her gaze angry, defiant, her lips

parted, her breath whistling in and out from between them. He felt his heart pounding, heard it in his ears.

He leaned closer and she turned her head sharply away. His cheek was against hers now, the sound of her breathing loud in his ear. He could smell her hair, her skin. He moved in closer still and pressed against her, and the soft, full warmth of her breasts against him was a kind of madness.

He took one hand from the wall and put it on her hip, then let it glide up, caressing her ribs, the swell of her breast, her neck, her cheek. He eased her head inward. She resisted for a moment, then turned with a strange sound, half growl, half cry, and met his lips, her mouth open, her tongue on his.

He took her head in both hands and kissed her hard, his heart pounding, a buzzing in his ears. He felt unmoored, as though he'd lost his hold on something and was rushing away through the dark. He was still pressed against her and now she was pressing back. He was so hard it actually hurt.

He wasn't thinking anymore, he just needed her naked, needed it. Nothing else mattered, nothing else was real. He took hold of the top of the camisole with both hands and pulled hard in opposite directions. The sound of the fabric tearing filled his ears, and then her breasts were in his hands, and they were beautiful, she was beautiful.

She put her fingers through the gaps in the front of his shirt and pulled, and the buttons popped off with a machine gun cadence. A part of his mind thought,

Shouldn't be surprised, look at the way she patted you down at Vesuvio, tit for tat, and then she was leaning forward, her mouth on his neck, her fingers working at his buckle. He dropped the holster as she was pulling his belt free. She fumbled with his zipper while he shrugged off his jacket and shirt, and then fuck it, he couldn't stand it anymore, he couldn't wait, he got his own pants open and stepped out of them. He kicked them aside and took her in his arms again. She wrapped a hand around him and squeezed and he felt it all the way through his abdomen.

He put his arms under her ass and lifted her. She gave a cry of surprise and wrapped her legs around his waist. He spun around, took two steps from the wall, and lowered her to the floor. He kissed her again, kissed her neck, her breasts, then broke away. Her panties were stretched taut across her hips and he wrapped his fingers through the fabric and pulled, tearing one side, then the other, then tossed them aside, watching her, looking in her eyes, seeing the hunger in them, the want, and then he was touching her, making her groan, making her writhe, and she was so wet this had to be real, it had to be, no one could be this kind of actress. He brought his knees forward, spreading her legs, then lowered himself onto her, wanting to fuck her so badly it obliterated everything else in his mind.

And then he was inside her, and thank God, there was nothing more, there was nothing better, he was like a drowning man gulping down mouthful after mouthful of lifesaving air. She gasped and moved against him, her ankles coming together behind his back, her hands on his face, pulling him to her, kissing him. They moved that way for a while and he willed himself to try to slow down, to be more gentle, and then he couldn't anymore, and he reached down with both hands and took hold of her ass and brought her up against him while he moved more deeply inside her, again and again and again. He closed his eyes and saw swirling colors, black and violet and green, heard her moaning and felt her hands in his hair and on his face and the heat of her body everywhere. Her legs tightened and she moved against him more urgently and she cried out into his mouth and he could feel her coming, coming under and all around him, and then he was coming, too, all the danger and uncertainty and insanity of the day tightening around him like a vise and then suddenly, miraculously, bursting open and letting everything go.

Slowly, carefully, he let go of her ass and brought his arms up, taking some of his weight on his elbows. She said, "No, I want to feel you," and he let himself relax a little. She circled her arms around his neck, her legs still around his back, and he could feel a sound coming with each of her panting breaths that was almost a purr. They lay like that, his heart slowing, his breathing coming back to normal.

He rolled off her onto his back and turned his head to look into her eyes. He wanted to say, **You're beautiful,** but he didn't. Instead he said, "I'm sorry."

She laughed. "I'm not."

"No, I meant—"

"I know what you meant."

He sighed. "I've had a bad week."

She turned on her side to face him, her elbow on the floor, her head propped against her hand. "I get the feeling it's been going on longer than a week," she said gently.

"What do you mean?"

She hesitated for a moment, then said, "You have a daughter, an ex-wife, and a brother, and you never see any of them, never even talk to them. That's more than a bad week."

"It's complicated."

"You know what they say: 'Take heart. The common denominator in all your dysfunctional relationships—'"

"'Is you.' Yeah, I've heard that."

Christ, she was tough. He imagined what it would be like to be in some kind of relationship with her. He wouldn't win many arguments, that was for sure.

"Look," he said, "you were right in the bar. I can't . . . I can't have them depend on me. I mean, what's worse, popping in on my daughter a few times a year, or just being gone entirely? All the first would do is make her aware of my absence, make her aware of some loss. With the second, there's no one to miss. So no loss."

"I don't get it. If no one depends on you, you can't let anyone down, is that it?"

"That's not what I'm saying."

"Want to know what I think?"

"Alex always asks me that. I always tell him no."

"Does he tell you anyway?"

"Of course."

"Then I will, too. What you're describing? It's like stealing. Stealing an inheritance the person doesn't even know she has. Will she miss the money? Will she even know it's gone, or feel diminished by its absence? No. But just because the person isn't aware of the theft doesn't make you any less a thief."

"They teach you that in law school?"

"What happened with you and Alex, anyway?"

"We drifted."

"Come on, no one drifts like that. He doesn't even know you were married, or that he has a niece."

He looked away from her for a moment, trying to decide what, or whether, to tell her. He didn't know where to begin. "We had a sister," is what came out. And he went on from there. He didn't mean to say much. But once he started talking, he found it hard to stop.

"Your poor family," she said, when he was done. "I thought mine had problems."

He laughed harshly. "What family? There's no one left."

"There's you and Alex."

"Alex blames me for the whole thing."

"He told you that?"

"Not in those words. But he does."

They were quiet for a moment. She said, "Did

you enlist to get away from what happened with your sister?"

"No. I had decided before the accident. My parents didn't want me to. They put a lot of pressure on me, but this is what I wanted. Since I was a kid."

"I think it's good you enlisted."

He looked at her, surprised. "Are you serious? I thought you thought I'm a sadistic, torturing baby killer."

"I don't think that. I was just trying to get under your skin. Anyway, that's not what I meant. I think it's good you enlisted because it's what you wanted. I wish I had your attitude about standing up to my parents. But . . . you were right in the bar, too. I don't know what I want."

He didn't respond.

She said, "Why are you helping Alex?"

He looked at her. "This is helping him?"

She laughed. "He doesn't have to know about this."

"Yeah, I think that's best."

"Why, though? I mean, you're so estranged and everything. And yet, here you are."

He thought about it for a moment. The bottom line was, he wasn't sure himself.

"He needs my help," is all he could think to say.

He wanted her to ask more. Maybe it would help him figure it out.

Instead she said, "You really think he's . . . interested in me?"

"Come on, look at you."

"That's all you're going on?"

"Believe me, that's a lot. But no. Like I said, I can tell. What about you? You were never interested in him?"

There was a pause. She said, "He's a good-looking guy, and there's a lot to like. But . . . I don't know, he reminds me of the guys I went out with in college and law school. I don't want to keep repeating myself."

"What do I remind you of?"

She looked at him. "You don't remind me of anything. But at the same time, you do."

He shook his head. "I don't follow you."

She smiled. "You don't have to."

"Yeah, but—"

"Shhh. Why don't you just apologize to me again?"

"I'm sorry."

She eased a leg over his body, then moved astride him, her hands on the floor on either side of his head. She leaned in close, her hair cascading down past his face, enveloping him, and looked into his eyes.

"That's not much of an apology," she said.

He put his hands on her waist.

"Let me rephrase it," he said.

26 LIKE A DREAM

After they'd made love again, Ben told Sarah he had to sleep for a while or he wouldn't be any good the next day. They'd crawled up onto the bed and he was gone almost instantly. Now she was watching him, exhausted herself, but too wired to sleep.

She'd never come like that before. Never. And now twice in one night. With her two previous boyfriends she had thought of intercourse as a pleasant option, but nothing indispensable. Now she finally understood what all the fuss was about. She ached in a delicious way, a physical reminder of how much pleasure she'd just had, and thinking about him inside her made her want to wake him and do it again. They hadn't used any protection, and she knew that was incredibly stupid. She knew she should be upset with herself about that, at least, and yet she wasn't. Maybe later she would worry about it, but for now she just couldn't.

She wondered what would happen between them when this was all over. Her two boyfriends were the only other men she'd been intimate with. She'd known them before anything happened, and there was structure and context for everything that happened after. The man lying naked beside her now . . . she didn't know him at all, and the little she did know was unnerving at best. He was a killer. He stood for—in fact, personified—things she abhorred. He was damaged, he was violent, he was the antithesis of everything she had previously conceived as suitable. So why? What was it?

She smiled. Why think so much? When he woke up, she would seduce him again. That would be enough for now, and after that, they could play it by ear.

She had wanted to ask more about his relationship with Alex. But he'd been reticent, and she didn't want to push.

She wondered, though. She didn't understand how Alex could blame Ben. First, because none of it seemed like Ben's fault to her, not really. And even if there was what lawyers called "but for causation," certainly there was no "proximate cause," the kind of cause that's legally blameworthy. And even if there were, how could someone hold a grudge like that? Against his own brother? She reminded herself she had only one side of the story. And Ben didn't exhibit a whole lot of brotherly love for Alex, either.

But why was he here, then? If Alex blamed him for what had happened to their family, was Ben's presence now a kind of . . . apology? Expiation? And if so, why couldn't Alex accept it?

She watched the rise and fall of his chest. Initially, she had thought he was a Neanderthal and nothing more, but now she realized he'd been feeding her that image, and that she had been all too ready to swallow it. He was actually extremely smart. The stuff he'd said about her in the bar . . . yes, he was trying to be hurtful, but he'd seen a lot.

She wondered for a moment whether she was giving him too much credit for his insights. Because if someone dumb had seen that deeply into her, it could only mean she was shallow. Better to credit his laser insightfulness than blame her transparent superficiality.

Or maybe she wanted a way to believe he was smart because if he was smart it would mean that earlier she'd been so wrong about him?

She chuckled softly. She was being an idiot, over-analyzing when what she really needed to do was just drop it and get some sleep. The sun was going to be up in just a few hours. She and Alex still had a lot to do if they were going to figure out what had made Obsidian so dangerous to them.

Alex. Could he really be in love with her? She'd never seen any sign. On the other hand, in his way, he was as tightly controlled as his brother. Look at the subterranean depths of his family history, something she'd never seen before, or even sensed. Who could say what other currents roiled beneath that smooth surface? Maybe she'd been taking him for granted. On the other hand, what else could she do when he showed so little?

Thinking about him made her feel guilty. If Ben was right, and if Alex sensed what had just happened here, it was apt to make their situation even more complicated.

Well, there was no reason for him to know. They certainly weren't going to tell him, and he wasn't going to find out.

She put her head on the pillow and let out a long sigh. She felt sleep descending, finally, and the last thing she remembered before surrendering to it was what Ben had said in the bar, that this was all going to seem like a dream.

27 WE'RE DONE

Alex sat hunched at the desk, his eyes roving over the laptop screen, reading Hilzoy's notes for what felt like the thousandth time. He'd been up all night, going through the notes forward, then backward, then randomly. He thought if he approached Hilzoy's thinking out of order he might spot something he and Sarah had missed. But nothing.

The Obsidian toolbar was designed like a typical commercial software application, with functions laid out horizontally, each clickable to reveal a drop-down submenu of options related to the primary menu function. You could customize the menu to add functions or hide them, but none of the functions allowed him to do anything but obvious variations of encryption. He tried every version of the menu he could think of. He customized it. He hid functions, then brought them back.

Hidden functions. That's what he was looking for. But where were they? Not in Hilzoy's notes, that was for sure. Alex practically had them memorized at this point. There was nothing there.

Was there another version, maybe? Something Hilzoy didn't even trust his lawyer with?

Maybe. But if there was some sort of double, secret set of notes, Hilzoy would have needed to back that one up, too. Why have Alex hold the backup for one but not the other? It didn't make sense. There wasn't another version. It all had to be right here.

Another version, he thought, rubbing his eyes. **Another version.**

He cursored up to the menu and scrolled through it. File. Edit. Tools. He selected Tools, then cursored down. Macros, Customize . . . Track Changes.

Track changes.

Track changes . . . from previous versions.

Damn. Could it be that simple?

He selected Show Previous Versions. Nothing happened.

Shit.

He scrolled down through Hilzoy's notes. Midway, the numerals one through ten appeared in blue alongside a list of functions, the functions all relating to creation of a macro. The numbers were out of order. Alex stared at them, not understanding. He scrolled through the rest of the notes, but there were no other changes.

He scrolled back up to the numbers. It looked like

in a previous version of the notes, Hilzoy had numbered these functions. But why? And why were the numbers out of order?

It had to be significant. If there had been any previous versions, Hilzoy had accepted all the changes, effectively erasing them all. Except for these numbers. He wanted a record of these. But a hidden record, apparently. That couldn't be an accident. It had to mean something.

All right, what if he just performed the functions in the order of the hidden numbers? Worth a try.

He followed the steps, one through ten, then hit enter.

Nothing happened.

Damn. He'd really been hoping there.

He scrolled up to the menu bar again, checking each function. File, nothing new. Edit, same. Tools . . .

He blinked and leaned forward. The Tools menu had three new entries: Creation. Concealment. Delivery.

"Holy crap," he said aloud. "This is it. It has to be."

Hilzoy had built an Easter egg into Obsidian. And not the usual, just-for-laughs version you could find in so many DVDs and so much commercial software. No, this looked like a whole new application for the technology.

But an application for what?

His heart pounding, he started working the keyboard. He got so immersed, he lost track of time, and didn't even remember where he was until light started creeping into the sky outside his window. What he found was electrifying.

At six-thirty, he showered and got dressed. He put the gun Ben had given him in his pocket, acutely aware of its weight and bulk. He couldn't imagine what it would be like to carry a gun—make that two guns—all the time.

He went across to the other room to tell Ben. The tough guy had walked out last night when things had gotten heated, but whatever. Alex wasn't sorry for what he'd said. Part of him wished he'd said more. Maybe that was the problem. Ben was obtuse. You couldn't expect him to understand something, especially something he didn't want to understand, unless you beat him over the head with it.

He tried his key card, but it didn't work. Shit, Ben must have engaged the privacy lock. He might still be sleeping. But the hell with it, this was worth waking him for.

Alex knocked, then waited. No answer. He knocked again, louder. After a minute, he heard Ben's voice.

"Give me a second. Gotta put some clothes on."

Half a minute went by, then Ben opened the door, wearing only a towel. He said, "You're up early."

"I did it," Alex said, walking in past him. "I cracked it. I know what Obsidian is really about."

Ben closed and locked the door behind him. "Hold on," he said. "I need to hit the head."

He disappeared into the bathroom for a minute.

Alex looked around the room. One of the beds had the covers pulled off it. There was a pile of clothes on the floor. Looked like the jacket and shirt Ben had been wearing the night before.

Ben came out wearing one of the hotel's robes. He sat down on one of the beds. "Tell me," he said.

"We have to get Sarah. She needs to hear this, too."

"She's probably sleeping, don't you think?"

Alex was a little surprised by Ben's solicitude. Yesterday he wouldn't even let Sarah stop to use the bathroom. Now he was concerned about not waking her?

"She'll want to hear this, trust me," Alex said. He walked over to the common door and opened it, then knocked on the door on the other side. "Sarah, it's Alex. Are you up? I found what we were looking for."

"I'll be right there," he heard from the other side of the door. A minute later, she came in, wearing a hotel robe. Her hair was tied back, she wasn't wearing any makeup, she was rubbing sleep from her eyes . . . and she was still beautiful.

It was funny that she and Ben were both in the robes. "Am I the only one who was getting anything done last night?" Alex asked. He meant the comment to be funny, but neither of them laughed, or even said anything. In fact, they seemed almost awkward. Well, he had just woken them both up.

"What is it?" Sarah said, leaning against the wall next to the door.

"I found an Easter egg," Alex said. "In Obsidian."

"Easter egg?" Ben said.

Alex nodded. "A hidden feature set. Something the programmer builds into the application but doesn't document, that's only accessible via a weird sequence of commands. Hilzoy built one into Obsidian. He documented the sequence in his notes, and hid the documentation so that it was only visible if you checked the current set of notes against a previous version."

"You're losing me," Ben said. "What are the secret functions? And why document them if they're supposed to be secret?"

"The sequence was complicated. It had to be, otherwise someone might have stumbled onto it by accident. Hilzoy was afraid he would forget it. So he included it in the notes in a kind of invisible ink."

"He wasn't worried someone would find it?"

"Of course not. No one else had the notes, they were just part of a backup copy of the program he kept with his lawyer, and why would his lawyer bother reading his programming notes? And even if I, or someone else, did read them, why would anyone think to look for earlier versions? And even if you did look for an earlier version, the clues he left wouldn't mean anything to you. You'd have to already know something was hidden, and be racking your brains trying to find out what it was, as Sarah and I were. And even then, you could easily miss it."

"Well, what is it?" Ben said.

Alex wondered why Sarah was being so quiet. Ordinarily, she got impatient with other people's explanations and was quick to add her own.

"The whole thing is a Trojan horse," Alex said. "On the surface, it's an excellent, efficient program for encrypting data. What it's really ideal for, though, is encrypting a virus."

"Cryptovirology," Sarah said, looking at him.

Alex nodded, pleased that she understood right away. "Exactly. Malicious cryptography."

"Sorry, guys," Ben said, "you're getting a little ahead of me here."

"Okay," Alex said. "You know what a computer virus is, right?"

"Sure. A piece of code that someone sneaks into a system to mess things up."

"Yeah, pretty much. Now, there are typically two ways viruses get detected and blocked—signatures and heuristics. Signatures basically means the antivirus software has a list of known viruses with instructions to block or isolate them. It's like the name of a suspected terrorist. It goes on a no-fly list, and if the name comes up, the guy can't get on the plane. It's the name you're keying on, or in the case of viruses, a kind of digital fingerprint."

"Okay . . ."

"The second method is heuristics. Here, the virus is unknown, and you try to spot it by analyzing typical virus behaviors. To stay with the airplane analogy, this would be like passenger profiling. The guy's name doesn't trigger any alarms, but is he doing things we associate with terrorist behavior. If so, he can't get on the plane."

"Okay, I get it."

"So the biggest problem for the virus writer is avoiding detection. If it's a new virus, you don't have to worry about its signature being detected, only viruslike behaviors. But if you eliminate all the virus-like behaviors, you're left with something that's no longer functional as a virus. Undetectable, maybe, but also useless."

"So we're talking about concealment," Ben said.

"Exactly. That's where the encryption comes in. You use the encryption to create a polymorphic virus."

Ben raised his eyebrows, and Alex realized he didn't understand. He paused for a minute, trying to think of a way to explain.

"'Polymorphic' means constantly changing," Sarah said. "We're talking about code that mutates while keeping the original algorithm intact. Which is, generally speaking, how encryption works. If you encrypt the virus, the viruslike behavior is hidden beneath a constantly shifting cloak. Antivirus software doesn't know what to look for."

"Why hasn't anyone done this before?" Ben said.

"They have," Alex said. "A Bulgarian virus writer who went by the name Dark Avenger created a poly-morphic engine years ago. And a couple of guys—Adam Young and Moti Yung—wrote a whole book on it. But there's always been a built-in limitation."

"You can't encrypt the whole virus," Sarah said. "If

you do, it's unusable. You have to leave an unencrypted portion that will decrypt and execute the encrypted portion. And it's that unencrypted tail the antivirus software tries to target."

Alex smiled, glad at her interruption. She'd been awfully quiet for a while. It wasn't like her.

"Obsidian encrypts the whole thing?" Ben asked. "How?"

"Maybe it won't work for all malicious applications," Alex said. "I haven't had time to test it adequately. But what it does work for—and brilliantly—is a virus that's instructed to carry out malicious encryption."

"I don't get it," Ben said. "An encrypted virus for encrypting? Why would someone want to do that? I mean, isn't the ostensible purpose of Obsidian encryption?"

To Alex, it was so obvious that he was momentarily stuck for an answer. "Well, yes," he said, "but the ostensible purpose is to encrypt your data voluntarily—and with your own key for decrypting it. Look at it this way. Imagine if this happened to you: you couldn't access your data. It would be like coming home to your house one day, and finding that someone had installed extra locks on all the doors—locks that you don't have a key for. Even if the perpetrator hadn't managed to defeat your locks and steal your stuff, he's prevented you from getting into your own house. You're locked out. Which means, effectively, your whole house has been stolen. You're homeless."

"So you would use this for what, extortion?" Ben asked.

"That's one possibility," Sarah said. "Or it could be pure destruction. Imagine if you locked up all the data at a major bank. Or the New York Stock Exchange. Or the Department of Defense. Or—"

"Don't those kind of institutions have their data backed up?"

"Sure," Alex said. "But you can create a virus that lies dormant for long enough to infect the backed-up data, too. And even if someone had backup, think of the disruption that would be caused if you could freeze their primary."

"Okay, I get it," Ben said. "I get it. Damn. Does it have other applications?"

"I'm trying to find out. I mean, locking up a computer network is bad enough, but if you could install an Obsidian virus and have it clandestinely transmit data, undetectable by anti-intrusion systems? Man."

They were quiet for a moment. Alex said, "So what does this tell us? I mean about who's behind this."

"It's someone with a lot of reach, I'll tell you that," Ben said. "Someone with a network capable of spotting Obsidian, assessing its hidden potential, and acting on a broad geographical scale to acquire it. If I had to guess, I'd guess the Chinese."

"Why?" Sarah said.

"Because in addition to their overall reach, they're so active in cyberwarfare initiatives. They managed to get some spyware onto the German chancellor's computer that was siphoning off something like a hundred and sixty gigabytes of information a day before anyone knew better. And not long ago, someone penetrated the office computer of the secretary of defense. The Pentagon thinks it was the People's Liberation Army. They've run war games in which they launch a first-strike attack on American computers, the objective being elecromagnetic dominance—crippling our military operations and disrupting civilian life."

"Come on, Ben," Sarah said. "You sound like a Pentagon PowerPoint briefing."

"Trust me, this is real. The State Department's computers are probed two million times a day. Two **million.** For the Pentagon, it's worse."

Wow, they were sure being congenial. Yesterday, when they argued about this kind of stuff, it had practically been a death match.

"I'm just saying we don't want to rule out the United States," Sarah said. "The government has an interest in this area, too."

Alex said, "Well, what's our next move?"

Sarah shrugged. "Why not publish it? Publish the executable, Hilzoy's notes, your conclusions."

"Are you crazy?" Ben said. "You just said yourself, anyone who knows how to use this thing could cause extreme destruction."

"We don't really know that. Alex has found some malicious applications, yes, but as far as we know it's never been field-tested."

Ben shook his head. "Absolutely not. All you're saying is that we know Obsidian could be destructive, but we don't know how destructive."

"Information wants to be free," Sarah said.

Ben laughed. "Come on, that's like saying a chair wants to be free. Information doesn't want anything."

"What I mean is—"

"I know what you mean," Alex said, "but viruses want to be free, too. That's not a reason not to contain them. We can't publish this. I mean, imagine the harm it could do. We can't take that chance."

"Fine," Sarah said. "But there's no way the people who are after this are going to just walk away if they think we know about Obsidian, or that maybe we have an extra copy. No way."

Ben looked at Alex. "No, they're not walking away. I went to the house last night. Someone was waiting there."

Alex felt a sick lurch in his gut, the memory of that night in the bathtub blooming darkly to life. "What happened?"

"I thought there was a chance someone might try to ambush you there, so I laid a counterambush. The problem was, there was an ambush—but it wasn't for you, it was for me. Or someone like me. I should have seen that coming. With what happened outside the Four Seasons, they knew you had some kind of professional help—a bodyguard, something like that. They outthought me. I was lucky to get away."

"You got away. What happened to the guy who was waiting?"

"He didn't come out of it so well."

Alex looked at him. He could feel himself not wanting to understand the implications of that last sentence. But he couldn't force the realization away. "You . . . you killed someone, at our house?" he managed.

"There's nothing there anymore, if that's what you're worried about."

"Well . . . yes, that is what I'm worried about."

"Great. Then you can stop worrying."

"But . . . shit, Ben, if this was self-defense, and I'm sure it was, we could have called the police! They would have believed us. There would have been . . . you know, there would have been a body. They would have taken us seriously, they would have to."

"Alex, self-defense is just that—a defense. I'm not going to get charged with murder and then hope a good lawyer will convince a jury my defense is valid. You're dreaming."

"Goddamn it, Ben, you just blew our best chance!"

Ben stood up from the bed. "I blew it? I drop three people in two days who are trying to kill **you,** and that's blowing it? You're not happy with my performance, is that it, Alex? You want me to, what, go to prison for you? Tell me, what the fuck do you want?"

They stood staring at each other. Sarah said, "Look, the question is, what do we do now?"

Alex only half heard her. He was so pissed he didn't

know what to do. His cocky, know-it-all brother, doing whatever the hell he wanted to, never consulting anyone, never mind the consequences.

"I have a way of finding out more about the guy Alex is so upset about," Ben said. "That is, if Alex approves."

Alex felt about a second away from telling him, **Fuck you, just fuck you,** then walking away and taking his chances with whatever happened after. Anything but more help from this prick he wished had never been born.

Sarah said, "I'm going to go next door so you guys can talk." She went back to her room and closed the common door behind her.

Alex looked at Ben. "Why do you have to be such a dick?"

Ben shook his head disgustedly. "You're unbelievable."

Alex stalked over to the wall. Why couldn't he get through to him? Why wouldn't he ever just listen?

He looked down at the pile of clothes on the floor. There was something funny about the shirt. He couldn't place what.

He leaned down a little. The buttons, that's what was funny. They were all gone.

What the hell? Why would the buttons on Ben's shirt . . .

Understanding flooded through him.

The robes. The weird feeling when Sarah had

walked in. The way she'd been quiet. The way she and Ben had dropped all the rancor.

He looked at the bed. There was no depression in the pillow. The sheets weren't creased. The covers had been thrown back, that's all, thrown back by someone in a hurry, someone trying to create the quick and superficial appearance that he had slept there.

That he had slept alone.

He looked at Ben. "You . . . you didn't," he heard himself say.

Ben held his gaze for a moment, then looked away. "Oh, my God. You did."

Ben licked his lips. "Look, after I got ambushed at your house—"

"What the hell does that have to do with it?"

"It's a post-combat thing, you get crazy."

"What are you going to tell me—after you killed someone, you had to have sex with Sarah? You didn't have a choice? Which—don't say it—it's some soldier thing I couldn't understand. Is that it? Have I got it right?"

Ben sighed. "Alex, I'm sorry."

And hearing those empty words, suddenly Alex hated him. Hated him more than ever. Hated him for everything he'd caused, for making Alex need him, for using the opportunity to . . .

"You're not sorry!" Alex bellowed, jabbing a finger at him. "You're never sorry. No matter what you do, no matter what you cause, you're never sorry!"

"What are you talking about? I just told you I was sorry."

"Oh, bullshit."

"Then what do you want from me, Alex? Tell me, right now, what the fuck do you want?"

"Nothing. There's nothing I want from you."

"Yeah, well, that's good. Because I don't owe you anything. And you've never been grateful for it anyway. All you know how to do is complain, assuming you even notice what I do for you in the first place."

"What you do for **me**? Jesus Christ, how can anyone be this blind?"

"Blind?" Ben said. "I'm blind? All I do is save your ass when you get in over your head. It's just like school, only now the people who are after you aren't just going to beat you up, they're going to kill you, and you think you have some kind of right to my protection, so much of a right it doesn't even occur to you to say thank you for it. Well, I'm sick of it. It's the same old shit and I'm sick of it."

"You want me to be grateful to you because you fended off a few high school bullies, Ben? You killed Katie. You killed her. Why don't you just—"

Ben moved in so fast Alex didn't have time to react. He hit Alex in the chest with both hands and Alex flew backward into the wall behind him. His head ricocheted against the plaster and he saw stars. Ben grabbed him by the fabric of the shirt and shoved him against the wall, his knuckles digging into his throat. Alex grabbed Ben's wrists and tried to tear them away, but it was useless. He couldn't speak. He couldn't breathe. Ben was roaring something incoherent, his breath hot on Alex's face, his teeth bared. Alex drew his arm back to punch him but the wall was right behind him and he couldn't get any leverage. He hit Ben in the jaw but it did nothing. He felt his lungs spasming for air and thought, **Oh God, he's trying to kill me, he's really going to kill me,** and he panicked. He brought a knee up but Ben's hips were turned, his groin out of reach. He clawed at Ben's hands, then at his face. The force of the knuckles grinding into his throat worsened.

A distant part of his mind whispered, **Gun. Gun. Gun.**

He groped blindly for the gun in his pocket. The contours of the room seemed to be receding behind Ben's face, clots of gray creeping in at the edges of everything.

Gun. Gun. Gun . . .

Ben shot a knee into his balls. There was an explosion of pain in his abdomen, a burst of light behind his eyes. Ben stepped away from him and he fell to the floor, choking and retching.

Ben squatted down and pulled the gun out of Alex's pocket, then stepped away from him.

"What are you going to do, Alex, you going to shoot me? Is that what you want to do?"

Alex managed to get to his knees. He clutched his throat and his stomach and sucked in a single sickening gasp of air.

"You want to shoot me?" Ben said again. "You think I killed Katie? And Dad? And Mom? You think it's all my fault? Well, here's your chance to avenge them. Go ahead."

There was a solid **thunk** on the carpet next to him. He glanced over and saw the gun Ben had taken from him.

He wheezed and fought the urge to vomit. **I'll kill you,** he thought.

"Come on, tough guy," Ben said. "Don't have the courage of your convictions?"

Alex picked up the gun and pointed it at Ben's face. He imagined squeezing the trigger, imagined Ben flying backward from the force of the bullet hitting him.

"That's it," Ben said. "That's the way. Go ahead, Alex. I'm the guy who killed our whole family, right? I did it all, it's all my fault. Go ahead."

Just pull the trigger. Pull the trigger. Wipe that smirk off his face for good.

Ben shook his head disgustedly. "I'm not going to wait forever, asshole. This is your chance. If you want to take the shot, take it."

Alex pulled himself to his feet, still sucking wind. He hated that Ben wasn't even afraid. More than anything, he hated that.

Then make him afraid. Do it. He tried to kill you. Do it. Katie. Mom. Dad. Do it do it do it DO IT.

The common door opened to his left. He glanced over. It was Sarah.

"Stop it!" she yelled.

Ben glanced over at her, then back to Alex. "Last chance," he said.

"Alex, are you insane?" Sarah said. "Put the gun down. Just put it down!"

God, he wanted to do it. And the thought of caving in to his sneering piece-of-shit brother brought up a fresh wave of nausea.

But he couldn't. He knew it. And the realization that Ben knew it, too, had known it all along, was infuriating.

Without thinking, he cocked his arm and hurled the gun at Ben's head. It cracked him in the forehead and Ben went down.

Sarah yelled, "Alex!"

"Okay," Alex said. "Now it's your turn. Go ahead."

Ben sat up. A rivulet of blood oozed from a gash in his forehead. He picked up the gun.

"You want to kill me?" Alex said, jerking his thumbs at his own chest. "You killed everyone else. Go ahead. Kill me, too."

Ben wiped his fingers across his forehead. He looked at the blood on them, then wiped them on his robe. "If I gave a shit about you," he said, "I would. But I don't. We're done. You're on your own."

He walked over to the pile of clothes on the floor, dropped the robe as though Alex and Sarah weren't even there, and pulled on his pants, then his shoes, then the buttonless shirt, and then his jacket. He picked up his bag and pulled Alex's and Sarah's cell phones from it. He tossed the phones on the bed and slung the bag over his shoulder.

"Ben," Sarah said. He walked right past her, into the bathroom, as though she weren't there. A few seconds later he came out with a washcloth pressed against his forehead.

"Ben," Sarah said again.

Ben paused and looked at her. "It was a mistake," he said. "Forget about it."

Then he opened the door and walked through it. It clacked closed behind him and he was gone.

The room was weirdly silent for a moment. Sarah said, "What the hell happened?"

"Nothing," Alex said, suddenly resenting her. He'd brought her along just to help her, because she might be in danger. And she repaid him by fucking his brother. Alex was up all night cracking Obsidian while the two of them went at it like bunnies. Well, the hell with that. He didn't need her. He didn't need anyone.

"I'm going home," he said. "I'll see you at the office."

"How can you go home?" she said. "Ben just told you—"

"I don't want to hear it!" he said, more sharply than he'd meant. "Just . . . like he said, forget about it. Just forget it."

He walked across the corridor to the third room to collect his stuff. He didn't care if people were still after him. He didn't care about anything. If someone killed him, it was going to be on Ben's head anyway. Just like the rest of it.

28 STAND DOWN

Ben walked the few blocks to the Chinese Hospital on Jackson Street, the morning sun low in the sky, the glare enough to make him wince. His head was throbbing from where it had stopped the flying Glock, and his emotions were roiled from everything that had happened just before, but he still took precautions along the way.

Alex throwing the gun had caught him by surprise. It was a reminder of how dangerous an amateur could be. Because no operator in the world would think to hurl a pistol, at least not one that was fully loaded and functional. It was just . . . counterinstinctual.

Of course, this one wasn't loaded, although Alex hadn't known that. While Alex was on the floor sucking wind, Ben had pulled the magazine and emptied the chamber. He knew Alex wouldn't spot the difference. And while he was only trying to shame and humiliate the little prick with his taunts, and was sure he wouldn't have the guts to pull the trigger, there was sure and there was **sure.**

He grimaced at the pain in his head. He had some QuikClot hemostatic bandages in his bag and could have used them to dress the wound and stop the bleeding, but he was this close to a hospital . . . might as well have it disinfected and closed up properly, and save the bandages for a real emergency.

Yeah, he'd been right about Alex's guts, or rather his lack of them. But he wasn't sorry he'd stacked the deck in his own favor just in case. What was that saying? The stupidest last words ever spoken are "You don't have the guts." No sense taking that kind of chance.

The real chance he'd taken was putting his hands on Alex in the first place. Because when Ben was that angry, starting was a hell of a lot easier than stopping. Already, he couldn't remember all of it. Alex had accused him of killing Katie, he'd finally said it out loud, just what Ben had known he'd been thinking for all these years. Ben heard the words and then . . . what had he done? There was a red mist, and then he was choking him, wasn't he? Yeah, choking him.

Choking? Say it. You were killing him. You knew it. You felt it. You wanted it.

But he'd stopped himself. He didn't know how, but he had stopped. That had to count for something.

He walked into the hospital emergency room

and filled out a form using a fake name and ID. He was lucky—no emergency cases ahead of him. They sat him down right away and went to work on his forehead.

Unbelievable. He'd been through two firefights in as many days—plus the thing in Istanbul a few days earlier, why not count that, too?—and he'd walked away from all of it without a scratch. It took his brother, who apparently couldn't tell the difference between a Glock 26 and a fucking rock, to do him some damage.

He almost laughed at the thought. Despite how pissed he was, he had to give Alex credit for showing some balls. At least he'd fought back. And he'd tried to use the gun, even though Ben had seen him reaching from a mile away and easily stopped him.

Five stitches and two ibuprofen later, he walked out of the hospital and picked up his car where he'd left it the night before. He thought about what he wanted to do. No new orders, and after Istanbul, he didn't expect to receive any for another couple of weeks at least. Maybe go to Bragg, use the range, stay sharp. Or fly to Cabo for a few days. Yeah, Cabo, do some diving, lie around on the beach, see what happens. That would be good.

He would just swing south on the way out. To see if he could find that Volvo. Not for Alex—fuck him. Just to satisfy his own curiosity, that was all.

Forty minutes later he was cruising the quiet morning streets of Ladera. It took him a long time to find the guy's car—a silver S80. He'd parked in a clever place, Dos Loma Vista Drive, only a half mile from Alex's house as the crow flies, but several miles away by car. The guy had clearly studied a topographical map and understood that with the night-vision goggles he could easily hump the short distance to Alex's house by cutting through yards, while keeping the car in a place where even someone searching for it wouldn't immediately think to look.

When Ben saw the Volvo's lights blink in response to the key remote, he parked and got out. Dos Loma Vista was a heavily wooded cul-de-sac. No one was around. No one was going to see him.

He checked the underside of the car for IEDs. It was clear. Then he examined one of the back doors. If someone had booby-trapped the car, most likely it was the driver's door that would be wired, but they'd outthought him once already, and he wasn't going to let it happen again. The back door was okay. He got in the car and did a quick search. The inside of the car was empty. No registration, not even any rental-agency materials. There was just one thing, in the glove compartment. A cell phone.

Gotcha.

Ben pocketed the phone and paused to write down the vehicle identification number from the dash under the windshield. Unlikely it would lead to anything other than the legend the guy had used to rent the car, but you never knew.

He drove away in his own car and parked in the Ladera shopping center. The phone was a Samsung T219, an entry-level model, probably a throwaway. He checked the log. There was a single incoming call entry—a 650 area code. Local. The call had come in just fifteen minutes earlier. Nothing else. The guy must have purged the phone before leaving the car for Alex's. Smart. But he couldn't stop someone from trying him after.

Ben pressed the Return Call button and raised the phone to his ear. There were two rings on the other end, then a man's voice: "I called you, just like you said. I still haven't seen him."

Ben's heart kicked harder. Goddamn it, the voice was familiar. But he couldn't place it.

"I know you called," he said, keeping his voice at a near whisper to disguise it.

"Where are you? Why are you talking so quietly?"

"I'm in a public place. I don't want anyone to hear. Where are you?"

"I'm at the office, where do you think? He's not here."

Son of a bitch. The office. That's why he knew the voice.

It was Osborne.

Thinking fast, improvising, Ben said, "There was a minor problem. I need to meet you."

"Now?"

"Yes. Go out to the parking lot and stand by your car. I'll be there in five minutes."

There was a pause. Osborne said, "I don't think this is a good idea."

"You will once you meet me and hear what just happened. Five minutes. We'll iron this out fast and you'll be good to go."

He clicked off, not giving Osborne a chance to reply. Ben had been making up the whole thing as he went, and had probably stumbled into a half dozen incongruities, maybe more. Right now, Osborne's unconscious was telling him something wasn't kosher. The trick was to make him feel under pressure, to give him no time to listen to that little voice telling him something was off. And if he did listen, if he did realize something was wrong, Ben didn't want him to have a chance to call in reinforcements. Five minutes was perfect both ways.

He took 280 to Page Mill and pulled into the Sullivan, Greenwald parking lot. If Osborne wasn't waiting, he'd get to him another way, it wasn't a problem.

But there he was, standing next to a shiny black Mercedes sedan, looking nervously left and right, absurd in his T-shirt and cowboy boots. Ben pulled into the spot next to him. Osborne watched him, his expression completely confused. Before he had a chance to process any of it, Ben was out of the car, the Glock in his hand. Osborne saw the gun and his eyes bulged.

"Don't say anything," Ben said. "Just unlock your car and get in the driver's seat. Do that, and I'll assume you want to talk to me. Don't do it, and I'll assume you want to be dead right there."

"I . . . I . . ." Osborne stammered.

Ben pointed the Glock directly at his groin. "Shut up and unlock the car."

Osborne took out his keys and pressed a button. There was a chirp and the lights flashed. Ben got in the back on the passenger side. He slid past a child's booster seat and sat directly behind Osborne.

"Now drive," Ben said. "Be smart, and this will be just a talk. Fuck with me and I'll kill you. Do we understand each other?"

Osborne said, "Where do you want me to go?"

"Right on Page Mill, toward 280."

They pulled out of the parking lot and onto Page Mill. Osborne said, "What's this all about?"

"I'll ask the questions. You just drive. Make a left on Coyote Hill Road."

"Coyote . . . why do you want to go someplace where there are no people? Why can't we just talk while I drive?"

Good instincts, Ben thought. And a smart question. Ben would never let someone take him to a secondary crime scene. Whatever the bad guy was going to do to you, it would be a hundred times worse when he had you someplace isolated.

"Do what I tell you, or I'll put a nine-millimeter round through the base of your skull. Your brain will blow up, but there'll be hardly any blood. I'll buckle you into the passenger seat and drive your corpse back to your law firm in the carpool lane. Sound good?"

"Fine, fine, Coyote Hill Road."

A minute later, Osborne was turning as Ben had instructed him. "That dirt road," Ben said, indicating a brown depression, lined by trees, that cut through the green hills to Deer Creek Road and some office complexes on the other side. "Turn onto it."

Osborne complied. They rolled a little way down the dirt road, and when they were out of view of Coyote Hill, Ben said, "Stop. Kill the engine."

"What do you want with me?" Osborne said.

Ben pushed the child seat onto the floor and slid across to the passenger side so he could see Osborne's face. "I want to know your angle on Obsidian," he said.

"I don't know what you're talking about."

"The invention Alex patented."

"Yeah, I know what it is, I just don't know what you're talking about."

Ben considered. There were two possibilities here. One, Osborne was running this whole thing with some impressive mercenary connections. Two, the outsiders were running him. But which was it? Osborne had to feel Ben knew more than he really did, that's what would get him talking, and to create that illusion, Ben needed to start out in the right general direction. Based on Osborne's responses, Ben's guesses would get increasingly specific. The whole act was an illusion, a lot like what fortune-tellers do to gull credulous customers, and just as for fortune-tellers, the key was to establish credibility, the appearance of knowledge and even omniscience, right at the beginning.

Osborne was afraid, that much was obvious. And yeah, he was being held at gunpoint, but his fear felt like something else.

"How'd they get to you?" Ben said.

"Nobody got to me. I told you, I don't know what you're talking about."

Ben smiled. He could see in Osborne's eyes, from the sudden beads of perspiration on his brow, that the question had terrified him. Okay, he wasn't running this thing. Someone had something on him. But what?

He glanced at the child seat on the floor. Had they threatened his family? No. Osborne's fear didn't feel righteous to him. It felt like something laced with . . . shame.

What did Ben know about him? He'd met him briefly. He'd been in his office for a few minutes. Alex had said something about Thailand, hadn't he? And there had been a photograph, too. Osborne and some Thai dignitary.

"It was Thailand, wasn't it?" Ben said, taking a chance, knowing if he was wrong Osborne would see he was fishing and make it hard to reestablish the proper momentum.

But he wasn't wrong. Osborne blinked rapidly and said, "This doesn't make any sense."

Yes it does, Ben thought. **That nervous blink is better than a polygraph.**

"Photographs?" Ben said. "Video? What was it?"

Osborne shook his head, saying nothing. His eyelids were going so fast it was exhausting to watch. Ben could actually smell the fear coming off him, a vinegary smell that filled the car's interior.

The car seat, Ben thought. **Guy with a family. A reputation. A position in the community.**

And a taste for something in Thailand. Prostitutes? Could be that. Lady boys? Kids? In Bangkok, you could get anything you wanted.

Well, it didn't really matter. He knew enough to work him now.

"There's something you need to realize," Ben said. "The people who've been blackmailing you are my enemies, too. Have you figured out yet what I do to my enemies?"

Osborne didn't say anything, and Ben went on. "So tell me what I need to know, and the people who've gotten into your life will go away. Permanently. Don't tell me, and I'll assume you're still trying to have my brother killed. Which would make you . . . my enemy."

"That's not true!" Osborne said. "I don't want Alex killed. I don't want to hurt anybody."

"Tell me, then. Convince me."

Osborne looked down. After a moment, he said, "A few months ago—"

"Don't look away. Let me see your eyes."

Osborne looked at him, his face twisting with fear and fury.

That's right, asshole. You feel it? You're hooked up to a human lie detector.

"A few months ago, I was leaving the office one night. There was a man waiting by my car. He called to me by name. 'David,' he said. 'Good to see you.' But I had no idea who he was. He . . . handed me a manila envelope. He said he had something he didn't want anyone to know about. That he could make sure no one would know."

"What was in the envelope?"

There was a long pause. Osborne licked his lips and said, "Photographs."

"Photographs of what?"

"Photographs from Thailand."

Okay, good enough. Ben was getting the picture now. Someone learns about Obsidian. Leave aside how for the moment; he knew from his conversation with Alex there were multiple possibilities there. The someone wants to vacuum the invention up. What are the nodes you have to hit? The inventor, the lawyer, the patent guy. The patent office. The patent filing system. The law firm.

"What did they want from you?" Ben asked.

"They wanted to know how they could get rid of Obsidian. I told them they couldn't, it was in the government's PAIR system, for God's sake, but they told me not to worry about that. How could they get rid of it at Sullivan, Greenwald? They wanted to know how our filing system worked, passcodes, backup copies, everything."

"And you told them."

"I . . . had to."

It made sense. They knew from the application that Alex was handling the patent. But for the information they needed to be sure of making the invention disappear, they needed an inside guy.

So how did they learn they could exploit **this** guy? Start with the firm's Web site. You get a list of partners and associates there, bios for all of them. You identify the likely prospects based on public information. You want married people, people with families, people with pressure points. Get a few national security letters issued, and get into their lives: tap their phones, examine their credit card statements, monitor their e-mail. Who's cheating on his taxes? Who has a mistress? Who's a closet homosexual? Who's set up a practice that requires frequent trips to one of the world's premier sex cities?

Now get into Sabre or one of the other online reservation systems to find out when he's traveling. What hotel? The guy's a partner in a major law firm, he's going to be at one of the three or four best in the city. Black bag job on his room. Pinhole camera. Hidden video. Or follow him on his way to somewhere else. Get the proof. Show it to him. Make him feel what it would be like if his wife saw these pictures. Or if the video wound up on YouTube, the URL e-mailed to everyone in his address book. You're holding his life in your hands now, his reputation, everything. You own him.

"Who was the guy whose cell phone you called this morning?"

"That's him. The same guy who was waiting for me in the parking lot that night."

"He have a name?"

"He told me to call him Atrios."

"Okay. Why were you calling Atrios this morning?"

"He called me yesterday. He was looking for Alex."

"What did you tell him?"

"That Alex had been in that morning, but I hadn't seen him since. He told me to call him if that changed, and that I should check in periodically regardless."

That checked out with what he'd said on the phone earlier, and with what Ben had run into in Alex's backyard. But who was Atrios? Who was he working for?

"Atrios," Ben said. "How did you communicate with him?"

"I have his cell phone number. That's all."

Ben thought about what he could do with that. Trace it back to the owner, sure, but Atrios had clearly been a pro and there was virtually no chance he had registered the phone, or rented a car, under a name that would mean anything. Damn it, it looked like killing the guy had closed off his only avenue of information. Not that he'd had a lot of choice at the time, but still.

His phone buzzed in his pocket. He pulled it out and looked at it. It was dark. He thought, **What the hell?** His pocket buzzed again.

Son of a bitch. Atrios's cell.

He pulled out the phone he took from the Volvo and looked at the display. It was a 202 area code. D.C.

"I'm going to answer this," Ben said. "Grip the steering wheel, look straight ahead, keep your mouth shut."

Osborne complied. Ben clicked the Answer Call button and raised the phone to his ear. "It's done," he said, in the same low voice he had used with Osborne earlier.

"Why the hell haven't you checked in?" the voice on the other end responded.

Ben had been prepared to improvise in a dozen different directions. But he hadn't been prepared for this. He froze, suddenly having no idea what to do or say.

The gravelly baritone . . . the rich Georgia coastal accent . . .

"Hort," Ben said. "What the hell?"

There was a pause. Hort said, "Who is this?"

"It's Ben."

Another pause. "Ben? What the hell are you doing, son?"

"Hort, what's going on here? Who was Atrios? Is my brother the target of someone's op? Am I?"

"Your brother . . . who's your brother? Oh, Jesus Christ almighty, are you talking about the lawyer?"

Ben desperately tried to sort through the bullshit. Was Hort playing dumb? What were the chances . . .

"What happened to Atrios?" Hort said. "How did you get this phone?"

"Atrios is gone."

"Oh, damn. You . . . oh, damn, Ben, you have no idea of the mess you're making."

"What mess? I'm in the middle of a mess. I'm trying to clean it up."

"Listen to me. You are to stand down. Immediately. Do you understand? Stand down."

"Stand down from what?"

"Are you still in San Francisco?"

Alarm bells went off in Ben's mind.

"Yeah, I'm still here."

"So am I. We need to meet."

"What are you doing here?"

"I'm running the op you've been fucking up."

"Your op has been targeting my brother."

"I think I understand that now. I didn't before. We need to straighten it out. Jesus Christ almighty."

"What do you want me to do?"

"I'm at the Grand Hyatt on Stockton. Meet me in the lobby in fifteen minutes."

Ben was ambivalent about the suggestion. On the one hand, fifteen minutes wouldn't give Hort time to set anything up. On the other hand, he never liked a face-to-face when someone else suggested the venue.

No. He needed to mix things up, give himself time to think, make sure he didn't surrender the initiative.

"I'm south of you right now," Ben said. "It'll take

me an hour to get there. Let's make it ninety minutes to be sure."

That would sound good to Hort. If Ben agreed to the place and was comfortable with a later time, it would mean he was feeling trustful. Although he very much wasn't.

"All right. Ninety minutes."

Ben clicked off. He looked at Osborne. Osborne kept his hands on the wheel.

"You knew about the inventor, right?" Ben said, his head beginning to throb again. "Hilzoy. You knew what happened to him."

Osborne stared straight ahead. When he spoke, his voice was an octave higher than usual. "The police say he was killed in a drug deal."

"Yes, that's what the police thought, it's what they were supposed to think, but I asked you **what you fucking knew.**"

Osborne didn't answer. And that was answer enough.

His head throbbed harder. This piece of shit knew what it was about. He knew they were going to kill Alex. Which was the same as if he'd tried to kill Alex himself.

A part of him marveled at his own inconsistency. A couple of hours earlier, he'd wanted to kill Alex himself, had on some level longed to do it. But that was different. Alex was his brother. Maybe that was a paradox, maybe it was screwed up, but there it was.

He tried to think whether Osborne presented any

further exposure. If taking him off the board would improve the state of play, he would do it. But he couldn't think of anything. He didn't know how to feel about that. Part of him wanted to do it anyway. And in fact, killing Osborne was exactly what he'd had mind when he'd forced him out to this deserted spot. But watching him grip the steering wheel, seeing and even smelling the man's fear, he found himself reluctant. He'd killed a lot of people—in combat, in self-defense, in cold blood. But he'd never killed someone when it wasn't sanctioned, or when it wasn't necessary. He'd crossed a lot of lines over the course of his life, and he was surprised to realize he didn't want to cross this one.

He looked at Osborne. "Get out of the car. Leave the door open."

Osborne glanced back at him, his eyes pleading. "Don't. Please don't."

"If that's what I was going to do, asshole, I would have done it already. And you wouldn't have seen it coming."

They both got out. Osborne raised his hands in front of him, half plea, half stick-'em-up.

"Put your keys and your phone on the seat," Ben said.

Osborne complied.

"Now move away from the car. You'll be able to find it back in your parking lot. Have a nice walk."

He drove back to Sullivan, Greenwald, parked the car, and got into his own. He wanted to trust Hort.

He always had. It made him sick that now he had doubts.

But maybe there was a way out of this. Maybe things could be straightened out. If he could sit down with Hort, hear what he had to say . . . Maybe there was an explanation. Maybe he could call off the dogs. Maybe.

But he needed to make sure Alex was on board first.

29 STING

Sarah took a taxi from the hotel to her apartment in the Mission. She was exhausted and felt strangely numb. The night before, with Ben . . . it had been overwhelming. She didn't know whether anything more could come of it, whether she even **wanted** anything more to come of it, but something had happened between them, and even in the midst of all the craziness, it had affected her profoundly. And then the next morning, he had walked out with about as much regard for her as for a comfortable chair he'd enjoyed sitting in. Because, what, he had a fight with his brother? That made her trash, to be just thrown away?

Or maybe the fight with Alex was just his excuse. She'd known he was damaged from the moment she met him, and she should never have done anything other than keep him at a sensible distance. She was as furious at herself for her ridiculous lapse of judgment as she was at Ben for treating her like she was some disposable thing.

Alex. She hadn't meant to hurt him. She hadn't even known she could. What was it going to be like now, when they saw each other in the office? Would he still want to work with her? Or would he blackball her somehow?

She realized the corporate and even the romantic concerns were mundane, probably her mind's attempt to ignore the real difficulty she was in. Because the people who wanted Obsidian were still out there. If she was in danger before, most likely she still was. But she didn't know what to do about it, so she was fretting about things that were far less consequential.

The cab stopped on Lexington Street in front of her apartment, a basement unit in one of the narrow, detached, tree-shaded houses that lined the street. She liked Lexington because it was only four blocks long and so attracted little traffic. Its sidewalks were menaced more by the Big Wheels and bicycles of the numerous children who lived in the neighborhood than they were by cars or trucks.

She paid the driver and got out. She'd been gone only, what, twenty-four hours? And yet the comfort and familiarity of the setting felt surreal to her.

She started up the flagstone walk toward the front door. A man called out from her right. "Excuse me, miss?"

She turned, surprised, because she hadn't noticed

anyone there when she'd gotten out of the cab. The surprise turned to alarm. What if they'd found out where she lived? Ben said it would be easy. Maybe they were waiting for her here.

But the man, a slim Asian in shades and a green fleece pullover, was keeping a respectful distance. He said, "If I wanted to get from here to San Jose, would I be better off taking 101, or 280?"

By reflex, her mind started working the problem, considering variables, imagining possibilities. "Well," she said, "it would depend on where you're going in San Jose."

Something suddenly felt wrong to her. Why would a pedestrian ask a question like that?

Because of the way it's calculated to momentarily engage your mind. It would distract you from—

Something stung her in the neck from behind. She clapped a hand to the spot and cried out. Something was stuck in her neck. She tried to turn, but strong hands gripped her shoulders. She struggled and the world seemed to lurch. From somewhere she heard a door—a van door?—slide open, and the last thing she saw before everything grayed out was the man in the sunglasses and fleece pullover moving quickly and purposefully toward her.

30 YOU ALWAYS HAVE

Alex was home in bed, but his eyes were wide open. Ordinarily, he wasn't prone to napping, but he hadn't slept at all at the hotel and he badly needed a few hours right now.

He'd walked all around the house looking for a sign of what had happened the night before. And he'd found it, in the backyard: the woodpile was knocked over, and a short distance away, the grass was trampled down and slick with something dark and sticky he immediately knew was blood. A trail of flattened grass led to the fence, and he imagined Ben dragging a body. It had really happened. Ben had really killed someone right in their backyard. The violence was done, but the signs of its occurrence terrified him. He'd restacked the woodpile and hosed down the bloody grass, imagining how he would explain it to Gamez when he was back in that windowless room for questioning. "Blood? I didn't see any blood. The grass just needed watering. Sure, there are sprinklers, but I sometimes water it by hand."

Finally, his exhaustion began to overwhelm his imagination. His eyes fluttered closed. He was in the backyard again, but he was a kid now, watching his dad water the garden. Katie was throwing a Frisbee to Arlo. A telephone was ringing somewhere . . .

He jerked awake. The phone. It wasn't a dream. Shit, he should have taken the damn thing off the hook. He picked up the handset. "Hello?"

"Alex, it's me."

Ben. A sickening surge of adrenaline coursed through him. He paused, then said, "Leave me alone."

"Alex—"

He put the handset back in the receiver and lay back down. A second later, the phone rang again. He ignored it. After three more rings, it stopped.

The trick, he decided, was to treat Ben as dead. Not to hate him, not to resent him, but just to place him in the same part of his brain where he kept his memories of Mom and Dad and Katie. Maybe he could even grieve for him. Then he could accept the loss, get over it, and move on. That's what he needed to do. Ben was dead. That was okay. That was good.

His agitation eased. His exhaustion rolled in again. He started to doze.

Someone pounded on the front door.

He sat bolt upright, total recall of that night in the bath flooding his mind.

"Alex!" he heard Ben call. "Alex!"

He thought about the gun Ben had given him. If he still had it, he might have shot through the front door.

He pulled a pillow over his head. **He's dead. This is a bad dream. He's dead.**

The pounding got louder. "Alex, open the goddamn door or I'll shoot the lock out!" Ben shouted. "You want to explain to the neighbors? The Levins? The Andrews? Mrs. Selwyn?"

Christ. Alex got out of bed and threw on a robe. He walked down the stairs and stood in front of the door. "Go away," he called loudly.

"Open the door."

"No! I don't want anything from you. Just go away!"

"Alex, I'm going to count to three and then I'm going to shoot the lock out. One."

Good God, it was like when they were kids again. Except with guns.

"Two."

"Okay, okay! Don't shoot, you idiot."

He opened the door, and damn if Ben didn't have his gun out. There was a bandage on his head that gave Alex a surge of satisfaction. Ben put the gun back in its holster and walked in. Alex closed the door behind him.

Ben looked around. Alex realized he hadn't been in the house in, what, eight years? Something like that.

"Looks the same," Ben said. He sniffed, his expression contemplative. "Smells the same."

"What do you mean it smells?"

"In a good way. It smells like . . ."

"Like what?"

Ben shrugged. "Like home."

Alex almost said, **Well, it's not your home.** Instead: "What do you want?"

Ben looked at him. "Your boss is involved in this."

Alex almost laughed. "Osborne?"

"They blackmailed him. He was their inside man."

"Good for you, Columbo. But it's too late. I don't even care. Just go."

"Alex—"

"We're done, remember? Seriously. Go."

"You don't understand."

"No, I do. I'm on my own, and so are you. Just go. Just go, Ben. Get out of my house."

He'd called it "my house" deliberately, but Ben seemed not to notice. "Alex, you need my help," he said.

"No, I don't need your help, I don't want your help."

"Yes, you do!" Ben shouted, spittle flying from his mouth. "Yes, you do, Alex, and you're going to take my help! You're going to listen to me, and if you don't want my help then, fine. I'm not going to be responsible for any more deaths. You're going to listen to what I have to say, you're going to do what I tell you to do, and then if you don't, it's your fucking fault, you killed yourself, you committed suicide on your own and it wasn't my fault! None of it!"

They stood staring at each other. Ben was panting, the muscles in his neck straining. "You think I don't hurt?" he said. "You think I don't wish I'd driven Katie home that night? Why do you want to torture me with that? You don't think I'm tortured already? What do you want me to do, say I'm sorry? Beg for forgiveness? Set myself on fire? What do you fucking want?"

His voice cracked and he stopped. Then he spun and slammed his palm into the wall. Alex heard a huge **crack!** and felt the shock reverberate through the floorboards. A hole appeared in the wall, plaster dust drifting lazily out of it.

Ben stood like that, his shoulders bunched, his breath heaving in and out. Then he wiped an arm across his face and turned and looked at Alex. His eyes were red. "What do you want?" he said.

Alex looked at him. He couldn't believe what he was seeing. Was Ben . . . was he **crying**?

"Why didn't you just tell me?" Alex asked. "Why didn't you ever . . . say something?"

"Because you blame me. You always have."

Alex couldn't deny the truth of that. And suddenly, he felt like the world's biggest jerk. He hadn't wanted Ben to be sorry. Or not just that, anyway. No, he'd wanted . . . he'd wanted to extract something from him. Punish him. Seeing Ben's tears, seeing the undeniable evidence of his brother's sorrow, made him realize that this was at least as much about himself as it was about Ben.

"Mom and Dad . . . they told me it wasn't your fault."

Ben laughed. "Yeah, they told me the same thing. But that's not how they felt. And they were right. And so were you."

"I don't think I was right," Alex said, surprised at the words. "I think . . . I don't know."

He'd almost said, **I think I needed to blame someone.** Was that it? He needed to think.

"And Dad," Ben said. "I wish I'd done that differently. It felt like my whole life was going to get wasted, like if I didn't enlist, the window would close or something. I look back and realize that was bullshit. I could have waited. I should have waited."

Alex didn't know what to say. He'd never felt so confused. "It . . . might not have made any difference," he stammered after a moment. "I think Dad . . . what he did, maybe he was going to do it no matter what."

Ben rubbed his temples. "Christ, I feel like I could sleep for a week."

Alex smiled. "How's your head?"

"It hurts. I wasn't really expecting you to throw the gun at me. Shoot me, maybe, but not throw it."

"It seemed like a good compromise at the time."

"I guess it was."

They were quiet for a moment. Alex said, "Osborne's really involved in this?"

"He is. Let's sit down and I'll brief you."

Alex sat at the kitchen table. Ben walked over to a cabinet, took out a glass, and filled it at the faucet. "You want one?" he asked. Alex shook his head, amazed at the familiarity of it. A simple thing like getting a glass of water.

Ben joined him and gave him an earful. They'd blackmailed Osborne. Ben's unit was involved. His commander was one of the people behind the whole thing.

"You're going to meet him?" Alex asked. "How can you trust him? I mean, he's been trying to kill me."

"He might not have known you're my brother."

"You believe that?"

"I'm trying to find out."

"If he had known, would it have made a difference?"

Ben sighed. "I don't know. That's one of the things I want to find out. I'm not going to meet where he wants, I'll tell you that."

"Where, then?"

"I'll figure something out. Do me a favor, go somewhere else for a few hours while I'm gone."

"Ben, I can't live this way."

"We're trying to fix that, that's the point. So you can go back to your life and not have to worry about someone coming after you."

"I don't know why you think you can trust this guy. I think meeting him is a mistake."

"I'm not trusting him. I'm being very careful, believe me. But I'll tell you what. You still have Obsidian and Hilzoy's notes on your laptop, right?"

"Right."

"Go someplace and take the laptop with you. That'll be a kind of insurance for me if things go sideways."

"Ben, seriously, I don't think this is a good idea. You're as exhausted as I am, maybe you're not thinking clearly."

"Trust me, okay?"

"What about Sarah?"

For an instant, Ben's expression was genuinely sorry. "You mean . . ."

"No, not that. Forget about that. Is she in danger?"

"No more than you, and probably less. But I doubt she's going to listen to me right now."

Alex sighed. "She's probably not going to listen to me, either."

There was a pause. Ben said, "I'm sorry, Alex."

Alex shook his head. He'd acted like a jerk at the hotel. It wasn't as though Sarah was his girlfriend. He'd never even had the courage to make a move on her, and he knew he never would. He'd just been jealous, that's all. But he didn't feel that way now.

"Are you sure this is a good idea?" he said.

Ben cracked his knuckles. "No. I just don't see a better one. Go somewhere. Relax. I'll call you in just a little while."

Ben left and Alex started to get dressed. He wondered where he should go. Another hotel? He was sick of hotels. And hell, he was so tired he could probably just put his head down at the library for a few hours.

He wanted to believe Ben could make everything right, but he couldn't. They'd killed two people for Obsidian. His own boss was part of it. They'd gotten into the patent office database, the law firm's filing system. These weren't the kind of people who could be talked out of what they were doing. Why did Ben think the fact that Alex was his brother was going to make any difference? It seemed more likely the connection would doom Ben than it would save Alex. Why couldn't Ben see that? And why couldn't Alex persuade him?

He pulled on a shirt and started pacing. Damn it, Ben was making a mistake. He thought about calling him and decided it would be useless. When Ben got an idea in his head, nobody could get it out.

He realized he was thinking only about what might happen to Ben. And then he realized something else: that's all Ben wanted him to think about. He didn't want Alex to be afraid for himself. He thought of the way Ben had led him gently from Katie's hospital room so many years before and wondered how they'd gone so wrong.

He kept pacing. What was he going to do, just sit around, hoping he was wrong, hoping Ben would somehow save the day?

This was crazy. He had to do something. He had

to take a chance. He grabbed his cell phone and called Sarah.

He got her voice mail. "Sarah," he said, "it's Alex. I'm sorry about this morning. Listen, I just saw Ben and he told me a bunch of things about what's going on that you need to know. And he's about to do something really stupid and I need . . . I need to figure out how to help him. Call me."

He grabbed the laptop and headed out.

31 SQUEEZED

Ben drove into Palo Alto to reconnoiter. He hadn't been here in damn near a decade, and even if the layout hadn't changed, which assuredly it had, he couldn't trust his recollections. He had looked at the world differently when he was living here, and absorbed different things. Before he'd seen neighborhoods. Now he needed to see terrain.

He walked the grid of streets downtown, observing without any sentimentality the things that had changed and the things that hadn't. He paid particular attention to alleys and where they led, to which streets were one-way, to the positions of banks and jewelry stores and other places with security cameras. When he felt satisfied with his new familiarity with the tactical layout of the town, he started looking for a suitable place for a meeting. He found it in a restaurant called Coupa Café. It had a patio in front, set back from the sidewalk, sheltered under a portico supported by thick pillars. He stood in front of one of the patio tables and noted that he had a good view of the entrance to the Citibank across the street and two stores down, and that positioning himself behind one of the pillars would offer some cover and concealment from the street. The tables were all taken, but something would open up. If he had to, he'd make the opening himself.

He went inside. The restaurant was a long rectangle, with the window facing the street on one of the short ends, the coffee counter along one long end, and a painted wall opposite. The tables were crammed close together, and even though it was getting into late afternoon, the place was packed. There was a room at the rear, accessible through a large open doorway, only partially visible from the front. He walked back and found what he was looking for: a fire exit, not alarmed, locked from the inside. It led to an alley that connected with other alleys branching out in three directions. If things went south at the front of the restaurant, he could haul ass back here and vanish in the alleys.

He got in line to order a coffee and called Hort from his cell phone.

"I can't get up there," he said. "I need you to come down here."

"What do you mean? Where's 'down here'?"

"Palo Alto."

"What's wrong? Are you nervous?"

"I'm always nervous, same as you. I'll be in the Citibank on Ramona Street in Palo Alto, between University and Hamilton."

"I see. Lots of cameras and tellers."

"Something like that. It'll be comfortable for both of us while we sort this shit out. Is it just you?"

"Just me and a driver."

"That's fine. Depending on traffic, should take you forty-five minutes. I'll be waiting."

He clicked off and shut down the phone. He stood by the counter and sipped his coffee and waited. When the people behind the pillar started to get up, he went out and took the table for himself. It was a good position. His back was to the wall, he could see up and down the street, he was camouflaged by the people around him, and he had a good view of the Citibank.

He sipped and waited and watched the street. The people walking past all looked like natives: confident, prosperous, oblivious. He felt nothing in common with any of them. He was like an emigrant returning from some faraway country to the land of his youth, only to discover he had forgotten the language, the dress, the customs, the code. He didn't belong here anymore, if he ever had. He was a stranger to this place, and it was a stranger to him.

A green Hyundai pulled up to the curb across the street in front of the Citibank. The passenger-side door opened. A black man got out and walked inside. Even if he hadn't seen his face, Ben would have recognized him from the large shaved head, the broad shoulders, the proud stride bordering on a swagger. Hort.

Ben watched the driver. The bone structure was Asian and he looked about Ben's age, with close-cropped hair and eyes concealed by sunglasses. From minute movements of his head, Ben knew the man was checking his mirrors. Not someone you could sneak up on. Not someone who was just a driver. The backseat seemed empty, but it wouldn't have been difficult to place one or two men low enough to be invisible through the windows. Still, Ben doubted there was more here than he could see. Atrios had been operating alone. He didn't think they had immediately deployable reinforcements.

He waited a minute, then called Hort's cell phone. Hort picked up immediately. "Where are you?"

"The restaurant. Coupa Café. Across the street."

"I hope you're not playing games with me, Ben."

"Just being cautious, sir. Like you taught me."

The line went dead. Ben watched him walk out of the Citibank and cross the street, his head moving, his eyes checking the same hot spots Ben would have checked. He saw Ben, gave a slight nod of acknowledgment, and walked over. He pulled a chair around so the two of them were at right angles, but Ben still had the better view of the street. The man's presence—his command aura—was almost overwhelming. Ben resisted the urge to speak, to explain himself, to ask for understanding.

"What do you want me to say?" Hort said in a low voice. "It was a goat fuck. The question now is, what do I need to do to set your mind at ease?"

"Just tell me everything," Ben said, amazed at his own temerity. "You've always been straight with me."

Hort nodded. "The first thing you need to understand is, no one knew it was your brother."

"Come on, Hort. How many Trevens do you know?"

"Until recently, only you. What you need to understand, though, is that I wasn't the one managing the target list. That was Atrios. All I knew was that he'd determined the mission required the removal of an inventor, a lawyer, and a patent examiner. I didn't need to know more than that."

"You didn't want to know."

Hort pursed his lips. "Maybe."

"Tell me the rest."

Hort glanced around, then leaned forward. "There's a special access program," he said, "being run directly out of the National Security Council. Its focus is cyberwarfare."

"What's the program called?"

"You don't need to know what it's called. You're not even supposed to know it exists. It's all sensitive compartmented information and I'm going out on a serious limb reading you into it without authorization."

"What's it called, Hort?"

Hort sighed. "You're going to make me pay for my sins, are you?"

"I just don't want to feel like you're holding anything back from me."

"The program is called Genie."

"All right. What does Genie do?"

"I don't know all the particulars. The only reason I know about the program at all is because of the invention your brother was trying to patent."

"Well, tell me what you do know."

"Apparently, all patent applications relating to cryptography are subject to a DoD national security review. Your brother's application for Obsidian received the routine look-over. But something about the invention attracted additional scrutiny. Long story short, the application got kicked upstairs all the way to the White House. And the Genie people in the NSC didn't like what they saw."

"Why not?"

"I don't know why not. All I know, all I'm supposed to know, is that if Obsidian were to fall into the wrong hands, it could pose a major threat to the whole U.S. network infrastructure."

"Okay, then what?"

"Someone in the White House made a decision. National security required that Obsidian be vacuumed up. All knowledge of it erased. The operation involved two prongs: electronic and real world. NSA was tasked with the electronic. We handle the real world elements."

"So the inventor, the patent guy . . . those were your ops?"

"Those were my orders."

"But Hort, those were . . . I mean, those guys were Americans."

"You know how it is, Ben. I don't make the rules."

Ben drummed his fingers on the table. "What I'm starting to wonder is whether there **are** rules. Not for the enemy. For us."

"I'm not happy about it, either. But the bottom line is, it's about saving lives. And sometimes saving lives involves collateral damage, you know that. It's a hell of a decision to have to make, but someone made it. And whether you or I agree with the decision doesn't matter. Our job is to carry it out."

"Look, Hort, I know what goes on. But it's one thing to pick people up, hold them in a navy brig incommunicado as enemy combatants, isolate them, keep them from talking to anyone. But just . . . executing them? Americans? When did we start doing that?"

Hort blew out a long breath. "I agree, it's a hell of a situation. No one would want to sign up for it. But we're not in this because it's easy. We're in it because it's a job that needs to be done."

"Yeah, but—"

"What are we going to do when one of our enemies gets a hold of something like Obsidian and uses it against us? When they shut down a power grid, or air traffic control? Are we going to apologize to the families of the people who burned to death in those flaming crashes because we could have kept the tools that caused it out of enemy hands, but we were too squeamish?"

They were quiet for a moment. Ben knew he was right, on one level, but . . .

He thought of Sarah, of what she had said about breaking the law a little.

He shook the thought away. "What about the Russians?" he said. "How do they fit into this?"

"They don't. That's just a bad coincidence."

"What do you mean?"

"We have a communications intercept from their embassy in Ankara. They're on to you for the Istanbul op. We're trying to find out how, and how much."

"What? How could anyone know who did that guy in Istanbul? I didn't leave behind anything, Hort. I was in and out of there like a ghost."

"Well, you left five bodies behind. Ghosts don't do that."

"There were going to be four bodies regardless."

"Iranian bodies. A dead FSB Russian is a whole different kind of problem."

"That still doesn't tell us how anyone could have pinpointed me for that guy."

"Like I said, that's what we're trying to find out."

"So who were those guys at the Four Seasons? They weren't FSB. They weren't that good."

"They were Russian mafia, operating out of Brooklyn. They do contract work for the FSB."

Ben thought about it. What Hort was saying wasn't impossible. But . . .

"Look," Hort said, "I can make it so your brother gets left alone. I need your guarantee—and you will be held accountable for that guarantee—that there are no copies of Obsidian, that no one can use this thing, that your brother will forget any of this ever happened and never say a word to anyone. Guarantee me that, and I can call in some favors with the NSC and make sure your brother is off their radar for good."

Ben considered. The truth was, this was just what he was hoping for. What, in fact, he was going to propose himself. It could solve everything. Give Hort the backup copy, tell Alex to keep his mouth shut. After all, it wasn't like Alex was an unknown quantity to them anymore. Alex's brother was an insider, a brother who could vouch for him.

He wondered for a moment what Sarah would make of that. She'd probably say something about how convenient it was not to be one of the little people, to have a relative in the party or on the politburo.

And what about Sarah? Were they still after her, too? Could Hort call them off?

"What about the girl?" he said. "Sarah Hosseini, the lawyer. Is she part of the op?"

"She worked on the patent, too," Hort said. "Compared to your brother, she was tertiary, but yeah, now especially there's a real concern."

"You can't get her off the hook?"

Hort laughed. "What do you think, I'm a magician? Sarah's not even her name. It's Shaghayegh.

Shaghayegh Hosseini. You want me to go to the NSC and tell them not to worry about a woman named Shaghayegh Hosseini who knows all about Obsidian?"

"You mean, you're going to kill her because of her name?"

"She was a security risk, Ben."

Ben felt something constrict inside his chest. "What do you mean, 'was'?"

"We picked her up this morning outside her apartment."

Ben looked at the table so Hort couldn't see his eyes. He tried to think. **Picked her up.** That meant she was still alive, right? If they'd dropped her, if she were already dead, Hort wouldn't have referred to the means. He would have just said, **She's gone.**

Christ, what were they doing to her to get her to talk, though? He could imagine. And he knew what they'd do when they were done.

Shards of fragmented thoughts sliced through his mind.

No, he's cool.

Okay, then. Later.

NO HE WAS NOT COOL AND YOU KNEW BETTER.

He put his fists to his temples. **Think. Think.**

But all he could think was that he'd come out here to help Alex, and instead he'd, he'd . . .

No. This wasn't going to happen again. He wouldn't **let** it happen again.

He looked at Hort. "What are you going to do with her?"

Hort waved a hand dismissively. "Forget about it."

"I asked you a question," Ben said, his voice as low as a dog's growl.

"And I answered it. The only way I can."

"Where are you holding her?"

"Let it go, son. You're already on thin ice."

Ben shook his head. "No," he said, his voice rising. "No. No. No."

"Ben, I trained you. We've bled in the same mud. We carry the same cost for the things we've done. Men like us—"

"Tell me where you're holding her, Hort. Tell me you're going to cut her loose."

A long, silent moment spun out. "Last chance," Hort said. "Will you vouch for your brother? Can I trust you?"

Ben flexed his hand. The knuckles popped. He'd never felt so boxed in. The feeling of pressure, of being **squeezed,** was almost physical.

He glanced left. A large man in sunglasses was leaning out from behind one of the pillars, his hand resting just inside a dark jacket, intent on Ben and Hort.

Shit. He glanced right. Another man had sidled up the sidewalk and was watching them with identical posture and focus.

There would be a third man inside the restaurant, or just outside the fire door. Obviously, he had badly underestimated Hort's manpower situation. And they'd moved on him, by either instinct or design, at the very moment he'd been most distracted by his own inner turmoil.

Part of him was enraged at his own naïveté. He should have seen this coming, but deep down, he'd trusted Hort. Stupid. Hort had always taught him the mission came before the man. Another part of him wanted to laugh. Five armed men a tendon twitch from a gunfight, and the yuppies around them were sipping their lattes and reflecting on the latest Pilates routines without the barest clue.

"How do you want to do this?" Hort said quietly.

Several scenarios played out in Ben's mind. None of them involved more than a ten percent chance of survival. He might have taken those odds if the only chips he was playing were his. But what would happen to Sarah? And to Alex?

"What are my options?" he said, still glancing left and right.

"You have two. You can come with me and we can work this out, or we can leave you here. I really didn't want it to be this way, Ben."

Ben drummed his fingers along the table. Going with them was the same as going to a secondary crime scene. How many times had he sworn never to let that happen to him?

He knew he could drop Hort before anyone could stop him. But he'd be dead himself a second later.

We'll do those steps another time, he thought. **When it's just you and me on the dance floor.**

A part of him knew the thought was just bluster. But it was all he had at the moment, and it was enough to get him through.

"All right," he said. "I'll come with you."

32 HEAD-ON

Alex was in his car, driving aimlessly, trying to figure out what to do. He had finally broken down and tried Ben, but there was no answer. He knew he was supposed to stay away from the usual places, and he was okay with that, but he wanted his cell phone on because maybe Ben or Sarah might check in, and he figured that meant he should keep moving in case someone was tracking the signal. But God, he was tired. He wished he could go somewhere, a park bench, anywhere, and just close his eyes for a few minutes.

He wondered what it would be like with Osborne when this whole thing was sorted out. How could he even look at the guy again, after what he'd done?

He thought about what Ben had told him, how they'd taken incriminating photos or video of Osborne in Thailand. Ben seemed pretty confident that it was no more complicated than that, but . . . could they really have picked Osborne out of all the Sullivan, Greenwald lawyers and identified, and then exploited, his vulnerability? The more he thought about it, the more far-fetched it felt.

He thought of Osborne's ego case, the photos of all those Valley and Washington players. The guy was connected. Well, maybe that's how they came to focus on him. He was known in Washington—he'd even testified to Congress a few times about visa quotas and capital gains taxes and other such issues near and dear to the Silicon Valley heart. Maybe . . . maybe he was more involved in this than Ben was giving him credit for. Ben was so arrogant about his skills, and he'd as much as told Alex that he thought lawyers were nothing more than a bunch of latte-swilling sheep. That arrogance would make him cocky, and blind him to just how shrewd and politically savvy players like Osborne could be. The more Alex thought about it, the more he thought Ben had missed something about Osborne's involvement. And the more sure Alex became that Ben was making a mistake about Osborne, the more sure he became that Ben was making a mistake about his commander, too.

He was going in circles, literally and figuratively. Enough. He was going to confront this head-on.

He drove to Sullivan, Greenwald but, mindful of Ben's admonitions, parked in the office and theater complex across the street. He crossed Page Mill on foot, used a back entrance, and headed straight to Osborne's office. He pushed away all the thoughts that were trying to crowd in—all the reasons he was being stupid, all the ways it could go wrong. He swallowed but his throat stayed dry.

Osborne was on the phone, his cowboy boots up on his desk. Alex closed the door and walked straight in. Osborne gave him a look—**Don't you even knock?**—and went on talking. For one second, Alex's doubts threatened to paralyze him. Then something broke through, and he strode behind the desk and depressed the receiver button on the phone.

Osborne swiveled his feet off the desk and planted them on the floor. "What do you think you're doing?" he said. He swatted Alex's hand off the receiver and started punching in a number. Alex picked up the unit and hurled it across the room. It crashed into the wall and shattered.

Osborne leaped to his feet. "Are you crazy?" he said, his eyes wide.

Alex looked at him. His heart was pounding but his head felt marvelously clear. "What do you know about Obsidian?" he said.

"I don't know anything. Obsidian was yours, remember? And your Bible-quoting brother already asked me all this. At gunpoint, I should add."

"You're lucky he didn't kill you."

"Yeah, well, you're lucky to be alive yourself."

And all at once, Alex knew Osborne had snowed Ben. There were no photos. He was afraid, yeah, maybe of exposure, but not of that. Otherwise he wouldn't have been looking at Alex as though he were no more than an annoying bug. He wouldn't have reverted to asshole mode so quickly.

There was a Lucite deal tombstone on Osborne's desk. Without thinking, Alex picked it up like a rock and belted Osborne in the head with it. Osborne cried out and fell, smacking his face into his desk on the way down. Alex stood over him, brandishing the tombstone, breathing hard.

Osborne rolled left and right, clutching his face, blood gushing from his nose. "You little shit," he gasped.

Alex smiled. He felt exhilarated. He was either flying or falling—he couldn't tell which and he didn't care.

"I made a copy of Obsidian," he said, improvising. "I've posted it to a Usenet newsgroup with full details of your involvement and everything else I know. Right now it's encrypted. But if I don't punch in a code within one hour, it decrypts and disseminates to a dozen other newsgroups. So you better tell me what you know."

Osborne tried to stand. Alex said, "Stay where you are or I'll bash your head in."

Osborne stopped moving. "You're done here, hotshot. And not just at Sullivan, Greenwald. When I'm finished making calls, you won't be able to get a job with a firm in the entire Valley."

Alex laughed. He recognized the technique—a

double-down, a negotiating escalation. He'd never negotiated using a heavy object before, but apparently the principles were the same.

"You know what?" he said. "Why don't you just tell the whole thing to the San Jose police? There's a Detective Gamez there who's investigating Hilzoy's murder. And he's in touch with the Arlington cops who are looking into the death of the patent examiner your people killed. How much do you think I need to feed them? They're going to get a warrant and examine your phone records, your e-mail; they're going to look down your throat and up your ass and whatever it is you're hiding, once they're pointed in the right direction, they're going to find it. They'll perp-walk you right out of here and I'll make sure the **Merc** and the **Chronicle** and KRON are on hand to get it on the evening news. So don't try to sell me that bill of goods about incriminating photos from Thailand. This was no hostile takeover, David. You're a silent partner. But you don't have to tell me about it. I'll just let that Usenet post run and then I'll be able to read all about it in the **Merc.** Yeah, that'll be fun."

He dropped the tombstone on Osborne and turned to walk out. The trick was to really believe the bluff. It was the same as walking out during a negotiation. Whatever part of your mind knew it was a tactic had to be walled off. You really **were** walking out. You **wanted** to walk out.

He was all the way to the door and actually had his hand on the knob when Osborne said, "Wait."

Alex opened the door and glanced back. "Forget it. You had your chance."

"All right, all right. You win. Just close the damn door and hear me out."

Alex closed the door but kept his hand on the knob, the posture communicating, **You have about ten seconds to change my mind.**

"I know some people in Washington," Osborne said. He grabbed a handful of tissues from a box and held them against his nose. "White House people. Focused on counterterrorism."

"Yeah?"

"One of the areas they're focused on is cyberwarfare. Systems security. So when you told me about what Obsidian could do, I made a phone call. Just trying to be helpful, that's all."

Alex laughed. "I admire your patriotism, David. I know it didn't have anything to do with political back-scratching or creating IOUs or sucking up to people who could steer government work to your clients. You're way too fair-minded for any of that to have figured in."

Osborne held the tissues away from his face, then reapplied them. "Think what you want."

"So what did the White House people tell you?"

"They told me maybe I'd read about a program in the newspaper."

"What program?"

"They didn't say. I figured it was the FISA stuff, the NSA domestic spying stuff. I'd seen something

about it in **The Wall Street Journal** and in **Wired.**
The Quantico Circuit, where some whistleblower
said the telecoms gave the government access to customer calls."

"What else?"

"They said a lot of private companies were cooper-
ating and they needed our help to fight terrorism.
And it's true, too. That's why the telecoms were helping, to listen in on al Qaeda—"

"Stop it. I don't care about the politics or about your
justifications. What did they tell you about Obsidian?"

"That it could help with the program."

Alex didn't get it. From what he'd seen of Obsidian, you could use it for sabotage, maybe extortion,
but not this other stuff. He wished Sarah were here.
She knew a lot more about what the government was
up to than he did.

"That it could help them spy?" he said.

"That was my understanding."

Alex thought. It was certainly possible Obsidian
had other uses. He'd recognized as much at the hotel
when he'd first cracked Hilzoy's notes. And the fact
that the government was playing defense in trying to
prevent other players from having Obsidian didn't
mean they weren't simultaneously interested in its offensive potential, too. Good God, Ben walked into
his meeting without knowing any of this. Where was
he? And why hadn't he called yet?

"What else?" Alex said. "What about Hilzoy, and
Hank Shiffman, the patent examiner?"

"I didn't know about any of that. I mean, they told me there were certain people they wanted to interview, but—"

Alex laughed. "'Interview'? They murdered two people you knew about. You expect me to believe you thought they just wanted to 'interview' me, too? David, if you weren't so pathetic, you'd be hilarious."

Osborne didn't respond.

Alex said, "What did they give you? What would make you . . ." And then he got it. The photos in the ego case. The new telecom client.

"Business?" Alex said. "You did all this . . . so they'd steer you business?"

Osborne wouldn't meet his eyes. "I was just trying to help."

"Tell it to the cops."

Alex opened the door and walked out. "Wait!" Osborne called out after him. "Alex!"

Alex was aware of the secretaries looking up from their bays as he passed, their eyes wide, their ears practically straining forward. He didn't care. He kept moving.

Osborne caught up with him and grabbed him by the arm. "Listen to me," he hissed. "I'll make you partner. With the work I've been bringing in, the management committee will do whatever I tell them. This year, no question."

Alex paused and looked at Osborne's hand. After a moment, Osborne withdrew it.

"You know," Alex said, "not so long ago, I would have believed you when you said that."

Osborne nodded vigorously. "Believe it. It's the truth."

"But that's not the point," Alex went on. "The point is, I don't care."

He walked on down the corridor, Osborne's entreaties following him all the way into the stairwell.

33 JUST A NEGOTIATION

Alex tried Sarah and Ben again from his car. No answer from either. He called Sarah's secretary. Sarah hadn't checked in. He was starting to get seriously worried.

He didn't know what to do. Maybe if he could figure out some of Obsidian's other applications, the ones the government seemed so eager to exploit? But he didn't have time.

What if they'd grabbed Ben? He'd seen the way Ben had been ready to trust his commander, seen that he **wanted** to trust. Alex knew the look. He'd seen it a hundred times in the eyes of clients who wanted the deal so badly that they caved on critical provisions, telling themselves the provisions wouldn't matter because everything was going to go smoothly, everyone would be making so much money there'd be no time and no reason for recrimination or regret. Probably it was the same look a rich man got right before his second marriage. **What the hell, we don't need a prenup. We're in love.**

Damn it, what was he going to do?

His cell phone buzzed. He looked down and saw it was Ben. Thank God.

He grabbed the phone, pressed the Answer Call button, and brought it to his ear. "Ben? Where've you been? I was getting worried."

"Ben's fine," answered a low baritone voice with a Southern accent. "You must be Alex."

Fear seized Alex's heart and throat. He felt it with horrifying total recall—**Oh no. Oh Please God no**—and he started shaking so badly he had to pull over to the side of the road.

"Who is this?" he managed to say.

"I'm someone who knows your brother well and doesn't want him to come to any harm. And you can help with that."

"How?"

"Hand over Obsidian, son. That's all we want. And everybody walks away. Ben, Sarah, everyone."

Jesus Christ, they had Sarah, too? He pressed the back of his phone hand against his mouth and hugged himself with the other, rocking back and forth in the seat, struggling to hold back tears. He was dead. They were all dead. If these guys could outwit Ben, with all his training and experience, what the hell kind of chance could Alex possibly have?

Stop it. Think. Use your brain.

Right. He still had Obsidian, didn't he? And if he had something they wanted, he could negotiate.

Framing it that way calmed him a little. It put him back on more familiar ground.

He took a deep breath and let it out. Another. Then he brought the phone back to his ear.

"I don't think we have a problem here," he said. "You want Obsidian, and I want Ben and Sarah."

"That's exactly right," the voice said. "No reason for this to be complicated. It's gotten too complicated as it is."

See? Just like a negotiation. You can do this.

Alex took another long, deep breath and slowly let it out. "What do you propose?"

"There's a parking garage on Bryant Street in Palo Alto, between University and Lytton. Meet me on the fourth floor in one hour."

"Let me talk to Ben."

"I'm sorry, son, I can't take that chance. I don't want the two of you passing messages to each other."

A good negotiator knows not to confuse means with objectives. The objective here was to make sure Ben was all right. Talking to him was only one way to do it.

"Ask him what was the name of the family dog," Alex said.

"I'm sorry?"

"I want to make sure he's all right. I understand why you don't want me to talk to him directly, but presumably you don't object to another way of my verifying that's he's okay?"

There was a pause. The voice said, "No, I don't object." Another pause, then, "Arlo."

"All right, good. And now . . ." He stopped. He didn't know a single personal thing he could ask about Sarah. Bizarrely, he considered, **What did you do to Ben's shirt?** But thankfully he came up with something better.

"Ask Sarah what brand of workout clothes she wears in the gym," he said.

There was another pause, longer this time. Alex thought he heard something in the background . . . a choking noise? He wasn't sure.

The voice said, "Under Armour."

All right. They were alive.

"I'll meet you," Alex said. "But there's something you need to understand." He fed the voice the same bluff he'd used with Osborne. Obsidian was encrypted and cued up to publish to a dozen Usenet newsgroups. If anything happened to any of them, Obsidian and everything else would be public domain.

"You're being careful," the voice said. "I understand that. I respect it. Just bring me what I want, and I promise everyone's going to be fine."

The line went dead.

Alex crossed his arms and rocked back and forth, fighting panic.

Think. Think. Think.

But he couldn't think of anything. If they'd only

had another copy of the source code, they could have just published it.

Wait. There **had** to be another copy. Hilzoy wouldn't have given the PTO the source code with the hidden functions. There were effectively two versions of the executable, which meant there had to be two versions of the underlying source code. Hilzoy was always careful about backing up the executable; he must have backed up the second version of the source code somewhere, too.

But where? There was nothing more in Hilzoy's notes, or if there was, Alex was never going to find it in time. And there was nothing more on the disc. Alex had been through it again and again, and the only extraneous thing had been that MP3. What was the name of the song? Sarah had recognized it. "Dirge," that's right. Christ, Hilzoy couldn't have picked a more appropriate title.

But there was nothing in the song. He'd been over it. It was just—

And then he had an idea. It was a long shot, a long, long shot. But he didn't have anything else, and in his near terror and despair, he clutched at it with fierce devotion.

He looked at his watch. There was time. He could make this work. All he needed was an Internet connection.

And a hell of a lot of luck.

34 DEAD MAN'S SWITCH

Ben listened to Hort from the back of the van, his frustration and rage growing. Alex didn't know what he was doing. He was coming to Hort like a fly into a Venus fucking flytrap.

They were in a seven-seat passenger van. Sarah and Ben were in the middle row, Sarah on the driver's side, Ben on the passenger's, their hands cuffed behind their backs. The Asian guy was driving and Hort was in the passenger seat. The two guys who'd flanked him outside Coupa Café were in back.

When Hort had asked him the name of the family dog, Ben had understood immediately what Alex was doing. Tactically, it was smart. Strategically, it was a disaster. What good was it going to do him to confirm that Ben and Sarah were alive, if the confirmation made Alex do something that would result in all of them dead a half hour later?

But he'd given up Arlo's name anyway. He might have been able to stand up to their trying to beat it out of him, but he didn't see what good it would do. They'd kill him and pick up Alex eventually anyway. He needed to bring this all to a head.

When Hort had asked Sarah about her workout clothes, she'd answered, "SourceForge." Ben recognized the name of the tech site from their earlier discussion at the hotel. She was trying to tell Alex fuck it, just disseminate the executable of Obsidian, it's better than nothing. Her instincts were good, but Hort didn't buy it. He nodded to one of the guys behind Ben, and the guy had slipped a sleeper hold around Ben's neck and started to strangle him. Sarah watched for less than two seconds before revising her answer.

Yeah, her instincts were good. Not just the tactics, either—the objective, too. Because nothing was going to save any of them as long as Hort still had a chance to recover Obsidian. Christ, if only he'd realized what was really going on when they were back at the hotel. Alex and Sarah could have done their thing, and Hort's op would have ended right there.

He looked at Sarah. She glanced up at him and gave him a tiny, sad smile. The smile did nothing to conceal the fact that she was scared shitless. She hadn't said a word since they'd disarmed him and loaded him into the van next to her. She was smart. She probably knew they were all going to die. She was probably right.

Now they were driving southeast on Foothill Expressway. Ben didn't know why—they'd told Alex to meet them in Palo Alto, the opposite direction, and apparently Alex had agreed.

He'd had time to think, and understood at least some of what had happened. Hort must have given him up to the Russians. But why? Live or die, he was going to try to find out.

"How did you know it was me?" he said. "You knew he was my brother, but how did you put it together?"

There was a long pause, long enough so that Ben thought Hort wasn't going to answer. But then Hort turned and said, "I wanted to keep you out of it, for everyone's sake, including yours. But then you put in that weapons request for San Francisco, after I'd told you to stay put in Ankara. It was a concern. Just being cautious, we got into some of Alex's communications. He'd called Military OneSource, and the army personnel center, and then we checked his e-mail, and we knew he'd been in touch with you. And why else would you be coming out here, if not to help him?"

"It's not as though I had a choice."

"That's exactly the point. There was nothing else you could have done. Blood is blood. But I didn't have a choice, either. I was responsible for a mission. And as understandable and inadvertent as your actions were, you made yourself a threat to that mission. For what it's worth, it was the hardest call I've ever had to make."

"So you gave me up to the Russians?"

"What difference does it make how I decided to get it done? Yeah, I was taking heat from the usual suspects for your killing that damn Russian in Istanbul. Some people wanted to hang you out to dry."

"So you did it for them."

"Like I said, what difference does it make?"

Ben imagined Hort contacting some Russian counterpart, telling him, **Hey, we found the rogue who killed your guy in Istanbul. It wasn't sanctioned. He's yours, if you want him. And here's where you can find him.**

It made a kind of twisted sense. You placate the Russians, appease the bean counters, eliminate Alex's protection, and create a cutout and a diversion from what's really going on with an op that's spiraling out of control.

"I guess you're right," Ben said, fighting back a bitterness that felt like the leading edge of despair. "But I should have seen it coming. You know why I didn't? I thought you were as loyal to me as I am to you."

Hort looked down for a moment, then met Ben's eyes again. "I am loyal to you, son. I'm loyal to all my men. But my first loyalty is always to the mission. You know that."

"Well, I know it now."

"I wish it hadn't had to happen this way, Ben. I really do wish that."

They came to San Antonio Road in Los Altos. One of the guys in back said, "Turn here."

They made a left. What were they doing in Los Altos? And then he realized.

They were tracking Alex's cell phone signal. They must have had the equipment in back. **Alex, goddamn it, I told you they could track you this way.**

"This is it," the guy behind him said. "Last place before the signal cut out."

"Drive around," Hort said. "We might spot his car."

Ben let out a long breath. Thank God, Alex had thought to turn the damn thing off when he realized what was happening.

But all it meant was that Hort wouldn't be able to take him unawares here. Presumably, Alex was still going to show up at the parking garage.

They drove along Los Altos's grid of streets, swinging in and out of parking lots. Every time they slowed in front of a dark M3, Ben felt his insides tighten with fear, but each time it wasn't Alex's.

After twenty minutes, the guy behind him said, "Wait, he's back online. In . . . Mountain View. Go down San Antonio and get on El Camino."

What the hell was he doing? He'd turned the phone off; why would he turn it back on?

"Wait, he's moving," the guy in back said. "Stay on San Antonio. Go to 101."

"Where's he heading?" Hort said.

"Palo Alto is my guess," the guy in back said. "The garage. Looks like he's heading toward 101."

Ben's phone rang. Hort picked up and said, "Hello." There was a pause. "Good, we're on our way, too. Thanks for checking in. A half hour from now, we'll have this whole thing sorted out and you'll all be good to go."

He clicked off. Alex must have gotten spooked that they'd been out of touch, and turned on the phone again to make sure everything was still co-pacetic.

"No, wait, he's taking Alma," the guy in back said. "Still heading toward Palo Alto." They swung off San Antonio onto the entrance ramp.

What the hell? Why wasn't Alex turning off the phone again?

Because he's driving. Jesus Christ, he thought they couldn't track him if he was moving? Ben tried to tamp down his anger. He couldn't expect Alex to know something like that. It wasn't his world. But goddamn it, they were going to take him by surprise, force him over to the side of the road, pull him into the van . . . If he'd been planning anything, anything at all tactical for the garage, they weren't going to give him the chance.

They headed west on Alma, two lanes of traffic in each direction. The midday traffic was light, but there were enough cars to provide plenty of concealment for vehicular surveillance even against someone who was tail-conscious, which Alex most definitely was not.

"That him?" the driver said.

Ben leaned left and looked through the wind-shield, his heart thudding. It looked like Alex's car, but he wasn't sure.

"Get a little closer," Hort said. "Just a little now."

The license plate came into view. Ben recognized it just as Hort said, "It's him. Back off now. Keep a few cars in between."

The thudding in Ben's chest got stronger. Adrenaline surged through his system. He flexed his thighs, his calves, his toes. He glanced left, right, ahead, measuring distance, calculating odds. He wanted to rotate his neck but didn't. He didn't want any sign that he was anything but resigned.

The only hope he saw was to disrupt them when they tried to take Alex. If Alex could see they weren't interested in bargaining, maybe he would understand his only hope was to disseminate Obsidian. If he could get away, if he figured things out, if he disseminated it . . . **Jesus Christ,** he thought. He had never tried to execute a plan so entirely composed of ifs and mights and maybes.

They followed Alex right onto Addison, a bucolic street of perfectly kept bungalows. Alex slowed for the traffic circle at Bryant. Hort said, "Take him."

The driver cut clockwise into the circle and accelerated into the street on the other side alongside Alex. He cut the wheel right and slammed into Alex's car. Metal whined and Alex went up on the sidewalk and straight into a tree. The driver hit the brakes and they screeched to a halt just ahead of where Alex's car had stopped.

The driver hit a switch and the passenger-side door slid open. The guy behind Ben moved up alongside

him and braced to leap out. In one smooth movement, Ben spun in the seat, planted the back of his
head and neck against the side of the passenger-side
seat, brought his knees to his face, and blasted both
heels into the guy's lower spine. The guy cried out
and went flying through the door, smacking his face
into the overhead jamb on the way.

Ben let the momentum of the kick bring him to
his feet. He dove through the open door, hit the
ground on his shoulder, and rolled to his side. He
brought his knees up and shoved his arms down, getting the cuffs over his ass. He straightened his legs
and pushed lower, getting the chain past the backs of
his knees, his calves . . .

Shouts came from the van. He heard a door open.
Come on, come on . . .

The chain snagged on his heels. He wriggled his
feet frantically and shoved his wrists forward with all
his strength. The cuffs bit savagely into his wrists and
he thought he wasn't going to clear it and then the
chain was over his boots.

He started to come to his feet and someone
grabbed him by the hair. He felt the knee coming in
time to turn his head and get his hands in the way.
The blow landed but he'd avoided the worst of it. He
tried to straighten, but the guy had a fistful of hair
and was twisting now, pushing his head down. All he
could see was ground and a pair of legs. One of the
legs retracted, setting up another knee shot. **Fuck
that.** Ben shoveled his arms up and snapped both

fists into the guy's balls, the knuckle of each thumb leading the way.

The guy grunted and the grip on Ben's hair loosened. He corkscrewed his head and tore loose. It was the other guy from the backseat. He tried to close and Ben threw his arms forward like a double jab, trying to plant the chain in the guy's neck but catching him in the teeth instead.

Sarah was out of the van, her hands still cuffed behind her. She looked at Ben. "Run!" he shouted.

The guy shoved Ben's arms to the side and slipped past him. He grabbed Ben by the hair again and whipped an arm around his neck. Ben jammed his fists up just in time to stop another sleeper hold. "Run!" he shouted again.

Sarah took off like a deer. A second later, the guy behind him yelled and his grip loosened. Ben spun and saw why: Sarah had run up behind him and bitten him on the arm. She was hanging on like a terrier. The guy drew back an arm to cuff her. Ben crossed his arms and brought his hands down behind the guy's head, catching his neck in the triangle formed by his wrists and the chain. He leveraged his wrists back and his elbows forward. The guy's eyes bulged and his tongue popped out. Ben felt cartilage grinding and squeezed harder, the chains cutting into his wrists.

There was an explosion of white light, and suddenly he was looking up at the sky, unable to account for what had happened. He was choking the guy, killing him, and then . . .

His head throbbed. Someone . . . someone must have pistol-whipped him from behind. He looked over at the van. The Asian guy was shoving Sarah back inside. And Hort . . . Hort was holding Alex by the hair, a gun at his temple.

No, he thought, but the words didn't come. **No.**

Alex was holding a laptop. Jesus Christ, he'd brought Obsidian with him? It was over.

"Get in the van, Ben," Hort said. "Or I'll decorate you with your brother's brains."

Ben got to his feet and took an unsteady step toward the van. It felt like someone had planted a vibrating chisel in the back of his skull.

"It's all right," Alex said. "I brought them what they wanted."

"Alex," Ben said, and stopped. He didn't know what to say. They were all dead.

This time they cuffed Ben to Sarah. His wrists were bleeding. "That was a hell of an effort," he said to her, because he wanted her to have something to feel good about in whatever time they had left. "For a lawyer." But she might as well have not even heard. He wanted to say something to Alex, too, but what could he? Alex had delivered Obsidian on a platter. It was game over.

They drove off. The guy Ben had kicked in the back was groaning as if someone had put thumbscrews on him, and the guy Ben had tried to strangle was coughing so much it sounded like he was going to bring up lung tissue. Whatever damage he'd done them, he hoped it was permanent.

Hort turned in the seat and pointed a pistol at Ben. "All right, son," he said to Alex. "Nice and simple. I want you to turn off that dead man's switch you set up."

Dead man's switch. What had Alex done, set up some kind of dissemination program that only he could stop? Christ, all he'd done was guarantee he'd be tortured before he was killed.

"I need an Internet connection," Alex said.

"Alex, don't," Ben said. "They'll kill us all the second you—"

"I'll kill you all if he doesn't," Hort said evenly. "Like I said, Ben, I didn't want it to be this way. But the mission comes first."

"Drive into Mountain View," Alex said. "Google has the whole town covered in Wi-Fi."

Ben grimaced. "Goddamn it, Alex—"

"Ben, I know what I'm doing."

"No more talk," Hort said.

Ben closed his eyes. His head was throbbing, his wrists ached, and they were one hundred percent out of options.

They drove in silence. Ben tried to focus on the pain, because what he felt in his body was infinitely easier than what was going on in his mind. He'd been a fool. Everything he'd believed about there not being rules . . . but that was to prevail against the **other** side. Well, this was the way it worked. Hort was just more ruthless. Which was why he was holding the gun while Ben was wearing the handcuffs. Why Hort was going to walk away, while the three of them would be dumped in some shallow grave. He'd always thought of himself as a realist, prided himself on it. And now, in his last minutes on earth, he'd been exposed, forced to confront the truth. Which was that he was nothing but a stupid, naïve dipshit, and the real realists had run rings around him and were now about to take away everything.

When they reached Shoreline Road in Mountain View, Alex opened the laptop. "Okay," he said. "I've got a connection."

They pulled onto a side street and stopped.

"Do it," Hort said. "And show me that it's done."

"It's already done," Alex said.

Hort frowned. "What do you mean it's already done? You told me you had to decrypt it, put in a passcode to stop a dissemination sequence."

"I only said that because I was afraid you'd hurt Ben or Sarah before I could show you what I'd really done."

Hort's expression was so steady it might have been frozen. "You did something else, didn't you?"

Alex nodded. For one crazy second, he looked like the little know-it-all he'd been as a kid. Ben felt a ridiculous surge of hope.

Hort swung the gun so that the muzzle was pointed at Alex's face. Ben's breath caught.

"What?" Hort said. "What did you do?"

Alex extended the laptop. "Here. You can see for yourself."

Hort ignored it. The gun didn't waver. He looked at Alex with machine eyes and Ben was so sure he was going to fire he couldn't breathe.

Then Hort lowered the gun. He took the laptop and watched the screen wordlessly for a moment.

"What is this?" he said. "StatCounter? I don't understand."

"Oh, that's just a Web site that tracks downloads and site traffic," Alex said. He leaned forward and pointed to the screen. "Look, you can see here how many people have downloaded the program from SourceForge. And here, that's Slashdot—wow, a hundred downloads in a half hour, that's pretty exciting. I also sent it to McAfee and Norton."

The pounding in Ben's head was so bad he could feel it in his stomach, too. He didn't know whether to laugh or cry or puke. Maybe all three.

Hort was clenching his jaw so tightly the muscles in his cheeks stood out like marbles. "Oh, you poor dumb son of a bitch," he said, shaking his head, his eyes glued to the screen. "You have no idea what you just did."

"I know what I did."

"You just unleashed anarchy, son. Anarchy. America is the most networked country on earth. This thing is going to go around like a virus, and no one is more vulnerable to it than we are."

"No, you don't get it. I didn't just post the executable. I posted the source code, too."

"We had all the—"

"No, you didn't. Hilzoy hid another copy. Hid it in plain sight, in a copy of a song he liked on a public file-sharing site. It took me a little while to find the right file—it was only a little bigger than the rest of them. But it was there. I decrypted it with Obsidian and now everyone has their own copy."

"Then we're fucked. You fucked our whole country."

"I'm not saying there won't be a few disruptions. But you know what? Right now, in a thousand basements and garages, more pimply-faced hackers and hobbyists than you can count are ripping this thing apart. Some will be trying to find out how to exploit it, yeah. Others will come up with ways to defend against it. The network is like an organism. The people are its T cells. You can't stop something like this, no matter how many people you kill. It's bits. It's information. And—"

"And information wants to be free," Sarah said.

"Anyway," Alex said, "the anarchy thing is only part of it. Or maybe it isn't part of it at all."

Hort watched him. "What do you mean?"

"According to your inside man, Osborne, the NSC wasn't interested in Obsidian because it could disrupt networks. They wanted it for a domestic spying program."

"Osborne told you this?"

"Ask him yourself."

There was a long pause. Hort's expression was grim. He said, "I believe I will."

Ben said, "They used you, Hort. They duped you. How do you like the taste?" It wasn't rational, but it made him feel a tiny bit better to know someone had fucked Hort the way Hort had fucked him.

Hort looked at the screen again. He shook his head slowly.

"Look at that," Alex said. "Another twenty downloads just since we've been talking. This is getting some buzz now. It's picking up speed."

"Genie's out of the bottle," Ben said. "Go back to Washington and tell them they can't get it back in. Tell them you did all this for nothing, you piece of shit."

Hort blew out a long breath. He closed the laptop and looked at Alex, then at Ben, then at Sarah.

"This op is over," he said. "The mission failed. I failed."

He glanced at one of the men in back. "Uncuff them. Let them go."

The man said, "But—"

"Do it."

The man hesitated, then leaned over and unlocked the cuffs. He inclined his head to Ben's ear. "This isn't over, asshole," he rasped.

"Maybe you didn't hear me," Hort said, and the interior of the van reverberated with his baritone. "This. Mission. Is. Over!"

Ben flexed his hands. They were numb. His wrists were slick with blood and flayed skin.

The three of them got out of the van. Hort rolled down his window and looked at them.

"Maybe Genie is out of the bottle," he said. "But some folks might still think that after what happened, certain people are a security risk. I'm going to tell them you're not. I think I owe you that. Don't do something to try to make me look stupid. You'd regret it if you did."

He looked at Ben. "It was the mission, Ben. And that's all it should ever be. Now you have to see if that's a standard you can aspire to. I won't try to make that decision for you."

Ben rubbed his wrists and nodded. The truth was, he didn't know what he was going to do. A minute earlier, he would have given anything to have one last shot at Hort. Now he wasn't sure.

"Go," Hort said, and the van pulled away.

Ben turned to Sarah. "You okay?"

"I need to go," she said, shaking her head.

"Well, sure, we could just—"

She held up her hands and took a step back. "No. I just need . . . I just want to be alone."

Ben said, "Sarah, wait."

She shook her head. "Like you said, it was a mistake."

Alex said, "Sarah, don't go. We need to—"

"Forget it," she said, turning and breaking into a run, not even looking back.

Caltrain was only a few blocks away. Ben guessed she was going home. "Let her go," he said.

"You think she'll be okay by herself?"

"I think if Hort were going to do anything, he would have done it now, while he had all three of us."

"He's not worried you'll come after him?"

Ben shook his head, trying to sort it out, feeling distinctly unsure of himself. "He might be, but—no, he wouldn't have let us go. Or letting us go knowing that I might want payback. It was like an apology."

Alex grimaced. "Not much of an apology, I'd say."

"Yeah, well, it beats some of the alternatives I was expecting. You know, he as much as told me he didn't want this mission. I think . . . maybe part of him was relieved to have a reason to stand down."

"You can't really know that. How can you trust a guy like that?"

Ben thought for a moment. All the answers that presented themselves felt stale and useless.

"I can't," he said, and the words brought up a fresh wave of pain and nausea. "I can't."

They were quiet for a moment. "Tell me what you did," Ben said. "You published Obsidian?"

"Yeah. But just on the tech sites. I didn't contact any of the political blogs Sarah told us about. There wasn't time."

"It's better you didn't. Disseminating it the way you did neutered Hort's op. Going political on top of it—that kind of scrutiny would have made him feel threatened. And a guy like Hort, you don't want him to think you're a threat. Anyway, how did you find the source code? I didn't follow that."

Alex smiled. "I could use a beer. You want to go someplace?"

Ben thought about that. A beer . . . with Alex?

"What about your car?"

"It's probably already towed. I'll say it was stolen."

"All right, then. A beer."

They started walking. "And after the beer," Ben said, "if you want, we could . . . go to the cemetery."

Alex glanced at him, then away. "You don't have to."

"No, I want to. I'd like to go with you."

They walked, the afternoon sun warm on their faces. "You know, I knew it was a trap," Alex said.

Ben laughed. "A **trap**? What movies have you been watching?"

"Well, I just knew you wanted to trust this guy, and that you shouldn't. I had to find some way to end this."

Without thinking, Ben slung an arm across his shoulders. "You did good."

Alex didn't answer. It took Ben a second to realize his little brother had choked up.

After a moment, Alex said, "Thanks."

Ben squeezed his shoulder and didn't say anything. He might have felt a little choked-up himself.

35 A BREAK IN THE ROUTINE

Sarah got to Ritual Coffee at six-thirty, a little after sunup. She hadn't been there since everything had happened, and should have been happy to be back to her routine. But rather than being a comfort, something about it felt . . . stale.

Going back to the office had been weird. Osborne was missing. Everybody was talking about it. She'd ducked into Alex's office and asked what he thought was going on. He told her, "I think it was a punishment to Osborne, and a warning to us."

"You don't think we should say anything?"

"I think we'd be crazy to say anything."

"What does your brother say?"

"The same."

She thought she should have been scared, but instead she felt depressed. She wanted to tell him she was sorry about what had happened with Ben. It ought to have seemed inconsequential after everything else, but it didn't. But maybe mentioning it would make things awkward, more awkward than they already were. So she'd nodded and left Alex's office, and they'd managed to avoid each other since.

She walked inside and there was Gabe behind the counter, just like every morning. "Hey, Sarah," he said. "Missed you the last few days."

"Yeah, I had some stuff going on."

"Hope it's all sorted out now."

"I think it is, yeah."

"Cool. The usual?"

She sighed. "The usual."

"Make it two," a voice said from behind her.

She spun around, already knowing.

"What are you doing here?" she said.

Ben said, "I wanted to see you."

"All right. You've seen me. Now you can go."

Ben handed some money to Gabe.

"I can pay for my own coffee," she said.

"You can get the next one."

She shook her head. She wanted to be angry. And she was—but more at herself now, for being excited to see him, than for anything else.

"Can we just talk?" he said. "I've been waiting out there for a half hour, freezing my ass off. I could really use a coffee. What did I just order, anyway?"

"A Black Eye."

"Sounds dangerous. What is it?"

"A cup of coffee with two shots of espresso."

"Damn, you drink one of these every day? I'd expect one a week would be enough."

Now he's charming, she thought. **Goddamn him.**

They moved down to the end of the counter to wait for the coffees. "I didn't get to thank you for what you did the other day," Ben said. "You should have run, but still. That took a lot of guts."

"I wasn't even thinking."

"Well, that much was obvious."

She didn't answer.

He said, "What is it?"

She looked away. After a moment, she said, "I should do something."

"What?"

"Go public. Contact the blogs. Tell them what I know."

"What do you know?"

"Cut it out. I know a lot. And you know it."

He gave her a gentle smile, utterly unlike the smirk he wore when he wanted to get a rise out of her. "Yeah, you know some things. But you don't think my unit's ever dealt with a public mess before? Granted, this is a bad one, but there've been others. And I can tell you, right now, while we're drinking our Black Eyes . . . records are being destroyed, aliases changed, alibis established. . . . It's practically a routine. These people know how to protect themselves, Sarah. They're good at it. Bigger players than you and I have tried to take them down, and so far they're still in business."

"And that makes you happy?"

"It doesn't make me feel one way or the other. It's just the way it is. Maybe information wants to be free, but freedom—freedom wants a unit like mine."

"You want to believe that."

He shook his head, and for a moment she thought he looked unaccountably sad.

"Look," he said. "At the moment, we've got a delicate balance going. I think Hort meant it when he said he was standing down."

"What about Osborne?"

"You know what happened to him."

"And it could happen to me, right?"

"If you give Hort a reason, yeah, it could."

"Are you threatening me?"

The sadness crossed his face again. "No. I don't want you to be afraid of me. That's the last thing I want."

She looked away. She knew he was right. She knew what the government could get away with—hell, she'd been watching it happen for years. Going public, she had to admit, was more about her own dignity than effecting any real change.

And there was another reason for her reluctance. She didn't want to hurt Ben. More than any other, that reason shamed her, and the shame was making her angry.

"Yeah, well, you've got a funny way of showing it," she said. "Sneaking into my room at the hotel, and now sneaking up on me here."

She looked away. After a moment, she glanced back at him. It looked like he was trying not to smile. Maybe it was the reference to the hotel room. She had to admit, it was hard to stop thinking about it.

"You really want me to grovel, don't you?" he said.

She thought for a moment. "Don't you think you should?"

His expression grew serious. "Look," he said, "what happened the other night . . . it couldn't have happened at a worse time for me. And it couldn't have been a better thing."

"That's it?"

"I don't know. I'm not used to groveling."

Now she was the one trying not to smile. "I think you should practice."

"Okay, how about this? I want to see you again."

She shook her head. "How's that going to work? Everything you stand for, I abhor."

He glanced away and shook his head. She realized she'd been expecting one of his patented snappy answers, and the fact that he didn't have one, or didn't want to offer one, suddenly fascinated her.

"I mean, I don't even know where you live," she said. "Where **do** you live? Do you live somewhere?"

"I move around a lot. But . . . I was thinking about spending some time in San Francisco for a while. Closer to home."

"Yeah? How long?"

"I don't know. How long could you stand me?"

"I'm not sure."

"It wouldn't be right away, necessarily. I wanted to stop in Manila first. Make sure my daughter knows she has a father. But after that. If you want."

She didn't answer. She wasn't sure what was happening. She felt like she wasn't keeping up.

Their coffees came. She put milk and sugar in hers. Ben took a sip. "Hooah," he said. "Is this how you bill all those hours?"

She shook her head. "I don't know how I do it."

He looked at her. "It's not really you, is it?"

"I don't know."

"What do you want to do instead?"

She sipped her coffee. "I'm working on that."

He shrugged. "Take some time off. Travel. Figure things out."

"You make it sound simple."

"It is."

"Oh, really?" she said. "Is that why you're going to Manila?"

"I have a few things to figure out, yeah."

"Like?"

His eyes narrowed, and she wondered whether she was pushing too hard. But damned if she was going to let him talk down to her.

"Like what the hell happened this week," he said, gravel in his voice. "Like whether I'm one of the good guys, like I always thought."

She looked at him. "Well, why don't you just admit that, instead of acting like the advice is just for me?"

His expression softened. "I'm not used to admitting things. It's like groveling. But I'm willing to learn."

She couldn't help smiling. They were quiet for a moment.

"You were right," she said. "Afterward, it seemed like a dream. The rest of it, too."

He nodded. "That's the way it works."

"And then you showed up here. Am I dreaming again?"

"You're not dreaming."

"Can you prove that?"

"Well, I could pinch you."

She looked at him. "My apartment is two blocks from here. Why don't you pinch me there?"

They walked fast. She knew this was a bad idea, but she didn't care. And maybe she would never see him again, but she didn't care about that, either. She could figure the rest out later. And she would. She would figure it out. She was sure of it.

ACKNOWLEDGMENTS

Once again I've written a book that has been made much better through the generous contributions of family and friends. My thanks to:

My agents, Dan Conaway and Simon Lipskar of Writers House, and editor, Mark Tavani of Ballantine, for seeing the promise in this story when it was not much more than an idea, and for helping me get it to where it is today.

Detective James Randol and Lieutenant J. R. Gamez of the San Jose Police Department, for answering all my questions, for providing some terrific ideas, for giving me a tour of the SJPD—and most of all for doing the incredibly important work they do.

Ernie Tibaldi, for continuing to generously apply thirty-one years of fieldwork with the FBI to the law enforcement issues in these books, and for helpful comments on the manuscript.

Warren Wolfeld of Haynes Beffel & Wolfeld LLP, for terrific tutorials on the inner workings of the U.S. Patent and Trademark Office and the whole process of applying for a patent, and for helpful comments on the manuscript.

Ashraf Hosseini, for sharing her family's story and answering all my questions about the Iranian immigrant experience in America—and for outfitting me in some stylish eyeglasses, too, at her wonderful Palo Alto store, A Site for Sore Eyes.

Hank Shiffman, for answering all my technology questions and coming up with quite a few excellent ideas of his own along the way; for expertly moderating my Web site discussion board; and for helpful comments on the manuscript. Come over to the dark side, Hank . . .

Dennis Volpano and Dave McAllister, for helpful background on network security and computer viruses, and Adam Young and Moti Yung for their excellent book **Malicious Cryptography: Exposing Cryptovirology.**

The extraordinarily eclectic group of "foodies with a violence problem" who hang out at Marc "Animal" MacYoung's and Dianna Gordon's www.nononsense-selfdefense.com, for good humor, good fellowship, and a ton of insights. A special thanks to Marc himself, for his continued insights into violence, operator mind-sets and behavior, and what makes people tick, and for helpful comments on the manuscript.

Vivian Brown, Alan Eisler, Judith Eisler, Montie

Guthrie, Tom Hayes, Mike Killman, Lori Kupfer, novelist J. A. Konrath, Naomi Andrews and Dan Levin, Doug Patteson, Matt Powers, Owen Rennert, Ted Schlein, and the Man Called Slugg, for helpful comments on the manuscript and many valuable suggestions and insights along the way.

Most of all my wife, Laura, for the usual input into the story and terrific comments on the manuscript, but even more than that for putting up with my occasional obsessiveness ("Occasional?" she might say here) with nothing but love and goodwill.

AUTHOR'S NOTE

Much of the backstory and many of the incidents recounted in this book are real. Here's a partial bibliography.

Defection of Iranian general Ali Reza Asgari: http://www.time.com/time/world/article/0,8599,16 01814,00.html.

National Intelligence Estimate on Iranian nuclear efforts: http://www.dni.gov/press_releases/20071203 _release.pdf.

Victor Litvinenko assassination by polonium radiation poisoning: http://www.timesonline.co.uk/tol/sport/football/euro pean_football/article756950.ece.

Rendition of Abu Omar from Milan: http://www.lrb.co.uk/v29/n15/foot02_.html.

Aviation hobbyists expose CIA rendition flights:

http://www.militaryphotos.net/forums/showthread.
php?t=65446.

Special operations "military liaison elements":
http://www.nytimes.com/2006/03/08/international/
americas/08forces.html?pagewanted=print;
http://www.specwarnet.net/americas/isa.htm.

Russia governed by **siloviki,** ex-KGB, and ex-
military: http://www.monitor.upeace.org/archive
.cfm?id_article=107.

Chinese antisatellite efforts:
http://www.globalsecurity.org/space/world/china/asa
t.htm.

Russian cyberwarfare efforts:
http://it.slashdot.org/it/07/05/17/1248215.shtml.

Eighth Air Force Cyber Command:
http://www.af.mil/news/story.asp?id=123030505.

CIA: Hackers to blame for power outages:
http://www.cnn.com/2007/US/09/26/power.at.risk/
index.html.

Wrongful prosecution of Iranian-American
businessman Alex Latifi: http://harpers.org/archive/
2008/02/hbc-90002484.

CIA/mafia connection: http://www.upi.com/
Security_Terrorism/Briefing/2007/06/26/family_
jewels_detail_castro_mafia_plot/6711/; http://www
.edwardjayepstein.com/archived/castro.htm.

Executive order prohibiting assassination:
http://www.washingtonpost.com/ac2/wp-dyn/
A63203-2001Oct27?language=printer.

Dark Avenger and the polymorphic engine: http://en.wikipedia.org/wiki/Dark_Avenger.

Adam Young, Moti Yung, and cryptovirology: http://www.cryptovirology.com/.

Chinese cyberwarfare initiatives: http://www.economist.com/world/international/dis playstory.cfm?story_id=9769319&CFID=1175260 7&CFTOKEN=ccdd4740076c5dc1-43B10757-B27C-BB00-012901C5EA08C4BB.

Abuse of national security letters (NSLs): http://www.salon.com/opinion/greenwald/2008/03/ 06/nsls/index.html.

National Security Agency domestic spy program: http://wsj.com/public/article_print/SB1205119733 77523845.html?mod=djm_HAWSJSB_Welcome.

FISA and warrantless eavesdropping: http://www.salon.com/opinion/greenwald/2008/02/ 14/fisa_101/.

The Quantico circuit and warrentless eavesdropping: http://blog.wired.com/27bstroke6/ 2008/03/whistleblower-f.html.

The Bay Area and Istanbul locations that appear in this book are described, as always, as I have found them.

About the Author

After graduating from Cornell Law School in 1989, BARRY EISLER spent three years in a covert position with the CIA's Directorate of Operations, and then three years in Japan, where he earned his black belt at the Kodokan International Judo Center. Eisler's thrillers have won the Barry Award and the Gumshoe Award for Best Thriller of the Year, have been included in numerous "Best of" lists, and have been translated into nearly twenty languages. The first book in Eisler's assassin John Rain series, **Rain Fall,** has been made into a motion picture starring Gary Oldman and will be released by Sony Pictures in April 2009. To learn more, please visit www.barryeisler.com.